Do you want to know what God is doing in the world today?

Then watch the 700 Club! You'll see the latest news and information on events unfolding in the world each day.

You'll get a Christian perspective on important issues. And we'll bring you stories about changed lives that will give you hope and inspiration you can use throughout your day.

For excellent spiritual resources, current news and inspiring information, log on to CBN.com!

Check your local TV listing for time and station.

THE
END
OF THE
AGE

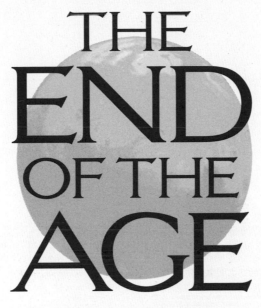

THE END OF THE AGE

A NOVEL

PAT ROBERTSON

W PUBLISHING GROUP™

www.wpublishinggroup.com

A Division of Thomas Nelson, Inc.
www.ThomasNelson.com

Published by W Publishing Group, a Division of Thomas Nelson, Inc., P.O. Box 141000, Nashville, Tennessee 37214.

Library of Congress Cataloging-in-Publication Data:
Robertson, Pat.
   The end of the age: a novel / by Pat Robertson.
     p. cm.
   ISBN 0-8499-4414-7
   1. End of the world—Fiction. 2. Prophecies—Fiction. I. Title.
PS3568.02498E5   1995
813'.54—dc 20

95-34672
CIP

Printed in the United States of America

02 03 04 05 06 PHX 9 8 7 6 5 4 3 2 1

To my wife, Dede, with thanks
for her encouragement
and support . . .

*"This is how it will
be at the end of the age."*

—The Gospel of Matthew

PART ONE

CHAPTER ONE

CARL THRONEBERRY was having a bad day. Agitated, restless, and hot, he turned off the television in his den and walked outside. He was hit immediately by a blast of dry heat. The meteorologist on the news had just reported that the temperature had hit a searing 112 degrees, as it had nearly every day for the past three weeks.

Not that it's all that much cooler inside the house, Carl thought as he stood on the front porch of his spacious Mediterranean-style dwelling, surveying what was left of his once-green lawn. Brownouts in southern California had become more and more frequent over the past several weeks, and despite the sweltering heat, the air conditioning was little more than a sometime luxury. There simply wasn't enough power in the system to support it.

Carl walked slowly around the grounds of his home, assessing the damage the heat had done to the hilltop lot he and his wife, Lori, had bought in Laguna Niguel ten years ago. The carefully manicured lawn was baked hard. The formal Italian gardens he and Lori had lovingly planted had been reduced to brown leaves hanging on brittle twigs. Not a single flower, not even a single blade of grass had survived the unremitting heat.

The combination of the heat, a severe water shortage, and the brownouts had made people short-tempered, angry, and even violent. The television report Carl had just watched had shown gangs in South Central Los Angeles roaming the streets and looting. Reports of domestic violence had risen dramatically, as had assault-and-battery cases involving neighbors. California was out of control.

He walked around the house to the back of the property and stopped on the terrace. What had once been the most beautiful part of his home was now a wasteland. Everything had turned brown, and the trees were as bare as any in the Minnesota winter landscapes he had known as a boy. What he wouldn't give for a cold Minnesota winter now!

"Honey, will you grill the chicken?" Lori called from the kitchen.

Carl stepped inside the door. "Are you sure you want to barbecue, Lori?"

"Yes," she said, as she started taking vegetables out of the refrigerator. "Don't you like the idea? We can eat on the patio and maybe get a breeze off the ocean when the sun goes down."

With her tanned, flawless complexion, her blonde hair, and light blue eyes, Lori was a striking woman. She was thirty-eight, two years younger than Carl. They had married when she was twenty and he twenty-two, and Carl thought she had grown more beautiful over the years. *Part of it's her personality,* he thought. She had a free spirit and an infectious laugh that made people want to be around her. And, despite the heat, she managed to be cheerful and upbeat. Her short, multicolored sundress made her seem young and vibrant in bright contrast to the oppressive weather.

Carl looked at his wife, gave her a quick hug, and said, "Okay. Barbecue it is."

While Carl cooked the chicken, Lori made a big salad. They ate outside on the terrace and lingered over iced coffee as evening descended on the ravaged landscape. The sun went down peacefully, and indeed, as if on call, a breeze off the ocean slipped gently in, bringing welcome relief from the scorching heat of the day.

The air was surprisingly clean, and the stars seemed to sparkle above them. Carl had studied astronomy at Cal Tech, and, deep in his heart he had always wanted to be a full-time astronomer. But his life had taken a different turn.

He had met Lori while she was an interior design student at the Pasadena Arts Institute. A mutual friend decided to get the two displaced Minnesotans together. They were married while Lori was still in school. Then, fresh out of college, Carl took the first good job he could find—as a copy assistant at the prestigious advertising agency, JPT Worldwide. Just over a year later, a senior account executive let him try his hand at writing a TV spot. That first commercial was so successful that more assignments came his way. The senior executives soon realized that Carl was extraordinarily gifted. Besides his ability to write, he was good-looking and charming. The execs saw that he could sell anything to anybody—from airline tickets to disposable diapers. And that's just what he did.

The ads Carl created were seen all over America. A stack of Addy Awards testified to his position in the industry. He could have had a high-paying job anywhere in the ad world, but JPT Worldwide snapped on his wrists a very attractive set of golden handcuffs—a $500,000 annual salary, generous performance bonuses, and enough stock options to squelch any thoughts he might have had of moving on.

Carl could dream of the stars in heaven, but for now he was a star in the advertising galaxy on Earth—and it appeared that nothing would ever change that fact.

"Look, Carl!" Lori exclaimed, pointing up at the night sky. "Look how bright that star is tonight! Isn't that Venus?"

Carl leaned back in his chair and looked up into the sky. "No," he said, "that's not Venus, my love. We can't see Venus from here tonight."

"Well, Galileo," she said, laughing, "what is it, then? It's not the North Star, is it?"

"No, I'm not sure what that is, honey. It's not a star at all. It could be a low-level satellite, I suppose. But if so, it's in the wrong place. It can't be a comet—it's moving too slowly. Maybe a weather balloon—or maybe it's an asteroid like the one that missed the earth by six hours about ten years ago."

"An asteroid? What are you talking about?" Lori asked, looking intently at Carl. "Are you serious? An asteroid missed the earth by just six hours?"

"Sure," he said. "Don't you remember? There were stories in the newspapers—after the fact, of course. There was even a TV documentary, and a big cover story in *Newsweek*. I'm sure we talked about it at the time, but an asteroid really did pass through Earth's orbit just six hours after Earth passed by. It was the closest near miss of that magnitude in recorded history. If there had actually been a collision, it would have been disastrous."

"I didn't hear anything about an asteroid," Lori said, sitting up in her chair. She looked at him closely. "You're putting me on, right?"

"No, I'm not, Lori. It's true. That big black expanse of space out there is full of rocks and debris—some big and some little. The little ones are called meteors. The big ones—some of them the size of little planets—are called asteroids. Usually when meteors hit the earth's atmosphere, they just burn up. We call them shooting stars, and usually only a small amount of debris ever reaches the earth. But sometimes fragments of meteors do get through, and those are called meteorites. You've seen meteorites, haven't you?"

Lori nodded. "Yes, I think so."

"Big ones, like the ones they've found in Arizona and Mexico, can leave huge craters in the earth's surface. But if an asteroid were ever to hit our planet . . . hold on to your hat. Honolulu and Nome, Alaska, would probably trade places!"

Looking up again, Carl paused, considering his own words. "If a meteor hit southern California, the ride would be so bumpy that not many of us would still be around to talk about it."

"Carl," Lori said, "you're so insufferably morbid! I think this heat has made *everybody* morbid." She reached over and touched his arm. "That little flyspeck up there isn't going to hit us—is it?"

"Don't worry." Carl laughed. "If we were in any danger, the national weather service and the disaster relief agencies would be all over the radio and TV, telling us to get out of here. If that thing was a meteor, the whole world would know about it by now. You couldn't keep something like that secret for long."

Lori's face brightened perceptibly, and as she slowly walked her carefully manicured fingers up Carl's bare arm, she whispered, "Carl, let's get out of here. Okay?"

"What have you got in mind?" he asked.

"Let's go to Colorado."

"You mean permanently?"

"No, of course not, silly." She gave him a seductive look. "Let's take a long weekend and get away from this heat. You need a break. I just finished that design job for the Forresters' new home, so I need a break. Let's just go. *Now.*"

Carl smiled. "Good idea, Lori, but you know I'm running the launch program for the new Hologram Sportswear campaign. That means big bucks for the agency and a healthy bonus for us. I'd like a break, but if I don't keep my eye on things the agency could really blow it. If that were to happen, JPT could kiss America's biggest advertiser good-bye."

"Carl, I know all that. But, for heaven's sake, going away for a couple of days to cool off won't make that much difference! Everybody knows how good you are, and Harvey will cover for you. Tell him you're going to sit on a mountaintop and meditate for a couple of days. And that you'll come back with a great new slogan for the world's greatest sportswear collection. He'll go for that."

"I don't know, honey," Carl said. "Even if we decided to go, and even if the agency wouldn't miss me for a few days, we couldn't possibly get airline tickets now—even if we turned over the mortgage to the house. Greg Peterson told me last week that every flight to the mountains has been double-booked for weeks."

Lori smiled mischievously, then lifted her placemat and held up an envelope. "Two first-class tickets from L.A. to Colorado Springs leaving at eleven o'clock tomorrow morning. Continental Airlines to the mountains and an air-conditioned luxury sedan waiting for us at the Hertz counter in Colorado Springs."

Carl looked at her in amazement.

"And besides," she continued, "we don't have to mortgage anything. I'm offering my love four days of cool mountain air, lush fairways, blue skies, and four nights of nuptial bliss. So, what do you say, handsome?"

"Are you serious, Lori? You already have the tickets?" Carl sat up in his chair, and Lori nodded, grinning at him like a mischievous child.

"You *are* incredible," her husband murmured. He leaned forward and gave her a kiss. "But please don't tell me how you got these tickets. I don't want to know." Then he added with a smile, "But *do* tell me you came by them honestly."

"Darling, you know honesty is the best policy. Haven't I always said that?"

Carl knew better than to ask any more questions. He wanted to get out of Los Angeles just as badly as Lori did, and suddenly here was the perfect opportunity. So the matter was settled. They were going to Colorado Springs.

AFTER A HASTY BREAKFAST the next morning, Carl and Lori eased their Mercedes diesel wagon onto the I-5 Freeway, which led, in turn, to the 405 Freeway and northward through Los Angeles. Most days, the Angelinos referred to the 405 as the largest moving parking lot in the world, and that day was no exception. Traffic was heavy, moving slowly without stopping. A light cloud of auto exhaust and pollution hung in the air around them.

Lori punched the radio dial to News Talk KABC. After a hardware commercial and traffic report was the weather forecast: "There will be no break in the heat wave," the announcer said. "The National Weather Service is warning California residents to prepare for more record-high temperatures—perhaps as high as one hundred twenty-four degrees in some places. No precipitation is predicted."

Carl reached over and gently squeezed Lori's hand. "We're getting out of this oven just in time," he said, smiling. "Only three hours to cool breezes and mountain streams!"

As he was speaking, a news bulletin interrupted the weather report. He reached over and turned up the volume on the radio. The reporter was saying, "Observatories in Australia, California, Canada, and the United Kingdom have been tracking a large meteor in space. According to Dr. Mack Collier, chief scientist at the Mount Wilson Observatory, the meteor is now on a path that could intersect with Earth's orbit in a matter of hours."

Carl and Lori looked at each other in shock. "That's what we were just talking about last night!" he exclaimed. "I can't believe this is happening!"

"Oh, no," Lori whispered and put her hand over her mouth.

The radio report continued, "Moments ago we spoke with Dr. Collier, who tells KABC News: 'The best we can determine at this point, an extremely large foreign body, perhaps as much as a kilometer in diameter, is on a path to enter the earth's atmosphere within the next several hours. There is a chance it will simply pass outside the gravitational field. But we must also consider the possibility that it may be drawn by the earth's magnetic field.'" There was a long pause. "'And, in that case, it would likely impact somewhere off the coast of California . . . between seven and eight o'clock this evening.'"

Carl and Lori looked at each other, wide-eyed. Simultaneously they said, "Seven o'clock."

The radio announcer continued, "This interview with Dr. Mack Collier was taped just moments ago. The Center for Emergency Relief requests that all southern California residents remain calm, and please stay tuned to this station for updates throughout the day as we track these developing events. In the meantime, residents of low-lying coastal regions are being asked to evacuate immediately and move to the east toward higher ground. We want to stress, however, that you should stay calm and move with extreme caution. There is no cause for panic at this point. We will keep you informed as events unfold."

Carl angrily snapped off the radio and maneuvered the Mercedes off the freeway, onto Sepulveda Boulevard, and then onto Highway 1, which would take them straight north to LAX without the freeway delays.

"Those dirty, lying idiots!" he blurted. "How could they do that?"

Lori flinched at his sudden outburst. "What, Carl? What are you yelling about?"

"Those jerks! I can't believe this! They didn't say anything until it was too late! They've been tracking that blasted thing for days, weeks even. And no warning whatsoever, until now . . . when it's too late to do anything. It's criminal!"

"Maybe they didn't want to start a panic, Carl."

"Panic!" he shouted. "Lori, all hell's going to break loose in less than ten hours. There will be *plenty* of panic then!"

"Maybe they didn't know it was coming so close," Lori persisted. "If they knew about that other one—the one you said came so close ten years ago—then maybe they thought this one would pass by the same way."

"Lori, listen to me," Carl said impatiently. "If that thing is as big as they say it is and if it hits anywhere near here, thousands of people— maybe hundreds of thousands—are going to die. It's criminal not to warn the people of California what's going on."

Lori shifted nervously. "What are you saying, Carl? What does this mean, really?"

Suddenly Carl wished he didn't know anything at all about astronomy—that he couldn't see what was coming. But over the years he had continued to educate himself about astronomy, keeping up with the latest books and articles. Reading about the movements of stars and the planets had always been a kind of intellectual consolation amid the mindless commercialism he lived with. But now he realized that if that huge chunk of rock came hurtling from the sky and landed off the California coast, it was going to wipe out everybody and everything for hundreds of miles. After that, a series of inevitable floods, fires, and earthquakes would leave a toll of devastation beyond human calculation. Nothing and no one could be saved, and it was already too late to help anybody else.

"Honey," he said, "what it means is we've got to hurry and get on that plane. Do you understand?"

Lori nodded, not trusting herself to speak.

As they approached the terminal, they could see hundreds of cars jamming every lane, in every direction. There was nowhere to park, so Carl pulled up onto the median and drove as far as he could before he stopped and turned off the engine. "Let's go," he said. "Grab your carry-on and just keep going straight ahead. Don't slow down and don't look back. Just keep moving, no matter what happens."

Carl reached over and touched his wife gently on the cheek. "Are you ready?"

She nodded again.

"Then, let's go."

They got out of their car and jogged the last hundred yards to the terminal, criss-crossing between cars and groups of people milling around on the sidewalk. When they entered the lobby, Carl took Lori's hand and pulled her through the crowds. At the checkpoint, they slipped into line, passed through the metal detectors, and made their way to the Continental gates with nothing but the bags in their hands. They were more than an hour early, but the flight was already in the final boarding stages.

Carl shoved the tickets toward the attendant behind the check-in desk.

"It's a good thing you're here early, folks," she said. "All airline equipment has been ordered off the ground and out of L.A. in the next three hours, and we're about to move this one within the next few minutes."

"Because of the meteor?" Lori asked.

"Yes, that's right. The front office is probably overreacting, but these airplanes don't come cheap, so Mr. Continental isn't taking any chances."

"So, is this plane still headed for Colorado Springs?" Carl asked.

"Yes, I think so." The gate attendant smiled. "The pilot will let us all know when we get to cruising altitude. But, wherever this flight goes, it will be better than L.A."

"You can say *that* again," Carl said. "Thanks for the information."

Still hand in hand, Carl and Lori walked quickly down the ramp and onto the plane. They took their seats in the first-class cabin and breathed a sigh of relief, not realizing that they would probably never see their friends, their business associates, their home, their beautiful possessions, their car, or the city of Los Angeles again.

CHAPTER TWO

A T 8:45 A.M., PACIFIC TIME, Manuel Quintana pointed his Jeep Cherokee up the winding road that led to the top of Mount Wilson. Manuel, whose friends called him Manolo, was the chief engineer of KTTV. The station had its transmitter at the antenna farm located on Mount Wilson—the highest point in the Los Angeles area, and less than a half-mile from the observatory.

Manuel wasn't accustomed to pulling transmitter duty, and if this hadn't been a special situation, he would have sent one of the technicians to take care of it. When the station called him at home that morning to tell him about the transmitter problem, he had been told that something was causing electrical arcing in the power supplies. Since his house was just a few miles from the foot of Mount Wilson, he had decided to drive up there and take care of the problem himself.

Manuel was from a blue-collar family, and he had always been a hands-on guy. The son of illegal Mexican immigrants who had slipped past the INS border patrol, Manuel had been born in the U.S. His father and mother, who had worked at various menial jobs, often said that their proudest accomplishment of all was that their son had been born on U.S. soil—a real American citizen.

Manuel graduated from the public schools in East Los Angeles, then went on to get a broadcast engineering degree from DeVry Institute of

Technology. After that, he breezed through the FCC broadcast license exams and was awarded a first-class Broadcast Engineer's License.

His first job was taking transmitter meter readings on the late-night shift. It wasn't much, but it was a start. To celebrate that first paying job, he married Cathy, his high-school sweetheart. Within a year came the first of three children—all boys, all like their father. Manuel adored them.

He was a hard worker and a quick study. Gradually, seniority came, raises came, and then one day the vice president of engineering suddenly quit and Manuel was given the job.

He could have sat at a desk and run the department, but Manuel liked being directly involved in the day-to-day operations. He loved the cameras and microphones and recorders and transistors and scopes and wave-forms. He loved and understood everything technical—the tubes and relays and printed circuits and wiring. He knew what made the sound and pictures that went into the homes of millions of Angelinos, and that was important to him.

Manuel had been there through the transition from analog to digital. He had witnessed the changes in the old-style color television as it was transformed into the new computer-based media. Satellites could now beam their signals to millions of receivers using tiny roof-mounted dishes not much bigger than pie plates. Wide-area computer networks were now linking tens of millions of users with real-time video, audio, and data, sending out millions of bits of digital information every second.

The new generation spoke of the old broadcast television of the late twentieth century as the horse-and-buggy service. Manuel had seen it all, and while he championed the new technology, he hadn't lost touch with the tradition and the ground-breaking work that had made all this possible. He never stopped believing that, despite all the new innovations, his transmitters and studios would continue to be the mainstream of the information age for years to come. So he was happy to check on the transmitter himself.

Manuel was halfway up Mount Wilson when he switched on the car radio. He listened in stunned silence to the same disturbing news report that Carl and Lori Throneberry had heard. His peaceful morning was immediately shattered.

Suddenly tears came to his eyes. "Oh, God, no!" he whispered. He knew that Cathy and the boys would be in danger. His precious transmitter could blow up, and there he was on a narrow road halfway up the mountain.

Cathy worked as a systems analyst for a computer software company not far from their modest home in Altadena. She had opted for flextime as the best balance between her demanding office job and the even greater demands of mothering three pre-teenage boys.

"Please," he whispered, "let her still be at home." Manuel gritted his teeth as he picked up his cellular phone and punched in his home number. He breathed a deep sigh of relief when his wife answered.

"Cathy. There's terrible news. I just heard it on the radio. A natural disaster is coming. There's no time to explain right now, but listen to me. I want you to do exactly what I tell you. Put all the food you can gather up into the car, especially canned foods, dried foods, and things like that. Fill up all the gallon jugs you can find with drinking water. Then I want you to get the boys together as fast as you can and meet me at the transmitter. Do you hear me? Don't waste one minute. I'll be at the transmitter in about twenty minutes. Just go fast, Cathy. And, remember, I love you."

"I love you, too, Manolo."

With that, a thoroughly bewildered thirty-five-year-old mother hung up the phone and went into a controlled panic. She grabbed up armloads of provisions and tossed them into cardboard boxes, garbage bags, and anything else she could find. Within ten minutes she was speeding toward the boys' school. Fortunately, she only had five blocks to drive.

She knew something awful must be happening. The whole town seemed to be in panic. People were running from house to house.

The streets were choked with cars. Red lights and stop signs were useless, and at practically every intersection Cathy saw cars with steam pouring out from under the hoods. She couldn't imagine what was happening, but it was obvious that people were in a state of alarm. They were trying to get away from something, but they didn't know which way to run—and all this chaos was taking place in the midst of blinding, searing heat.

Cathy parked at the curb and raced through the school until she found her three boys, one by one. First she located Miguel, twelve, then Ricardo, ten, and last, little Juan, seven. None of the teachers said anything or tried to stop Cathy as she ran into their classrooms, said one word—"Emergency"—and grabbed her boys. She knew she must look like a madwoman, but she didn't care. The three youngsters ran out of school behind their mother, aware that something big must be happening.

"It's life and death," she gasped as they piled into the car. "We have to meet your father on Mount Wilson. He said he'd explain later. Buckle up, boys. And pray that we can get out of here before the streets are all shut down."

As she edged the car into the street, she glanced down at the gas gauge and saw that she had a full tank. *My Manolo, the engineer*, she thought. *Thank God he has always insisted that the gas tanks be filled every night, "In case of an emergency."*

She drove as fast as she could to the 210 Freeway, but from the service road she could see that all four lanes were jammed. So she cut back through Pasadena and Des Canso Gardens to connect with Highway 2, which was a straight shot up to the San Gabriel Mountains and the Angeles National Forest.

Miraculously, the loop east and north toward Mount Wilson was still passable. Despite stalled cars and people running hysterically along the road, Cathy picked her way through the traffic and northward, slowly, mile by agonizing mile. After what seemed an eternity, she reached the Mount Wilson access road and turned back to the south and began the ascent. She longed to turn on the radio to find out what was happening, but she didn't want her sons frightened by the news. Instead, with her right hand she reached for the rosary beads hanging from the rearview mirror. Silently, she began to pray.

MANUEL HAD ALREADY ARRIVED at the transmitter site near the summit. He unlocked the building door and stepped inside. The heat was unbearable. A quick glance at the gauges showed that the transmitter was unable to hold its assigned frequency. The dials and meters were dancing crazily, like a drunk weaving in and out of traffic on a crowded freeway.

Manuel quickly punched the number for the private telephone line of Mike Hennessey, the station president. After what seemed like an eternity, Mike answered.

"Mike," he said, "this is Manuel. I'm at the transmitter, but there's no way I can hold frequency in this heat. If we stay on the air with the frequency jumping like this, the FCC will be all over us. . . ."

After a moment of silence, a voice boomed back, "*Forget the FCC! We just got a news bulletin out of Washington, and a meteor is travel-ing through space toward us. It's going to splash down before dark tonight somewhere out past Catalina.*"

"Yeah, Mike," Manolo yelled back. "I heard about it on the radio. Go ahead."

"The traffic chopper says the freeways are packed and all the access roads are completely choked off. And, get this . . . people are so freaked down here, they're dying of heart attacks just sitting still in traffic. Can you believe that?"

Mike continued, "I don't know if we can do anything more, but maybe we can save some lives. Are you with me on this?"

With tears in his eyes, Manuel said, "Yeah, Mike. I'm with you, man."

"We owe this town something, so let's just keep the station on the air until this thing is over." There was a pause on the line, and Mike's gruff voice softened slightly. "And, Manolo—if I don't see you again, God bless you."

"God bless you, too, Mike. I'll keep us on the air as long as I can. But please start evacuating while you can. Don't take any chances."

Manuel switched off the portable phone and began going over a mental checklist of all the things he had to do. He was sweating— more from fear than the heat, he realized. He pushed his damp, dark hair back from his face, rolled up his sleeves, and prepared to get to work. As he yanked off his tie, he said out loud, "Okay, Manuel, you're a professional. You can do this. There's a job to be done here. Just stay calm and do it, man. Just do it."

As he raced through the procedures, reducing power and setting up his equipment, Manuel remembered the basics. Traditional analog broadcast television transmitters receive sound and pictures produced by microphones and cameras, then direct the sound and pictures into a frequency band called a channel. The sound and pictures are amplified, one stage after another, until they are combined and passed through an electronic pipe or wave guide, then to a broadcast antenna that, in turn, multiplies the power of the signal by a factor of ten or twenty or even more, and then sends the signals through the air to receiving antennas connected to the television sets in millions of homes.

Manolo knew that the average television viewer couldn't care less about the technical details as long as he or she got a clear picture. But if something broke down and the system malfunctioned, then those same viewers would start screaming. His only task now was to keep the rig working the best way he knew how.

The first thing he did was to roll a giant five-foot shop fan across the room to blow directly on the crucial mini-transmitters called exciters. Next, he disabled the fail-safe mechanisms designed to automatically shut down parts of the transmitter in the event something went wrong.

Manuel had orders to keep the facility up and running, and that's just what he planned to do. Both he and Mike knew that, despite his best efforts, the tubes, circuits, and power supplies would all fail sooner or later. The rig would probably shut down for good within an hour or so. At that point, KTTV would be off the air until the crisis was over. But this was truly a matter of life and death, and they were prepared to lose everything to keep the station on the air until the last minute.

Just as he finished disabling the fail-safe devices, Manuel heard a car horn outside. He dropped what he was doing and bolted out the door. Cathy and the boys were just getting out of the car. He stretched out his arms and encompassed them in one big hug. "Thank God, you're all safe!" he cried. "Thank God you got out of there in time."

"Oh, Manolo, it was horrible down there!" Cathy exclaimed. "You can't imagine what's happening to those poor people."

"I know, Cathy," he said. "I just talked to Mike, and he said it was going to be real bad. Come on inside where we'll be safer. Come on, boys."

THE TRANSMITTER FACILITY was equipped with a two-way microwave relay, a satellite receiver dish pointed at the Galaxy satellite, and a propane-fired auxiliary generator. In the days when FCC regulations required on-site transmitter engineers, the KTTV crew had set up a spartan living area with a bed, bathroom, and a utility kitchen. They had a small stove, a microwave, and a refrigerator, which could run on auxiliary power. To help the fellows fight boredom, there was also a moderate-sized telescope, which Manuel had learned to use reasonably well.

After they had transported all the groceries and supplies from the car, Manuel explained what was going on to Cathy and the boys. He told them about the meteor and the possibility that it would hit sometime that evening. The boys were all surprised and incredulous.

"A meteor—wow!" Ricardo exclaimed.

"Cool!" said his older brother, Miguel. "Just like in the cartoons."

Manuel realized that reality would hit all too soon. He decided to say nothing more.

After a few minutes, and discussion of sleeping arrangements, Cathy and Manuel went back outside carrying the telescope and tripod. They went up the stairs onto a tiny observation platform overlooking the city. Manuel adjusted the eyepiece and scanned the sky without the scope to find the target. The bright ball in the sky wasn't hard to find. Manuel turned the barrel of the telescope toward the onrushing meteor, then carefully adjusted the focus.

"Good Lord, Cathy," he whispered. "It's huge and it's blazing hot! Take a look."

For the first time in his life, Manuel understood the fear of death. Fear, real fear—and overwhelming dread. How could one puny engineer hope to survive what was coming in just eight hours? But, survive he must. He also realized that Cathy and the boys couldn't be allowed a window on his real feelings. He didn't know how he was going to do it, but he determined to stay calm and told himself that, one way or the other, he and his family would survive the night.

When Cathy focused in on the monstrous object through the telescope lens, she let out a sharp cry, "Oh, Manolo, we're going to die! All of us!"

"No, we're not going to die!" Manuel insisted, hoping his voice sounded more confident than he felt. "We are *not* going to die. We are going to come through this thing. Alive!"

He embraced his wife briefly, then turned to the telescope and moved the lens back toward the sprawling city below. Words could not describe the chaos he saw. It was as if every vehicle in Greater Los Angeles had moved onto the freeways. None of them was moving. Hoods were up on many vehicles, and geysers of steam poured out of overheated radiators.

Just beyond the freeways, he could spot puffs of smoke rising into the blistering sky. *Fires,* he thought, *in the bone-dry woods and fields.* To the southeast, he could see whole neighborhoods engulfed in flames. There was no way firefighters would ever reach those places. It was just a question of time until the whole city would be ablaze.

Manuel went back into the transmitter building, leaving Cathy on the observation deck. He said softly to himself, "It's all gone. The life's work of ten million people. Everything they've struggled for, and everything they've fought so hard to get. Up in smoke. Wiped out by a huge chunk of hot rock from outer space. Why? Why is this happening?"

He snapped out of his reverie long enough to see that the transmitter was wavering and about to shut down. At this point it had less than ten minutes of life left in it. But what he saw on the picture monitor made him wish he had cut the thing off hours before. The station was showing live and taped feeds from its chopper.

Temperatures at street level were reported to be in excess of 140 degrees. Some people had stripped off their clothes and were running naked in the scorching heat, screaming for help. One reporter estimated that the number of heart attacks alone had already passed one hundred thousand.

According to the reporter, deaths from heat prostration were approaching the same level. There were gruesome close-up shots of the dead, their faces puffed up and contorted. Dead bodies were hanging out of the windows of cars stalled up and down the freeways.

A large group of people were on their knees crying out to God that this tragedy would somehow be averted. Some begged for death—anything to escape the hellish heat that descended from the sky. Radiation, like steam, shimmered before their eyes. The pavement, concrete buildings, and every metal object were now scorching hot.

Thousands of men, women, and children were hurrying through the streets with no clear destination in mind. Some were like lemmings running toward the ocean, seemingly oblivious to the repeated warnings being broadcast throughout the area to evacuate the coastal regions. *Of course,* Manuel thought, *evacuation is now a physical impossibility for most of the population.* The broadcast warnings from official sources could not even begin to describe the hideous watery grave that awaited those who were still alive at seven o'clock.

Manuel watched as the cameras picked up a nondescript black-and-white mongrel dog lying on the side of the road. Her eyes were open and staring blankly into space, her tongue hanging out of her dry, parched mouth. A half-dozen puppies, no more than a week old, had been nursing beside her when they died.

A picture, someone said, is worth a thousand words. *That picture says it all,* Manuel thought. That was the last picture his station, KTTV, would ever transmit.

Manuel's work was over as quickly as it began. He followed shut-down procedures for the transmitter to allow the blower fans enough time to cool down the big tubes in the final output section of the transmitter. Then, to avoid electrical fires, he threw the main breakers to cut off all power into the building. The automatic shut-over mechanism fired up the auxiliary generator at reduced power. He said a silent prayer, hoping that the propane tank was buried deep enough to be shielded from the heat.

The job was over, but he couldn't afford to slow down now. Survival came next.

Manuel went to the storeroom and opened a metal cabinet. He took out two long-handled shovels and walked outside. He called the two oldest boys and said, "Okay, you guys, this may be the most important job you'll ever have. I want you to take turns digging."

He led them to an area off to the side of the hill. "We're going to need five trenches, each one big enough to lie down in. I know it's going to be hard work, but I want you to dig five big foxholes, each one about four feet deep. Can you do that? If there's too much rock down there, we'll just have to mound the dirt up. But we've got to make them at least four feet deep."

Miguel and Ricardo took the shovels without complaint.

"This may not work," said their father, "but it's the best chance we've got."

"How much time do we have to dig all five holes, Dad?" Miguel asked.

"It looks like we've got about five hours," Manuel answered. "We'll all pitch in. But you guys go ahead and get started, and do the best you can, okay? I know it's going to be hard work, but it means everything. So, you'd better go ahead and get started now. I'll be back soon to help."

"Okay, Dad," Ricardo said. "You can count on us."

CHAPTER THREE

THE CONTINENTAL 767 carrying Carl and Lori Throneberry taxied down the main east-west runway at LAX, then climbed straight out over the Pacific. At five thousand feet, the plane banked left, leveling out on a course heading east-southeast, then climbed to clear the Santa Ana Mountains south and east of the city. After about twenty minutes, the plane reached cruising altitude at thirty thousand feet, and immediately it encountered clear-air turbulence.

The cabin speakers came on, and a reassuring voice said, "Ladies and gentlemen, this is your captain. We have entered the jet stream at this altitude, and the flight center tells me that atmospheric disturbances caused by the meteor approaching the West Coast at this hour are going to be causing us some rough weather for the next few minutes. So I want you all to please remain in your seats with your seat belts securely fastened. Flight attendants, please remain seated until further notice. I want you all to remember that this aircraft is built to survive severe stress. We may have a bumpy ride for a bit, but please stay calm and relax—you're going to be completely safe."

At that moment the plane banked sharply to the left, shuddered, and dropped five hundred feet before stabilizing once again. Several passengers grabbed frantically for the air sickness bags in the seat-back pockets. With all of the tensions they had already experienced, the sudden jolt of air turbulence was more than most on board could tolerate. It wasn't long before the cabin took on the unsavory smell of a charity hospital.

The pilot came back on the intercom. "Sorry about that, ladies and gentlemen. We're going to try to gain a little altitude and see if that will help smooth things out for you. As you know, this flight was originally scheduled for Colorado Springs. We're getting reports from the tower, however, that there are some dangerous conditions ahead of us—including a number of rapidly spreading forest fires in the Rockies, along with high, gusty winds around Colorado Springs. It looks like we're going to be diverted."

There was animated conversation in the forward cabin as people realized their plans were being changed. After a brief pause, the captain continued, "We have been rerouted to Albuquerque. I'm sorry to change plans on you like this, but I hope you'll understand the importance of these emergency procedures. On our present course, we'll be landing in Albuquerque in about an hour and twenty minutes. There will be airline employees at the gate to assist you and help you make any additional travel arrangements you may require."

Suddenly it felt very cold inside the first-class cabin. Despite the debilitating heat they had survived in Los Angeles, Carl felt a shiver run the length of his spine.

Within a couple of minutes the captain came back on the intercom. "During the remainder of our flight," he said, "I'll do my best to keep you up-to-date on the situation on the Coast. . . . I can tell you now that I've just learned that all civilian and military aircraft on the West Coast, as well as those in Hawaii and Alaska, are now being evacuated with full passenger loads to cities in the Southwest, the Midwest, and the East Coast. The authorities can't give us any estimates at this time of how many hours are left before the air navigational network begins to malfunction, but we anticipate no problems or delays on our flight directly into Albuquerque this afternoon."

Hushed conversations could be heard throughout the plane. Some passengers were wondering aloud about the prospects for finding a place to stay in Albuquerque, of getting rental cars, or of making contact with loved ones and friends. One older woman was saying loudly that she knew it would come to this. Her thoroughly embarrassed middle-aged daughter was doing her best to change the subject.

"Well, I always wanted to go to Albuquerque," Carl said, trying to keep his tone light. He didn't even get a smile from his normally ebullient wife.

Before long, the captain came back on the intercom and said, "I'll give you as much information as I can about what's going on before we touch down in about an hour. But, folks, you should all be advised that the situation in Los Angeles is much worse at this hour. Whatever your religion, and whatever you may believe personally about God, I suggest you all pause to thank your God that you got out of L.A. safely today."

Lori reached over, took Carl's hand, and looked straight into his eyes. In all their years together, he had never seen that expression.

"Carl, the pilot's right. I think we should thank God that we got out alive."

"Thank God?" he snorted. "What has God got to do with it? We're on this plane because you wanted a vacation in Colorado. You bought the tickets and I agreed to come."

Lori was more serious now than at any time in her life, and she would not be put off. "Carl, stop and think about what's happened to us this morning. What if the emergency bulletin we listened to on the radio had been broadcast sooner? What if we hadn't heard the news? Or what if our car had broken down on the roadside somewhere because of the heat? What if we had shown up for our flight on time instead of an hour early? Don't you see? Millions of people are going to die back there, and you and I are safe. Somebody has been watching out for us!"

"Lori, I love you, and you know I respect your opinions. But, let's face it. Everything we've accomplished came from our own hard work. We bought the house and the cars and all the things we own. Nobody gave us anything. You bought the plane tickets because you wanted us to have a mini-vacation. And even if you did it as a surprise, you and I paid for these tickets. That's why we're here. What did God have to do with any of that? Be serious, will you? We were just lucky."

For the first time since their ordeal began, Lori showed signs of genuine grief and fear. Her eyes filled with tears, and Carl could feel her hand trembling before she pulled it away. Without meaning to, Carl realized he had hurt his wife deeply. He wanted to say something, to apologize, but he didn't know what to say. In truth, his own world was collapsing too. He realized that his tough words were mostly a front to cover up the helplessness he felt inside.

But Carl didn't have to worry about Lori. He could see that the day's events had somehow kindled a fire in her spirit that no casual remark could ever extinguish.

"Do you remember my aunt Josephine?" Lori asked after a long moment of reflection. "The one who retired to Phoenix?"

"Vaguely."

"Aunt Jo was the one who used to talk to us kids about the Bible, and she would tell us about all the spooky stuff in Revelation."

"What's revelation?" Carl asked.

"You know. The last book of the Bible . . . the one that talks about beasts and plagues. Surely you know about that—the Four Horsemen, the Last Judgment, and all that stuff?"

"Okay," Carl said warily. "I guess I've heard something about it. So what?"

"Well, I was just thinking. Aunt Josephine used to tell us about all those things in Revelation, describing what would happen on earth at the end of the age . . . before Jesus comes back."

"Lori, what are you talking about?" Carl laughed. "What has that got to do with the situation we're in? This is not some made-up story, you know. This is *real*. Here we are, right here on this airplane—headed for Albuquerque, New Mexico, of all places. And the city of Los Angeles, along with everything we own, is about to be wiped off the map!"

"Carl, don't you see? It's not a made-up story. Revelation was a prophecy about what would happen at the end of the age, and in one part it says that an angel is going to throw a burning mountain into the sea, and lots of people—on ships and on the land—are going to be killed. Don't you get it? A flaming mountain? A meteor? Millions of people are going to die!"

"Lori," he said in a somewhat patronizing tone, "I love you, but you know that I don't buy that stuff." He looked at his wife. She was so earnest, he couldn't help but feel the intensity of what she was saying. He owed her more than a cynical put-down.

"Okay," he said, "you've got my attention. What *else* did Auntie Jo tell you about revelation?"

Before Lori could answer, the cabin speaker clicked on once again.

"Ladies and gentlemen, this is your captain. We are about forty-five minutes from Albuquerque at this moment, and I have just received an update on the situation back in L.A. The word is that the meteor is expected to impact in the Pacific Ocean at a point west of Catalina. Impact time is still expected to be approximately seven this evening, Pacific time.

"The scientists are saying," he continued, "that the size of the object is estimated to be over a kilometer in length, half a kilometer in height, and perhaps as big as three-tenths of a kilometer in width. They are calling it a fireball." As the captain spoke, a loud murmur swept through the plane, along with sounds of crying, prayers, and expressions of anguish and concern.

"I hate to say this," the captain said, "but scientists are estimating that the intensity of the impact will be equivalent to one million megatons of TNT. That's a force almost impossible for anyone to imagine—but if they're right, it will send a wall of water at least a mile high across all of southern California. . . ."

Lori reached over to Carl with tears welling up in her eyes. Carl was biting his lower lip to keep from crying himself. The captain continued, "Nothing in the southern half of the state is expected to survive. It's still too early at this point to estimate what the effect of the impact may be on the rest of the Pacific region or the states east of California, but we'll try to get more information on that for you by the time we reach Albuquerque."

For the first time, Carl realized that everything he had worked for in life was suddenly gone. No home, no cars, no security. He didn't even have a job to go back to, and furthermore, he had no idea what would come next. He had never felt so lost and cut off from reality.

As the captain switched off the intercom again, Carl could hear people all over the plane crying and praying loudly. Carl twisted in his seat and looked straight into Lori's eyes.

"Lori," he said hoarsely, "I don't understand any of this. It's a nightmare! This can't be happening!" Lori nodded and brushed tears from her eyes. "What that man just said," Carl continued, "definitely seems to describe a mountain-sized rock, burning with fire, falling into the ocean. You know I've never been religious, but, honey, what's happening is just like what your aunt told you."

Lori spoke slowly and deliberately. "Aunt Josephine said that the Book of Revelation, which was written almost two thousand years ago, told about a time when a series of violent disasters would shake the earth. Most people don't really understand much about Revelation, but Aunt Josephine was convinced that an angel was going to throw a burning mountain into the sea and that it would kill millions of people someday."

"Does that mean the end of the world? Are we all going to die?" Carl asked, not sure he wanted to know the answer to his question.

"No," Lori said. "Aunt Jo said that when all the disasters were finished, Jesus was going to come back to the earth for a second time. That's what they mean by the Second Coming."

"What then?" he asked. "What's Jesus going to do to the earth then?"

"I don't remember all of it, Carl," Lori said, "but I think He's going to tie the devil up somehow, put an end to all the wars, and then begin something like a golden age of peace on earth."

Carl felt he was going into information overload. They had just lost everything. Every material object he had worked so hard to pay for was gone. He could never recoup his losses. Now Lori was trying to tell him about things that he had resisted or ignored all of his adult life.

He looked at her and asked angrily, "If Jesus Christ wants peace on earth, why doesn't He just make peace? I don't get it. I thought angels were supposed to be good guys. Why do they have to kill all these people?"

"Carl," she replied, "you know I'm not religious either. For sure, I don't have the answers. But here's what I remember. People like you and me ignore God until we come to a crisis in our lives. Aunt Jo said that God might give the human race as much as two thousand years to accept His love voluntarily. But after that, God was going to bring things to an end, in two ways. First, the Christians would be given a short time to tell everybody in the world about God's love. That would be like a big revival, I suppose. When they finished doing that, God was going to send some kind of terrible punishment on the rest of the people because of the way they had been living. Everybody would be given a chance to believe in Jesus, but not everybody would listen. Look, we know that's true. Some people have been too busy making money and doing other things with their lives—people like *us*."

Carl looked at her in amazement. "Lori, in all the years we've been together, you've never said one word about all this stuff to me. If you believe it so much, how come you never mentioned it until now?"

"Until today," she said, "it never exactly came up. Anyway, I thought most of it was a fairy tale. Aunt Josephine was . . . well, she was one of those evangelical Christians. Mother always said she was a little weird. Anyway, she died a couple of years ago. But, Carl, before she died, Aunt Jo told me that she was praying—for you and me. . . ."

"What are you saying?" he asked.

"I'm saying that those prayers may have gotten us on this airplane."

They both fell silent for several minutes, lost in thought.

Carl felt another shiver run down his spine. He had never been a particular believer in God, but he and Lori were alive, and millions of other people were in immediate danger. Why? He reached across and took Lori's hands in his. "I don't know anything about all this, but after all we've been through today, I *do* want to find out."

One of the things Lori loved about her husband was that he was incredibly inquisitive. She was grateful that he hadn't dismissed her aunt as some sort of religious lunatic, that he was keeping an open mind. She gave Carl's hands a squeeze. "We'll find out together," she said softly.

They leaned back in their leather seats and tried to relax for a few moments. But before either of them could relax completely, the pilot came back on the public address system: "Ladies and gentlemen," he said, "we are beginning our descent into the Albuquerque International Airport. Barring any unforeseen delays, we should be on the ground in about twenty minutes. Please remain in your seats with your seat belts fastened.

"We are being told by the tower," he continued, "that airplanes are landing in Albuquerque every three minutes, so we can expect some further delays and inconvenience before we get to the gate. But, we'll do our best to look after your needs. I've been told that there will be a complete briefing for you in the terminal, along with an update on the situation on the West Coast."

CARL FLIPPED TO THE BACK of the in-flight magazine and found maps and several paragraphs on the various airports in the region. The Albuquerque airport, he learned, was a joint-use military/civilian facility situated at 5,352 feet above sea level. It had four active runways, two of which were able to accommodate landings by any planes now flying. Runway 26/8, the east-west runway, was 13,755 feet long. Runway 35/17, the north/south runway, was 10,000 feet long. *Obviously this is a very large facility for a relatively small town,* he thought, realizing they had probably been rerouted to Albuquerque because the Albuquerque runways could handle all kinds of air traffic.

Looking out the window, he could see that the air traffic controllers were using both runways in an attempt to handle hundreds of big jets coming in for landings. Planes were parked at the civilian terminal, at ramps intended for corporate aircraft, as well as at the military facility.

Ground crews appeared to be exerting superhuman effort, pumping jet fuel into waiting aircraft. Carl assumed that they were going to reposition those planes to other areas, perhaps to the big Dallas/Fort Worth Airport, or even farther east before the anticipated navigational blackout. There were military personnel and air force buses everywhere. Obviously, emergency crews had been brought in to help unload passengers and baggage and to transport them to the terminal.

After deplaning several hundred yards from the main building, Lori and Carl got on one of the military buses and rode to the terminal. Once inside, they had to push their way through the crowds. About halfway down the concourse, the public address system in the terminal and the few television monitors in the waiting areas began broadcasting a message from the president of the United States.

Lori grabbed Carl's arm. "Look at this, Carl," she said, pointing to a TV they were just passing. They stopped to watch.

Sitting at his desk in the Oval Office, the president looked exhausted and very grave. *He seems much older and grayer now,* Lori thought.

His forehead was creased by deep lines. "My fellow Americans," he began, "it is my sad duty to inform you that in less than six hours our nation will experience the most devastating natural disaster in its history. At seven P.M. Pacific time, a meteor—a fireball weighing more than three hundred billion pounds—will impact the Pacific Ocean somewhere off the coast of California. I am told that it will strike the earth at a speed in excess of twenty-five thousand miles per hour."

During the emotional pause that followed, the president wiped tears from his eyes. Carl could hear cries of surprise and alarm echoing throughout the airport.

"My science advisers tell me," the president continued, his voice breaking, "that such an impact will send a wall of water a mile or more in height across all of southern California. . . ." There was another long pause. "I'm sorry," he said. "This is very hard for me. Similar waves will cause tidal waves throughout the entire Pacific Basin. Seismologists have told me that the impact may also cause other natural disturbances, including movement of the tectonic plates under the entire Pacific Rim. If they are correct, this will, in turn, set off a series of major earthquakes with unknown and generally unpredictable consequences all across the Pacific."

By this point there were hysterical shouts, moans, and weeping in the terminal. It was so loud that, at one point, Carl and others had to yell for quiet. Everyone could see that the president was visibly shaken. Carl noticed the haunted look in the president's eyes and briefly wondered if the president might just stop talking and walk away. But he continued.

"We are expecting, in addition, volcanic eruptions in the Pacific Northwest, British Columbia, and Alaska. . . . This is terrible," he said, looking away from the cameras briefly. "From there, our scientists anticipate that further eruptions will be triggered in Japan and the Philippines. I wish that were the end of it, but it's not. Within days, I am told, clouds of volcanic ash will fill the earth's atmosphere to such a degree that the sun and the stars will be obscured—for months, possibly even years."

The president paused, visibly pained and grief-stricken, then slowly continued his somber words, interspersed with tears and labored breathing. "I regret to tell you that our American ships—including United States Navy vessels located in the Pacific, and particularly those within fifteen hundred miles of the West Coast—are going to be in terrible danger. I understand that many will likely capsize and sink within hours of the meteor's impact. There is, in addition, a high probability of serious damage to commercial and military shipping between the West Coast and Japan—as far east as Southeast Asia.

"All civilian and military aircraft located anywhere in the Pacific area have been ordered to evacuate as many passengers as possible to designated locations of safety."

Lori and Carl were being jostled by the crowds gathering around the television monitors. The talking, crying, and yelling were growing increasingly louder by the minute until several airline personnel, who were also standing by watching the broadcast, called loudly for quiet.

"In just the past few minutes," the president said, "I have ordered all our United States armed forces and national guard units to maximum alert status. Our military personnel are ordered to take all necessary steps to save lives and minimize suffering. At the same time, civilian relief agencies are authorized by me to spare no expense or effort to try to render aid wherever they are able to do so."

Drawing his hand across his eyes, the president gasped audibly, and tears began streaming down his cheeks. Suddenly his eyes took on the look of a hunted animal. "I have been told by my advisers that there is no realistic hope of evacuating the inhabitants of Greater Los Angeles tonight. All freeways and feeder roads in and around the city are clogged at this hour with stalled and abandoned vehicles. No significant assistance to the population of southern California is possible from this point on. . . ." Then sobbing, he added, "Unless there is some dramatic change in the situation, and none is expected,

I fear that millions will die and there is nothing either I or your government can do to stop what is about to happen. . . . Absolutely nothing!"

As they listened, Carl and Lori clung to each other. It was almost impossible to comprehend what was being said. The scope of the damage predicted by the presidential advisers was beyond human understanding. Carl was visibly shocked and stunned by every sentence, but at the same time he realized that the people standing around them were embarrassed and angry that their president was making such a spectacle of his own emotions.

The president continued his address in a halting voice, his head and shoulders visibly shaking, but what followed was unscripted. The tone of their leader's voice had changed. "I know you all remember that three years ago I vetoed a bill submitted to me by the Congress to finance development of nuclear-tipped interceptor missiles that would have been capable of destroying asteroids and meteors in outer space that might threaten the earth. It was my considered judgment, as your president, that the technology was too unreliable at that time, and the cost was beyond the demands of a balanced budget. I realize now that I made a terrible mistake.

"We in government learned of this approaching meteor just seven days ago. No immediate disaster management plan was put into effect because, again, I ignored the advice of my own science adviser and chose to believe the academic experts who said that this object was not going to be captured by Earth's gravitational field. They convinced me that it was going to pass by harmlessly in space, much as others have done in the past.

"But even after the location of the Impact Zone seemed certain, I delayed announcing this impending event for fear of arousing unnecessary panic in southern California and in world financial markets. . . ."

At that point, the president of the United States began to weep uncontrollably. "I delayed the announcement," he said, sobbing, "because of my fear of the political consequences if the experts were wrong. I am very sorry to say tonight that my own cowardice and indecision will now cost the lives of millions of innocent people."

As he stared into the television camera, he reached his right hand slowly and deliberately inside his suit coat. "My fellow Americans, I have failed you, and I cannot go on living with the guilt I feel for what I have done."

At first the Secret Service agents standing behind the cameras thought he was reaching for a handkerchief to dry his tears. Then they saw the gun. They lunged toward him, but he already had the 9-mm Beretta in his hand. They reached the desk a fraction of a second after the bullet entered the president's right temple.

The president's body thrust back convulsively, a ghastly grimace frozen on his face. His arm shook violently, and the gun clattered to the floor. There was blood everywhere, and pieces of his skull were blown away. But before the nation could grasp what they had just seen, the president of the United States slumped forward . . . dead.

Shrieks and cries went up throughout the crowd where Carl and Lori now stood, embracing each other even more tightly. Chaos erupted all around them. The world seemed to have gone crazy. They were facing a moment of world crisis like nothing in recorded history, and their president had just entered the history books—as the first chief executive of the United States to die by his own hand.

Chapter Four

WORD SPREAD LIKE WILDFIRE that the president of the United States had just committed suicide before the eyes of the entire nation. The crowds in the Albuquerque International Airport had witnessed the entire spectacle in stunned amazement. Some people cried out loud. Others moaned or spoke in hushed tones. Out of the crowd, a burly man dressed like a construction worker yelled out, "I'm not sorry for the bum! The sniveling coward was a mass murderer! This country's in serious trouble right now, but we're sure better off without *him*."

"Yeah, that's right," someone yelled out. "I'm *glad* he's dead!"

Carl Throneberry reacted impulsively. "What are you people saying? You're glad the president is dead? Have you all gone crazy? We should be glad to be alive at this moment. Enough people are going to die tonight without you standing there gloating over the death of the president."

Several voices answered back—some supportive, but others obviously angry. Suddenly a tall, athletic-looking, young black man stepped up beside Carl and held up both hands. "Hey, come on, people," he said, pointing to Carl. "This guy is right. We're gonna be losing something very precious today, and this is no time to be bad-mouthing anybody—least of all the president of the United

States. Let's just get on with business, what do you say?" There were a few angry murmurs, but they were overwhelmed by a chorus of agreement. Then the crowd began to disburse.

Lori instantly recognized the tall young man. He was Dave Busby, the star forward for the Los Angeles Lakers basketball team. Moving closer, she reached out her hand, "You're Dave Busby! I can't believe it's you!" He smiled and took her hand.

"I'm Lori Throneberry," she continued, "and this is my husband, Carl. We're big Lakers fans. . . ." She paused. "Well, actually, *I'm* a big Lakers fan. Carl has done some ad campaigns for the Lakers, but I'm the real fan in our house!"

Even as Lori was speaking, a wave of sadness rushed over her. In the instant she recalled the fun and excitement of going to the Lakers games, she also remembered the tragedy of their situation and the fact that the Lakers and basketball and Los Angeles itself would soon be things of the past. "In fact," Lori continued, "I've followed you ever since you played at North Carolina State, Dave. I'll never forget the time you scored forty-nine points against Phoenix in the playoffs! But how odd to finally get to meet you here—and in this situation."

"Thanks, Lori," Dave said. "I'm glad to meet you too. It's always good to meet a fan. But you're right. This is weird."

Carl reached over and took Dave's hand. "Thanks for standing up for me, Dave," he said. "Actually, we've met before. You probably don't remember, but I was the guy who set up your Cadillac endorsement about three years ago. I'm the account exec from JPT Worldwide."

"Oh, sure!" The big man smiled. "I remember you, Carl. It's a small world. But, hey, come on—let's get out of this crowd." Dave led the way, and Carl and Lori followed him to an open space near a check-in counter.

Carl looked down instinctively for his luggage, then realized he had nothing but the flight bag in his hand. Lori had a shoulder bag and her carry-on suitcase. Dave wasn't carrying any luggage at all, but he held a large black book in his hand.

"Dave," Carl said, "do you have a suitcase or bags or anything to pick up?"

"No, man," the athlete responded. "I got out with this—my Bible. That's it."

"A Bible?" Carl asked. "That's all?"

"That's right," Dave answered. "I always use my travel time to read it. Looks like that's going to be the most important thing right now, anyway." Dave smiled and looked into Carl's eyes. "Are you folks believers?"

"No," Carl replied, "I guess I'm what you would call an agnostic. But a day like this can sure make a guy stop and think. You know, on the flight from L.A. Lori was telling me about a book of prophecies in the Bible called Revelation. It tells about how a meteor is going to strike the earth someday. At least, that's what Lori's aunt said. Have you ever heard of that?"

"Oh, yeah," Dave said, "I've heard of it. But, listen, we've got to get out of this mob and find a place to stay. If you don't already have other plans, I know this guy who has a big house near here. He's an old basketball coach and a good friend. I think he'll put us up for a couple of days until we can find out what's going on. If you're up for it, I think we can go over there and camp out, and then we can talk about Revelation if you want."

Lori and Carl nodded agreement, and Dave looked around quickly for a phone.

There were long waiting lines at all the pay phones in the terminal, and just when it looked as if they might have to give up on calling Dave's friend, the tall player walked over to the ticket counter, looked down at the agent, and boomed out, "Hi, I'm Dave Busby of the Lakers. Would you please call this number for me so I can get a place to stay tonight?"

Taken completely by surprise, the agent immediately forgot all his usual excuses and meekly punched up the number, then handed the phone to Dave.

Dave put the phone to his ear and waited until there was an answer on the other end. "Charley," he yelled, "this is Dave. What do you know, man? I just got out of L.A., and I'm at the airport with a couple of new friends. Do you have any room at your place for three refugees?" He paused briefly. "Really? That's great, man, but just one more thing. Would you be able to pick us up at the airport?"

Dave looked at Carl, smiled, and gave a thumbs-up sign. "That's terrific, Charley. You're a good friend. And, yes, I *am* praising the Lord that I'm alive! We'll see you outside in about ten minutes."

The three travelers pushed through the crowds of confused people and made their way down the concourse and to the front of the terminal. In less than ten minutes, a big, new BMW sedan pulled up, and a tanned, athletic-looking man in his sixties got out of the driver's side. "Hop in," he said. "You've been through quite an ordeal. I'm glad I could be here for you."

Once in the car, Dave introduced everyone. On the way to his home, Charley was like a machine gun, firing questions at them about the situation in Los Angeles, the news on TV, and all the things that had been going on around them during their eventful journey.

But as soon as they were settled in at their host's opulent adobe hacienda, built in the style of the old high-beamed ranch houses, it was Carl and Lori's turn to start asking questions. "Charley," Carl said, "Lori and I have just gotten out ahead of what may be the worst natural disaster in human history. I'm not a religious guy, but I've always been innately curious. Back at the airport Dave said he knows about the Book of Revelation, and that's something I'd like to hear more about. Was this thing—this meteor—predicted two thousand years ago, like I've heard? And, most important of all, do you guys know what's coming next?"

Charley let out a loud guffaw, then caught himself. "Carl, I'm just a sixty-five-year-old ex-coach who made some good investments a few years ago. Dave here is a pretty talented hoop jock who happens to be a committed Christian and student of the Bible. Actually, we're both students of the Bible, but we're not the ultimate experts in any of this. We'll be glad to help you as much as we can, but please understand that we don't have all the answers either."

"Okay," Carl said, "but surely you can help give us a better idea of what this is all about, can't you? If what Lori has been telling me is even half right, then it's worth talking about."

"Of course it is," Dave said. "But what about something to eat first? I mean, I'm ready to talk, but let's eat while we're doing it. Is that all right?"

"Sure. Good idea," said Carl.

"Good idea is right," said Charley. "Come on. Let's go into the kitchen and make some sandwiches—then we can talk. And even better, tomorrow morning I'll take you guys up to the mountains to meet somebody who can take you to the next level. The guy's an old friend of mine who has spent practically his whole life studying the Bible. Pastor Jack can tell you a lot more than either of us ever dreamed of."

Lori turned to Charley. "Before I eat, do you mind if I call my parents in Minnesota? They and my sister are going to be worried sick about Carl and me."

"Of course," Charley said. "There's a phone in my den. I'll show you where it is. We can make lunch while you're talking to your parents."

Lori turned to Carl. "Should I call your mother too?" Carl's mother lived in Minnesota as well. "That would be great," Carl said. "Tell her I love her and that I'll call her later."

While Lori was on the phone, the others went to the kitchen. Charley started taking bread, lettuce, tomatoes, and lunch meat from the pantry and the refrigerator. As Dave and Carl pitched in to help, Charley flipped on a TV set on the counter. "I understand that in about an hour the vice president is going to be sworn in as our new president. I'm sure we all want to hear what's he's got to say."

By the time Lori returned, lunch was ready. "Did you get in touch with our parents?" Carl asked.

"Yes," Lori said, "and they're very relieved that we're okay and that"—she smiled at Charley— "we have such a good place to stay."

They settled down around the giant table in Charley's spacious, wood-beamed kitchen to a platter of sandwiches and chips and a large pot of coffee. The kitchen was warm and inviting, with colorful Spanish tiles and traditional decor. It was a great place to relax and a good place for Carl and Lori to start getting some answers to the questions that burned inside them.

Carl's mind was racing now more than ever. There were so many gaps to fill in. Why was the L.A. tragedy happening? Was all this just a freak of nature, or was it really something more? Why were their lives being spared? Was it possible that there was, after all, a God in the universe? And, if so, was it possible that the meteor and the heat wave and all that had been happening to them were acts of God, as so many people seemed to believe? He was perplexed. There was a certain fatalistic comfort in believing God was a myth. But if He did exist, what possible purpose could He have in letting all these bad things happen to people? And, more troubling, what was His purpose for their lives? Carl realized that, in light of their current predicament, these were things he needed to know.

CHARLEY SAID A BLESSING over the food and invoked God's care—not only for himself, his guests, and their loved ones, but for all those on the West Coast who were standing in the way of unimaginable tragedy. Both Carl and Lori found themselves sniffling and wiping tears from their eyes as Charley talked to God in such an intimate way.

He seems to know God personally, Lori thought, as she listened to Charley pray. As he prayed, she thought about people she and Carl had known for years. She thought about all the people and places they loved back in L.A., most of which would soon disappear forever. She remembered all the good times and the good friends. She thought of the things she wished she had never done, words she had never spoken—old wounds that would never be healed. She glanced briefly at Carl and recognized from the expression of deep sadness on his face that he was feeling the same way too.

Dave Busby's family was mostly on the East Coast. He wasn't worried about them for the moment, but he was thinking of all that he was losing on this day of terror and tragedy. He looked up while Charley was still praying and thought about the concerns of the people in that room. *Surely God must have a purpose for our lives. Surely this is not some tragic mistake. Surely—*

Charley finished his prayer, and everyone quietly echoed, "Amen."

The conversation was subdued while they were eating, but little by little the talk grew more animated, and they returned to their earlier discussion. Lori came back to the point first. "By all rights, Charley, Carl and I should be victims along with everybody else back in L.A. tonight. This just keeps running through my mind. But instead, we're here with you guys in a very nice place—relatively safe, I hope. I don't know about the rest of you, but I'm having a very hard time with all this. Charley," Lori said, "I just want to know what's happening. Can you help me?"

Carl looked up and nodded in agreement. "Me too," he said. "This is all pretty unreal for me right now—like a bad dream."

"That's right," Lori continued. "Not that we don't appreciate you guys, Dave and Charley. You're great. But I keep hoping I'm going to wake up in a few minutes and find out it was just some kind of terrible nightmare. I want my home back. I want my happy life in Los Angeles. I want my old friends—Ginny and Brigette and Tom and Nancy and all the people we may never see again." She paused and brushed the tears from her eyes. "This just can't be happening to me—to me, to Carl, or to you guys either. But it is!

Why?" Lori wept quietly but openly, and the hearts of the three men in the room reached out to her. They also knew what it was to lose everything. They knew what she must be feeling, and each shared a deep sense of her pain and suffering.

Carl slid closer to his wife and put an arm around her shoulder. "Lori's right. I feel the same way," he said. "Our lives, our home, our property, our friends—everything we ever worked for and lived for are gone. My life, my career. Kaput. Just like that! I've got to face the fact that for the first time in my life I'm not in control—and I'm both angry and terrified. I don't know what's going to happen next. Do you hear what I'm saying?"

Charley nodded and sat forward in his chair. "Yeah, Carl," he said. "I do. We were all caught off guard by this thing. At this moment, I think I have a sense of peace about it, but I know exactly how you feel. I'm also concerned about what comes next."

"I guess you must think we're a little crazed," Lori said, "but we've got to get some answers. Can you help us? I have been trying to remember what my aunt told us kids about the end times, but it's been so long ago. Where in Revelation does it talk about meteors?"

"Let me get you something first," Charley said. He pushed back from the table and left the kitchen. A minute later he returned, carrying three Bibles. He handed one to Lori, one to Carl, then opened the biggest one.

"Okay," he said. "Have you ever looked at any of this before?"

Carl shook his head, "No. Never."

"Well, then open the Bible to the very last book. That's Revelation." He sat down in his chair again, flipped the pages of his Bible open, and waited for the others to find the place. "Got it? Now turn to chapter eight. If you look down the page you'll see a series of verses where it tells about the seven angels ready to sound their trumpets. Do you see that?"

Carl ran his finger down the page over the first five verses. "Okay," he said. "Here. I see it. But where does it tell about meteors?"

Charley and Dave both laughed out loud. "Man, you *do* get straight to the point, don't you?" Dave said.

"Look at verses six and seven," Charley said. "That's where it tells about the first angel who is to bring a scorching heat wave to the earth. We've been feeling the effects of that already. But that just sets the stage for what's coming next."

"Oh, look!" Lori exclaimed. "Here's what my aunt Josephine told me about! Carl, look at verses eight and nine." She read the verse aloud, slowly. "'Then the second angel sounded: and *something* like a great mountain burning with fire was thrown into the sea, and a third of the sea became blood. And a third of the living creatures in the sea died, and a third of the ships were destroyed.'"

"I see it!" Carl exclaimed. "That's what the president was talking about on TV before he—he killed himself. He said that there was going to be a tidal wave caused by the meteor that would capsize even the biggest warships. The president didn't talk about this specifically, but the pressure from the concussion would certainly wipe out the fish—even the big whales in a large part of the Pacific Ocean. Charley, this is incredible! Who wrote this stuff?"

Charley McAtee let go another booming laugh. "Carl, you sure give me a lot of credit for knowing all the answers. Here's what I've been told. The Book of Revelation was written after the time of Christ by one of His apostles named John. John was in exile on a little rock— actually, a penal colony—off the coast of Greece called Patmos. He said that Jesus appeared to him with a message for the church and his job was to write it down faithfully. In some sort of spiritual sense, John was caught up into heaven where he saw and heard all these things dealing with the future." As he looked around the group Charley saw that they were all hanging onto his words.

"The book he wrote," he continued, "is what the early church called the Apocalypse. That means 'the unveiling.' John sent copies of this book to all seven of the early churches in what we now know as Turkey. Later, it was made part of the New Testament. Believers haven't always understood what it means, and there has been a lot of debate over certain parts of the book. But we're certain it is a faithful and true witness of what will happen at the end of the age."

"So, you're talking, like the first century?" Carl asked.

"Yeah, Carl. That's when it was written," Dave answered. "Probably around eighty or ninety A.D. So, the things taking place today were actually foreseen by the prophet nearly two thousand years ago."

"Wow!" Carl exclaimed. "What comes next?"

Charley smiled and continued. "Next, after the meteor falls and the ships are sunk in the Pacific, we're told about another angel who gives a signal for a star called Wormwood to fall to earth and poison a third of the waters of the sea. So, at that point we see another tragedy taking place because the people who drink that poisoned water will all die."

"Wormwood?" Lori asked. "What is that?"

"Nobody really knows for certain at this point, Lori," Charley said. "But God may have given us a clue. You remember back in the eighties when the Ukraine was part of the old Soviet Union? There was a nuclear power plant located at the city of Chernobyl near Kiev. Well, that plant malfunctioned, and when it did, a lot of deadly radiation escaped into the environment. Many people got sick or died—eventually tens of thousands of people were affected by it. Clouds of radioactive material traveled as far as Western Europe, England, and Ireland. It was a real tragedy."

"But, Charley," Carl interjected, "I don't get it. What has the nuclear accident at Chernobyl got to do with Revelation and Wormwood?"

"That's why I said God may have given us a clue to the mystery, Carl. You see, Chernobyl in Russian means *Wormwood*."

Carl and Lori stared at each other. Then Carl turned to Charley. "Do you mean that Revelation is talking about poisonous radiation getting into the drinking water?" Carl asked, then quickly answered his own question. "Of course, I see it now. This meteor that's about to hit somewhere out in the Pacific Ocean may very well start setting off earthquakes all over the world."

Lori picked up the thread. "And those earthquakes could cause meltdowns in nuclear power plants all over the world!"

"Good Lord!" Carl exclaimed. "The radiation fallout could kill millions!"

"Which is precisely what the groups protesting nuclear power plants have been trying to tell us for years," Dave Busby chimed in.

Carl fell back in his chair, took a deep breath, then continued, "Charley, this apostle John couldn't possibly know anything about nuclear power plants and radiation fallout. Everything fits, but how did this guy learn all these things?"

Dave said, "Don't you see, Carl? John probably didn't have a clue, but God knew about nuclear power. After all, He put the sources of power there to begin with. John for sure understood bitter, poisonous water."

"That's right, Dave," said Charley. "For one thing, he read about that in the Old Testament, which told the history of Israel. John used the term *bitter water* instead of nuclear radiation, but I believe that God slipped in the code word, *Wormwood,* which could only be understood by people living at the end of the age—people who lived after the Chernobyl meltdown."

Carl shook his head. "Are you telling me that the God of love was forecasting, two thousand years in advance, that a time would come on earth—perhaps in our time—when He would personally oversee the natural disasters that could kill a billion or so people?"

Charley looked him squarely in the eye. "Carl, God sent His only Son to die to save everybody. For centuries, He has sent His servants all over the world to warn people and to offer them forgiveness. He actually begged people to turn from their selfishness and immorality so He could forgive them for their sins, but they haven't listened. Over the past five years or so, Christians all over the world have been carrying on a maximum effort to bring God's love to the world, and there has been a tremendous harvest."

"But most people," Dave joined in, "have thumbed their noses at God and turned their backs on Him. Right? So please don't blame God for what's about to happen to the world. He's given people every opportunity to turn to Him."

"I don't guess I have much room to talk," Carl said. "I've done everything I could to steer clear of the Bible and people—no offense—like you guys, who read it. But you're serious? There's been a—what—a revival or something going on for the last five years?"

"That's right," Dave answered, "but we'll talk about that when we have more time."

"Carl," Charley said, "let me ask you something. Have you ever lied?"

"Of course," Carl said and smiled. "I'm in advertising."

"Have you ever taken something that didn't belong to you?"

"Sure, I suppose so." Carl shrugged.

"Have you ever cursed and used God's name in vain?"

"Of course," came the answer. "All the time. But what are you getting at?"

"Carl, here's the deal," Dave Busby broke in. "You just admitted to breaking God's laws. Any one of those things would earn you a maximum sentence. But how many billions of people do you think have done exactly what you've been doing, and worse? Every one of those people has had a chance for a full pardon. It's always been there, but they've turned it down. Now, they're coming up on 'J Day'—that's Judgment Day. It's a bad scene now, man, but hang on to your hat. After the next few years are over, Jesus Christ is coming back to set up His kingdom on earth. Are you ready for that, brother?"

Lori jumped in. "Please, you guys, stop getting off the track and let's talk about Revelation. I want to know what's next. When I look down here, it says, 'A third of the sun, and a third of the moon, and a third of the stars will be darkened and not shine.' That's terrible. But what does it mean?"

Before Charley could answer, Carl stepped in. "I studied astronomy in college, and I've tried to keep up with it ever since. I may not know everything, but I do know this: nothing is going to happen to the sun, the moon, and the stars. If this is true, it probably means that they just won't shine on the earth."

Suddenly it was Charley's turn to ask the questions. "Why not, Carl?"

"Very simple," he replied. "When Mount Krakatoa, a volcano in Indonesia, erupted about a hundred years ago, the sky was so full of smoke and ash that the sun's rays didn't get through to much of the earth for nearly two years. If the meteor sets off volcanic activity throughout the Pacific Rim, from Central and South America all the way around to Borneo, then I have no doubt there will be enough ash in the sky to shut out the sunlight for a year or more—or several years, for that matter. And if that happens, the earth will enter a long winter, a global night."

"I don't want to think about that, Carl," Lori said, shuddering as she closed her Bible.

"I'm afraid we don't have a choice," Charley said. "Carl is right on track."

"But just think," Carl continued. "Think how that will destroy agricultural production. It means millions of people will starve. Talk about hell! There will be hell on earth, not to mention what it will do to the economy of the whole world. If I'm right, Charley, I bet there won't even be one of the present governments standing three years from now."

There was silence in the room as the group considered the implications of Carl's words.

"Listen, Charley," Carl continued, "you, Dave, and Lori's aunt Josephine know about all these things that I've never even thought about before. But I'll tell you right now, in my opinion the Bible simply could not be this accurate unless it was written by someone with intelligence beyond anything we know as human. And if that's so, the Bible has to hold the mystery of what's next. So, are you guys gonna help us to find out what's next?"

Charley sat forward on the edge of his chair and replied softly, "You have my word, Carl." Then he stood up, and as if on some unstated signal, the others stood up too.

"Are you an investor, Carl?" Charley asked.

"Yeah," he answered. "You know . . . a little of this and that, but I'm not a pro at it."

"Dave *is* a pro at it," Charley said. "At least, he has some good pros working for him. But when I first began to see that times were going to get tough around here, I bought fifty thousand bushels of soybeans and rented a storage facility to hold them. I went long a thousand contracts of September beans, and it looks like I've turned a pretty good profit. We should have enough supplies and extra cash to help a lot of God's people."

As they walked back toward the center of the house, Carl threw an arm around Charley's shoulder. "I don't believe you and Dave! One minute we're talking prophecy and worldwide disaster, and now *this!* Sure, Charley, you're just a poor, simple, barefoot ex-coach—who just happened to pick up a cool ten million dollars on one phone call. You two guys amaze me!"

Dave laughed. "Come on, Carl. Let's go to Charley's den and see what the new president has to say in his first official speech."

AT THREE IN THE AFTERNOON, Manuel Quintana stopped work so he and the boys could take a short lunch break. His muscles ached from the unaccustomed work of digging, and his hands were stiff, raw, and swollen. He looked at his boys' hands. They were blistered and bleeding, but no one complained. The five short trenches were almost complete. They went inside the transmitter building where Cathy had made lunch.

Manuel moved the big warehouse fan closer to them to help create a more constant breeze, and then as the family sat down at the table, he reached over and flipped the channel selector to one of the satellite stations just in time to watch a replay of the president's speech on CNN.

The boys were stunned silent by what they saw. The past few days had been very difficult for them. The heat was stifling. But the day's events left them speechless. And there was something else too. Because it was television, there was an aura of unreality to what they saw taking place on the screen. They knew that this was a deadly serious time. They had seen the terror in the streets of Altadena earlier in the day; yet they were aloof, distant. "Dad?" Juan asked. "We *are* going to make it, aren't we?"

Manuel looked at his youngest son and reached over and gave him a hug. "Yeah, I think we'll make it, Juanito," he said. "The meteor is going to hit somewhere out there in the ocean. We're high enough on this mountain to escape the surge of water. At least, I think we are.

"But the problem," he said, "is going to be the heat. That thing is really hot and getting hotter. If we can just survive the heat, then I think we'll be okay. But we need to keep praying, boys. We're alive so far—and with God's help, we can make it. But, let's eat now and get back to work. We have to finish digging those holes and then fill up all five pits with water as fast as we can."

The boys ate their sandwiches and then went back to work. Manuel gave Cathy a hug, then started dragging several large rolls of commercial sheet plastic out of the storage room. With his pocket knife, he cut off five huge sheets of film and quickly fashioned five makeshift linings—one for each of the shallow trenches. He was careful not to cut or tear the film, and as each boy finished his digging, Manuel shoved the plastic down into the hole so that it extended over the rim. The boys weighted the sides and corners down with rocks, logs, and other heavy objects they found lying outside the transmitter building.

By five o'clock, they could all see the clouds of smoke billowing up from hundreds of forest fires to the north and south of their location. Forest fires would pose a whole new set of dangers for them, provided they survived the impact.

Cathy, who had been silent most of the afternoon, took Manuel's large hands in her own tiny ones and kissed each of his fingers. "I love you, Manolo," she said. "If we don't make it, I want you to know that I've always loved you, and I've never ever loved anyone like I love you right now."

Manuel put his arms around Cathy and held her in a desperate and tearful embrace. "Cathy. . . ." He looked into her beautiful brown eyes, but there was nothing to say. No words would come. He simply buried his face in her long, dark hair and held her close.

When he turned back to his work, Manuel wiped sweat and tears from his eyes and called the boys together. "You know, guys, none of us may come out of this thing alive. But I'm hopeful, and here is the only survival plan I can think of. It's going to get really, really hot around here in a little bit. The worst will only last for two or three minutes, but if any one of us is exposed to the direct heat. . . . Well, just make sure you keep down low in the trenches, and stay underwater as much as you can.

"I want each one of you to kneel down, up to your nose in the water. Okay? And when that thing comes down, whatever it is, I want you to hold your breath and duck all the way down under the water until you feel the impact. Can you do that?" All three boys nodded. "I think the dirt and the water will shield us. But if you get out of your trench or if you stand up, you won't be able to take the heat. So, please boys, stay down. And you, too, Cathy. We all have to just stay down in the trenches and don't panic."

His wife spoke up. "Manolo, you know we trust you, but will this idea of yours really work? Do you think there's any hope for us?"

"Cathy," he replied softly, lifting her chin slightly with his right hand, "it's the best plan we have right now. Nothing like this has ever happened before." He looked at each of his sons, then drew them all together. "I don't know if it'll work. It's just a chance, guys. But we have to try it, okay?"

They nodded.

"Okay then, that settles it," Cathy replied. "I believe that God has let us come to this mountain for a purpose, and we are going to ask for His help right now. Manolo, my husband, will you pray for us?"

Manuel thought, *I am an engineer, not a priest. But this is something I must do for my family*. Then he began to pray aloud.

"Padre Celestial, we five are on this mountain today facing death. If we are going to die, then we ask that You would forgive us our sins. Because of the sacrifice of Your Son, Jesus, we know You will forgive us. But, if You would, please, dear Father, let us live so that we can glorify You. Thank You, Father, for hearing our prayer. Amen."

When he finished, four other voices whispered, "Amen," and four other hands followed him in making the sign of the cross. Tears flowed down all five faces as they hugged and kissed one another—perhaps for the last time. Now all they could do was wait.

Manuel walked quickly over to the shed and pulled out a long water hose connected by a pump to an underground storage tank. He dragged it over to the edge of the clearing and filled the survival trenches to a point less than a foot below the surface. He took each of the boys by the arms and lowered them down into their trenches. First Juan, then Miguel, then Ricardo. Finally, he came over and held Cathy's arms as she stepped down into the water.

"Thanks, Dad," said Miguel. "Thanks, Dad," the others echoed.

Then Manuel put his hands down on the side of the last trench and lowered himself into the water. He could hear the others dipping their heads under the water every few minutes to cool off. Then they all waited silently, and they prayed.

Chapter Five

Vice President Ted Rust was an imposing figure. He was a former movie actor who had been cast as a political hero in several of his films. He had done such a good job of acting, speaking his lines with such conviction, that the voters of his home state felt he had the makings of a real politician. In yet another case of life imitating art, they elected him governor by a landslide.

Approaching middle age had only accentuated Rust's image as a leader. His hair was brown but going salt-and-pepper. His voice had become even richer and more distinguished. Millions would gladly have followed him anywhere. In reality, nothing could have been more absurd. Ted Rust was emotionally unstable, insecure, and in need of constant affirmation.

Yet, despite many flaws, he had the good sense to surround himself with capable supporters—including a brilliant chief of staff and two equally brilliant young speechwriters. The chief ran the office while Rust delivered prepared television speeches flawlessly. So flawlessly, in fact, that his approval rating as governor hit 80 percent. He was nominated by acclamation for second place on his party's winning national ticket.

The vice president learned of the president's suicide through his encrypted satellite telephone aboard Air Force Two. They were over the Caribbean at the time, en route to Chile for the state funeral of General Pinochet. His first inclination was to keep on going, but after a moment's thought, and the prompting of his flight crew, the vice president realized they had no alternative but to turn around and return to Andrews Air Force Base near Washington.

Vice President Rust left his stateroom in the forward part of the airplane and signaled for Vince D'Agostino, his chief of staff; the air force brigadier general assigned as his military aide; and his speechwriter to come with him. He appeared to be in control, but, in truth, he was on a short fuse. As they gathered hurriedly around the table in the conference room near the center of the plane, a fax was coming through that contained the text of the president's message to the nation.

The document included a candid assessment from the office of the Federal Emergency Management Agency (FEMA) and the Joint Chiefs, describing the impending disaster on the West Coast. As soon as they took in the information they had received, and as they measured the gravity of the situation, the chief of staff started going back over the facts quickly, in a sort of impromptu vice-presidential situation briefing.

Little by little, the color drained from Ted Rust's face. As D'Agostino laid out the details concerning the meteor threat, the death of the president, and their own sudden change of plans, Rust stood up, mumbled to himself, then yelled at the top of his lungs, "Hold on! Stop it!"

There was a long, uncomfortable silence as Rust visibly struggled to come to grips with his own situation. He was running both hands through his now disheveled hair and marching restlessly back and forth across the width of the plane.

When he stopped pacing, he said through clenched teeth, "Are you telling me that I am going to go back there and take charge of the government of the United States during the worst crisis in history?" Again, there was a long, awkward silence.

Shuffling a stack of papers on the large table, his military aide tried to speak. "Mr. Vice President—I mean, Mr. President . . ."

Rust spun on his heels and shouted abruptly, "Shut up, you!"

Everyone froze, and nervous glances were exchanged around the room. When Vince D'Agostino tried to speak, the vice president exploded once again. "I cannot handle this, Vince, and I am not going to allow myself to be put into this situation! Do you hear me? I will *not* be put into this situation!"

Unbelievably, tears were welling up in the vice president's eyes. Not the tears of a man grief-stricken by impending tragedy, or even the tears of one horrified by the reported suicide of the nation's chief executive, but more like the tears of a child terrified by his own vision of reality. The facade of self-confidence and calm was shattered. All pretense of power, leadership, and eloquence was gone. All those disaster movies, after all, were just make-believe. Suddenly Ted Rust found himself face-to-face with a real-life tragedy, a real global crisis, real responsibilities, and he could not deal with any of it.

"Get me a drink," he barked to no one in particular. "Make it a double bourbon on the rocks." He wiped the sweat from his forehead with his shirt-sleeve. "No, bring me the whole bottle. I'll pour my own." The speechwriter got up and returned a few minutes later with a bottle of bourbon and a glass of ice. The vice president immediately poured a double and downed it.

The group in that little room knew very well that the vice president of the United States was a borderline alcoholic. They knew also that his home life was in shambles, held together by political expediency. He sought solace through compulsive alcohol abuse and equally compulsive womanizing. Rumor had it that his wife fought back by absenting herself for extended periods of time, to engage in secret liaisons with assorted lovers—male and female.

Vince D'Agostino, the chief of staff, was a streetwise Italian from the Lower East Side of Manhattan. He had fought his way through New York public schools, went on to New York University where he graduated Phi Beta Kappa, and was then awarded a full scholarship to Fordham Law School, where he was editor of the *Law Review*. After passing the New York state bar exam, he was romanced with heady offers from several prestigious corporate law firms.

But Vince decided he wanted something else. He worked one year for a Federal Appeals Court judge on the United States Second Circuit. Later he earned a name for himself as a tough litigator, working for the United States district attorney in lower Manhattan. That's where he had first met Ted Rust.

The two men were thrown together at a political strategy meeting. D'Agostino saw Rust's political potential and offered to help out in any way he could. He worked on the campaign for the state house, then left his law career to become the new governor's chief of staff.

When Ted Rust moved to Washington four years later, Vince came too. He was a Catholic, a hard-nosed idealist who wanted a big family when he married his wife, Angie. But, try as they might, they were unable to have children.

As the vice president reached for the bottle to pour a second drink, Vince quickly took both the glass and the bottle away. Before Rust could protest, Vince leapt to his feet, his eyes blazing. "Listen to me, Ted Rust, and you listen good! Millions of grief-stricken Americans are going to be waiting on you when we get back to Washington. They've got their eyes on you, watching for some sign of hope. They'll be looking at you, and they'll be expecting something from you. They're going to get it too! Heaven help me, their new president is not going to stand before the American people as a stumbling drunk!"

Rust settled back in his chair, visibly cowed by Vince's sudden burst of anger.

"We'll get you a speech," Vince continued. "We'll give you something that will touch the hearts of the whole world. We'll have a Supreme Court justice swear you in. But you are going to pull yourself together, and you are going to give the performance of your life—so help me God. And, if I catch you boozing again, I'm going to kick your butt all over this airplane. Is that clear, Mr. President?"

"Okay, okay!" Rust mumbled. "I'll do it. You don't have to be so hostile. You people work out the details. But I'm going up front." He stood up and moved slowly toward the door. "I've got to get myself ready for . . . the performance of my life."

TED RUST'S CHIEF OF STAFF had his work cut out for him. Vince grabbed the felt-tip pen from his shirt pocket and began jotting down a laundry list of things he had to get done in the next hour and a half: He needed to speak to the judge who would administer the Oath of Office, place a call for the vice president to express condolences to the dead president's widow, arrange a press conference with the networks, and help frame a short, passionate speech. And that was just for starters. There was too much to do in such a short time, but he had no choice. These things simply had to be done.

Some of the tasks on his list were things only he could do. Others, he could delegate to his colleagues back at the White House. But time was precious.

Once he had completed several phone conversations and made a number of secure calls back to members of the executive staff, Vince went forward to the vice president's stateroom to inform Ted Rust that he had placed a call to the president's widow. He stayed while Rust took the call, and after the customary words of condolence, Rust hung up the phone.

"She's really torn up," he said. "We've got to get her some help."

"You're right," Vince replied. Then he moved quickly to the rear of the plane, where thirty-five members of the media were waiting to attack him like a school of barracudas going after a hunk of raw meat. ABC-TV had responsibility for the pool camera on the trip. The rest were assorted print reporters hoping to get lucky, to be on the scene of an assassination, a riot, or some other diplomatic screw-up. No courtesy or respect was to be found in this crowd.

The first to launch a salvo at D'Agostino was Sven Larson of the *New York Times*. A sixties Marxist who had idolized Che Guevara in print, and who seemed unable to cope with the fact that Fidel Castro was finally gone, Larson was always looking for an angle. It was no secret that he despised capitalism, Western-style democracy, and particularly the free-market system that had spawned such a thoroughgoing success in Chile—especially when Marxism had failed so conspicuously in Cuba. Even though he was an editorial page writer by trade, Larson had asked for this assignment as one last effort to trash the now-dead Pinochet.

"Why have we turned around?" Larson snapped at D'Agostino. "Have you people screwed up again? Have you lost your map, or is this tub going to crash?"

Vince glanced at him sarcastically, then held up both hands to quiet the babble of questions. He started the spin control. "Ladies and gentlemen, the vice president is in his stateroom, overcome with grief at the news we have just received from Washington. The president of the United States is dead—he has just committed suicide."

There was an audible gasp from everyone in the cabin, but before anyone could speak, D'Agostino called for quiet. "Listen, please. Obviously, this is a terrible tragedy, but the vice president's first thought was of the president's widow, and he has just spoken to her and offered his condolences. We're returning to Andrews at this moment, and you all know what comes next. Vice President Rust will be sworn in as president of the United States the moment we return. There will be a brief ceremony on the tarmac at Andrews, and you will be allowed to cover it."

Before anyone could jump in, Vince held up both hands, looked from face to face, and paused for the effect of his words to sink in. "You know, of course, that you're very lucky to be in this position.

But there is one more thing you need to know. We have been told that a huge meteor, big enough to cause very serious damage, is due to impact somewhere in the Pacific Ocean off the coast of California at around seven o'clock, Pacific Coast time, tonight. You will be fully briefed at Andrews."

There was pandemonium in the passenger cabin. Reporters jumped into the aisles shouting questions, gesturing and waving, and demanding more information. Tape recorders snapped on, and strobe lights flashed, but Vince ducked out of the passenger compartment before any of the reporters could get to him. Once through the door, he ordered two Secret Service agents to block the passageway forward. No one was to go in or out of the media compartment until he gave the order.

Vince walked quickly back to the conference room where the speechwriter was already working at top speed on the new president's address. Vince read the draft, penciled through a sentence or two, changed wording as needed, and marked up the text. In less than fifteen minutes, they had hammered out the best speech President Ted Rust would ever give to the American people. He pulled a large-print copy of the text from the onboard computer and, once again, entered the stateroom of the vice president.

Ted Rust's hands were trembling visibly when the chief of staff entered the room. "Vince," he moaned, "I need a drink."

Vince was hard. "Ted, I told you. No booze."

"Listen to me, Vince! This is no joke!"

"I'll give you enough black coffee to charge up an elephant," he said, "but absolutely no booze." Vince sat down in the vice president's swivel chair and leaned toward the sofa where Rust was seated. "Here's your speech, Ted. Read through it quickly, and let's start rehearsing your lines. There's a place in there where you've got to get teary and choked up, and it has to be perfect. Can you do it?"

"You *know* I can do it," the vice president answered sourly.

As Rust read through the speech, Vince took the headset and ordered the air force colonel in the cockpit to cut the flight speed to make sure that the plane would be stationed at the ramp with the stairs in place and in front of the ceremonial platform at precisely 7:55 P.M., eastern standard time.

WITHIN TEN MINUTES OF LANDING, the official party filed ceremoniously down the stairway. They waited briefly while the traveling press unloaded from the rear of Air Force Two and joined a mob of Washington press corps representatives around a podium about thirty feet in front of the steps. On either side of the red carpet were assorted cabinet members and leading members of both houses of Congress. At the foot of the steps was Ted Rust's wife, Valery. They embraced briefly and whispered a few words in each other's ears. Cameras captured the moment, strobe lights flashed, and the press reported to the American people that a tender exchange had taken place between two deeply devoted people.

In reality, Valery had whispered, "I don't know how you'll pull *this* one off, super boy. Just remember that everybody will be watching you from now on, so you'd better keep your pants zipped."

Ted smiled, pinched her cheek, and muttered in return, "Thank you, Mommy dearest. I knew I could count on your support in a tense situation. Now, put on your best face, will you? We don't want anybody to see what's underneath that war paint."

Arm in arm, the new first couple stepped up to the platform. Millions of Americans watched as Ted Rust placed his hand on the Holy Bible held by the chief justice of the Supreme Court and swore the constitutionally mandated Oath of Office to become president of the United States of America.

There was polite applause. A military band played a presidential fanfare, then President Theodore Rust walked to the microphone to give a performance worthy of Laurence Olivier. His voice rose and fell almost magically. He cried on cue, just as he had been carefully rehearsed to do.

When it was over, the president and first lady were safely ensconced in the bullet-proof presidential limousine. President Rust was on his way to his first cabinet meeting at the White House. But, moments later, when the limousine did not move quickly enough, the new first lady addressed a harangue to the Secret Service agent at the wheel that was coarse and salty enough to make a longshoreman blush. The agent and his partner were sworn to secrecy about what they heard between the president and first lady, but they were under no obligation to endure personal humiliation.

After he stopped the car under the White House portico, the driver got out, leaving the motor still running. He walked over to one of the Secret Service cars following the limousine. His supervisor rolled down his car window, and before he could say a word, the driver handed him his badge and his weapon. "I quit," he said, and started to walk away. Then he stopped, turned on his heel, and said, "If some crazy wants to pop these clowns, I sure don't want to stand in the way."

AFTER THE PRESIDENT'S brief but stirring inaugural address, Charley McAtee flipped off the television in his spacious den and looked at the expressionless faces around the room. "Well," he said. "What do you think?"

"He's very charming," Lori Throneberry replied, "and, I must say, he appears as presidential today as he ever did in the movies. But something isn't right. I can't quite put my finger on it."

Dave Busby had spent too much time in what he called "the hood" to be taken in by one speech, and he was nodding his head vigorously. "I agree, Lori," he said. "I think you're right on target. I have a bad feeling about this dude. I've seen some ringers before, but this guy's as phony as a three-dollar bill. We're not going to have a country much longer if they put *him* in charge." He looked at Charley and said, "We'd better make some plans real soon. Know what I mean?"

Charley smiled. "Dave, I trust your gut instincts better than anybody I know. I wasn't sure if it was just me or what, but both of you saw what I saw. It looks like we've got about two hours until the next bombshell hits on the West Coast, but I don't know which I fear most— the meteor or Ted Rust. God only knows what will happen next, but all we can do right now is wait. Wait and pray. And in the meantime, I think you and I need to see if there isn't some way we can help Carl and Lori get some answers to their questions. Okay?"

"Sure, Charley," Dave said. "You're right."

"There's going to be a lot of work to do tomorrow," Charley added. "This may be our only chance to talk at length, so let's get down to business now while there's still some light left."

Carl and Lori followed Dave Busby and Charley McAtee back into the kitchen. Charley poured out four steaming mugs of hot coffee, and then, as everyone around the table began putting milk and sugar in their coffee, the questions began. Carl started talking first. "Charley, as I see it, what you and Dave have been telling us is that the Bible predicted what was going to be happening at this time in history. If I'm following you, what you're saying is that at the very end of the age there's supposed to be a period of intense warning by Christians to people living all over the world. Then, after that, there will be some indescribable disasters. Is that right?"

"Yes," Charley said, taking a sip of his coffee, "that's exactly right."

"You've shown us," Carl continued, "a prophecy—a revelation, if you prefer—concerning a scorching heat wave, followed by a fiery meteor, followed by what might be poisonous nuclear radiation of some kind. Then after that you're saying there will be, or could be anyway, an indefinite period of global night probably caused by extensive volcanic activity set off by the meteor."

Charley shrugged his shoulders and nodded. "It appears so," he said simply.

"This is the most horrible thing I can conceive of," Carl said. "Yet, considering what's been happening today, it's all perfectly plausible. We're sitting here waiting for some type of meteor to vaporize the West Coast, and the president of the United States blew his brains out on national TV. What more can happen?"

"Depending on the extent of the damage," Charley said, "chances are we're going to see earthquakes, tidal waves, nuclear disasters, volcanoes, and maybe even a worldwide famine before it's all over, Carl. At one point in Revelation it says that as many as two billion people could die on this planet in the next two to three years. And that's—"

"Oh, great!" Carl interrupted. "That's just great. Now, we've got a worldwide famine too!"

"It sounds gruesome, doesn't it?" Charley conceded.

"Oh, yeah." Carl shook his head in disbelief. "But there's one more thing, Charley. How come God doesn't get you Christians out of all this? If you guys are so special and if your God has all this stuff worked out, then why are you all still here, anyway?"

"Whoa, Carl!" Dave interjected. "Let's take our coffee back to the den. Come on, man. This is getting pretty heavy, and I think we all need to take a closer look at the Book."

"Okay, Dave," Charley began, once they were all seated in the comfortable den with Bibles in hand. "Here we go. We'll start with chapter six." He waited while Carl and Lori flipped the pages, then continued.

"As you can see, John the Apostle is writing here about a time when four mystical horsemen—representing war, revolution, famine, and death—terrorize the earth. They are called the 'Four Horsemen of the Apocalypse.'"

"Yeah, I know about that," Carl said. "That image has been around a long time."

"That's right," Charley said. "In fact, I believe strongly that the terrible ride of the Four Horsemen was fulfilled during the twentieth century. It's not going to happen in the future because it has *already* happened."

"Is that right?" Dave Busby asked.

"That's the way I see it, Dave," Charley said. "But if that sounds odd to you, just stop and think what all has happened during the past hundred years. Wars, one right after the other, along with revolutions, disasters, and terrors of every kind. More than fifteen million people died in World War One. Before that, the Muslim Turks slaughtered practically the entire population of Armenian Christians in Eastern Europe."

"Gosh, that's right," said Dave. "I read somewhere that the Bolsheviks wiped out at least forty million people during the Russian Revolution, between 1917 and about 1940."

"In China after the end of World War Two," Charley said, "Mao Tse-tung butchered sixty million more in his revolution."

"That's over a hundred million people!" Lori exclaimed. "You're right, Charley. That's hard to believe, isn't it?"

"Hard to believe, Lori, but that wasn't the end of it. World War Two saw the killing rise to new heights. The combined death toll in Europe and Asia was at least fifty million people from just that one war, and that includes both soldiers and civilians. On top of that, Adolf Hitler was a demon-possessed madman who ordered the execution of at least six million innocent Jews, along with another million non-Jews, Christians, Poles, and others. And even before Hitler, upwards of a million people lost their lives in the Spanish Civil War."

Carl stirred restlessly in his seat. "Charley, is that true? The last century was the worst in history? I mean, worse even than Rome or Greece or the Dark Ages?"

"It's a simple matter of technology, Carl. It would have been impossible to kill so many people at any other time in history. The Romans had swords. They didn't have guns or bombs. It took two thousand years of science to give mankind the expertise to wipe out millions of people in such a short period of time."

"Doesn't say a lot for technology, does it?" Dave added.

"Just think what happened during the second half of the twenti-eth century," Charley said. "We lost hundreds of thousands of lives in Korea, then another million in Vietnam. How about revolution and famine in Nigeria and Ethiopia, Somalia, Angola, Mozambique, Sudan, and Rwanda, as well as Bangladesh, Cambodia, and Bosnia? By all reports those revolutions and famines cost from fifteen to twenty million lives. If you add all those numbers together—and I don't even want to try—it becomes readily apparent that the death and misery of the last century was—well, incalculable."

As Charley paused to sip his coffee, Dave said, "Charley, you paint a pretty gruesome picture, but you haven't mentioned the Middle East. There were something like three separate Arab-Israeli wars, weren't there? And I know that hundreds of thousands of people had to have died there. Not to mention hundreds of thou-sands more in Lebanon, Syria, and the Persian Gulf War. In some college class back there, I learned that a million or more died in the Iran-Iraq war. So I hear what you're saying. That was one bloody century."

"So now you understand," Charley continued, "why I'm convinced the Four Horsemen have already come and gone. It was as if some kind of madness was let loose on the whole world during the twen-tieth century. We had the most deadly weapons of all times, and whether they were placed in the hands of Fascists or Communists or Islamic terrorists or brutal dictators of some kind, the savagery was unimaginable. At one point in the 1970s there were as many as a hundred wars taking place simultaneously."

"The thing that disturbs me, Charley," Lori said, "is the idea that God personally engineered all of this. How could He do something like that? Why would He want to make this a terrible century of slaughter and bloodshed all over the world?"

"On the contrary, Lori," Charley answered. "God *didn't* engineer it at all. Rather, He allowed the natural instincts of sinful men to have free rein, to reap the penalty of their own behavior to the fullest extent possible. Instead of doing good, men used their God-given freedoms to destroy their fellowmen. Of course, God knew that this would eventually happen, but He also knew that this was the very thing that would help bring our troubled world to the end of the age."

"So," Lori continued, "from now on there won't be any more wars or revolutions anywhere in the whole world?"

Charley paused and thought for a long moment. "Okay. I'm going to take the easy way this time, Lori. My answer is 'yes and no.' I believe that at least this part of the prophecy in Revelation had its culmination in the twentieth century. There's still one big war left to go, but it's very different from the others.

"We'll talk about the next war later. I don't want to confuse you guys right now."

"Confuse us?" Carl snorted. "Are you kidding? I've been in information overload all day!"

The laughter that filled the room seemed to clear the air and bring everybody back to the reality of the moment. But before they could change the subject, Carl quickly picked up his train of thought. "Charley," he said, "before we move on, I want to go back to what I asked you earlier. Are Christians going to be spared or not?"

"Forgive me, Carl," Charley said and chuckled, "but once again, I have to say 'yes and no.' I know that's not much help, but since you're so determined to keep this dialogue going, why don't we take a look at Revelation again. Okay?"

"Yeah," Carl said. "Good idea."

"In the ninth verse of chapter six," Charley picked up, "John says, 'I saw under the altar the souls of those who had been slain for the word of God and for the testimony which they held.' Then look at verse eleven where it says that the souls of the dead were told to rest a little longer 'until both *the number of* their fellow servants and their brethren, who would be killed as they *were,* was completed.'"

Lori grimaced. "No way out!"

"Look, guys," Charley said, "you've got to understand one simple fact. Christians have been slaughtered by Romans, Communists, Fascists, the followers of Islam, and even by other Christians during the Inquisition. So this is nothing new. Our brothers and sisters have been massacred by the thousands by dictators throughout history. It *is* horrible, but in one sense, it isn't necessarily all that bad."

"Oh, yeah?" Carl broke in. "It sure sounds bad to me. Why isn't death bad?"

Charley smiled. "You see, the Bible tells us in many places that when a Christian dies, he or she goes to be with the Lord, where there is utter bliss for all eternity. For believers the issue is not whether you die physically, but whether you die in the Lord. After all, a Christian can only die once. So from that point of view, what difference does it make whether Christians have heart attacks or get shot or drown? Their spirits go to be with the Lord, and they will live and reign with Him forever."

"Charley," Lori protested, "no offense, but I'm scared of dying. And what we've been talking about scares the willies out of me."

"I hear that, Lori," Charley replied. "The human part of us fears death. That's only natural. But the eternal part—the spiritual part— has something more to look forward to, and that's what gives us confidence—peace, if you will—in the face of death. My sincere prayer, Lori, is that you and Carl will give your hearts to Jesus Christ and come to know Him personally. I know that you're going through a traumatic experience, and you have a lot to think about. But that's what it's all about. Once you find security in Christ, you won't have to be afraid anymore."

"Yeah—maybe," Carl said softly.

"But, Carl," Charley continued, "you wanted to know if Christians will be among the multitudes who may be dying today, tomorrow, next week, and two years from now. The answer, my friend, is yes. Christians will die tonight in Los Angeles. The innocent will suffer with the wicked. But that's where the similarity stops. The eternal spirits of those who belong to Jesus Christ will be taken up immediately to be with the Lord for all eternity. On the other hand, the spirits of those who die without Christ will be taken to hell to await judgment before the throne of God, where they will have to answer for everything they have ever done during their lives. The Bible says that their own consciences will be their accusers as they stand before a holy and righteous God."

"Hold on, Charley," Carl said. "You mean that if that meteor had killed me, my spirit would have to stand before God and answer for every rotten thing I've ever done?"

Charley couldn't help smiling at Carl's assessment of himself. He nodded.

"Everything?" Carl persisted. "With no exceptions?"

"You got it, Carl," Charley said. "After you die physically, your spirit will have to answer for everything that you've done while you lived on earth."

"Holy —" Carl stopped himself. "Excuse me, but I can do without that."

They all smiled, but the room suddenly grew silent until Carl said very softly, "You know, I left L.A. an agnostic. I don't understand it all, but I do believe what you've been telling us, Charley. But it's all so new to me that I need to think about it. I know one thing, though. I don't want to face the judgment. There has got to be some way out of this deal for Lori and me!"

Dave Busby, who had been silent for several minutes, spoke up. "I believe that what is coming is called the 'Day of the Lord.' It's also called the 'Day of God's Wrath.' Isn't that right, Charley? In one place the prophet Isaiah called it the 'Day of Vengeance of our God.'"

"Okay, Dave," Carl said, grimacing, "I get the point."

"All over the Old Testament," Dave continued, "the prophets were warning the people that a terrible day of judgment was coming. One prophet called it the 'day of gloom and darkness.' What comes through loud and clear, though, is how short this day is going to be. In one place Isaiah talks about 'an acceptable year of the Lord,' but he says it is to be a 'day of vengeance.'"

"Good, Dave!" Lori laughed. "Keep it up. This is getting scarier all the time."

Dave stood up, "Look! What we've been talking about today is going to happen fast, you know. No messing around—just splat. Then shake, rattle, and roll."

"That's good, Dave," Charley said, shaking his head. "Can you be any more graphic? There's no way any of this can be seen as funny, but the suddenness and the speed of it all really is part of the good news."

"Within the next thirty days, max, I'd say," Dave continued, "and the whole job will be done. In my church we sing a song called, 'Our God Is an Awesome God.' I mean to tell you, that's the gospel truth. He is some kind of awesome God!"

"Dave," Lori asked, "what is this time we're in now? Does the Bible give it a name?"

"Yeah," he said. "It does. It is called the 'Great Tribulation.'"

"And are we in it?" Carl asked.

"It sure looks like it to me," Dave said.

"It sounds to me," Carl said, "like the last hundred years with the Four Horsemen and all could be called a tribulation. What about the Jews and Chinese and Russians Charley was talking about? You had Armenians and Biafrans and Laotians, too, didn't you? Just to name a few. Call it what you want, but it sure sounds like tribulation for those guys in the rice paddies in Vietnam, the beaches of Normandy, Iwo Jima. That's about the limit of my history, but you're saying we're in tribulation now. So what was it back then?"

Charley stood up and moved around to the sofa where Carl and Lori were sitting. "Carl, you know, you may be on to something. After all, God doesn't send an angel down with a big gong to announce the beginning of the Tribulation, then another gong when it's all over. The fact is, on this earth we're never going to get the whole picture—

just parts of it. The apostle Paul said we are like people who are trying to make out shapes on the other side of a foggy window. But I still have to agree with Dave. The time of God's wrath is short, even though it is horrible beyond imagination."

"You know what amazes me," Dave said, "is how people in America, from the Supreme Court all the way down, thought they could insult God and get away with it. Even most Christians in America have been acting like God is some kind of big, easygoing teddy bear in the sky who's going to let them get away with trashing all His sacred laws."

Carl nodded his head, took a sip of coffee, then almost sobbed, "Charley, I've got to tell you, I never saw it like this before. My job was to sell stuff. I was part of the Hollywood media scene. I'm an ad man. Sure, I thought I had some standards, but when it came to selling stuff, success was all that really mattered." He was getting visibly upset, and he took a deep breath to calm himself. Then he continued, "You know, if I saw that the big audiences were going for shows that trashed God and religion, or if they were turned on by naked chicks jumping in and out of bed with naked guys, then that's where we put the dollars. It was just good business. I mean, I figured I wasn't a priest. People's morals weren't my job. Whatever people wanted, that's where I put the bucks."

"Don't be so hard on yourself, honey," Lori said, putting an arm around Carl's shoulders. "You were always very careful to pick the best people."

"Oh, yeah, right," he continued, his pain evident in his voice. "You can be sure I fought like a tiger for the rights of producers and writers—so they could be as free, crude, and blasphemous as they wanted to be. We thought you Christians were no better than right-wing thought police. In fact, it never occurred to me that you were trying to protect us from the wrath of God."

As Carl spoke, the four people in that room drew together quietly and naturally, both because they needed one another in this difficult hour and because they felt the genuine sorrow in Carl's words.

They understood the hurt, the fear, the emotion that lay at the back of his thoughts.

"For years, none of us listened," Carl said, with tears in his eyes. "Now, it's too late to do anything about it."

"I hear you, Carl," Charley said, "but that's not exactly true. Even if two billion people die because of the things we've been talking about, another four billion will be left. I'll be the first to say that you and most of your Hollywood pals have been fools. But from now on there's a lot you can do before the Lord comes back. You can't buy God's love, but you *can* demonstrate the changes taking place in your heart."

Spontaneously, Charley, Dave, and Lori reached out and took Carl's hands in theirs. They stood there for one brief moment, a lot like a basketball team in a moment of silent prayer, then quietly moved apart again.

"Carl, I do love you," Lori said quietly.

"Me too, Lori," he responded, bending slightly to give her a kiss on the cheek.

Charley looked at his watch. It was 7:00 P.M. mountain time, and 6:00 P.M. Pacific time—which meant they still had one hour before impact. Charley picked up the empty coffee cups and took them out to the kitchen, and one by one the four of them returned to the den to see what they could learn from the TV news.

CHAPTER SIX

THE CABINET WAS ASSEMBLED in the long White House Cabinet Room. An air of impending disaster hung in the atmosphere. As they realized the magnitude of the tragedy about to strike California, the nation, and the entire world, the members of the cabinet and the presidential staff could only think about the betrayal that they had allowed to be perpetrated on the American people.

"The people will never trust us again," the secretary of housing and urban development said.

"I don't see how a cover-up like this was possible," the secretary of energy added.

"If we had known in time," said the secretary of transportation, "we could have launched a mass evacuation, but—the president just didn't give us any time to warn the people. It was—it was criminal!"

"I think we're all jumping to conclusions," the secretary of state said in defense of the late president. "I honestly don't think he had enough advance warning either. I truly believe that. By the time the White House learned about it, and by the time all the fluff was blown off this thing, it was just too late to say or do anything, or to warn anybody. You all remember what was going on around here. The president feared, and I think legitimately, that if he spoke prematurely he would start a panic!"

There was polite debate and conversation as the speaker defended his statements.

When President Ted Rust entered the Cabinet Room from the Oval Office, the group rose formally, and each offered congratulations prefaced with the deferential "Mr. President." Rust walked around the massive table and shook the hand of each cabinet member, beginning with the secretary of state and moving completely around the room.

For a moment he seemed genuinely warm and human, but as he sat down in his own leather chair he reached into his coat pocket and withdrew a stack of note cards. "Ladies and gentlemen," he read stiffly from the three-by-five cards in his hand, "our country is facing a grave national crisis. In just one hour, a tragedy of unimaginable proportions will be inflicted upon southern California and the entire Pacific Basin. In order to deal with this crisis and to administer emergency procedures from this office, I am asking each of you to remain on board as members of my cabinet. And I would also ask of you the same dedicated loyalty and professional service that you gave to my predecessor."

This statement was greeted with mild applause and a variety of comments and modest acknowledgments around the room. "We're with you, Mr. President," said one man. "You can count on us," said another.

"With less than an hour before the meteor's impact," President Rust continued ceremoniously, "I would now like to ask our science adviser, Dr. Eisenblatt, to brief us on the current situation."

Jerome Eisenblatt was a highly regarded theoretical physicist. He had graduated at the top of his class from MIT, took his Ph.D. at Cambridge, then entered government service. He was generally considered to be apolitical—at least, he was as neutral as possible in the Washington environment. His views were generally in the mainstream of modern science, and his briefings were always concise and lucid. Unlike the majority of cabinet officers who gained their stripes by inside service to the ruling party, Eisenblatt's position was due more to a true dedication to the task of harnessing scientific knowledge for the good of mankind. He was trusted by all who knew him, which had, in turn, made him a respected adviser to administrations of both major parties.

Dr. Eisenblatt rose slowly, took a deep breath, and began. "Thank you, Mr. President. As you all know by now, at this hour we are working around the clock to establish reliable intelligence and communications links on all levels: television, radio, short wave, microwave—essentially all major military and civilian frequencies—and many other specialized resources. Everything is being called into service. Our three main IntelSats are currently processing more than a hundred thousand simultaneous events, and two of those satellites have the capacity to observe and photograph the surface of the earth with extraordinary clarity. So that is a main area of focus at this moment."

Eisenblatt walked a few paces to a large easel that had been set up behind him. He drew back the cloth that had been covering it to reveal several charts and graphs. "One of our most sensitive satellites," he said, pointing to a sketch at the top of the page, "is in geosynchronous orbit to allow detailed photography of southern California. Right here," he said, pointing to a glossy photograph, "is a still-frame picture taken this morning. It shows just how very good and how very precise the satellite imaging actually is. This particular technology can magnify virtually any object. . . . This, for example, is the warning label on a package of cigarettes, as seen from space."

There was a spontaneous reaction from the cabinet members. "That's incredible," said the secretary of energy. "I knew they were good, but I had no idea . . ."

"Naturally, our main concern," Eisenblatt continued, "is the size, shape, trajectory, and velocity of the approaching object—the meteor, for lack of a better definition. Our most high-powered terrestrial telescopes have been tracking the object's entry into earth's atmosphere.

We want to know as much as we can at every second. Then, to be certain that we leave no stone unturned, we also have helicopters in the air at this moment with sophisticated photographic capabilities."

"Vince." President Rust looked around for the chief of staff. "Vince, will you please dim the lights so we can see the pictures Dr. Eisenblatt has brought us?"

The lights went down, and the presentation began with a highly magnified image of the meteor recorded on videotape earlier in the afternoon. Everyone leaned closer and began talking in hushed tones of surprise and fearful anticipation. There were loud gasps from some around the table as many came to grips for the first time with the magnitude and the true horror of what was approaching the West Coast at that moment. Somehow these closeup pictures of a massive object hurtling through space, looking more like the sun than their previous image of a meteor, brought home the terror of the situation.

Next, Eisenblatt showed them a composite of videotape and still photographs of the tragedy that had been unfolding on the ground in Los Angeles over the past twelve hours. They witnessed the panic, the hysteria, the effects of the heat, thousands of bodies being processed by medical and emergency teams wearing specialized heat-resistant gear, and helicopter footage of freeways and highways clogged with vehicles.

They saw the bodies of dead children, houses and entire neighborhoods on fire, and the wrenching transmissions from an affiliate station in the northern suburbs of Los Angeles, KTTV, which showed some of the most moving pictures of the real-life drama unfolding on the streets of that doomed city.

Ten minutes into the video presentation, the president's hands began to quiver. He suddenly put a hand over his mouth as if he were about to vomit. He coughed, wiped sweat from his forehead, then noisily shoved back his chair and bolted from the room.

Dr. Eisenblatt stopped the presentation in deference to the president and took questions from around the table while the group waited for the chief executive to return. But, safely inside his private bathroom, Ted Rust was vomiting uncontrollably. He was terror-stricken by the terrible images he had just witnessed and the realization that he was powerless to help in this moment of crisis. What he wanted most to do was to escape, to scream out, or to run as fast and as far as he could go. Instead, he pulled out the flask of bourbon he had hidden inside his suit jacket before he got off the plane and poured himself three fingers in a wide-bottomed glass. After a quick glance at his ghostly profile in the mirror, he downed the whole glass neat.

He leaned against the sink, shivering, until the whisky began to work, then he poured an equal amount and gulped it down too. Despite his practiced tolerance for alcohol, which had been built up over many years of hard drinking, the president's empty stomach was no match for what hit it. Slowly, he braced himself, straightened his tie, and took one more slug straight from the flask for good measure.

The president was clearly staggering when he reentered the Cabinet Room. Seeing the situation, one of the executive staff switched on the lights, but it didn't help. Rust pulled back his chair, tried to sit down, but missed the seat and fell with an absurd gurgle to the floor. His aides rushed over to pick him up, but he slapped at their hands and pushed them away.

"I'm fine," he protested. "Get back. Get back to your places!"

Some members of the cabinet expressed concern for the president's fall. Others chuckled politely, trying to ease the tension of the moment. A few thought they had observed an understandable mishap caused by the lights coming on so suddenly in the darkened room. But all such notions quickly vanished when the new president of the United States opened his mouth.

"Thish—is a most terrible thing—" he said, pointing to the video screen and wagging his head from side to side. "It's a terrible, terrible, terrible thing—and we're gonna —we're gonna get it—we're gonna get a big, red bouncing ball crashing down on Hollywood, California— jush like in the movies. . . ."

Vince D'Agostino was on his feet in a split second. At his signal, two aides grabbed hold of each of President Rust's arms and physically lifted him from his chair, propelling him from the room. As he was seized, Rust roared in anger and flailed his arms. "Turn me loosh—you little pipsqueaks!" But before he could say another word, he was out of the room with the door closed behind him.

The cabinet members were aghast at what they had just witnessed. But before anyone could get up, speak, leave the room, or respond in any way, the chief of staff returned and immediately took control of the situation. "Please excuse us, ladies and gentlemen. As you can see, the president is not himself today. Clearly, he is overcome with grief and fatigue. He has been through so much in just the past eight hours or so, as have we all. I hope you will understand the situation and be sympathetic. After a good night's rest, the president will be himself again and will be in command once more. But for now, if you will allow me, please, I will stand in for just a moment. Can we please continue—Dr. Eisenblatt—ladies and gentlemen?"

There was concern in the eyes of those in the briefing room, but Vince was so surprisingly polished and capable, and so firmly in charge, that no one could argue. One by one, they settled back in their seats and returned to the present order of business.

"Basic business," Vince continued, breathing more easily. "We need to take care of basic business. First of all, I would like to request on behalf of the president that Mr. Augustus and his staff in the Defense Department, especially in light of all we have seen so far—be prepared to move forward with full implementation of their disaster relief plans."

"Yes, sir." Al Augustus nodded. "We are prepared to do that."

"Good," said Vince. "I know you are. And I recognize, too, that all of you in this room need to coordinate your activities and come to some sort of agreement among you as to how you propose mounting relief operations and engaging your various departments for this—this *tragedy*. What else can we call it?" Vince could see that his words were having their desired effect and that calm was being restored to the meeting.

At that moment, however, he was much more concerned about the other disaster that was taking place in the president's private office next door, and he was anxious to get back to calm the chief executive and salvage what was left of his career.

"Ladies and gentlemen," he continued, "I think you understand that, as chief of staff, I really need to be with the president at this moment, so I would like to defer to Mr. Augustus, our secretary of defense, to direct the remainder of this meeting and to make sure that our original directives are carried out. Does that—"

"Go on, Vince," someone chimed in.

"Hey, we understand, Vince. You go ahead," offered another.

"Thank you," he replied stiffly. "Please excuse me. The president needs my help."

He withdrew before anyone could ask embarrassing questions. The secretary of defense stood up to continue the deliberations. Vince thought, *At last the relief effort is in good hands.*

WHEN VINCE ENTERED the Oval Office, President Ted Rust was sitting on a couch, sobbing, with his head in his hands. Vince was furious at what they had just been through. There was no doubt in his mind that the story of the president's showing up stumbling, confused, and drunk at his first cabinet meeting would be all over Washington within minutes after the cabinet adjourned. He had been around long enough to know that there were no secrets in this town.

He couldn't cover up for Ted Rust anymore. There was every possibility that Rust had condemned his own presidency to failure, and Vince hated him for that. The chief of staff walked over to the sobbing, drunken president and snarled, "You sniveling, cowardly drunk." Then he drew back his right arm and delivered a full force slap across the president's face.

The blow had the desired effect. It served to snap Ted Rust out of his maudlin reverie. But what he did next shocked them both. He rose to full height, looked down at his chief of staff, and roared, "I am president of the United States of America! No one can talk to me like that! You cannot strike me! *No one* can do that. Do you hear me?"

Caught completely off guard by the president's reaction, Vince stumbled backward.

"I don't need you around here," Rust continued, gesturing wildly. "I don't want you, and I don't need you. Do you hear me, Vincent D'Agostino? So, clean out your desk and get out of here. You—are—fired!"

Dazed, Vince shook his head. Then, after the briefest pause, he began to laugh. "Sure thing, Mr. President. No problem. I'm just leaving," he shot back. "But, please understand, I won't be back. It's all yours now, Mr. President, and you've bloody well earned it. Ted Rust's America. And with you in charge, may God save this venerable nation!"

Having fired his final salvo, he strode out of the office, slammed the door, and walked away. He went to his own office and, pausing briefly at his reception area, told his secretary what had happened, and asked her to pack up his personal effects and send them to his house.

Then he went into his private office and closed the door. His blood was still pumping rapidly, and a thousand thoughts went through his mind. He knew this would likely be the last time he would be there as a privileged insider in the White House. He had been accepted here and treated with deference.

But now, as suddenly as it had all begun, it was over. He had this one last moment to savor his rise to power, before he would have to think about his precipitous fall. But at the same time, the disaster on the West Coast was on everyone's mind, and he wanted to catch up on what was happening. So he flipped on the television set in his office and watched. What he saw shook him to the very core of his being.

Later, Vince called his wife, Angie, and broke the bad news about losing his job. She was equally disturbed, but they agreed to talk later about what they would do next. After he hung up, he breathed a simple prayer for the victims and their families. Then, on his own behalf, he added, "God, this is all too much for me. It's so big, and so sudden, nobody knows what to make of all this. I've been a very lucky and privileged man, and I know I'm living during one of the most dramatic times in history. Everything I ever thought was important is suddenly collapsing all around me."

With tears welling up in his eyes, he muttered, "God, if You have a purpose for me in all this, I'm ready to do whatever You say. Just show me the way. . . ."

ONLY MINUTES AFTER the chief of staff departed the Cabinet Room, a slender man slipped out another door. He was the personal assistant to the president's national security adviser. He had been receiving promises from the most powerful newspaper publisher in Washington of favorable treatment in exchange for leaks of certain confidential White House information. Other high-ranking officials had received threats from the same paper of severe political retribution if they didn't provide information. It was one of Washington's dirtiest little secrets; but, despite what some critics would call criminal extortion, the *Post* was so powerful that it routinely operated above the law.

On any other occasion, the story of a new president appearing drunk and disoriented at his first cabinet briefing would have rated a front-page banner headline. But news of the tragedy in California so dominated the news that this particular story of the presidential mishap was buried on page A-3. Without the customary media attention, it lay there like a land mine waiting to explode from the computer of any news hawk or political enemy doing a little background check on President Ted Rust.

OF ALL THE PRESIDENT'S CABINET, Albert Carlton Augustus was the most qualified. He first became nationally famous when he put together a $10 billion merger between the missile guidance company he headed and the acknowledged giant of the defense industry, Consolidated Aviation. His stock options in the deal had netted him a cool $100 million after taxes. He had been looking forward to some serious tarpon fishing off Bimini in his new forty-five-foot Bertram yacht when the call came from the then president-elect, offering him the post at the Defense Department.

Al Augustus was born in Columbus, Ohio. He was the oldest son of a privileged family and a high achiever in school and in varsity athletics. After high school, he had gone to Yale, where he received a bachelor's degree in political science, then went on to Harvard Business School. From childhood, his mother and father had instilled in him a sense of his patriotic duty. So when the president of the United States called, he knew immediately that fishing would have to wait.

He had said yes to the president. Then, Al and his wife, Barbara, bought a spacious Colonial townhouse in upper Georgetown and became part of the Washington scene. Now he was acting director of the entire U.S. government during its most severe domestic crisis in history.

As he stood looking around the room at the other cabinet members, he was aware that the information he was about to divulge was even darker than that shared by Jerome Eisenblatt. "Best estimates from the secretary of the navy," he said, "indicate that we are going to lose three-fourths of our Pacific Fleet. After we gave up the Subic Bay facility in the Philippines, we pulled all our forward-based ships back to Pearl. There's a carrier task force in the Indian Ocean that we are hoping will be able to ride this thing out. But I'd like to hear what the scientists have to say. Dr. Eisenblatt, what is your estimate of the damage to Hawaii?"

The science adviser remained seated as well, but opened a folder of confidential information. "We have never dealt with anything of this magnitude, Mr. Secretary, so my projections are mostly theo-retical. But, depending on precisely where this object strikes the Pacific—and I'm certain now that it will be somewhere west of Catalina Island—I believe the most dangerous effect," he said, "will be a tidal wave that will likely be traveling in excess of five hundred miles per hour. At about a thousand miles from impact, it will slow perceptibly, but we need to understand that the frontal wave height of this type of wave, or tsunami, will be in excess of five thousand feet at impact. Ladies and gentlemen, I am not exaggerating when I tell you that we may see a tidal wave anywhere from one to three miles in height moving across the Pacific in all directions from the point of the meteor's impact."

"My God," said the secretary of transportation. "Jerry, do you know what that means? It means that all of the low-lying areas of Hawaii, including our entire naval facility, will be swamped! There will be nothing left."

"I'm sorry to say that you're exactly correct."

"Jerry," the speaker added, "I—I've got family there!"

"Yes, I know," Dr. Eisenblatt replied. "I'm sorry. We will all be impacted by this, but we have to do the best we can in this situation. And, please understand, ladies and gentlemen, that we have just hours—a very few hours—to do everything we can to prepare for disaster."

There was a murmur of alarm and concern among the members seated at the table. Once again, the reality of the situation was slowly beginning to penetrate their studied resolve and professional decorum.

"Please," Dr. Eisenblatt interrupted the scattered conversations. "Please, we must return to the issue. There is more. An even more serious danger to Hawaii and the Pacific Basin will come from earth-quakes and volcanoes. As you know," he continued in clinical fashion, "the islands of Hawaii came into being because of volcanic eruptions beneath the ocean floor. The entire area is still geologically unstable, as we have seen many times over the past two decades. But the impact of the object—the meteor—is sure to trigger a chain of seismic events throughout the Pacific Basin."

As he spoke, computer simulations were being displayed on the large-screen monitors.

"I hasten to add that no one has available the empirical data to predict with certainty whether seismic shocks will occur, or how far they will travel. These disturbances," he said, "will theoretically radiate at speeds up to twelve thousand kilometers per hour through the tectonic substructure in that region. The tidal wave, on its own, will set off seismic shocks in Hawaii. Add to that the fact that the concussion from California will likely reach Hawaii in three to four hours, and then we will see a cascading effect as the subsurface action reaches the Aleutians, then closer to home in Seattle, and straight down the Pacific Coast into Mexico.

"I'm sorry, Stan," he said, speaking to the secretary of transportation, who was showing signs of strain and exhaustion, "but I must continue. Please forgive me, but I have to give this as straight as I can."

"Go on, Jerry," the other man responded. "I understand."

"If this chain of events continues as I've described it so far, then we should not be surprised to see parts of Hawaii swamped with water, then torn apart by simultaneous volcanic action. The shock will be so intense that very likely most of what we know today as the Hawaiian Islands will disappear under the Pacific Ocean. Islands and atolls from the Aleutians to the Marianas will no doubt meet the same fate.

"But, Stan," he added, reaching over to touch the secretary of transportation on the shoulder, "I also hasten to say that a lot of this is still conjecture, based on our best scientific analysis. You and I both know that we have never faced this exact situation before, thank God. But this is what I anticipate."

Al Augustus rose from his seat. "Thank you, doctor. But one more thing. Will you please amplify on what you see as the earthquake threat?"

"Mr. Secretary, as you know," Eisenblatt responded, "I am a theoretical physicist, not a geologist or seismologist. What I'm telling you now comes from briefings and conversations that I participated in earlier today."

"Yes, we all know that, doctor," Augustus said. "Proceed."

"The Baja Peninsula of California," Dr. Eisenblatt continued, "was once part of the mainland. A violent earthquake split that peninsula away from the mainland. Then the intervening space filled with the body of water known as the Gulf of Baja. But the fault line that runs northward from that fissure continues northward into southern California. Most of us know about the San Andreas fault, but you may not know that California is literally criss-crossed with east-west fault lines, diagonal fault lines, as well as the main San Andreas fault, which runs northwest and southeast.

"Even our best theoretical models are inadequate to predict with precision which faults will move and with what intensity. However, as we plan for crisis management, we must take into account not only the swamping of southern California, but also earthquake action of such intensity that the entire western portion of California, from San Francisco to San Diego, might become a peninsula separated from the mainland.

"If that were to happen," Eisenblatt said, using his pointer to indicate an area on the map, "a new body of water will be formed there, both by the influx from the Pacific after the geological events have subsided, as well as by the retention of a portion of the seawaters that have inundated the state. Again, let me add that an earthquake of this scale is so devastating as to leave loss of life and property virtually beyond calculation."

"We are losing most of our Pacific Fleet," Al Augustus said. "We will lose the aviation production capability of Lockheed and Northrop. If this thing swamps the Sea-Tac area, Boeing is as good as gone. That means only McDonnell Douglas and Grumman will be left. Obviously, we run the risk of losing Silicon Valley, along with the heart of Intel and Microsoft. This is going to put tremendous stress on all our systems."

As he looked around the table, the defense secretary could see that several men had taken off their coats and ties. Others were wiping their foreheads with handkerchiefs. The secretary of agriculture had his hands over his eyes and was shaking his head in disbelief. The formality of the meeting had slowly disintegrated, and the level of emotion had dramatically intensified. Everyone in that room was painfully aware that the world as they knew it would never be the same again.

Chapter Seven

B Y 9:50 P.M., EASTERN standard time, the tension in the presidential Cabinet Room was palpable. Several cabinet officers had placed calls to their staffs to check on progress in their areas of operations. White House couriers and Secret Service agents had delivered confidential packets containing updated information and reports from the field. None of the news was good.

Al Augustus loosened his tie and turned toward the secretary of energy. "We now have less than ten minutes until impact, Madame Secretary," he said. "Can you give us an appraisal of what we're looking at, relative to energy matters?"

The secretary of energy, Marsha McGovern, was an attractive woman in her mid-fifties who had once headed a large southern university. She was a capable administrator, but her critics contended her cabinet appointment was more a reflection of her gender and voting address than her actual ability.

As she stood, the lights dimmed and charts were displayed on the large-screen monitor. "Until today," she began, "the electric generating capacity in the state of California has been on the order of fifty million kilowatts, with annual production of some one hundred eight billion kilowatt hours of electricity. Nearly seventy percent of the electricity in the state is generated in thermoelectric plants that depend on petroleum and natural gas resources."

Looking around the room, the secretary continued, "As you know, there are currently four nuclear power facilities in the state. Half of the state's electricity is produced by hydroelectric installations, including the Colorado River, Owens Valley, and San Francisco aqueducts. In terms of total output, Mr. Secretary, the state of California has been the most productive of the fifty states for the past twenty-five years in both general economy and energy matters.

"Of this nation's total capacity," the secretary continued, "which is in excess of three trillion kilowatt hours of electricity, the states of California, Oregon, and Washington together account for more than one-third of our total production. Sixty percent of the energy being produced in this country is derived from coal. However, petroleum, natural gas, nuclear power, and hydroelectricity are also vital to current production levels. Even with an acceleration in the amounts of oil and gas we can bring in from international suppliers, the loss of the production capacities and particularly storage facilities in California will, quite frankly, cripple energy production capabilities in this country for the foreseeable future."

Secretary Augustus shook his head with visible concern as he listened to the energy secretary's report. "Secretary McGovern," he asked, "what are we doing to limit the breakdown of systems in the states adjoining California?"

"Mr. Secretary," she said, "as you know, we maintain a western power grid to provide systems within the region with the energy resources they need to cope with emergencies. However, I have ordered disconnects between all systems and California to block sudden surges of power that could knock out our other systems in that grid. What we don't know is whether there has been time enough to get the job done.

"In addition," she continued, "I have ordered all valves shut off in pipelines between California and other states. No one knows for sure if the valves will hold under extreme pressure. Neither do we want a flood of seawater heading into refineries up the lines, and we certainly don't want fires and explosions from natural gas!"

The secretary of the interior broke in. "Please, what are the nuclear risks at this time?"

Secretary McGovern opened a thick briefing book lying in front of her. "Our principal concern must be the reactor units in southern and central California, Mr. Secretary. Diablo Canyon Number One is operated by Pacific Gas and Electric Company, twelve miles west-southwest of San Luis Obispo. It went on-stream about fifteen years ago and produces thirty-three hundred megawatts of power, on average."

"The other is the San Onofre Two operated by Southern California Edison Company and the San Diego Gas Company four miles southeast of San Clemente. It went on-stream about seventeen years ago with essentially the same capacity as the Diablo Canyon Unit.

"Without question, both of these units will be swamped and may experience some type of meltdown. What we *don't* know is how much radiation will escape into the atmosphere after the floodwaters recede." She paused. "Nor do we know the extent that poisonous radiation will penetrate seawater or fresh water throughout the region. The much more serious problem for residents of the United States will be the radiation fallout from the meltdown of reactors in Japan, Korea, Taiwan, and mainland China if earthquake activity of the estimated magnitude strikes the entire Pacific Rim."

"Madame Secretary," Al Augustus interrupted, looking at his watch, "excuse me for stopping you at this point, but we need to turn our attention to the monitor. I've just been informed that there will be a satellite feed piped in here momentarily to give the members of the cabinet a firsthand view of what's unfolding at this moment on the West Coast."

The large screen in the Cabinet Room had the capacity to receive civilian satellite pictures, as well as a range of real-time pictures from various government satellite sources. The information was sent in millions of digital bits, which allowed computer processing and editing of information to suit the tastes of the viewers.

The room also had remote control equipment that permitted an operator in an adjoining room to adjust the cameras on-board a satellite, either to scan a large portion of territory or to zoom in for detailed closeups. Since there had long ceased to be coverage on the ground, nongovernmental news agencies were now dependent on government sources, plus the commentaries of scientific advisers hastily assembled for the purpose.

The first pictures that came up on the monitor caused an intense reaction in the room. There were moans, cries, and even sobs as the cabinet looked at an earth-based view of the fireball hurtling toward impact. The picture then switched to satellite coverage of the southern California coastline, followed by a fast zoom shot giving a closeup view of the impact—and then an equally fast zoom-out to show the magnitude of the hellish scene.

They watched in horror and shock as picture after picture flashed before them, each more terrible than the preceding one. The secretary of state seemed transfixed. He kept repeating over and over again, "Oh, my God! This is the end! Oh, my God! This is the end!"

As they watched, billows of roaring, fiery waves engulfed the Los Angeles Basin. One closeup shot brought tears to many eyes as walls of water engulfed the tall buildings in West Los Angeles like a deadly, malevolent force, smashing them to pieces in mere seconds, then roaring on by as fast as the eye could follow, to claim more and more victims.

THE FIRST INDICATION Manuel Quintana and his family had of the approaching horror was a steadily increasing roar in the distance. At precisely 7:00 P.M. they heard what sounded like a loud ripping sound as the meteor plunged through the atmosphere. They huddled silently, shivering in fear at the rush of the wind that preceded the three hundred billion pounds of fiery rock hurtling through space toward the surface of the ocean.

By 7:01, Pacific Coast time, the entire sky overhead was lit up like the light from a hundred suns. The roof on the transmitter building burst into flames, and then the gas tanks in both their automobiles exploded. Manuel could hear the three boys gasping and crying softly in their trenches, but he was relieved that they were staying down in the water.

At 7:02, they heard distant thunder that sounded like the roar of ten thousand jet engines. The sky screamed overhead, and the wind whipped over the top of their mountain like a hurricane. To Manuel, it felt as if some great vacuum had been created in the heavens that was sucking up everything in the atmosphere. From one second to the next Manuel did not know if he wanted to live or die. Surely nothing alive could possibly survive what was taking place at that hour.

Every member of the Quintana family was fully submerged under two feet of water like creatures in suspended animation. The life-saving fluid around them was growing hotter by the second. But at the moment of impact, they were still alive.

In the distance there was a tremendous explosion, and the earth shook like nothing they had ever felt before. Seconds after the meteor struck the water, they heard a deafening roar and an explosion thousands of times louder than anything they had ever heard in their lives. *Outside the water,* Manuel thought, *surely our ears would have been shattered. Surely we would have been roasted alive!* The scalding wave of heat shot over their mountain at that instant. But the Quintanas stayed low in the water, praying silently, shaking, and waiting. Waiting to see what would come next.

There was no logical explanation why the water in their shallow hiding places did not boil them alive or simply evaporate—or why the resulting shock waves did not collapse the fragile walls of their tiny makeshift trenches. Later, when they were asked about their harrowing experience, Manuel and Cathy Quintana would simply say, "God must have wanted witnesses to what happened out there that night. He put His hand down on top of Mount Wilson to protect us. That's all we know. We have no other explanation."

WHAT THEY DISCOVERED after it was all over, was that at 7:03 P.M., Pacific Coast time, three hundred billion pounds of blazing rock plunged into the cold waters of the Pacific Ocean, then immediately pounded the ocean floor with an explosive force equivalent to five thousand of the most powerful nuclear warheads on earth. Geysers of scalding hot steam shot up miles into the evening sky, followed immediately by a circular wall of water that rose over one mile above the earth's surface, then spread out in every direction at lightning speed.

Within minutes of impact, petroleum products stored in California depots from Long Beach to San Luis Obispo burst into flame. Fuel lines leading from offshore oil wells had ruptured at impact. The crude oil and natural gas from deep offshore had been ignited, setting the sea itself ablaze.

Towering waves were crowned with blazing crude oil, and the massive tidal wave from hell raced across the Los Angeles Basin, burning, drowning, and destroying everything in its path. Nothing could stand against it. Nothing could have lived in its wake.

Minutes later, the boiling, surging seawater overflowed everything from San Diego to Santa Barbara. Every inch of Greater Los Angeles and Orange County was suddenly under five thousand feet of water. The waves lashed against the San Bernardino Mountains to the east, then poured into the Imperial Valley and the Mojave Desert. Floodwaters poured through tunnels and mountain passes into Bakersfield and the San Joaquin Valley to the north.

Steadily, like the hand of a death-dealing monster, the second surge moved up the coast toward San Francisco, Berkeley, Oakland, and San Jose.

Like concentric rings on a pond, massive walls of water were hurled northward toward Alaska and the Aleutian Islands; southward along the coast of Mexico and further south toward Peru and Chile; westward toward Hawaii and the islands of Polynesia; and then on to the west, where they were soon to encompass Japan, the Philippines, Korea, and the islands of the Pacific. The havoc unfolded like clockwork, and even the most hardened disaster trackers knew that nothing like this had ever before been witnessed by mankind.

Pressure from the underwater blast had been so intense that all fish and marine life within a thousand-mile radius of the Impact Zone were instantly killed.

No ocean vessel, no military or civilian transport, and no other craft at sea, no matter how sturdy or how skilled her crew, was able to survive in that area of the Pacific lying between the West Coast of the continental United States and Hawaii. Every single ship in the water capsized, was broken apart, or simply sank under the sudden and relentless deluge. No human being could withstand the awesome force. Everyone on the sea that day, whether they were there for business or pleasure or official duty, died. There were no survivors.

THE UNFOLDING PANORAMA of horror was more than any human being could take in. The men and women in the White House Cabinet Room watched as what appeared to be the entire contents of the tidal basin came crashing against the side of the tallest mountains in the San Gabriel and Santa Ana mountain ranges. They watched as surging fingers of water laced with fire dashed through the low-lying passes and tunnels, then flooded beyond, over, and through them. Nowhere in that raging, steaming, roiling inferno was there any sign of life. No possibility of survival, and little or no sign of hope.

But as the satellite cameras scanned the mountain ridges, something moving caught Dr. Eisenblatt's eye. "Stop!" he yelled to the operator. "Quick, back up and zoom in—over there!" He gestured with his finger to a point on the screen at the rim of a mountain.

There in the midst of charred ruins, a man, a woman, and three young boys were huddled together.

"This is—it's unbelievable. How did they survive? How *could* they survive in that place?" Dr. Eisenblatt asked no one in particular. Then, in answer to his own question, he said aloud, "They must have been covered by the hand of God Himself." No one in that room whispered an objection to his unscientific assessment. What else could they think?

From a headset on the table, they could hear the voice of the technician. "That's the antenna farm on Mount Wilson, Dr. Eisenblatt. I can't detect any other movement out there, but they appear to be standing by what used to be a television transmitter site."

"Tomorrow we've got to get a chopper in there," said the science adviser. "We've got to get those people out of there—alive."

"Consider it done, Jerry," said the secretary of defense.

For the next hour, as long as there was light in the western sky, the cabinet members watched as the tidal wave spread out at great speed from the impact area. In less than twenty minutes Los Angeles was no more. In no more than a half-hour, southern California was inundated by the sea and buried under a mile of water. It might as well have been part of the Pacific Ocean. Now the stalking rivers of death were moving steadily inland to endanger the rest of the world.

When the signals finally faded and flickered out, Al Augustus turned up the lights in the room. "Ladies and gentlemen," he said softly, "like you, I am horrified by what we have just witnessed. Our prayers and our assistance must be offered to the surviving families of those who have perished in this terrible tragedy. Our nation and all our allies and friends are facing a time of great peril. And we have a long night ahead of us."

AFTER SEVERAL ANXIOUS MINUTES, Manuel crawled slowly out of his trench. He looked below them toward the coast in awe. A crown of steam and water rose majestically in the air, then rushed outward. He was awestruck. For that one moment, he had been given, as it were, a ringside seat to witness the power of creation itself. He had seen what no other man had ever seen, and he had lived through it.

The water moved at ferocious speed. Banks and brokerages, oil companies and movie studios, hotels and restaurants, department stores and car lots, government offices and churches, along with schools and beautiful homes were now at the bottom of an ocean of water. The rich and the poor, the beautiful and the ugly, the powerful and the weak, all met the same fate. The primal forces of the universe were totally unimpressed by human wealth and prestige. The forces of nature showed no mercy for the vanities of man.

Before Manuel realized what had happened, the ocean waves were breaking against the sides of his mountain. The waters rushed onward and crested just below him. But since there was nothing to the west to hold them there, the boiling, frothing waves of seawater poured back into the ocean basin, dragging everything solid with them and leaving behind mountains of dead fish, animals, people, and a horrible layer of crude oil mired with twisted and mangled masses of steel and concrete that had once been a great city.

Suddenly aware that other dangers were to be expected, Manuel crawled back over to Cathy and the boys. One by one, he helped them, drenched and shaking, out of their hiding places. As the five of them clung together, the ground began to shake. Violent movements of the earth's crust had been set in motion. There was a rolling and twisting of the land, then a terrible crash and splitting open of the earth, from Baja, California, south of the Mexican border, north through the San Francisco Bay.

As they huddled together in a circle, Cathy sobbed quietly, "Manolo, we've lived through the worst of it. We're not going to die now, are we?"

He put his arms around his beautiful wife and drew her close. "Cathy, I don't know what to say. None of us should be alive now. We could be like any one of those poor dead people down there. But we are going to live. I believe that with all my heart. God has allowed us to survive. Somebody is going to come for us, believe me. In a few days either a helicopter will pick us up, or we'll walk out of here when the water recedes and these quakes stop. We'll make it. We have to make it. We saw it all."

The little family sat together in the dirt while the earth continued to shiver and shake beneath them. The air was full of the sounds of explosions and rushing wind and strange noises of every kind. They were dirty, wet, frightened, but still alive.

"Cathy," Manuel said after a long pause, "what we've witnessed tonight is a turning point in human history. It's a terrible disaster. Look around. You see what I see?" He pointed to the wall of water to the west. "We can't begin to imagine what is going to happen on the other side of the ocean, over there.

"We don't know what has happened to the rest of our country. There will be some big changes everywhere. Who will be able to deal with what has happened here? Things will never be the same."

His shoulders lifted slightly, and a smile crossed his face. "And, you, *mi esposa y mis jovenes*, will be around to tell the world that God answered our prayers and kept us alive." His family all watched him. They tried to smile. "Now, let's get some sleep," Manuel said. "We're going to be in a whole new world tomorrow."

LOOKING AT THE SECRETARY of energy, Al Augustus began, "Madame Secretary, this is a tense moment for everyone, and I have no doubt that pandemonium is breaking loose outside this room at this very hour, but these issues are simply too critical for us to stop at this point. Can we please have the rest of your report? In particular, I'm concerned about something you said earlier. You say you ordered all power plants and utilities shut down on the West Coast. Is that right?"

"Yes, that's correct," she said.

"Will you please tell us more about that?"

"We knew that the meteor would be generating heat anywhere from five thousand to twenty thousand degrees Fahrenheit at impact. It appeared that some type of electrical shorting could develop with possible damage to our generating stations in the western states. So, basically, I exercised my emergency authority and ordered all power companies in these states to notify their major customers and then begin shutdown throughout the area, to be completed not later than five P.M., Pacific time."

"So you mean that, as of this moment, there has been no electrical power in California, Oregon, and Washington for better than three hours?"

"Yes, sir. That's true in those states," the secretary of energy replied, "and, also in Nevada, Arizona, Utah, and Idaho."

"For three hours," the secretary of transportation pursued the question, "there has been no power for air traffic, street lights, electric trolleys, subways, or anything else anywhere in the western United States?"

"That's right," the energy secretary replied. "And, I might add, that means no power for television, radio, factories, or office buildings. Some facilities, such as hospitals, will of course have emergency generators. But fortunately the shutdown is taking place at the end of the day while there is still some daylight left. It's the best we can hope for under these conditions."

"I think we need some clarification on this, Madame Secretary," Al Augustus said. "We're in the midst of a civil defense emergency in northern California, Oregon, and Washington State. The level of chaos we have been witnessing out there is like nothing we could ever have imagined, but if I understand what you've just said, we will be unable to give those people any further broadcast warnings or instructions, and there is essentially no means of communication with roughly twenty percent of the United States population at this very moment. Is that correct?"

"I'm afraid so," she said. "Mr. Augustus, my staff and I were faced with an impossible decision. We could not selectively apply power in order to leave the emergency warning mechanisms operating while we shut down the rest. I know that it makes our job a lot more difficult, but the choice was between temporary notification to the civilian population or preserving the long-range power capabilities of the region. We chose the latter. Absent serious earthquakes and tidal waves, the power should be back on in most of the states by tomorrow morning."

In the midst of increasing tension, a navy captain assigned as aide to the secretary of defense entered the room and handed the secretary several documents. Augustus scanned them quickly, then stood up. "The situation is much worse than we feared. I've just received word that the remaining population of the western states is now in a state of uncontrollable panic. The meteor fireball was clearly visible in the evening sky. The noise of its entry into the atmosphere and its ultimate impact were audible for thousands of miles. In some places, apparently as far east as the Rockies, trees actually exploded into flames. Smoke from forest fires has reduced visibility in some regions to near zero. Cities and towns close to forests are also beginning to burn.

"As we now know, they have no electric power and are without their normal sources of news and information. To compound the problem, armed gangs are taking advantage of the darkness to loot stores, rob banks, and terrorize people.

"Ladies and gentlemen," the secretary of defense said, "I have no choice but to order all our state militias to full alert status to try to restore order. Madame Secretary, part of the danger to power plants that you feared is now past. I respectfully request that you have your department instruct the power companies to reactivate all power in those states as quickly as possible."

The energy secretary nodded and walked immediately to the telephone to relay appropriate instructions.

Al Augustus addressed the science adviser. "Dr. Eisenblatt, have you been able to learn anything further about the physical circumstances at this hour?"

Eisenblatt stood. "Yes, Mr. Secretary, I have. We'll be getting a satellite feed momentarily, but in the meantime I can tell you that the worst disaster imaginable is now taking place all over the Western Seaboard. At this moment the tidal wave is devastating all of the coastal areas of California north of the point of impact. The surge is being contained on the east by the coastal mountain range. However, it is being channeled toward the north at tremendous speed. It will overflow Monterey Bay at approximately ten-thirty P.M., Pacific time. Then there is no doubt that it will hit San Jose, Oakland, Berkeley, and San Francisco not later than eleven P.M., perhaps sooner.

"According to documents given to me just moments ago, it appears the waves will crest at something over three thousand feet in height, which means they will most certainly demolish all manmade structures in that region. Subsequently, it is reasonable to expect massive earthquake activity in the San Francisco Bay area as well. As I indicated earlier, we must still entertain the possibility that a significant portion of the state of California may very well separate from the mainland—or perhaps submerge completely.

"On a more pleasant note, I am able to report that several Corps of Engineers units have been able to deploy their sky hook helicopters along the main roads leading north and east from the San Francisco Bay area to lift stalled vehicles off the roads and, where possible, to higher ground. The emergency relief agencies have also ordered all available city buses and major transportation equipment commandeered to complement our military vehicles to get people out of there.

"We are working in the dark at this hour," he continued, "and against impossible odds to evacuate as many people as possible in San Francisco before the wave hits. This will sound terribly grim and I apologize, but if we are lucky, we will lose only fifty percent of the population. Of course, the bridges, the airport, the elevated highways, the subways, the downtown office buildings, the houses, and even Candlestick Park will all be destroyed."

The distinguished older man shook his head sadly. Fatigue lines were now etched in his face. "Whatever else we may know," he said, "this part of America is gone forever, ladies and gentlemen. Gone forever"—his voice trailed off—"forever. . . ."

The head of the Federal Emergency Management Agency (FEMA) had been called to the meeting. He arrived during the satellite display, but remained silent out of deference to the more senior officers. But, seeing the science adviser overcome by emotion, he stood to report on the next target—Seattle.

"If I may, ladies and gentlemen," he said, "we expect the situation in Seattle and the Pacific Northwest to be very much like that in San Francisco. A wall of water between one thousand and fifteen hundred feet in height will flood Puget Sound at approximately two tomorrow morning. Bremerton will be destroyed. The Boeing Aircraft factory, which is in a low area between Seattle and Tacoma, will be destroyed, which means that all equipment, along with the jet transports currently in production, will also be destroyed.

"Fortunately, we have time to organize a massive evacuation of the population in that area using private vehicles and military vehicles provided by the combined armed forces. If Secretary McGovern is able to restore power in the region soon, I'm confident we can effectuate an eighty percent evacuation. However, without electric power, the gasoline pumps will not be working, and transportation will be effectively halted."

There was a brief stir in the room and several loud comments, but the director of FEMA went on. "Especially troubling at this point are the numbers of confirmed reports of people who have died of heart attacks brought on by the fear and panic that we all must be feeling today. There are tens of thousands of them, and the hospitals are jammed to capacity. They are working off auxiliary power, but they can only continue for a limited time under these conditions."

The secretary of agriculture spoke up. "Take us back to California for a moment, will you, sir? My people tell me that the crops in the San Joaquin Valley north and south of Fresno from Modesto to Bakersfield are already gone from the heat. Heaven knows what will happen if saltwater floods those farms. It may be years before they're producing again."

"It's the same story in Oregon and eastern Washington, Mr. Secretary," said the director. "Fruit trees are dying, and the land there is bone-dry."

The agriculture secretary paused, then asked, "Even if you can get them out, how are you planning to feed the hundreds of thousands of people streaming inland from the San Francisco Bay and Puget Sound areas? What about shelter? Toilet facilities? This thing could get to be as bad as that mess in Rwanda a few years ago."

"It's difficult to imagine the magnitude of the problems we're facing, Mr. Secretary," the director of FEMA answered. "We were set up to deal with isolated emergencies as a supplement to existing infrastructures. Tonight, we will be forced to deal with hundreds of thousands of desperate people, many of them armed. We must evacuate them with a complete absence of electrical power.

"The air further inland is stifling hot and choked with smoke from forest fires. We have a shortage of rations, a shortage of tents, a shortage of doctors, and a shortage of containers for drinking water. We will be assembling crucial supplies all night and hauling them in truck convoys and military airlift to designated assembly points at first light.

"How to care for the displaced in the short term is a real challenge to all our systems. The long-term problem is simply beyond our capacity to consider. We can only pray that the law of the jungle won't take hold of these frightened, desperate people before we can get our relief effort in place."

Al Augustus turned to the director. "Thank you for your report." Then he looked at the entire cabinet. "Thank you, all of you," he said.

"It's getting late, and there is little more we can do tonight. But before we adjourn, we need one more critical piece of information." He turned to the secretary of the treasury, who had been silent throughout most of the evening. "Secretary Wong," Augustus said, "what are the financial implications of all this?" Then he caught himself. "But, first, James, do you have any word about your wife's family?"

Wong answered slowly. "They all got out of California safely, Mr. Secretary. Her brothers are in Asia on a business trip. Her father and mother are vacationing in Scottsdale. They flew the rest of the family out by company jet. But," he added, with obvious sadness in his voice, "they will lose their real estate, their savings and loan, and whatever else they had in California. It's all gone."

The appointment of James Wong to head the Treasury Department had been an acknowledgment of the burgeoning financial power of Asia. Born in Shanghai, he was the eldest son of a wealthy Chinese family who had lost all their holdings during the early days of Mao Tse-tung's regime. They had managed to escape to Hong Kong where, over the years, they had regained their fortune many times over by hard work, excellent contacts, and shrewd investments in real estate and banking in Hong Kong, and cement, plastics, and shipping in Taiwan.

Wong came to the United States as a student, winning degrees with high honors from Stanford in economics and international banking. He went to work with J.P. Morgan in New York City. Soon, he was marked as a rising star. Within ten years, he was promoted over the heads of more senior officers to become managing director of Morgan's entire Asian operation.

At college, he met and fell in love with Joyce Cumberland, the daughter of a former governor of California. Before they were married, Wong opted to become an American citizen. His family was fabulously wealthy and well-connected. Her family was very wealthy and even better-connected. James did not need to work, but he had a golden touch and enjoyed making deals. It was the sport, not the money, that really mattered to him. He and Al Augustus had become fast friends in Washington. They played tennis together. They socialized together. Their wives were close. They were the strength of the cabinet.

"Now, for the bad news," Secretary Wong began. "There are about fifteen hundred banks and thrifts in California with total assets of six hundred billion dollars. The Bank of America is the nation's second largest bank. Wells Fargo, based on the West Coast, is number fifteen. In industries such as banking, energy, aerospace, high-tech manufacturing, health care, construction, agriculture, and, of course, entertainment, California has been the leader. The state produced in excess of three hundred billion dollars in wholesale sales and a hundred billion in retail sales each year during the late 1990s. The best estimates suggest that total annual output of the state may have been in excess of eight hundred thirty-five billion dollars. Many California-based firms are listed on the Big Board or NASDAQ. In addition, we collect nearly sixty-four billion dollars in federal taxes each year from California, which is twelve percent of the total. We haven't got all the numbers on total market capitalization, but it is massive, and the loss of that market is going to send shock waves worldwide.

"Now all that is gone," he said, "and I can't begin to calculate the economic toll this will take on the rest of the country. How will we calculate what claims California residents had on other parts of the country? Who is entitled to the assets? How will we treat losses by those in the rest of the country who were owed money by someone in California? How do we process claims against insurance companies for damage caused by fire and flood? Such claims could bankrupt every insurance company doing business in California.

"We have learned that although most banks, insurance companies, and commercial businesses kept duplicate computer records in safe storage, only a few were kept out of state. Some data went out earlier today by high-speed data transmission, but such panic developed that the flow of data soon stopped." He paused with a helpless look on his face.

Al Augustus asked pointedly, "Where will these evacuees get money?"

"They won't, Mr. Secretary," said Wong. "There *is* no money. Where there are no computer records, there is no money. Unless they have deposits outside of the West Coast, they are now wards of the government. But can you grasp what is happening? Millions of feet of timber are going up in flames, vegetable production has had it, we have lost a huge chunk of the nation's productive wealth, millions of people are dead, and hundreds of thousands more are homeless refugees. With the spectacle we witnessed earlier tonight in this room, I suppose we have to ask whether or not we have the stomach for what must follow. Can our nation survive?

"Tomorrow we will have to halt trading on listed stocks that are West Coast-based or have significant West Coast exposure. Selling may be so heavy that we may be forced to close the markets. We will pour liquidity into the banking system to stave off a panic. We will declare force majeure to get the insurance companies off the hook to avoid mass bankruptcies. And, we will do everything we can to provide emergency cash payments to survivors so that they won't have to beg. I also know that the commodity markets will be up to the limit for lumber, soybeans, corn, and wheat minutes after opening. Once that happens, gold, silver, and platinum will follow. I'll leave it to the board to decide what happens after that.

"Beyond that," he said with remorse in his voice, "we must acknowledge that, at least for the foreseeable future, California, Hawaii, and parts of Oregon and Washington are gone. There is not enough money anywhere to undertake a disaster loan program. What is lost . . . is lost."

James Wong sat back then, and said nothing more. The entire room was silent.

Then Al Augustus said, "I have just been handed a message. It indicates that several heads of state of our Pacific allies have been placing urgent calls to the president and getting no response. I don't know where Vince D'Agostino is at this hour. However, I recommend that we adjourn until seven-thirty tomorrow morning. In the meantime, please continue to move forward on all your department initiatives to assist the refugees and victims. The Pentagon will work closely with FEMA and the state police, national guard, and relief agencies. All these people will be working through the night, but I suggest we each try to get some rest so we can deal with what comes next."

One by one, the cabinet members filed from the room, weary, disheveled, and emotionally exhausted by their ordeal.

CHAPTER EIGHT

CHARLEY MCATEE, DAVE BUSBY, and Carl and Lori Throneberry watched the horror in Los Angeles on big-screen television as much as they were able for over two hours. They had been mesmerized and virtually speechless throughout most of it, but when it was clear they were all reaching a saturation point, Charley touched the remote control, and the set went dark.

He stood up and shook the knots out of his spine. "There is nothing we can do to help the situation now," he said, "except pray for the families of the dead and those who are still alive north of L.A. But there is still a lot we can do personally to get ready for what's coming."

Dave Busby leaned back and extended his arms and legs to their full length. "I'm getting too old for this, Charley," he said. "Basketball's demanding, but this business is much, much harder." Standing up, he said, "When we first got here, you told us we were going to meet an old friend of yours, didn't you? When is that going to happen?"

"Good for you, Dave," said Charley. "I'm glad you asked. We need to be up at five o'clock and rolling out of this place no later than six."

"Five?" Lori gasped. "You mean, like, five o'clock—in the morning?"

"Yep." Charley nodded and smiled.

"Whew!" Carl whistled. "That's pretty early, Charley. Where are we going at that time of day?"

"We're going to pick up three truckloads of supplies and diesel fuel to take to a special place in the mountains called El Refugio."

"El Refugio," Lori repeated. "That's interesting. The refuge. Sounds like the right place for a bunch of refugees like us. . . ."

"You're right, Lori," Charley said, "and this will be a chance for you and Carl to meet the man I told you about earlier. He built El Refugio with his own money. Most people call him Pastor Jack. His real name is John Edwards. He's a descendant of Jonathan Edwards, who was one of the great early preachers, back in the middle 1700s. He's really proud of that heritage. Three hundred years later, Pastor Jack's still carrying on the tradition." Charley yawned and stretched. "Anyway, let's get some sleep. What do you say?"

With little coaxing, they all went to their assigned quarters and fell fast asleep.

IN WASHINGTON, VALERY RUST was watching the television news when two Secret Service agents showed up at the door with her husband in tow. She looked up, amazed to see the president home so early in the midst of such a crisis. He was expected to be at a top-level meeting with the entire cabinet through most of the evening. But Ted Rust was too groggy to think about the crisis facing America. And he was obviously in no condition to meet with anyone.

Since their move to the White House had been delayed until the widow of his predecessor could make the move back to her home state, President and Mrs. Rust had elected to stay in the Victorian mansion on Naval Observatory Hill that had served as the official residence of American vice presidents since the time of Vice President Gerald Ford, in the mid 1970s.

The agents who helped him up the steps put their arms around the president's back and supported him as he stumbled into the entry hall and settled down in one of the overstuffed chairs in the hall. Once they had deposited their burden, the agents turned quickly, said good night to the first lady, and left the chief executive to his fate.

There was fire in her eyes as Valery approached her husband. "What are *you* doing here?" she demanded. "Why aren't you with the cabinet? What are you doing about the crisis?"

"Leave me alone," he mumbled. "I couldn't take it anymore, so I left."

"You what?" she yelped. "You couldn't take it anymore—so you *what?*"

"Shut up, Valery," he protested. "I don't want to talk about it."

"Oh, no, Ted!" she exclaimed. "What have you done? You couldn't take what you saw at the briefing so you just—you just left? I'm sorry, Mr. President, but the West Coast of our country has just been blown off the map, and the president of the United States can't take it—and just left!"

"Look," he said. "It's not what you think. I had a couple of drinks to steady my nerves. That's all. Vince slapped me, so I fired him."

"Oh, Ted. You didn't!" she exclaimed. "You fired Vince? The man who has propped you up since your first campaign, and you sent him packing for doing what anybody in his right mind should have done? Ted, you've got to stop this thing—now. Without Vince D'Agostino you couldn't run a garbage truck, much less the United States. What are we going to do?"

"I think I'd like to go to bed," he muttered.

"Good! Terrific! That's just great. You screwed up your first cabinet meeting, deserted your post in a time of crisis, fired the one man who is indispensable to you, and now you want to go to bed." She looked at him in disgust. "*That's* the Ted Rust I know."

"Try and stop me, shady lady," he said, rising unsteadily to his feet.

"Good, Ted. Yes, you go to bed. In the meantime, maybe I can do something about fixing the mess you've made."

Ted stumbled noisily up the stairs while Valery walked back quickly into the little sitting alcove off the main entrance hall. She sat down on an ivory love seat and pondered for several minutes, then dialed a number she knew by heart.

"Tauriq?" she said. "Valery Rust. Can we talk now? I have a problem, a matter of great concern, and I'd like you to come over to the residence right away. Can you do that?" She paused briefly, then added, "Good. I'll tell the guards to expect you."

Within thirty minutes, there was a knock on the door. Valery opened the door herself to admit a tall, immaculately dressed man of about forty-five, with high cheekbones and aquiline features. One look into his eyes and nothing else about him seemed to matter. His eyes were deep, dark brown, and they seemed to burn like hot coals. They were a paradox: attractive, yet strangely repellent; malevolent, yet kindly.

The man standing before her was Tauriq Haddad—resident of Washington, Palm Beach, Paris, and New Delhi. By profession, he was a commodities dealer, oil trader, arms merchant, soldier of fortune, ladies man, and reputed billionaire. His Washington parties were legendary, as were the bribes and blackmail that went along with them. It had been rumored that he was the most powerful behind-the-scenes figure on three continents.

Valery smiled as Tauriq entered. She turned and closed the door behind her. "Thank you for coming, my friend," she said, as they walked into the sitting room. She motioned to a chair, then sat down on the sofa across from him. "Forgive my sudden call, and so late in the evening. But I have a serious problem, and I am very much hoping that you may be able to help me."

"How could I ever refuse the first lady?" Tauriq smiled. "I am yours to command. Please—how may I serve you?"

"It may not be simple, Tauriq," she said, drawing close and speaking quietly. "Ted has just come back from the White House, and he told me that he has fired our man Vince D'Agostino, who has served

Ted as chief of staff for many years. Vince has been invaluable to us. I cannot tell you how much he has helped Ted over the years. I'm afraid my husband is not a very aggressive man. He needs someone strong, like Vince, to depend on. He'll be helpless until we can find a suitable replacement—someone strong, intelligent, and politically astute."

"Yes," Tauriq mused, "I do see your dilemma, madame. You require someone who is not only intelligent and astute, as you say, but who can help direct the nation and her allies in a closer union during these times of world crisis." Folding his hands delicately on his lap, he added, "Yes, I do see your dilemma. But, surely there is just such a man."

Valery was pleased by the gentleman's manner and his exotic charm. "Exactly, my friend," she said. "I'm so pleased that you have grasped the urgency of the situation so quickly. It may not be a simple matter to find the person I have in mind, someone who can help—how did you say it?—direct America and her allies into a closer union during this time of crisis. But your gifts are legendary, Mr. Haddad. I know I can count on you."

Tauriq Haddad rose, looked into her eyes momentarily, then kissed Valery's hand. "My dear first lady," he effused, "I assure you that I will have the perfect man for you by nine o'clock tomorrow morning. Not one minute later." After bowing ever so slightly, he turned quickly on his heel and was gone.

Thirty minutes later, in the luxurious study of his elegant townhouse on Kalorama Road, Haddad picked up the handset to an encrypted satellite telephone and dialed a number in Antwerp.

"Panchal," he said, "sorry to wake you. Get your people ready. Tonight the gods have given America into our hands."

After leaving the Cabinet Room, Al Augustus went to find the president. It was morning in Asia, which meant that the Japanese, Koreans, Taiwanese, Filipinos, Chinese, Vietnamese, Indonesians, and every official in every other Southeast Asian nation had viewed the California disaster and were in various stages of panic. All those nations customarily looked to the United States for leadership, yet none was forthcoming. Every Asian leader had been frantically calling the White House, but they all received the same stock answer: "The president of the United States is personally directing the relief effort and cannot speak to you at this moment. He will return your call at the first opportunity."

The secretary of defense knew that it was crucial to share data with the Asian allies in order to save lives. The duty officer informed the secretary of defense that the president had left some time ago for his residence.

Al Augustus walked briskly from the Oval Office down the hall, through the reception area, and then turned left toward the office of the chief of staff. As he entered the outer office, the secretary motioned for him to go on into Vince's private office. Once inside, he found Vince sitting alone, watching a small wall-mounted TV set, as he had for the past two hours.

"Vince, what is going on? The president's gone home, and you're hiding in here watching TV."

Vince turned slowly. "He fired me. I'm out."

Al was shocked. "When did he fire you? When you followed him out of the room?"

"You've got it."

"Why, for heaven's sake? He depended on you. He couldn't even open his mouth without you!"

"I got mad and slapped him. So he slapped back."

"You can't be serious."

"I am. Dead serious. Ted Rust is an alcoholic, a coward, and a bad actor."

"I had my suspicions," Al said, "but nothing like this. You've always done such a great job of propping him up."

"Sure," came the answer. "If I hadn't done such a good job, he wouldn't be holding this office—the highest office in the greatest nation. Al, what are we going to do?"

Secretary of Defense Augustus thought for a few minutes, then spoke. "There are two keys—the new chief of staff and the new vice president. With a suitable vice president in place, we can probably maneuver an impeachment. But if we lose the chief of staff, we'll probably lose the selection of vice president."

Vince was growing very uncomfortable. "Are you thinking what I'm thinking?" he asked.

"I am, if you are thinking that Valery will control the selection of a new chief of staff," Al answered. "With the chief of staff, she gets to select the vice president."

Vince moaned. "I totally agree with you. But do you know how spooky she is? I'm not talking about her girlfriends, but all that mystical New Age stuff she's into. If her psychic buddies get their veep candidate voted in by Congress, hold on to your hat. They could very easily pop the president and wind up owning the candy store."

Al Augustus winced. "Ouch!" he said. "You're exactly right. Vince, old friend, you are talking twenty-first century coup d'état. That's a pretty sinister scenario, but, with all we've been through—who's to say? The problem is that if something like that were, in fact, to happen, and if they were to get away with it. . . ." He paused. "We had better be prepared to fight. Better still, we had better fight before it happens."

Vince leaned back in his chair. "What do you have in mind, Al?"

Al smiled. "I know you've been fired, Vince, but for the good of America, will you please return the calls of those panic-stricken Asian leaders who've been burning the wires all night?"

"I'll do it on one condition," Vince answered. "Buy me a pizza on the way home. I'm ravenous."

"Done."

WHEN JAMES WONG RETURNED from the cabinet meeting to his big corner office in the Treasury Building overlooking the south lawn of the White House, he knew what lay ahead of him—a long, virtually sleepless night. It was going to be grueling trying to calm the American markets. Having witnessed the president's disgraceful performance, he was now plagued with his own doubts about the future of the American economy. The nation was riding the crest of the worst crisis of its history. But, on top of all that, why had fate dealt America such a cruel blow, sending a buffoon to lead the nation in such a time of tragedy?

It was well after eleven at night in Washington, and the data from Asia was telling the story of widespread financial panic. The Japanese Nikkei stock index had dropped from 18,000 to 6,000 within thirty minutes. Investors sensed that the major Japanese banks would, with few exceptions, be insolvent. Property companies were in free-fall. After two hours of financial carnage, the government stepped in and closed all markets for the weekend.

Despite the massive problem in California, James Wong knew that the dutiful Japanese workers would already have headed off to work as if this were just one more business day. They would have packed themselves into the trains or driven their cars over the jammed highways, as if nothing had changed in the world overnight. In the minds of the average Japanese worker, America was a degenerate, crime-ridden, inferior nation, which clearly deserved whatever it got. Such a tragedy would never happen in their country. They would be shielded.

As he reflected on the developing picture in the East, the buzzer sounded on James Wong's office phone. "Mr. Secretary, Minister Nomura is calling from Tokyo."

Wong pushed the blinking button and quickly picked up the receiver. "Kubi, my old friend, how are you?"

Kubayashi Nomura, finance minister of Japan, had become a trusted friend to the treasury secretary over the years. Wong and Nomura had first met through a series of currency crises, trade disputes, and fishing wars. Nomura had traveled extensively in the United States and Europe, and was known as an urbane, cultured individual. From James Wong's perspective, he was also the most reasonable and reliable member of the Japanese government.

"James," Kubi Nomura began, "please allow me to express the profound sympathy of both myself and my government for the most terrible tragedy that has struck your great nation. Tell me of your wife's family. Are they safe?"

"Yes, thank God. They left California before the tragedy, and they are all safe."

"I've watched the TV and read the wires. But please tell me—how bad *is* it?" Nomura asked.

"Kubi, you just can't imagine. It is inconceivably bad. In all of human history, there has never been anything like this tragedy. The loss of life on the West Coast has been staggering. The losses in property and market value are well into the trillions. But what about Japan?"

"I know that you have been watching the news," Kubi said. "Our markets were chaotic, so I was forced to close them for the weekend. All over Asia, the story is the same. In Hong Kong, the Hang Seng is down fifty percent and still dropping."

James Wong's voice softened. "Kubi, the tidal wave coming your way is massive. The experts have never dealt with anything like it before. Their best guess is that a tsunami will also hit Japan sometime early Saturday morning, your time. The wave height may be as great as five hundred feet—it could be more. I fear for you, my old friend. Every coastal city will be obliterated. Surely your own experts have briefed you fully and you have seen the television news."

There was silence on the other end of the line, then, "Our government has kept most of this from our people, James. What else can you tell me?"

"We're having earthquake activity in California at this moment. You can expect the same. Seismic activity and the tsunami will hit like a one-two punch. There's even a chance that, in your area, the earth-quakes will hit first." There was a long silence on the other end, but James Wong continued, "Kubi, our markets are chaotic, but the U.S. is still intact. All those government bonds you have been buying will be good. You won't lose anything if you hold onto them. They'll give you something to rebuild with."

"James," Kubi Nomura whispered, "I fear this will be the end of Asia."

James Wong was a naturalized American, but in his heart he was Asian. Only two hours before, he had suffered the loss of count-less dear friends, not to mention his wife's massive family fortune. Now, the horror confronted him that in just over twelve hours, tens of millions of his fellow Asians—including Chinese, Japanese, Indonesians, Malaysians, and Filippinos—would perish in the churning sea.

"Kubi," he said in a voice that lacked conviction, "this is *not* the end of Asia. We who are left will rebuild together." Then he paused, "For now, you have more advance warning than we had. You must mobilize immediately. Throw in all your resources to save as many lives as you can. Tell the prime minister to take steps this very hour to move key parts of the government to a secure place in the mountains."

There was no answer on the other end, but James Wong con-tinued to plead his case. "If you will have your assistant call back in one hour, I will arrange to have a battery of top-secret computers on-line to store any financial records you want to transmit for safe-keeping here. They will be kept safe and secure for you. You have my word." Then, with strained emotion, he said, "Please, Kubi, listen to me. You must get a government helicopter and take your family out of Tokyo to some place high, where there are no volcanoes. Do you hear me?"

"You are a great friend, James," Japan's finance minister said hoarsely. "We will rebuild together." James held the phone to his ear until the line went dead.

No sooner had he hung up the phone than James's assistant announced another call. This time, it was the managing director of the bank clearing house in Brussels known as the Society for Worldwide Inter Fund Transfers, or SWIFT.

Unlike the previous call, James Wong feared what this one might bring. For the past five years, all of the major banks had been clamoring for a system to transfer money without checks. The cost of physically transporting checks and bank drafts, verifying information, and processing paper ran into hundreds of millions of dollars annually. How much better to have all banking transactions handled by wire— computer to computer. Then, in the bankers' perfect world, there would be no cash—only a card for consumers—a smart card—with balances updated with each use.

In that checkless, cashless world, there would be no money, per se. Only computer entries controlled by a cascade of regional computer systems, finally terminating at the World Inter Fund computers in Brussels.

There was just one problem with this perfect world, however. The genius who designed the system had failed to reckon with what would happen to SWIFT if all the banking computers were destroyed in a state whose economy was equal in size to the seventh largest nation on earth. Would transfers originating in California be honored? If they had been honored, should they be canceled? If they were canceled, what institution in existence was capable of making good on the financial obligations? Then, what would happen if the computers that controlled the world's eight largest banks, situated in Japan, the world's second largest economy, suddenly crashed?

The answer was simple to James Wong. The whole thing would shut down, and the world would be out of credit. Trillions of dollars of financial assets would be on hold until swarms of computer programmers could recreate every transaction. Then, hordes of lawyers would have to sort through the legal ramifications of who owned what and where.

He smiled as he thought of the jubilant speculators who thought they had made billions playing the market crash and gambling on the impending shortage of commodities. Thinking of the financial carnage, he realized that no one with sufficient money would be around to honor those options, neither the shorts nor the longs, the puts nor the calls.

And then he recalled the words of an ancient prophet, "It will be the same for the seller as for the buyer, for the borrower as for the lender, for the debtor as for the creditor, the earth will be completely laid waste and plundered." How odd to know that today he was the man who would see the fulfillment of those words as perhaps no other had ever done.

Yes, he thought, *it doesn't matter which side of the trade they were on. Everybody comes out a loser*. But his thoughts were interrupted by his intercom buzzer again. "Mr. Secretary, it is Raoul Gaston in Brussels with SWIFT. He's still waiting on line one."

James couldn't delay talking to him any longer. He picked up the phone. "Yes, Mr. Gaston, how can I help you?"

"Mr. Secretary, something terrible has happened," he said. "Our computers are spitting out nonsense. Nothing balances. We are holding up the money flow of the world. Have you any suggestions? We are in a most desperate situation."

"Mr. Gaston," James replied, "I want you to listen to me very closely. For several months now, I've been considering this very possibility, and I've been contemplating what kind of contingency plan might be needed in case there was a breakdown in your system. I have an answer for the problem, but you must do as I say."

"Please, Mr. Wong," Gaston exclaimed, "tell me now!"

"First, notify your correspondent banks to discontinue SWIFT clearances immediately. Then resume the regional transfer mechanism. Leave in place all transactions prior to the catastrophe. As quickly as possible, then, you will need to have your people rebuild the computer records and track down those legally responsible for payments."

"Yes, I understand," Gaston replied. "Please continue."

"I am afraid that California is a total loss, and it also looks as if both Japan and Hong Kong will be out of the picture by this weekend. So, please, plan around that prospect."

"Oh," the European reacted in surprise. "That too?"

"After we have time to assess the extent of the damage," Wong continued, "the surviving governments will try to inject liquidity into the system to restart our world again. We won't fund the profits of those who have been speculating on tragedy, nor can we repay losses. So for now, I recommend that, as quickly as possible, you wire urgent notices to your network, then shift to a simpler system. When my counterparts have met, we will give you more specific directions. Does that help you, Monsieur Gaston?"

"Yes, Secretary," he said. "We have no other choice. Thank you. And please stay in touch with us."

"I will. Just stay calm. Good night."

"Good night, Mr. Secretary," said Gaston. "I am glad you are in charge."

By now James Wong was exhausted, but he had to go on. In rapid succession, he had his assistant put through calls to those of his Asian counterparts in the path of danger. The message was always the same: "A tragedy of immense proportions is unfolding. . . . Save what lives you can. . . . America will survive. . . . We will rebuild together."

By now it was almost two o'clock in the morning. His brain was numb. His body screamed for rest. He would be no good to anyone unless he could sleep a few hours, take a shower, and put on clean clothes.

He called down to have his limousine brought around, grabbed his jacket off the coat rack, and turned off the light on his desk. Just as he was walking out of the office, an assistant called out, "Mr. Secretary, it's the secretary of defense. What do you want me to tell him?" Reluctantly, Wong picked up the phone and stabbed at the flashing button with his finger. "Al, I was just leaving. What's up?"

A worried Al Augustus responded, "James, we've got a political crisis that could hurt us worse than the meteor. I've got to see you right away."

"Al," the secretary moaned, "I've been on the wire to Asia and Europe all night long. I'm dead tired. Can't it wait until morning?"

"Okay, Jimmy. I guess you're right. We'll both think more clearly after a few hours' sleep," the equally weary secretary of defense replied. "Your place is only two blocks away from mine. What do you say? Can you come by for breakfast at six-thirty? We may be a few minutes late for the cabinet meeting, but I'll ask the good lady from Energy to hold the fort until we get there."

"Al," James asked, sensing the gravity of his friend's late-night call, "what's this all about?"

"Not on the phone, Jimmy," he said. "Just come over tomorrow, and I'll fill you in."

"I'll be there at six-thirty," James Wong replied. Then, he quickly hung up the phone, took his private elevator to the street floor, walked to his limousine, got in, and promptly fell asleep in the backseat on the way home.

CHAPTER NINE

SECRETARY JAMES WONG arrived at the lovely Georgetown residence of Al Augustus at 6:30 on the dot Friday morning. His body was beginning to ache from fatigue.

The door was opened by a German woman in her sixties who had been with the Augustus family for decades. She ushered Wong into the elegant dining room with its eighteenth-century furnishings and sparkling crystal chandelier.

Al rose from the table and greeted him, then nodded to the German woman to withdraw. "Welcome, James," he said warmly. "Help yourself."

James was too keyed up even to consider a large breakfast. He went over to the sideboard, selected a large blueberry muffin, poured a cup of coffee, then sat where his host motioned for him to sit. "Al, what's all the mystery about?"

Al leaned across the table and said, "James, you are one of the few people in Washington I trust implicitly. As you know, the offices and cars in this town get bugged a lot. I sweep my home regularly for bugs and wiretaps. We can speak freely here."

"Fine, Al. That's just fine," James Wong replied and took a sip of his coffee. "But what are we to speak freely about?"

"It's a coup d'état," Al said.

"A what?" James shot back.

"Jimmy, I'll give it to you as concisely as possible," Al continued. "You remember what a jackass the president made of himself last night?" Wong nodded. "Well, after the cabinet meeting I went looking for Vince to find out exactly what happened with the president. I found Vince in his office. It turns out that he was so steamed about it, he followed the president into the Oval Office and slugged him."

James Wong was aghast. "What? The chief of staff struck the president of the United States?"

"Well," Al answered carefully, "he didn't slug him exactly. He slapped him with his open hand across the face."

James Wong was now wide awake. His mind was racing. "Then what happened?"

"The president fired Vince. Vince claims that Ted Rust is a drunk. Actually, I know now that it was Vince who was the one making Rust look good all along."

"Is the firing going to stick?" James asked.

"Looks like it to me," Al replied. "Rust holds the trump card. Drunk or not, I don't think he will countenance any frontal attacks on his personal image of grandeur. Anyway, I'm reasonably sure that Vince would never come back—even if the president asked him to."

James spoke quickly, "Al, Vince D'Agostino is only the newly designated presidential chief of staff. What is all this coup d'état nonsense?"

"It's not nonsense, Jimmy," Al replied. "We both watched Ted Rust in action last night. He is a cowardly drunk. I'd be willing to bet you that his wife has seized on this incident as a way to get power away from her oaf of a husband."

He paused and then spoke very deliberately. "As sure as you and I are sitting here, Valery Rust has been working all night to fill the void in the executive staff. You can count on it. It wouldn't surprise me to learn that she's presenting Ted Rust with her choice for chief of staff along with his coffee and doughnuts this very morning."

James Wong whistled. "Oh, man," he said, "we don't need that."

"You know it," said the secretary. "The next step would be to land her choice for vice president. If she succeeds, my friend, our constitutional system will be left in tatters. And, that really would be a de facto coup d'état."

"So, what do we do?"

"We do nothing if my suspicion is ill-founded," Al replied. "But," he paused, then spoke slowly and deliberately, "if it *is* true, we must take very careful steps to deny them the use of the military power of the United States. I don't have a plan yet, but whatever we decide to do later, for now this discussion must be treated with absolute secrecy between us."

"You have my word, Al."

"There's a national crisis to manage, and we'd better get moving." Al Augustus stood, and James Wong followed. "I'll see you at the cabinet meeting," Al said. "And, Jimmy," he added as he took his friend's hand, "may God help us to help America."

TED RUST WAS A LATE RISER, but this morning he was dressed and coming downstairs for breakfast at 8:30. He had entrusted his headache to a couple of extra-strength painkillers and was looking forward to strong, black coffee and his customary large glass of fresh-squeezed orange juice.

Valery met him at the foot of the stairs. "I've got good news," she said cheerily. "I've found the perfect replacement for Vince D'Agostino."

"What are you talking about?" he replied warily. "Why would I want a replacement for Vince?"

Valery stared incredulously, then realized that the previous night must have been another blackout for her besotted husband. "Ted, I don't want to be the first to tell you, but you fired Vince last night. Remember? Vince is gone. *History.*"

"Okay, I remember vaguely," he said as he pushed by her. "I've got to get some coffee. Talk to me in the dining room."

He helped himself to coffee and a muffin from the sideboard, then sat down at the elegant mahogany table. After taking several sips of coffee, he asked, "What do you mean, you've found a replacement?"

"Just the right man for you, Ted," she said. "He's fabulous. Just the kind of person we've needed. He'll make you look great."

"I'm listening," Ted mumbled. "Tell me more."

"He grew up in San Francisco, earned a law degree at Yale, took a turn at Covington and Burling, then went to work for the State Department in the Far East. He served briefly in Brussels before being promoted to chargé d'affaires at our embassy in New Delhi. He's been a policy analyst, a contributor to *Foreign Policy Review*, and, from what I hear, he is extremely well-connected in this town."

The president took a bite of his bran muffin. "Tell him I'll see him at the White House sometime this morning."

"I can do better than that," Valery responded with a sly smile. "He is here right now. I'll bring him in."

Before Ted Rust could object, he found himself greeting a wiry, handsome, impeccably tailored young man in his late thirties. In a deferential tone that bordered on the obsequious, the young man spoke. "Mr. President, I cannot express to you the honor I feel at this meeting. My name is Benjamin Benares. The first lady has indicated her desire that I offer myself for your service. I have prepared a detailed résumé, along with a dossier containing recommendations from people whom you know personally."

As he handed over the papers, he stared directly into Ted Rust's eyes. Rust had warmed to the thought of a chief of staff who would take orders, instead of always giving them. As he looked into this stranger's eyes, he felt instantly drawn to him . . . a strange and powerful presence. As he examined the documents in his hand, a strong desire swept over him—almost a compulsion—and he knew that he must have Benjamin Benares as his chief of staff. No further discussion of the matter was needed.

He tried to shake it, but the urge he felt was like a narcotic that left him somewhat dazed. He smiled at this young man and briefly scanned pages of glowing references. "I respect my wife's opinions," the president said with no conviction. "And, I like the looks of all the important names you have here—many important people seem to think very highly of you." He fought not to say it, but he was powerless to stop the words that flowed from his mouth. "Subject to an independent verification of your credentials, Mr. Benares, and subject to our standard FBI security check, I would be pleased to have you join my team. We'll be in touch."

"Thank you, Mr. President," Benjamin Benares said meekly. "You will never know how happy you have made me—and my family."

Valery showed Benares to the door. He looked knowingly into her eyes. "It is well done, indeed," he said softly. "Our good friend Tauriq will be pleased." Then he was gone.

BY THE TIME THE NEW YORK Stock Exchange opened, news of the meteor disaster had created a feeding frenzy in the world markets. Every stock on the Big Board, NASDAQ, and the AMEX had begun selling off the previous afternoon. Then, computerized trading programs began sending massive sell signals that, in turn, brought on frantic telephone redemptions by holders of mutual funds and equally frantic selling by fund managers desperately needing cash.

James Wong, the treasury secretary, left the cabinet meeting early to deal with the financial crisis. He had already halted trading in all stocks and funds with exposure in California the moment the severity of the crisis was known. As the situation worsened, he halted trading in all bank stocks and insurance company stocks. He contacted the desperate chairman of the Federal Reserve board, who was paralyzed into inactivity—not knowing whether to inject money into the system to instill confidence or to drain money out of the system to instill confidence. So, the Fed sat on the sidelines and did nothing.

By 11:00 A.M., East Coast time, the tape was running ten minutes late as a record eight hundred million shares had been sold on the Big Board. The Dow had dropped a sickening twenty-five hundred points with no floor in sight. By then, nearly two trillion dollars of investor value had been wiped out. James Wong ordered all U.S. markets closed.

Shrewd traders were amassing fortunes on paper by shorting the stock indexes like the Standard and Poor's 500, the 200, the 100. Holders of put options and short positions were popping champagne corks to celebrate their incredible good fortune.

In the commodity pits, the story was just the reverse. Sensing the impending shortage of lumber and agricultural commodities, speculators had bid up to the limit every available contract in lumber, corn, wheat, soybeans, oats, and cotton. This type of trading required very little money to control option contracts on enormous quantities of goods. As prices accelerated, paper profits available to margin more option contracts also increased. With the increased paper profits, the smart speculators stayed fully margined, which meant that their profits were accelerating geometrically.

In the stock market, there were only sellers. In the commodities markets, only buyers. All this frenzied activity was transmitted instantaneously by satellite data link to trading rooms in Tokyo, Hong Kong, Manila, Taipei, Singapore, Kuala Lampur, Jakarta, and Bangkok, where frantic traders were making urgent calls in the middle of the night to notify wealthy clients and to receive instructions.

Before all of the chaos began, Secretary Wong had tried to explain in the simplest possible terms the subtleties of the international markets to two new personal assistants. "It begins with the idea that the earth rotates on its axis toward the east," he said. "That is why sunlight arrives first in countries that are situated to the east.

Since each twenty-four-hour day has to start somewhere, the world's scientific community decided, for the sake of clocks and calendars, to draw an imaginary line in the Pacific Ocean and call it the International Date Line. At this point, the old day theoretically ends and the new day begins. On the eastern side of the date line, when it's Thursday, it's Friday on the western side.

"The time difference between Washington, D.C., and Manila in the Philippines is twelve hours when we're on daylight savings time. So nine o'clock Thursday night in Washington is nine o'clock Friday morning in Manila. But consider what the global time shifts mean to the world financial markets. If the French stock market closes at four P.M., it is ten A.M. in New York, but nighttime in Asia. When New York closes at four P.M., it is one P.M. in California, and very early morning in Hong Kong. When West Coast markets close, the markets in Asia are about to open. Then, market openings travel with the sun around Southeast Asia to India, to Europe, and back to New York.

"With a global economy comprised of trillions of dollars worth of stocks, commodities, bonds, currencies, and options, the world becomes a twenty-four-hour-a-day casino that only closes down on weekends. For serious traders in the big casino, sleep gets to be a rare luxury—even more so in a time of crisis."

It was common knowledge in the high-stakes investment community that even the slightest delays in transfers could cost tens of millions of dollars, and funds transfers were often just as costly. When the alarms were given, some of the wealthiest Asians were astute enough to order their stored gold bullion to be carried to corporate jets whose pilots had been told to plan predawn flights to inland high ground located at least two thousand miles to the west. Others received calls, but deferred action until morning. By then, it was too late.

Over the years the creation of wealth had become an Asian obsession. As the supreme leader of China, Deng Xiaoping, put it before his death, "To be rich is glorious." During the 1980s and 1990s, an Asian frenzy had developed to buy and sell the real estate in the coastal cities. In one transaction, which was not that extraordinary by Asian standards, a one-acre plot of land in Hong Kong sold for $2,000 per square foot, which translated to $88,000,000 per acre. James Wong had watched as property values in Japan had been bid to ridiculous heights, reaching a mind-boggling fifteen trillion dollars at one point. There was a time when the estimated market value of the land dedicated to the grounds of the Imperial Palace in Tokyo was higher than the sum total of the market value of all the property in the entire state of Florida. Any rational trader would have seen that this was an unreal market valuation that was bound to lead to chaos.

The valuation did not stop there, however. Japanese banks loaned money based on stratospheric land valuation. The market price of Japanese industrial stocks was bid up based on valuations of corporate land holdings. The major Japanese corporations began supporting the overall stock market valuations by buying one another's stocks and bonds. A giant financial pyramid was erected that, in turn, rested on the value of land whose fate depended on the continued peacefulness of the ocean called by that name . . . Pacific.

Now, it's no longer peace, but fury that's roaring their way, James thought. *As Benjamin Franklin put it, "The prospect of hanging concentrates a man's mind wonderfully."* As another workday was about to begin in Asia, the minds of Asian leaders were riveted on how the California meteor would affect them. James doubted, however, that most of the leaders could fully comprehend that all the money, all the stocks, all the real estate in Asia would mean nothing, once the tsunami hit.

CHAPTER TEN

CHARLEY, DAVE, LORI, and Carl awoke in the darkness Friday morning, showered and dressed quickly, and by 5:30, they were eating a healthy breakfast of whole-grain cereal and melon. Then they climbed into Charley's high-powered, four-wheel-drive pickup and headed for a garage on the edge of town. Inside the flat, tin building were two nondescript flatbed trucks with removable stake siding. They quickly loaded ten empty fifty-gallon drums onto each truck and lashed them securely with ropes.

"Charley, what's this all about?" Dave asked. "I thought we were going to see some Bible teacher."

Charley laughed. "We are! But, in light of what's coming, we're going to need a lot of diesel fuel. El Refugio is too far out in the hills for regular deliveries, so we'll have to make sure we've got what we need . . . when we need it."

Charley and Dave drove the big flatbed trucks. Carl and Lori took the pickup. They drove to an all-night service station, topped off the tanks, then pumped a thousand gallons of diesel fuel into the drums. As Charley paid the bill, he paused to talk to the attendant. "We've got some serious dozer work up in the hills," he said. "How are you doing?"

The attendant shook his head. "I can't stop thinking about all those people in Los Angeles last night. They say that San Francisco was practically washed away during the night. Seattle's next. Only the Lord knows how bad it's finally going to get."

"Ed," Charley answered, noting the nametag on the coveralls, "all we can do now is trust in the Lord."

"You got *that* straight, mister. Thanks for the business."

The little convoy moved north out of Albuquerque, then west to a branch of the Rio Puerco into the foothills toward the Continental Divide. After a three-hour drive, they entered a lovely mountain valley. Through a grove of trees was John Edwards's impressive spread, El Refugio.

THE CENTRAL BUILDING at El Refugio was a large multipurpose structure with the natural log-and-adobe design of the region. The living room, a large den and meeting room, kitchen facilities, and guest rooms were all on the first floor. Upstairs were several bedrooms. Farther up, at the top of the long, winding stairway, was John Edwards's private study. Flanking the residence on either side were two rustic bunkhouses. To one side of the main building was an impressive array of communications equipment, including a satellite telephone antenna, two satellite TV receiver dishes, and a satellite TV and data transmission dish.

John Edwards came out to greet them, dusting off his hands on his blue jeans. He was a tall, powerfully built man in his early seventies with gray hair pulled back into a ponytail, revealing a deeply lined and tanned face. He looked like a cowhand with faded jeans, rough hide cowboy boots, a blue workshirt, and denim jacket.

He hugged Charley, then warmly greeted Dave, whom he recognized instantly, and the couple, whom Charley introduced as Carl and Lori Throneberry.

"Pastor Jack," Charley began, "Carl and Lori are from Los Angeles. They barely got out of the horror that hit the West Coast last night. They told me they wanted to learn more about the Bible and what's going to happen next. So that's why Dave and I brought them up here to you."

"Well, that's quite a story, Charley," their host said. "I'm glad you've come."

"But before we go any further, Jack, we've also brought you twenty barrels of diesel fuel for your dozers and your generator. Do you want us to unload them?"

"Charley, you're top drawer," John Edwards said warmly. "We can sure use it. Carlos and my fellows here will take care of the diesel in a bit. But you folks come on inside and let me get you something cold to drink."

When they were seated in the large, open living area, Lori whispered something to Carl. Their host reappeared a few minutes later with a large tray on which there were glasses and a pitcher of iced tea. He put the tray down on a large coffee table and began pouring the amber liquid into glasses for each of them. Then Lori addressed the question she had shared with Carl to their host. "Pastor Jack, I know you from somewhere, don't I?"

He smiled. "Well, maybe you do, after all. Lori, a few years ago, the church I started on the East Coast became one of the biggest in America. I was on television, and from time to time my picture appeared in various newspapers and magazines. That's probably why you think you know me."

"That's right," Lori said.

"John Edwards," said Carl. "Of course. I know that name. You're the big-time minister who made all that money—some kind of investment, wasn't it? What happened? You didn't lose it all, did you?"

John Edwards let out a booming laugh. "No, Carl. I didn't lose it all. I guess you might say I lost and I gained. It all started about ten years ago. My wife, Charlotte, was coming home from a weekend visit to her sister. Our twenty-seven-year-old son was driving. It was late and it was dark, and he was passing a slow-moving truck on a hill when his car was hit by a speeding tanker truck coming in the opposite direction. The car was torn up pretty badly, and—well, there were no survivors."

"I'm so sorry. I didn't know."

"That's all right, Carl. I've gotten accustomed to it now. I was devastated at the loss. But, you know, I turned to God in a way I never had before. It was then that God's Spirit really started showing me some of the things that were about to start happening on earth."

He took a sip of his iced tea, then continued. "In 1995, the Lord gave me a clear understanding of the relation between Bible prophecy and our present situation. A couple of years ago, following what I believed to be His leading, I left my church, sold some of my most profitable investments, gave some money away, and then I bought this place. I've been up here praying and studying so that I could be a resource for people all over the world who, like you, are looking for answers during the chaos that's about to grip the world."

"It's certainly a great place," said Lori. "You've got everything you'll ever need right here."

"Thanks, Lori," he said. "And you're right. That's why I have all this communications gear." After a brief pause, he said, "You know, Lori, I can talk to every continent on earth from these mountains. Satellite communications still amaze me."

"Me too," Lori said, smiling.

"Mr. Edwards, " Carl said, "if I heard what you said correctly, you indicated that you already knew this hell was going to break loose on the West Coast. Is that right?"

"Well, yes and no, Carl," was the answer. "By the way, please call me Jack. I knew it was going to happen soon. I also knew that a short period of indescribable suffering was going to grip the earth. That's basic teaching, as you probably know. However, I didn't really know when, or where it would start."

"I buy that," Carl replied. "But tell me how you knew five years ago, back in 1995, what was coming and what was going to happen from that time on."

"Carl, I'm willing to tell you the whole truth, but I want to ask you two questions, as well. Do you have the time to learn the truth? Think it over. If not, then there's not much point in my going further with this. But if the answer is yes, then I need to know one more thing. Are you ready to face the consequences of that truth?"

Carl and Lori looked at each other, then nodded their heads in unison. "Jack," Carl said, "take all the time you need. Lori and I are both ready. Believe me."

"Okay, then let's get started."

Both Carl and Lori had a pretty good idea what was coming next. More Bible study. But this time, unlike their first indoctrination with Charley, they were looking forward to it.

As John Edwards moved the tray and pitcher out of the way, Charley and Dave took several Bibles from a nearby bookcase and passed them around.

"Good job, Charley, Dave," John Edwards said, falling back into his chair. "What I'd like to do is start with the good stuff, so let's take a look at Revelation."

Lori and Carl laughed. "We know about Revelation, Jack. Charley has given us the Cook's tour."

"Is that right?" he said. "Well, if you spent the night at Charley's, then I'm sure that he brought you up to speed on what the apostle John wrote about the meteor."

"It was fascinating," Lori murmured. "But let's keep going."

"Okay. First, I want you to understand that at the end of the age, two distinct and widely different things are going to take place. Open those Bibles to Revelation, chapter six, where it tells about the Four

Horsemen. These are the angels that are to bring war, revolution, famine, and death to the world."

"We've done that, Jack," Carl interrupted. "Charley went over the Four Horsemen with us last night."

"Fine. What did he tell you they represented?"

Lori spoke first. "He said that, in his opinion, these horsemen rode through most of the twentieth century."

"It was the bloodiest century in history," Carl added. "War, revolution, mass killings—and famine, I think—but maybe that's still to come."

"I can't quarrel with any of that," John Edwards replied. "Well, in that case, look at verses fifteen through seventeen of that same chapter." Everyone turned to the chapter. "Lori," said their host, "why don't you read the verses for us?"

Lori began to read out loud. "'And the kings of the earth, the great men, the rich men, the commanders, the mighty men, every slave and every free man, hid themselves in the caves and in the rocks of the mountains, and said to the mountains and rocks, "Fall on us and hide us from the face of Him who sits on the throne and from the wrath of the Lamb! For the great day of His wrath has come, and who is able to stand?"'"

"Lori," John asked, "what does verse seventeen say to you?"

Lori reread the verse to herself, then said, "It seems to say that the great day of God's wrath has come, and no one can stand against it."

"When does that happen?" he asked.

"After the ride of the horsemen?" she asked.

"That's right," said John Edwards. "You're absolutely correct. But what takes place after the horsemen ride and before the great day of God's wrath? Take a look at chapter seven."

"I see it," Carl spoke up. "An angel keeps any harm from coming to the earth. It looks like John is saying that there's to be a sort of supernatural protection over us until the angels have sealed the servants of God on their foreheads."

"But do you know what sealing means? And why foreheads?" John asked.

Carl hesitated. "Got me, Jack. Unless a seal is like a sign of ownership."

Lori said, "Could it be that the forehead—symbolizes the mind or the will?"

"Excellent, Lori. You two are very quick."

"Well," Lori explained, "that's what my aunt Josephine told me. God would not send destruction on the earth until He'd placed His seal of ownership on people all over the world."

"There's just one problem," Carl said. "We've already had the meteor. So when did the sealing take place?"

John Edwards was amazed at the insight and intelligence of his new guests. He was beginning to understand that Carl and Lori were not just a couple of lucky travelers who had dropped in out of nowhere. They seemed to have some special calling on their lives.

"When did the sealing begin?" Jack mused. "Now, *that's* a good question."

IN HIS MIND'S EYE, he was standing on a huge platform on the Mall in Washington, D.C., between the U.S. Capitol and the Washington Monument. He was fifty years old, in the height of his ministry. Before him were assembled five hundred thousand evangelicals and Roman Catholics from all over America. It was the largest Christian gathering in the history of America. The people had been called together by a committee organized by a Puerto Rican pastor who had once been jailed as a heroin addict.

"Now, join your hands together all over this great assembly," he was saying. "Then, let's pray. Father, we have sinned. Our nation has sinned. We repent before You. We humbly ask Your forgiveness. Come, O Father, heal our land. Hear our prayer, Father, and let righteousness flow like a river over the great land. . . ."

Then the cheers, the shouts of joy, the applause, the tears of joy—
God had heard their prayer.

JOHN EDWARDS SNAPPED out of his reverie. He looked at Lori
and said, "I believe, and it's strictly my opinion, that the sealing in
preparation for the end times started on April 29, 1980, at a great
meeting of a half-million Christians in Washington, D.C. This was
the anniversary of the prayer meeting of the Jamestown settlers, when
they landed on the Atlantic shore in Virginia on April 29, 1607, and
claimed America for the Lord."

"From 1980 on, millions of Americans were energized with
faith. Huge churches sprang up all over the country. Some were so
popular that people actually ran to the sanctuaries from the parking lots on Sunday morning to be able to get good seats. In the
1980s, the airwaves in the United States were filled with church
services, evangelistic meetings, Christian teachings, Christian tes-
timonies, and prayer for the sick. The nation had never known
anything like it."

"Yeah, but that bubble sure burst before the decade was over," said
Carl, somewhat cynically.

"Not really, Carl, though it might seem that way. The Bible tells us
that judgment begins at the house of the Lord. God had a much greater
role for the Christian people in the nineties. How could a holy God
use a corrupt church to offer forgiveness of sin to people all over the
world? There were, indeed, a few highly publicized Christians who
were guilty of conduct that was decidedly un-Christian. They were
disgraced and severely punished. Then, the church grew stronger,
not weaker."

Carl shook his head. "That's not what I read in the newspapers."

"You're absolutely right, Carl," John replied. "There were many
key people in the media in the United States who considered the
rise of the Christian faith to be a dangerous thing. They hoped to

persuade Americans to reject Christianity by trumpeting the sins of several errant evangelists."

"I remember it well," Carl replied. "In a sense, I was one of those media people myself. The things I produced appeared in all the media, and I was one of those who condemned all Christians because of a few corrupt leaders."

Charley nodded. "Then, you may remember what happened next. Most Christians quickly saw through the media bias and ignored what was being said. The believing church kept on growing. People like you, however, seldom heard about the positive things because the media refused to report them."

Lori spoke up. "But, Jack, what has all this got to do with sealing people before God's wrath started?"

John smiled. "Lori, America was the source of seventy percent of the money for missions. During the seventies and eighties, American evangelicals gained great skills in communications. They produced television and radio programs. They produced films. They used satellites. They acquired large full-color presses. They learned cultural and language skills.

"Then, in 1989 and 1990 when Communism fell, an enormous spiritual vacuum developed all over the world. At that time, God directed certain groups within the evangelical church in America to use their skills and finances for quick and massive outreach around the world. One leading evangelical organization produced a first-class film of the life of Jesus. They mobilized traveling teams who showed that film with foreign language soundtracks to a quarter of a billion people in over a hundred countries.

"Another American ministry broadcast a message of God's love in thirty-two languages to an additional quarter of a billion people living in seventy nations. From those broadcasts, fifty-five million people came to faith in Jesus Christ. In five years, from 1990 to 1994, this one American-based ministry led twenty-five times as many people to faith in Christ as it had in its previous thirty years of existence."

"Pastors, teachers, evangelists, church groups from all over America traveled throughout the world holding meetings, training workers, distributing Bibles, Christian literature, and electronic messages. One well-known evangelist held a crusade in Puerto Rico that was beamed by satellite to over a hundred and thirty halls and stadiums all over the globe."

"There was another extraordinary movement in 1997. The Pope, the head of the Roman Catholic Church, called on every cardinal, archbishop, bishop, and priest around the world to begin three years of concentrated prayer and evangelistic effort. The Pope wanted to cause every Catholic believer to begin to live a holy life and for every nonbeliever in the world to accept Jesus Christ in faith. He wanted to prepare the church and the world for the new millennium."

"There has never been anything like it in the history of the world, yet the American press completely ignored what was happening."

"Jack, I'm astounded," Carl said. "I've never heard a word about any of this. Those of us in Hollywood told each other that Christians were money-grubbing, Bible-thumping, fundamentalist crazies. You're telling us today about a dedicated army of people following divine direction who went all over the world offering God's pardon before serious calamity hit the earth."

"But, Jack," Lori asked, "what did God show you personally?"

"Lori," he answered, "I was up to my neck in this very work from 1990 until 1995. In all of my life, I had never seen anything like it. It was as if God had strapped a rocket on my back, then ignited the after-burner. Yet, in 1994, God showed me that I had to accelerate everything that I had been doing, that we had five years to complete the worldwide spiritual harvest."

"Then," he continued, "I learned that he had placed the same sense of urgency on many of my fellow ministers. Part of it, perhaps, could have been explained by the approaching end of a millennium. But, somehow, this was different."

Charley interrupted. "What do you mean, it was different?"

"Well, Charley, too many signs of the times were being fulfilled in the world. We all felt that we were moving close to the end of the age."

"Signs of the times? What are signs of the times?" Carl asked.

"Signs of the times are those conditions or events told about by Jesus Christ that will take place before He returns to earth," John Edwards answered.

"And, you think His coming is close?" Lori asked.

"Yes, I do."

Carl was insistent. "What signs? How did you know?"

"Just be patient. I'll get to the signs shortly, but let me finish about 1995. When I do, I'll give you the most important sign of all."

He looked at his watch, then stood up. "We'll talk some more over lunch. Maria, my housekeeper, should have it ready. I hope you like Mexican food. Oh, and bring the Bibles with you!"

They went outside to a covered patio. The smell of wood smoke from distant forest fires was heavy in the air. As they sat down to a lunch of flour tortillas, rice, black beans, and chicken, John Edwards bowed his head. The others followed suit. "Lord, we smell the smoke arising from the tragedy. We pray for protection for the survivors and comfort to those who are grieving. Please, Lord, bless this food and our fellowship, and, Father, please help us to fulfill the purpose that You intended when You kept us all alive. Amen."

John Edwards looked up and smiled at his guests, "Before we begin, let me introduce my wonderful housekeeper and Christian sister, Maria. Maria is a Mexican citizen who has lived around here for the past forty years. She never bothered with all the formalities of the immigration laws, so I guess she's technically an illegal, but that doesn't keep her from being a great cook and friend."

"Maria," he said, introducing her to the new arrivals, "*mia hermana, estos son mis amigos y hermanos de Albuquerque y de Los Angeles.*"

Maria smiled broadly. "*Bienvenidos,*" she said, welcoming the guests. "*Con mucho gusto, señores,*" she said with a smile, then left them to their discussions.

Charley, Dave, Carl, and Lori, who had not eaten since breakfast early that morning, were more than ready for lunch. As they devoured the well-prepared meal, Jack renewed the previous discussion.

"By 1995, I was only one of many people around the world who sensed the urgency of the times. It was spontaneous. In Asia, in Africa, in Latin America, in Europe, in North America, small groups, then multitudes of people, began to pray. Christian leaders began to fast for revival."

Between bites of a tortilla, Lori asked, "What exactly is revival? I mean, what does it really mean to have a revival?"

"Revival literally means 'life again.' Real revival comes when God Himself becomes a living reality to His people, not just something they read about in a book. When there's revival, Christian people begin to live like God is real for today. When they do that, God pours His power through them, and non-Christians turn to Him in droves."

"Did such a thing happen after 1995?" Carl asked, as he cut into the chicken.

"Carl, it was incredible! Students in evangelical schools in the United States were gripped by such a powerful sense of God's presence that they stayed up all night praying and confessing their sins. In China, Korea, Indonesia, India, England, and Canada there were reports of supernatural visitations of God to assembled groups of Christians. There were dramatic healings, creative miracles, and many manifestations of God's power.

"I know personally," he continued, "of a banker in India who reported that Jesus Christ personally appeared to him and called him to an extraordinary ministry. The visitation was accompanied by supernatural signs. In 1995, Jesus told him that there were only five years left to finish bringing millions of people to faith."

"Jack," Carl asked, "do you honestly believe that Jesus Christ appears to people?"

"Jesus appeared to people like the apostle Paul," Jack replied. "The apostle John says Jesus appeared to him. He has never appeared to me, but He speaks to me all the time. I have no reason to doubt the word of the many people all over the world who report seeing Him, talking to Him, hearing His voice. We are told in the Bible that one day 'every eye shall behold Him.'"

"I would love to see Him," Lori said reverently. "Is it possible?"

"Lori," John Edwards responded, "with God, *everything* is possible." Then he chuckled, "Much as I would like it, the Lord hasn't given me the authority to grant visions. But, I promise you, today you and Carl will meet Jesus Christ.

"Now, let's look at Revelation. Please turn in the Bible to the fourteenth chapter of Revelation. Carl, would you read verses fourteen, fifteen, and sixteen?"

Carl carefully turned the pages and then read these words, "'Then I looked, and behold, a white cloud, and on the cloud sat *One* like the Son of Man, having on His head a golden crown, and in His hand a sharp sickle. And another angel came out of the temple, crying with a loud voice to Him who sat on the cloud, "Thrust in Your sickle and reap, for the time has come for You to reap, for the harvest of the earth is ripe." So He who sat on the cloud thrust in His sickle on the earth, and the earth was reaped.'"

"Who did the apostle say that he saw?" John Edwards asked.

"He says it was someone like a son of man with a gold crown on his head, sitting on a cloud," Carl answered.

"Who do you suppose it may have been?" John asked.

"Could it be Jesus?" Lori questioned.

"He called Himself the 'Son of Man,'" John replied, "and a crown is the sign of a king. He also told those at His trial that they would see Him coming on the clouds. What did John see Him doing?"

"He took a sickle to reap the ripe harvest of the earth, and He harvested it," Carl answered. Then he followed with a question of his own. "Jack, what is this all about?"

"Before I tell you," John answered, "how about reading the next three verses?"

Carl picked up the Bible and read, "'Then another angel came out of the temple which is in heaven, he also having a sharp sickle. And another angel came out from the altar, who had power over fire, and he cried with a loud cry to him who had the sharp sickle, saying, "Thrust in your sharp sickle and gather the clusters of the vine of the earth, for her grapes are fully ripe." So the angel thrust his sickle into the earth and gathered the vines of the earth, and threw *it* into the great winepress of the wrath of God.'"

"Okay, what happened here?" John asked.

Carl paused to think, then responded, "There seems to be another harvest. This time an angel did it with grapes. He then threw the grapes into a crushing mechanism that represents God's wrath."

"So, what do we have here, then?" John asked.

"I see it!" Lori exclaimed. "They are harvests of people! One is a good harvest, which Jesus Christ conducts. He's bringing people to love and forgiveness. When that is over, God sends an angel to bring people who disobey His laws to some kind of punishment."

Before John could answer, Carl broke in. "Remember, Lori, that novel by Steinbeck called *The Grapes of Wrath* about the dust bowl and the migrant farm workers? He must have taken the title from this part of Revelation."

Lori nodded in agreement.

John didn't want to be distracted by a discussion of American literature, so he turned to Lori with a smile. "Lori, that's exactly what God made clear to me in 1995. He showed me that the good harvest was almost over. I was led to believe that there must be one supreme, massive effort to mobilize the resources of the Christian church to win people to Jesus Christ all over the world."

"I felt that we had only five years before indescribable judgment was going to hit the earth. And now we have this terrible tragedy taking place on the West Coast." He was silent for a moment, thinking. Then he said, "I have to tell you, I find no satisfaction at all in realizing that I knew in advance what was coming."

Dave Busby had been silent through most of this discussion. Now he had some questions of his own. "So, you had five years to work. Do you feel you got the job done?"

"Only God knows everything that was accomplished during those five years. I believe over one billion people accepted Jesus Christ as their Savior. There wasn't one continent that did not feel God's power.

"The big news was in Asia. In 1995, there were at least seventy-five million Christian believers in mainland China. When the Communists began to welcome Christian beliefs as a counterbalance to Hollywood, another two-hundred-fifty million Chinese became believers. China quickly developed the largest and strongest Christian church in the world.

"In India, it was the same story. Christian meetings took place all over the country, attended by throngs of people. Millions more were converted after watching Christian television programs and movies. In India, at least a hundred million people professed faith in Christ.

"The largest church in the world, with a million members, was in Seoul, South Korea. This great church published Korea's largest daily newspaper. Then they began sending missionaries to Japan, other parts of Asia, and the United States.

"Thousands of Christians in the Philippines volunteered as missionaries to Hong Kong, China, Malaysia, Indonesia, India, and the Persian Gulf."

Dave stopped him. "Whoa, man! That's more than I can handle. How did you do that?"

John Edwards chuckled. "Dave, I didn't do it. A sovereign God caused millions of people all over the world to get involved. The Bible says that Jesus is the head of the church and the church is His body. Every Christian is like a cell in a human body. Each cell grows according to the DNA built into it. But it moves because of signals from the brain.

"When you think about it, the church did the harvesting. But since Jesus is the head and the church is His body, then the apostle John was exactly accurate in saying that Jesus was the one who was swinging the sickle."

Dave was awestruck. "You know, man," he said, "I played ball. I belonged to a church. I believed in Jesus and tried to live for Him. But I had no idea that all this was going on. The Lord is something else!"

"Now, Jack, for the sixty-four-thousand-dollar question," Carl said seriously. "If that was the good harvest, did yesterday start God's harvest of wrath?"

"You must understand," John said, "that I don't sit at God's hand to learn what stops and what starts. But from the best of my knowledge of Scripture, God's day of wrath has come. Certainly for the past ten years there have been very serious natural disasters to warn the world of what was coming."

Two questions—really, two parts of the same question—kept eating at Carl and pushing him. *Why were we spared? What purpose is there for us?* Yet, the answers still eluded him. He rocked back in his chair and reflected on what he was hearing, then looked at John Edwards. "Charley showed us some things last night about the meteor, about the waters that were poisoned, which he said could be radiation fallout, about earthquakes and volcanoes, and about darkness and famine. Horrible enough. But is there more?"

Charley answered the question. "Carl, I would like to say no, and I'd like to assure you we've seen the worst of it already. But I'm afraid there *is* more. With Jack's permission, I'd like to go back to what we were talking about last night. Let's look at chapter nine." Each of them flipped back to the text. "Okay," said Charley, "I'll read just the first six verses."

"'Then the fifth angel sounded: And I saw a star fallen from heaven to the earth. To him was given the key to the bottomless pit. And he opened the bottomless pit, and smoke arose out of the pit like the smoke of a great furnace. So the sun and the air were darkened because of the smoke of the pit. Then out of the smoke locusts came upon the earth. And to them was given power, as the scorpions of the earth have power. They were commanded not to harm the grass of the earth, or any green thing, nor any tree, but only those men who do not have the seal of God on their foreheads.

"'And they were not given authority to kill them,'" Charley read more slowly now, "'but to torment them for five months. Their torment *was* like the torment of a scorpion when it strikes a man. In those days men will seek death and will not find it; they will desire to die, and death will flee from them.'"

Charley looked up from his Bible. "Carl, do you have any idea what this is about?"

Carl shook his head. "I haven't got a clue."

"If you realize what we witnessed last night, with a meteor falling from the sky and the destruction that catastrophe has begun to unleash," Charley said, "I think you begin to get a hint of what's being described. But the deeper meaning will become clearer in a minute. How about reading verse eleven?"

Carl slowly read the words, "'And they had as king over them the angel of the bottomless pit, whose name in Hebrew *is* Abaddon, but in Greek he has the name Apollyon.'"

"Who is this, Charley?" Dave Busby asked.

"Abaddon means 'destroyer,'" Charley answered. "This is another name for the king of demons we call the devil."

"You mean the one with the red suit, horns, tail, and a pitchfork?" Lori asked in jest.

John Edwards stepped in quickly. "It's really not a joking matter, Lori. The devil—or Satan or Lucifer, as he is sometimes called—is the most powerful angel that God ever created. He was called Lucifer—the light one—because he was an angel of light. He was so close to God that he actually covered the very holiness of God Himself. Then Lucifer rebelled against God and took a third of the angels with him.

Those rebellious angels became evil beyond comprehension. We call them demons. The demons and demon princes are responsible for the strange New Age religions that have been springing up in recent years. Demons are behind most of the unexplained cruelty and perversion that exist in our world today."

Carl spoke up. "Wait a minute. Twenty-four hours ago I hardly believed in God. Now, you're trying to get me to believe in a devil and fallen angels?"

Now it was the coach's turn. "Carl and Lori, you're asking us how the game comes out. We're trying to tell you. It's played in four quarters with no break for half-time. During the first half, God controls the action. In the first quarter, the good guys run up a score that you can't believe. Then, the second quarter gets very physical, and a lot of players get hurt. In the third quarter, the opposing coach sends in a whole crew of hairy-legged, muscle-bound gorillas who beat up the good guys and then scare the socks off every fan in the bleachers. In the fourth quarter, God sends in a fresh team of special good guys with wings and halos. They round up the gorillas and lock 'em up. Finally, God's team wins the trophy and gets to keep it for all time!"

They were all laughing by now. "Okay, coach," Carl said, chuckling, "tell me about the hairy-legged gorillas."

"Maybe *I'd* better take over at this point," John Edwards said with a smile. "What the apostle was writing about here follows the terrible natural disasters that we all saw take place last night. That was the beginning. The inhabitants of earth who are still alive believe that it can't possibly get any worse, but it can. And it will.

"Up to this time in history, Satan's activity has been restrained by God's Holy Spirit—by law and order—by the natural morality that exists in the heart of virtually every human being. Of course, there have been the Hitlers and Stalins, but the world has reacted against their conduct. But after the disasters that we will be experiencing, the restraining equilibrium will be removed. People will be so confused, so fearful, so desperate they will do anything to survive. In that spiritual vacuum, the devil will be revealed as Abaddon, the destroyer, and he will loose a flood of demon power on earth that has never been experienced in history.

"These demons," he continued, "will have no power over those people who belong to God—those who were previously sealed by Him. But, to the non-Christians still living in the world, the demonic torture of their minds and bodies will be so intense that they will beg to die. Death by floods and earthquakes cannot begin to compare with the inhumane torture that people will go through for five months."

Lori cried out, "Jack, please stop it! I can't stand the thought of what's coming next. Why would God let all this happen?"

"Lori," John Edwards said solemnly, "our hearts cry out in pain to think about it, but you've got to understand. God is letting all the survivors experience for just five months what hell will be like for all eternity. You see, my dear friend, in hell, people can never die. They will beg to die to escape the torment. They will scream for death, but death will elude them—forever."

"During these five months on earth, in order to escape they have only to call out to God, admit that they are sinners, and ask for His pardon. Then, they, too, will be sealed and never have to face hell."

"But, Lori, please read what John says their reactions will be. You'll find it in verses twenty and twenty-one."

Lori's hands were trembling; tears were rolling down her cheeks. She was overwhelmed by the enormity of what was about to happen. She could hardly comprehend it, yet she knew these kindly men were telling the truth. Her eyes were blurred with tears, and she had to wipe them before she could turn to the page.

Finally, she began to read, "'But the rest of mankind, who were not killed by these plagues, did not repent of the works of their hands, that they should not worship demons, and idols of gold, silver, brass, stone, and wood, which can neither see nor hear nor walk; and they did not repent of their murders or their sorceries or their sexual immorality or their thefts.'"

Lori looked up. "It says they would rather keep on rebelling against God and breaking His laws than change the way they were living and be forgiven. Jack, why are people like that?"

He smiled at her and took her hand. "I suggest you ask the Lord that question when you meet Him, Lori. That's too much for me. But," he added thoughtfully, "there is something else. After the attack by the horde of demons, people will no longer be thinking rationally. They'll be willing to give political power to anybody who's able to restore order and get the world moving again. Then, the devil will bring out his satanic savior, the man of sin we call the Antichrist. For a short time, he will rule the world."

"Then comes the fourth quarter," said Dave Busby, jumping to his feet, "and the good guys win!"

CHAPTER ELEVEN

MANUEL QUINTANA, his wife Cathy, and their three sons had seen hell face-to-face and lived through it. Very possibly, no human being since mankind appeared on earth had come so close to the primordial force of the heavens and survived. As darkness fell, they had heard the roaring of the ocean, the crashing of giant waves, and the grinding and cracking of giant portions of the planet's surface as it was ripped violently apart by the incredible power of the earth's internal forces released by the meteor.

The experience had drained every vestige of emotional and physical strength from them. Seen against the vast caldron seething below them, they were like five tiny flyspecks, huddled together for safety. Yet, not even their fear could hold back the sleep of exhaustion.

Dawn reached their mountaintop while the remains of Los Angeles were still shrouded in shadows. As the giant wave collapsed back into the ocean, it had set up a vacuum that sucked air from all directions. Fierce winds howled about Mount Wilson during the night, but the Quintana family was wrapped in the sleep of oblivion. They noticed nothing until the sun's rays began to warm their faces.

They had grown up as native Angelinos. Smog to them was a part of daily life. On some days, it was thick and acrid; on others, hardly noticeable. But there was always smog.

Manuel liked the old Jimmy Durante line, "I don't trust any air I can't see." *But today is different,* Manuel thought. *The air is clear—no smog, excellent visibility.* He realized it was only a question of hours before the smoke of distant forest fires would once again pollute the air.

Fortunately for them on this sparkling morning, they knew nothing of a coming global winter. There was just this day: the sun was shining, the smoke was gone, and—thank God—all five of them were alive.

"Manolo," Cathy said. "Do you remember the old song from when we were kids? 'Morning has broken like the first morning. . . .' That's how I feel this morning. Don't you? It's like we've got a ringside seat at the first creation."

"Yeah," Manuel replied. "It may look like creation, but those big waves are on the way to Asia right now. Before they're finished, I'm afraid millions of people will be drowned. I don't even want to think about how many of our people in Mexico are going to die before it's over."

The day before, Manuel had carefully taken apart the tripod and telescope and buried them in a large sheet of plastic to protect them from the heat and the moisture. As he and Cathy talked about the prospects for getting out of there, he dug the parcel up again and was delighted to find that the telescope was still in perfect shape and that it worked. He set it up again and trained the lens on what used to be downtown Los Angeles.

The scene below them was shocking. There was little or nothing left of the city they had grown up in. No landmarks, no large buildings, no traffic, nothing to help him get his bearings. Hardly a building was left standing in what used to be downtown L.A. The hotels and office towers of Century City were gone. The golf course at the Los Angeles Country Club was now a small lake. No doubt the glitzy shops on Rodeo Drive were gone as well, their priceless merchandise forever lost and destroyed amid the rubble. The mansions of Beverly Hills and the single-story houses in South Central L.A. were all flattened.

From his vantage point, it appeared that someone had actually exploded a nuclear device over the city.

There was no way to see beyond the smoke and fires in the east, but Manuel felt certain the valleys over there had to be underwater now. In particular, the Mojave Desert and Death Valley, which lay about three hundred feet below sea level, would almost certainly be inundated, turned into a vast inland lake. He could see water coursing to the east into the valley, and he wondered if there might not also be flooding up in the mountains as well, and on to Nevada. What if the Hoover Dam had burst from the pressure? Upstream pressures along the Colorado River could even create problems as far away as Lake Mead and throughout Nevada and Arizona.

As Manuel continued to peer through the lens, he realized that his TV station was gone. The television and motion picture studios of Hollywood were too far away to see from there, but surely they were gone as well. As far as the eye could see, there was an enormous panorama of devastation—vast fields piled high with broken bricks, stone, wood, and cement and the shattered frames of buildings surrounded by twisted steel and overturned automobiles. Nothing he had known as a child, and none of the places where he had lived and worked his whole adult life were even recognizable anymore. No matter where he looked, everything was lost.

Little lakes appeared in what used to be simple ravines and depressions. There were still oil and gas fires burning in scattered locations. There were also clearly visible cracks in the earth's crust. Serious tremors were still shaking the earth—which, as an Angelino, Manuel knew was a forewarning of more serious quakes yet to come. To the north, it was obvious that the tectonic plates had not moved three feet or even thirty feet. They had moved *three hundred yards* and were apparently still moving farther apart. Water was flowing into the vast separation.

Although from that vantage point Manuel could not see the full extent of what had happened to his city, it was obvious that a huge part of coastal California was forever severed from the mainland.

As he swung the scope to the south, Manuel focused on what was left of the giant stacks marking the San Onofre nuclear power facility. Manuel thought, *This thing is just south of San Clemente. It must have been directly in line with the place where the meteor hit. It's probably starting meltdown. God has kept me and my family alive so far. Surely He wouldn't now let us all be killed from radiation!*

Cathy and the boys said they wanted a turn at the telescope, so Manuel stepped aside. What Cathy saw broke her heart. By nature she was tender and emotional, but throughout the ordeal she had been stoical. *Numbed* might be a better description. Now she wept uncontrollably. "Manolo," she cried, "they are all gone . . . friends . . . neighbors . . . our relatives . . . the city. Everything's gone! Why did God leave us alive to see all this? I can't stand it any more, Manolo! I can't take any more."

Manuel, who had just caught a glimpse of a slow, lingering death through nuclear radiation, took his wife in his arms. "Cathy, I told you that we were going to make it, and we are. I know it's horrible, but we've got to live. These boys need us. Please don't fall apart on me now."

Once again, the couple drew their sons into a circle with their arms around one another. Once again, Manuel began to pray. "Padre Celestial," he began, "we did not die. You chose to let us live. Now, Father, please send Your angel and take us to safety. . . ."

No sooner had the word "Amen" passed his lips than Manuel heard the first faint sounds of a motor in the distance. He looked up but saw nothing. Yet as the sound drew steadily closer, he knew that they were not alone. Finally he saw it. A plane was coming from the east. But in this vast mountain range, he wondered, would anyone see them there? Suddenly he had an idea.

He tugged the large sheets of plastic out of their crude trenches, which had now largely collapsed, and began spreading them out on the ground in the clearing.

"What are you doing, Dad?" Miguel, his oldest son, asked.

"Quick, Miguel!" he replied. "There's still some more plastic on those big rolls. You and Ricardo go see if you can find it, quick. We'll spell out H-E-L-P on the ground. Maybe that plane will see us."

But this time, the engineer's makeshift efforts were not needed. The slow-moving aircraft was heading straight for them.

It appeared to be a fixed-wing aircraft. It buzzed their outpost and dipped its wings to acknowledge that they had been spotted. But when the aircraft reached their position, everyone was surprised to see that this was no ordinary plane. First, it hovered overhead, then the engines and propellers began rotating upward so that the airplane actually became a helicopter. On the fuselage was painted the U.S. insignia, a star with beautiful blue lines, and the single word "Marines." Manuel realized it as an Osprey, a unique type of forward support aircraft he had heard about but never seen. It had been added to the nation's military arsenal just six months earlier.

As the Osprey gradually descended, Manuel broke into a broad smile. "Cathy, we're safe. It's a miracle!" Then he reached inside his collar, pulled out the little gold crucifix hanging from a chain around his neck, and reverently kissed it. "Thank You, Padre," he said softly. "Thank You from the depths of my heart."

The wheels of the Osprey had touched down. The giant engines were roaring like a high-powered fan. A door opened suddenly, and a crewman jumped out to help the Quintanas inside the aircraft.

"Thank God you came!" Manuel shouted over the noise. "How did you find us?"

"Last night," the crewman replied, "the president's science adviser saw you on a close-up scan by one of our satellites." He motioned for Manuel to put on a headset with earphones and a small microphone.

When he had slipped the phones over his head, the pilot looked around and said, "Hey, man, getting out here was the easy part. But the hard part was your staying alive. How did you do it?"

"It was a miracle!" Manuel said. "We prayed a lot."

"I hear you. That was Dr. Eisenblatt's guess too. I'll tell you one thing: There's nobody else out here. By all odds, you folks should be dead. I'm Major Paul Burns. Welcome aboard!"

"I am Manuel Quintana, and this is my wife Cathy, and my sons, Miguel, Ricardo, and Juan. I can't tell you how glad we are to see you, Major."

The Osprey was still resting on the mountain, its props turning. The two-man crew seemed transfixed by the sights below. Manuel tapped the pilot on the shoulder. "There's a nuclear reactor south of here, Major, near San Clemente. For sure, it's in some stage of melt-down right now. Pretty soon there will be something more than ocean breezes blowing up here. You probably ought to get us out of here. We may all be in danger of radiation poisoning."

"Don't you worry, my friend," Paul Burns said. "You folks are Exhibit A for Washington. I don't have any intention of letting any-thing happen to you!" He looked back one last time and yelled over the noise, "Okay, buckle up." With that, he shoved the throttle forward, and the Osprey rose slowly and majestically above the sanctuary of Mount Wilson and headed back to the east. At two hundred feet above the top of the mountain, the engines of the hovering craft slowly rotated forward and were locked into posi-tion. In seconds the helicopter was once again an aircraft, and headed for safety. Major Burns pushed the craft up to thirteen thou-sand feet, then reached maximum cruise speed.

"Where are we headed?" Manuel asked.

"The airports in Nevada are pretty well torn up right now," Burns said. "There's a supply depot set up in the desert, and that's our desti-nation. They've had a huge shuttle operation going back and forth all night. It's probably too little, too late, but the government is trying to get supplies in and people out wherever possible. We're using C-130s and C-117s for civilian relief in northern California and Oregon. Those birds can land almost anywhere."

"Where do we go from there?" Manuel asked again.

"Not sure," Paul Burns replied. "But my guess is they'll fly you on a Herc down to Albuquerque. That's the major staging area. By the way, we brought along several box lunches and some bottled water. Thought you guys might be hungry. Back there in the ice chest. . . . Please, dig in!"

THE FLIGHT FROM MOUNT WILSON to Nevada was short but exhilarating. Manuel couldn't help smiling at his sons' excitement over their first plane ride—and in an Osprey, at that. He knew that the reality of their situation would hit them later. But for now, he was delighted they were still smiling. Food, safety, and the friendly crew cheered them all enormously. Manuel knew that for years he and Cathy would relive the terrible ordeal of the night before—the fire, the heat, the explosion—and the loss of their friends. Yet he also felt a sense of joy that they were still alive. And best of all, the five of them were together. No one had died. No one had surrendered to panic.

Manuel Quintana, Cathy Quintana, the three Quintana boys—they had met the beast, and they had lived! Millions had died, but they had lived.

But why me? Manuel wondered. *Why not someone else more holy, more worthy, more capable?* Cathy sensed Manuel's thoughts, for they were her own. She reached over and took his hand. "Manolo," she yelled over the noise, "soon enough we will learn the reason why our lives were spared, I imagine. But right now, let's enjoy life and thank God." The couple continued to hold hands until the Osprey touched down in a desert area, not too far from Nellis Air Force Base in Nevada.

What they saw as they jumped from the rear of the plane amazed them. A piece of raw desert had been transformed into an air base. A runway had been marked out on the desert floor, and one after another, U.S. Air Force cargo planes were coming in to land. A portable ground control system had been set up. Tents had been hastily erected for offices, mess areas, and temporary sleeping quarters. Clouds of dust rose in the air as columns of tanker trucks loaded with jet fuel swung in off the nearby highway. Convoys of eighteen-wheelers were rolling in with food, medicine, tents, blankets, and drinking water.

Manuel remembered from news clips at the TV station that the C-130, with various upgrades and modifications, had been the work-horse of the armed forces since at least the 1950s. Because of its lifting capacity, the C-130 was called the Hercules, or "Herc." The C-130s could haul over fifty thousand pounds of cargo. They could drop into short-field hostile environments. They could also deliver specially cushioned pallets of cargo from the air by parachute. The C-117, the upgrade of the C-130, carried more cargo and flew farther and faster, but hardly enough to justify the threefold increase in price.

Some planes were landing empty, but they were being quickly loaded with cargo, refueled, and sent off to help flood victims.

Manuel could not believe that anything run by the government could be so efficient. Major Burns had radioed ahead, and within minutes the Osprey was met by a handsome, athletic-looking officer in a flight suit with the silver star of a general on his lapel. "Hey, you incredible people," he said with a big smile, "I'm Archie Gladstone. Came out here yesterday from Pope Air Force Base in North Carolina to head up this joint effort. I just had to meet you all. And Secretary of Defense Al Augustus sends his personal greetings. He asked me to make sure you get whatever you need to make yourselves comfortable." The general opened the door of a waiting van, and they all stepped inside.

"General," Manuel said as they drove to one of the neatly positioned tents, "I'm a transmitter jockey—an audiovisual engineer. Been in the TV business most of my life. But I'm curious how I rate all this personal attention from the secretary of defense."

"Well, sir," General Gladstone replied, "you and your family are personal eye witnesses to the greatest natural disaster in American history. We couldn't be happier that you made it through alive. And the secretary wants to talk to you about it, himself."

"Secretary Augustus?" Manuel asked.

"That's right."

"Did he plan this relief effort?"

"Yes, sir, he initiated the effort," General Gladstone replied. "He was three steps ahead of everybody on this deal. But then, he usually *is* three steps ahead! We've never had a secretary of defense like him. He's a hero of mine, I'll tell you."

The van stopped in front of the headquarters tent. "We've got a C-130 headed for Albuquerque in about sixty minutes. There are tents like this at the airport where you and your family can stay. If you can find better accommodations, be sure to leave a telephone number where we can reach you. But your contact in Albuquerque will be Master Sergeant Anthony O'Reilly. He's the best we've got. Whenever I need anything special, I call Sergeant O'Reilly."

"General," Cathy Quintana spoke up as everyone was piling out of the van, "I hope this Sergeant O'Reilly can help us find someplace to get a shower. We are all filthy."

"Ma'am," Archie Gladstone replied, "we haven't had time to rig up showers here, but if it'll help I can sure get you a couple of buckets of hot water, some soap, and towels. Maybe even a razor for your husband. But if you can wait until you get to Albuquerque, Tony O'Reilly will show you where you can get hot showers, new clothes, and even spending money! Come on now and have a cup of hot coffee, some doughnuts, and some soft drinks for the boys, all courtesy of the United States Air Force."

Chapter Twelve

W HEN THE BUZZER sounded on the desk of Percy DuVal, the head of the office of White House personnel, he responded abruptly. "Yes, Miss Kaminsky," he said. "I'm here." *What now?* he wondered. Since Ted Rust had been named president, there had been a flurry of resignations.

"Mr. DuVal," said his secretary, "do you have time to take a call from Mr. Haddad?"

DuVal sighed heavily. As much as he wanted to, he could not refuse to take this call. "Yes, Marsha," he responded. "Put him on."

Then, lifting the receiver, he spoke in even, mellow tones, "Tauriq, my good friend. To what do I owe this pleasure?"

"Peace to you, my good friend, and most gracious greetings to you," Tauriq Haddad intoned on the other end of the line. "A very simple matter, Mr. DuVal. I am calling as a loyal and supportive citizen of this great country. I understand that the president has chosen a new chief of staff. I hear also that his résumé and references will be coming to you shortly. It would give me great pleasure to know that this exceptional young man will be cleared quickly so that he may begin to serve the president and the nation in this time of great physical and emotional stress."

"A new chief of staff? What is his name, my friend?" Percy DuVal asked.

"His name is Benares—Benjamin Benares—and he comes highly recommended."

"Yes, I'll make a note," said DuVal. "But please understand, Tauriq, that this is not a simple matter. This is a very sensitive post. You know how thorough the FBI review will be; and the Secret Service checks are even harder. The process will take time."

"Of course it will, my dear friend," Tauriq Haddad replied. "Thank you for your consideration. And, by the way, I hope you and your wife will join me for dinner very soon. I have just purchased some fascinating home movies that we can . . . view together. *Au revoir*, my friend." Haddad laughed softly, and the line went dead.

The blood drained from Percy DuVal's face. He had been in charge of the presidential personnel office for three years. During his tenure there, he had used every trick in the book to fill the highest government positions with those who shared his lifestyle and philosophy.

Yet, he had been very successful in hiding his own lifestyle choice. To maintain his cover, he had even married a former secretary, who, in exchange for a platonic relationship, complete freedom, and a very comfortable position in the government, played with consummate skill the role of adoring wife and hostess.

Everything had been going so well . . . the two lives of Percy DuVal. His one slip had occurred months earlier, at a party in the lavishly decorated home of a Middle Eastern ambassador. Percy got carried away with the excessive, decadent atmosphere and indulged his erotic tastes too much. He drank too much, enjoyed the entertainment too much, and he allowed himself to be enticed into group sex with a number of very young Ethiopian boys who had been brought to America specifically to fulfill the sordid desires of the ambassador—an old and highly respected friend of the United States government. Percy regretted the episode, but assured himself that it would go no further.

Unfortunately, the entire incident was on videotape, and his proclivities had been recorded in graphic detail and in living color.

Within twenty-four hours, the tape had been passed, in exchange for a considerable sum of money, into the hands of Tauriq Haddad.

At first Tauriq had used intermediaries to inform Percy in the subtlest of ways of the existence of the tape. He never used it. He never mentioned it again. He simply held onto it for . . . a suitable occasion.

Tauriq Haddad was himself a man of immense wealth, charm, and mystery. He had amassed his fortune thanks to one extraordinary attribute—his remarkable patience. He never bought too soon, never sold too late. And, he never tried to pick and eat a half-ripe fruit. He knew that one day the baubles, trinkets, and videotapes he collected would have their desired effect: to give him control over one or more powerful departments of the government. But how could he have dreamed that one day his most distinctive character trait would bring him the White House itself?

Thus, he had waited patiently, until this particular day.

For Percy DuVal that videotape meant public disgrace. Worse than that, it meant the threat of prosecution for a federal crime. DuVal knew that Tauriq Haddad was absolutely ruthless. If Benjamin Benares failed the security test, Percy DuVal would be destroyed. On the other hand, Percy had ample reason to believe that Tauriq Haddad was no petty extortionist. When Percy delivered on this request, neither he nor anyone else would hear of the incriminating tape again.

After all, Percy thought, *what real difference does a chief of staff make?* The president could fire him anytime he wanted to. The chief of staff was only an adviser, not a policy maker.

So, armed with what he believed to be impeccable logic, Percy DuVal called in one of his highly trusted colleagues, a Secret Service supervisor. "Daniel," he said, "this is a rush confirmation from the White House. The file is on the way. The man's name is Benjamin Benares, and he's the first pick. It's already cleared by Number One, but I need something to paper the files. Please see what you can do, and make it quick."

"Yes, sir, Mr. DuVal," replied the supervisor. As he walked away, his mind focused on one thing. *That little pervert can kill any promotion coming my way. I know what he wants, and it's unorthodox, to say the least. But if I don't do as he asks, my career is dog meat. If I play ball though, it could mean a promotion or even a raise.*

Thus, the circle of Washington's bureaucratic protectionism went into high gear. It was just one career bureaucrat protecting his career. Then, in natural progression, another career bureaucrat protected *his* career. Then another and another, until, in record time, out came a glowing security clearance for a man with certain questionable credentials. And from that clearance came a new White House chief of staff—Benjamin Benares—appointed without proper security checks or references. Appointed with no real concern for the welfare of the United States. Appointed by manipulation and extortion.

MARK BEAULIEU HAD JUST stepped out of the shower when his portable telephone rang. He wrapped a towel around his slender waist and picked up the receiver.

"Mark," the heavily accented voice said, "I have wonderful news! When can we meet?"

"Name the place, my good friend," said Beaulieu.

"There's to be a memorial service for the West Coast victims—the National Cathedral at seven o'clock this evening. I'll see you there."

As Mark hung up the phone, he said softly, "I wonder what news Tauriq Haddad has that could be so important?" Tauriq and Mark Beaulieu had deliberately avoided contact with each other for the past ten years. So, why now?

Mark Beaulieu happened to be one of Washington's most fascinating young men. He was a descendant of an aristocratic French family that had sent two of its promising sons to America shortly before the French Revolution. They had embraced this new nation as their own, married American wives, and entered into business.

They began exporting American agricultural products to Europe on a small scale and importing, in turn, the European silks, satins, furniture, and machinery that the newly independent nation craved. With their profits, they commissioned the construction of one ocean vessel, then another, and another. In time, they started a bank to finance their trading and shipping enterprises.

Successive generations of Beaulieus carried forward the dreams of their first American ancestors. Beaulieu Brothers became a power in American finance. After the Civil War, the new breed of American capitalists turned to the Beaulieu family to float public stock offerings in Europe and America. Their funds paid for the construction of American railroads, steel mills, public utilities, and refineries.

Beaulieu Brothers floated the stock of vast enterprises for a fee. And along with their fee, they were careful to reserve for themselves a share of the equity of each enterprise they financed.

By the beginning of World War I, the Beaulieu family had prospered to such a degree that it was ranked alongside the Rockefellers, the Mellons, and the DuPonts as one of the wealthiest families in America.

Mark Beaulieu, as one of dozens of Beaulieu cousins, was the beneficiary of generously endowed trusts. But he had no desire whatsoever to enter the family business. Had he wished, he could have lived out his life in luxury without working a single day. Like so many children of great privilege, Mark Beaulieu realized he had not earned the luxury that he enjoyed. And that knowledge created in him a sense of guilt. Then, over time, there followed a loathing for the possessions that had brought him only guilt and anguish. From that point, his mind made a completely illogical transition. He began to loath the free-enterprise system that spawned his wealth, as well as capitalism, the United States, Christianity, and the whole of Western civilization in general.

He hated it all. Yet, like scores of others in his position, he did not hate it enough to tear up the checks worth hundreds of thousands of dollars that were mailed to him each quarter from the trust company. As a young man, Mark wore imported Italian suits, Gucci loafers, and Ferragamo neckties. He drove a high-powered Porsche and lived in a luxuriously furnished Fifth Avenue co-op. To assuage his guilt, he consorted with Marxist radicals, New Age gurus, and intellectual extremists, and lent his name and influence to many leftist causes and manifestos.

After he graduated with a Bachelor of Arts degree from Columbia, he tried for a couple of years the life of the pampered playboy. Then he joined the Peace Corps, and from that point everything changed.

He was sent as a Peace Corps volunteer to a city in India north of Madras called Rajahmundry, "The City of the Kings." In this city, amid disease, squalor, and shocking poverty, Mark Beaulieu attained what he felt was ultimate spiritual enlightenment.

In the center of Rajahmundry is a statue of Shiva, the Hindu god of destruction, whose consort is Kali, the goddess of death. According to legend, the task of Shiva was to destroy the world and rebuild it to perfection. Around the head and shoulders of the stone god, the artist had carved a cobra with its head outstretched as if it were imparting wisdom to Shiva. As Mark Beaulieu stood in front of that enigmatic statue and stared into the face of the pagan deity, something icy cold coursed through his being. Then he felt that the statue spoke to him—he was sure it was more than his imagination—and Shiva promised him what he truly wanted: wisdom and power.

The people of Rajahmundry believe that the river that flows alongside their city is the sperm of Shiva, their patron deity. Many natives of the town come early in the morning to bathe in the polluted, muddy river, hoping to receive the life force from their god.

Day after day, Mark Beaulieu watched the devotees of Shiva. Day after day, he stood in front of the statue of Shiva and studied the cobra. Day after day he seemed to receive enlightenment and spiritual wisdom. And day by day, the consciousness grew in him that Shiva would give him the wisdom and power to destroy the corrupt nations of the world—including America and all its greedy capitalists. Then one day he would rebuild it all in beauty and harmony.

From Rajahmundry, located in the state of Andra Pradesh, Mark Beaulieu journeyed north and west to the ashram of the famous guru, Raj Baba. According to Indian legend, Raj Baba could levitate. Raj Baba could tell the future. Raj Baba spoke wisdom received from ascended masters—the ancients who supposedly had been reincarnated many times, until they had attained a state of perfection. Even the prime ministers of India came to the ashram during the last decades of the twentieth century and fell on their faces before Raj Baba. They venerated him as an extraordinary person and sought his wisdom.

When Mark Beaulieu first learned of the guru, he decided to go to him and learn from him. He set out on the road from Rajahmundry, and, after a series of rides in assorted vehicles, he reached the village where Raj Baba lived.

Raj Baba was seated on a raised platform. His disciples were gathered around him. When Mark Beaulieu appeared at the back of the assembled crowd, Raj Baba's head jerked violently back and forth, his mouth and jaw grew slack, and spittle drooled out of the side of his mouth. His eyes ceased to look human. Then, something overpoweringly malevolent stared out at the crowd. His mouth began to move, and those seated before him heard a voice that seemed to be coming from an echo chamber. "You have been chosen by Shiva," the voice said. "Shiva will give you power and wisdom to destroy, then create again. You will rule your people in the name of Shiva."

It was over in a minute. Raj Baba returned to his normal state. He pointed a finger at Mark Beaulieu, "You, young man! That message was for you. You must live here with me, and I will teach you the secrets of the ascended masters."

Mark Beaulieu did not fully understand what had happened to him. Without his conscious knowledge, a powerful demonic spirit had entered the very core of his being.

Two assistants appeared at Mark's side, took his knapsack, and ushered him politely to rustic quarters. "You, sir," one of them told him, "have been specially chosen to receive many secrets. Stay here and meditate. Then, Master Raj Baba will call for you."

Thus, Mark Beaulieu, wealthy playboy, pseudoradical, seeker of truth, was introduced to occult secrets few Westerners have ever dreamed about. When he left six months later, he was controlled and directed by powerful demonic forces that far transcended his human understanding. Only upon his return to America did Mark Beaulieu realize the power he now possessed over people.

BACK IN NEW YORK, Mark Beaulieu entered a world he had never known before. A cosmopolitan group of businessmen, diplomats, and politicians were thrown across his path. It seemed that everything was happening by chance until one day he learned what was taking place.

He was attending a social gathering held at a fashionable Upper East Side townhouse, when a distinguished man approached him and said, "Mr. Beaulieu, I am Tauriq Haddad. I know of you and the claim that has been put upon your life by the lord Shiva.

"When unusual opportunities come your way, recognize the source. The followers of Shiva are active all over the world. They will help you. But now, your opportunity has come. I have been asked to inform you that there is to be an open seat in the United States Congress. You are to run for it. Don't worry, you will not be opposed."

"I don't understand—" Mark began.

"Not now, my good friend. We will talk again." As suddenly as he had appeared, Tauriq was gone.

Indeed, in February, the incumbent congressman representing a so-called silk-stocking congressional district in Manhattan announced his plan to retire. Mark Beaulieu filed for the nomination of a major party for the open seat. To everyone's surprise, all other potential candidates for the nomination failed to file a declaration of candidacy.

Mark knew nothing about running a political campaign and, according to pollsters, was trailing by thirty points three weeks before the general election. Two weeks out, the steering mechanism on his opponent's car failed while he was crossing the George Washington Bridge on his way home from a fund-raiser in North Jersey. The vehicle had been traveling very fast, hit the guardrail, and crashed into a concrete barrier. Mark's opponent was hospitalized in a coma. Eventually his name had to be withdrawn from the race.

Consequently, Mark Beaulieu won by default and was sworn into office.

EVEN BEFORE HE CAME to Washington, Mark Beaulieu had assembled a staff that was acknowledged to be the most astute, most politically savvy ever to be working on Capitol Hill. From the start he drew committee assignments that were undreamed of for a first-term congressman—among them, a seat on the Foreign Affairs Committee and another on the highly sought-after House Appropriations Committee.

His floor speeches were brilliant. His analysis of complex problems was flawless. His positions on the major issues were so unassailably centrist that he drew kudos from both sides of the political spectrum. His previous radicalism was quickly dismissed as youthful exuberance.

In short order, because of his previous foreign experience, he was chosen as a member of important United States delegations to foreign nations. Everywhere he went, he managed to develop warm friendships with the key officials who were at the heart of their nation's foreign and domestic policy apparatus.

Mark purchased a showplace estate off Foxhall Road, then staffed it with Indian and Japanese domestics. With a $3 million loan advance from one of his family trusts, he was able to give generously to Washington cultural and civic charities, and it was soon apparent that his star was rising. It would be impossible to conceive of a more desirable member of Washington society than this brilliant, successful, well-traveled heir to one of America's great fortunes.

Now, ten years after Mark had been ensconced in the capital network, Tauriq Haddad had suddenly come back into his life. As Mark Beaulieu knelt in prayer in the National Cathedral, he felt someone slide in beside him, praying fervently for the families of the West Coast tragedy. It was Tauriq Haddad, who had even arranged this seat by calling in some long-forgotten favor from the head usher. *Tauriq will stop at nothing*, Mark thought. *He even bribed someone to get a seat at a prayer meeting*.

They shared a hymnal during the closing hymn. During the singing, Tauriq leaned close to Mark Beaulieu and said, "Congratulations, Mr. Vice President. Your uncle Shiva is working on your behalf." After the benediction, he left ahead of Mark and was gone without further comment.

After that came a series of discreet telephone calls from Tauriq Haddad to key members of Congress. Each call followed the same theme. "I understand that the president is going to recommend Mark Beaulieu as his new vice president. It would give me great pleasure to know that this exceptional young man will be approved quickly so that he may begin to serve the president and the nation in this time of great physical and emotional stress. Don't you agree that he will be a superb vice president?"

Each recipient of that message had also been the recipient of corporate PAC money—bundled $1,000 individual checks, bank loans, and immense soft-dollar contributions—all of which had been arranged by Tauriq Haddad.

WHEN TED RUST ARRIVED at the Oval Office later that night, accompanied by his interim chief of staff, the Speaker of the House was on the phone. "Mr. President," he said, "we are with you in this emergency. I'm calling about the vice presidential appointment. I hear you're considering Congressman Mark Beaulieu. We'll miss him over here, but he's a fine choice. I just want to assure you that the nomination will sail through." Next was the Senate majority leader, who offered a similar message.

Ted Rust was so occupied with the enlarging Pacific disaster that he had ignored the need to fill the vital office of the person who would succeed him in the event of another tragedy. He had heard of the brilliant Congressman Beaulieu, but he hardly knew him.

"Benares," he called to his chief of staff. "Tell me something about Mark Beaulieu. What kind of vice president would he make?"

"Mr. President," Benjamin Benares replied, "this man is well known to me because of his tremendous skill in foreign policy. He would be a splendid representative for you at official meetings abroad." He paused. "And if I may say so, sir, he would help you greatly with the youth vote in the next presidential election. He has a lot of appeal to younger voters."

"But what about some of the other candidates?" Ted Rust asked. "Surely there must be others. What about the secretary of defense, Al Augustus? He's certainly very capable."

"Indeed, he is, sir," Benjamin Benares answered. "Very capable. But, sir, Augustus is indispensable to you at the Department of Defense. How could you replace a man like him in such a crisis?"

"That's right, Ben," Ted Rust answered. "Didn't think of that."

"There's another point," Benjamin Benares said. "A sitting member of Congress can get approval overnight. I don't know how long it might take to confirm someone else."

Rust warmed to the thought. "Beaulieu. Vice President Mark Beaulieu. It doesn't sound bad, does it? Ben, get my wife on the phone, then see if you can get Beaulieu over here ASAP."

"Yes, sir, Mr. President," Benjamin Benares replied as he bowed ever so slightly and exited the room.

Within minutes, the president's personal buzzer sounded. "Your wife is on the line, Mr. President."

Ted snatched up the phone. "Valery!" he said. "I like this Benjamin Benares you got for me. Got a level head on his shoulders. But tell me something. What would you think of a congressman named Mark Beaulieu for my new vice president?"

Valery, who had already been briefed on the plan by Tauriq Haddad, tried not to appear overly enthusiastic. "Mark Beaulieu? That's interesting. Who suggested him?" she asked. "Surely, you didn't come up with his name by yourself."

"Came up in a call from the Speaker. Benares seems to like the idea too."

"Beaulieu," Valery mused. "Mark Beaulieu, huh? Rich, good-looking, quite a speaker, and gets rave reviews in the press. Ted, you could do a lot worse."

"Does that mean you approve?"

"Sure, I do. The selection of a New York congressman like Beaulieu would look like a stroke of genius. I think you should go for it."

"Good, Valery," Ted replied. "Thanks. I knew I could count on your advice."

Ted Rust could never be accused of having an analytical mind. Nor could he ever be charged with overcaution. He charged through life following his instincts, which were like putty in the hands of those who wished to exploit him.

That night, he forwarded to the Congress the name of Congressman Mark Beaulieu to be the constitutional successor to the president of the United States. The next day, by acclamation, Mark Beaulieu was confirmed by Congress as the new vice president of the United States.

From that moment on, Ted Rust's days on earth were numbered.

CHAPTER THIRTEEN

FTER LUNCH JOHN EDWARDS excused himself, saying that he had work to do in his study. He told Lori and Carl that they should feel free to roam the grounds, to watch TV, or just to relax if they could. "I'll be putting you to work soon enough," he said cryptically, then disappeared into his study.

Dave and Charley went outside to see if they could help the ranch hands.

"We haven't checked out what's happening today," Carl said. "Let's see what the news reports are saying."

"I'm not sure I want to know," Lori said. Nevertheless, she followed Carl into the living room and sat down beside him on the sofa as he picked up the remote control and turned on the TV.

The situation was even worse than they feared: Los Angeles was gone, earthquakes were ripping California apart, and a massive tidal wave was decimating Hawaii. Massive flooding was occurring in Oregon and Washington. It was being predicted that half the populations of Japan, Taiwan, and the Philippines were being wiped out. No one could be certain what would happen after that, but it was predicted that before the disaster was over, coastal areas of Europe would experience flooding and, to a lesser extent, the East Coast of the United States.

Finally, Lori could stand no more. She started to sob. "Turn if off, Carl, please," she said, tears running down her face. "I can't take anymore."

Carl, who was more upset than he was willing to admit, turned off the TV and put his arms around his wife. He wanted to comfort her, to say that things would be all right. But he couldn't. The world that he and Lori had known was gone forever.

Lori cried until she was drained. "I need a tissue," she sniffled.

"I'll get you some," Carl said, getting up. "Be right back." He returned a few moments later with a box of tissues.

"Thanks," Lori said as he sat down beside her again. She wiped her nose, dried her eyes, then said, "I think I must have been in shock yesterday. It didn't really hit me 'til today that we've lost everything, Carl."

"Not everything," Carl said softly. "We still have each other—and we're alive and safe."

Lori gave a deep sigh and rested her head on Carl's shoulder. "You're right," she said. "We may have lost our home and our possessions, but we're here, *together*, in this beautiful place, and with good people who care about us—"

"And studying the Bible," Carl interrupted, grinning, "as if we didn't have a care in the world."

Lori laughed. "It *is* surreal, isn't it? But Pastor Jack seemed to be pretty clear that this is going to be about the only time we have to *learn* about Revelation—that we're soon going to be too busy with other things." She looked up at Carl. "What do you think he means?"

Carl's expression was pensive. "I don't know, Lori. I wish I did. I just keep asking myself, 'Why us? Why were our lives spared?'"

"I know," Lori said. "I don't know why either. But I will never stop thanking God that we were spared."

Just then John Edwards walked into the living room, followed by Charley and Dave. Dave was carrying the Bibles they had left in the kitchen after lunch. "Are you two ready to take another crack at Revelation?" John Edwards asked, sitting down in a comfortable oak chair across from Carl and Lori.

"Not only are we ready," said Carl, "but I have a question for you."

"Not another one!" Dave Busby laughed as he sat in the chair next to Jack.

"What's your question?" John asked.

Leaning forward, Carl looked at John Edwards and said, "At lunch, you mentioned the 'signs of the times,' as you called them, that helped you know what was coming next. I'd like to know if these are signs of judgment or signs about this Antichrist person you were talking about."

"Actually, Carl," John responded, "the signs of the times are indicators pointing to the Second Coming of Jesus Christ. In fact, His disciples asked this very question: 'What are the signs of Your coming and the end of the age?'"

"There you go again!" Carl smiled. "That's another term you've used a lot. What exactly does it mean—the end of the age? Is it the end of the world?"

"Not as I see it," John replied. "Jesus Christ was the Messiah of Israel. His disciples expected Him to set up a kingdom that would defeat the empire of Rome. Instead, He spoke to them about a spiritual kingdom composed of people who voluntarily made Him King of their lives. His spiritual kingdom did not supersede the Roman Empire or any world government that followed Rome. His kingdom was in the midst of the other kingdoms, but it was a secret kingdom. Although He was leaving earth physically, He promised that one day He would return and establish a worldwide, visible kingdom in which God's law would govern and people would live in peace, love, and prosperity."

"When He returns," John continued, "the present age will end, and the new age of God's kingdom will begin."

"But isn't that part of the New Age religion and that Age of Aquarius stuff we used to sing about?" Lori asked.

"Lori," John replied, "the Bible tells us that the old age will end in the cataclysm we've been talking about. It's like the birth pains of a new order. Satan understands exactly how this present age will end, so he has set out to trick people into believing that his kingdom will be the surviving kingdom instead of Christ's kingdom. That's why the psychics and gurus who take direction from demons are telling us that they hold the key to the New Age, the New World Order, the Age of Aquarius, or whatever else they decide to call it."

Lori brightened perceptibly. "Carl, do you remember what I told you on the plane from L.A.? This was part of it. One of the things Aunt Josephine told me when I was little was about a time called the Millennium. Jack, isn't this new age also called the Millennium?"

"Lori, what I'm telling you now is hardly new. Evangelical Christians have always known about most of this. What happened yesterday just snapped the entire picture into focus. I believe the final countdown has begun to usher in the return of Jesus Christ to earth. Yes, some people call His reign on earth the Millennium. That word comes from Latin—*mille,* meaning 'thousand,' and *annum,* meaning 'year'—a period of one thousand years."

John Edwards picked up his Bible. "I want us now to see exactly what Jesus Christ Himself said would be the signs of the times. I like Matthew's account of it, so turn in the Bible to the Gospel of Matthew, chapter twenty-four."

There was a rustling of pages. "We've got it," Carl said. "Where do we begin?"

"Try verse three." John read aloud. "'As Jesus was sitting on the Mount of Olives, the disciples came to Him privately. "Tell us," they said. "When will this happen, and what will be the sign of Your coming and of the end of the age?"'"

"They asked Him two questions, maybe three," John said. "So, His answer takes in all of them. What were they asking?"

Carl had already glanced at the preceding verse, so he answered, "It looks like, first, they wanted to know when the temple buildings were going to be thrown down. Then, they wanted to know the sign of His coming. If it's a separate question, I suppose they wanted to know also what the sign was of the end of the age. Maybe they thought His coming and the end of the age were one and the same."

"Carl," John said with a big smile, "you surprise me. But I wouldn't be surprised to learn that God may have sent you here to learn, so that you can help teach others. You're very good at this."

It was just an offhand compliment, but John's words hit Carl like a thunderbolt. Could it be that God had kept him alive to use his years of experience in advertising and promotion so he could help Pastor Jack persuade people to try God's way instead of Satan's way? If so, what an incredible irony! Nobody in L.A. would have picked Carl for a Bible-thumper! But in crisis times, somebody had to package the message so ordinary people could grasp it. *No jumping to conclusions now*, he thought. *Let's just wait and see what comes next.*

"I promised I'd show you the one absolutely certain sign that would precede the end of the age," John said. "Read a few more verses and see if you can find it."

After a few minutes, Dave Busby stretched his long legs and spoke up. "I think I've got it, Pastor Jack. A lot of things are going to happen, but to me they look like the preliminaries. The main event is down in verse fourteen, where it says, 'And this gospel of the kingdom will be preached in the whole world as a testimony to all nations, and then the end will come.' This is what you've been talking about, isn't it?" he asked. "For five years, the gospel of Christ's kingdom has been preached all over the world. You said earlier that something like a billion people have responded. That was the sealing we talked about. It was the harvest by the man with the crown . . . sitting on a cloud." Then he flashed a wide grin. "Did I get it right?"

"Right on every count, Dave," John Edwards answered with a laugh.

Carl gave Dave a high-five. "Good job, Champ!"

"You see," John Edwards went on, "God was not going to let the terrible judgment we've been seeing come upon the earth until the whole world had a chance to hear the good news of His love. There were a number of us who felt that God actually was holding back judgment from America because so many ministries in this country were leading the harvest and they needed America's resources to do the job.

"Isn't it ironic? The work of the evangelicals was protecting everybody by holding off God's judgment, yet the secularists were doing all in their power to hinder the work that was, in fact, keeping them alive."

"Anyhow," he continued, "you asked for signs. This is the big one—the sure one. It's flashing as brightly as a casino marquee in Las Vegas."

"But is that all, Jack?" Carl asked, "There must be a number of other signs that told you what was coming."

"You're right, Carl. Of course there were," John answered. "You can't imagine how busy we were in the eighties and nineties verifying the signs. It was perfectly clear to anyone with an ounce of biblical understanding that humanity was heading toward some kind of collision. A person would have to be blind not to see it. And to those of us who had spent our lives studying and teaching the Word of God, the signs were screaming at us."

"Like what?" said Carl. "Name a few."

"Okay, Carl," said John Edwards. "I'll try to outline the events that seemed uppermost to us in the mid-nineties. The first was the sign of Jerusalem. . . ."

JOHN RECALLED A DAY IN 1967—June 5, to be exact. It was 10:00 o'clock in the morning. Behind him, bulldozers and construction workers had gathered to begin the construction of a new, enlarged sanctuary for his church. There was to be a small ceremony. The church board and a few local officials had gathered for the event. Just before it got underway, the last member of the board arrived.

"They've started a war in Israel," he shouted breathlessly. "The Egyptians and Jordanians against the Israelis. They're fighting in Jerusalem."

Then, over the next five days, they followed the news reports. There was a brilliant Israeli strike, right through the center of the Egyptian line in the Sinai, followed by brutal fighting up the sides of the Mount of Olives.

King Hussein of Jordan rejected Israel's offer of neutrality and joined the battle against Jerusalem, only to be driven back, humiliated. The television cameras showed a haggard King Hussein conceding defeat. John watched the stirring scene of General Moshe Dayan standing at the Eastern Gate of Jerusalem . . . the high priest blowing the ram's horn, the shofar . . . Jews once again at the wailing wall. It was called the Six-Day War, less than one week from start to finish.

As the events unfolded, John Edwards announced publicly that this was the most significant prophetic event in recent history. For the first time since King Nebuchadnezzar of Babylon conquered Jerusalem— in 586 b.c.—the Jews were once again in control of Jerusalem. For Edwards and his people, there was a sense of destiny. The start of their church building coincided with a prophetic event of great significance.

SUDDENLY JOHN EDWARDS REALIZED that everyone was waiting for him to speak. With a slight shake of his head, he dispelled the memories and returned to the present. "Flip over to Luke's gospel, folks," he said. "I want to look at the twenty-first chapter and the twenty-fourth verse." He read these words to them: "'They'—that is, the Jews— 'will fall by the sword and will be taken as prisoners to all the nations. Jerusalem will be trampled on by the Gentiles until the times of the Gentiles are fulfilled.'

"In 1967, that prophecy was fulfilled," he continued.

"It was?" asked Lori. "How do you know?"

"Because," said John Edwards, "for the first time in twenty-five hundred years, the Jews were actually in charge of their own capital city."

"I don't see it," Carl said. "I know there's been a lot of flack over Jerusalem, but what does a little old town in the Middle East have to do with the end of the age?"

"Carl, the Lord established the Jewish people to be His prophetic time clock about four thousand years ago. Three thousand years ago, Jerusalem became their capital."

"Yeah, but that doesn't really answer the question," Carl said.

"Jerusalem is now the spiritual center for Jews and Christians alike," said John. "So, what happens in Jerusalem has great spiritual significance. I'll show you in a minute.

"Later," he continued, "the Jewish nation split in two. Ten tribes formed the northern region called Israel, two tribes formed the southern region called Judah. In 721 B.C., virtually the entire population of Israel was carried captive into Assyria. Later, in 586 B.C., Judah was carried captive into Babylon. The descendants of those who came back from Babylon, seventy years later, rebelled against the Romans in A.D. 70. The Romans, under the Emperor Titus, crushed them, and that was the end of the Jewish nation for nearly two thousand years. But, as if by a miracle, in 1948, a new Jewish nation was formed at the very site of ancient Jerusalem, just as the ancient prophets had promised would happen. Ever since that time, Christians have been waiting for this prophecy about Jerusalem to take place."

Lori said, "Jack, I'm sorry, but I still don't understand why this is such a big deal."

"Here's why it's so important, Lori," John answered. "Jesus said that the age of the Gentiles, which is the age we're living in now, would be over whenever the Jews got control of Jerusalem again. I believe the Jewish victory in 1967 started what I would call the generation of the end of the Gentile age. A Bible generation is forty years. So, that puts the end of the Gentile age around 2007."

"Whoa, Pastor Jack!" Dave exclaimed. "Do you mean it's all gonna be over in seven years?"

"Dave," said John Edwards, "you know the Bible well enough to realize that none of us can tell the exact date when Jesus will return. But we can certainly look at the signs, because He put them there to point us in the right direction.

"There's something else interesting," he continued. "Do you remember, I told you that America began as a nation on April 29, 1607, when a prayer of dedication was offered by the first English settlers? If you measure four hundred years from then—that's ten Bible generations—it takes you to the year 2007. The United States of America is the greatest Gentile power in history. I find it fascinating that the end of forty generations of U.S. existence and the end of the Gentile age take place about forty days from each other in 2007."

Carl spoke up. "I'm beginning to see what you meant when you told us earlier that God had given you insight into Bible prophecy and the present world. It's astounding that all this fits so perfectly. But I'd be curious to know what else you found out."

John said, "Well, let's see what else Jesus had to say about it. Luke twenty-one roughly parallels Matthew twenty-four. Carl, why don't you read Luke twenty-one, verses ten and eleven for us?"

Carl turned some pages, found the verse, and read, "'Then he said to them: "Nation will rise against nation, and kingdom against kingdom. There will be great earthquakes, famines and pestilences in various places, and fearful events and great signs from heaven."'"

"Good," said their teacher. "Now, turn back to Matthew twenty-four, which describes the same thing. But something has been added. Please read verse eight."

Again, Carl turned the pages until he found these words. "'All these are the beginning of birth pains.'"

"I've never had kids," said Dave Busby, "but I know a lot of people who have. And what they say about birth pains is, they're short little pains at first, maybe thirty or forty minutes apart. Then they start coming quicker, and they also last longer and get more intense. And labor can last a long time. When my sister, Julie, had her first baby, she said the pain was so bad that when she was in the middle of labor, she decided she didn't want to have any more babies. But the minute the doctor put the baby in her arms she forgot all about the pain. Now she's got five kids!"

"That's great, Dave." John Edwards laughed. "Once again, you're right on target. The signs keep coming closer and closer together and with more intensity until the delivery comes."

Lori laughed too. "You're too much, Dave!"

John continued, "The next sign of Jesus' coming that I saw in the 1990s was the frequency and intensity of war, which we've already talked about. But there has been more carnage in the last one hundred years than in all the previous history of the world combined. I believe that a century filled with so much war and destruction can, in itself, clearly be a sign. The wars were, however, only the beginning—not the end."

He looked at Carl. "What's next?"

Carl looked down at his Bible. "It looks to me to be great earthquakes," Carl replied. "Which brings us back to where we are, doesn't it? I mean, I can't even imagine how many earthquakes this meteor is going to cause. But I know there were plenty before these, weren't there?"

"Of course, there were," John replied. "Just as there have been wars throughout human history, there have also been earthquakes. However, because of the growth of cities near earthquake faults during the eighties and nineties, the damage caused by earthquakes has been much more serious in recent years. As you may recall, the most costly earthquake in history happened in 1995, in Kobe, Japan. Just seven months before that, an earthquake struck Bolivia that was considered one of the most powerful ever recorded. It occurred four hundred miles under the earth's surface, so no surface damage occurred, but tremors were felt as far away as Toronto."

"The Pacific 'Ring of Fire' was very active during the last decade—just remember what happened in San Francisco, in Los Angeles, and Northridge, California, and in Kobe, Japan. There's been an unprecedented amount of earthquake activity during the last two decades. We can't even conceive of the kinds of shocks that will be hitting the Pacific Basin as a result of yesterday's meteor. I doubt seriously if there has been anything like it in human history."

Charley, who had been watching and listening silently for some time, addressed the teacher. "I'm intrigued by all this, and you're showing me things in this book I never knew were there. But there's something else I'd like to know. You mentioned that God showed you some things back in 1995 that really opened your eyes to what's happening now. Is this what you were talking about? And, if so, was there ever any question in your mind where the world was heading?"

John took an unusually long time to answer. Finally, he said, "I didn't know the exact time or place when things would happen. But I never doubted from 1995 on that God had shown me His program and that everything would take place exactly as the Bible said it would. Of course, it's easy with the benefit of hindsight to say I knew. The tough part is knowing in advance. Yet, I have to believe that God had prepared my heart and mind, and what you see here at this place is the evidence of that."

John Edwards continued, "There's something else very important that I learned was a key sign. It's there before you—see if you can figure out what it was."

Carl looked at the Bible, then answered, "It says here, 'pestilences in various places.' Is that what you mean? If so, I'm sure not the expert. What's your take on pestilence?"

John responded, "As I understand it, a pestilence is an epidemic of a contagious or deadly disease. We surely had our share of them in the late 1990s. The two most deadly came out of Africa, probably from the country of Zaire. In the 1950s, scientists working for a European research institute discovered a polio vaccine made from monkey serum. They gave the vaccine by oral spray to about two hundred thousand people in Zaire.

"But something terrible happened that the researchers had not bargained for—the monkey serum carried a virus that was unknown to human beings. It caused a shutdown of peoples' immune systems. Once it got into the human population, the virus spread rapidly through sexual contact, particularly among homosexuals. The appearance of this virus among humans coincided with what we called the 'sexual revolution.' This virtually guaranteed that it would spread like wildfire all over the world. Right now, ten million people have the virus, and at least a million have already died from it. I'm sure you already know what I'm talking about. Acquired Immune Deficiency Syndrome, or AIDS."

Carl spoke up. "You believe that AIDS is a sign of the times?"

"Yes, I do."

"So, is it a biblical pestilence?"

"Of course, it is," John replied. "And, so far, there's no cure for it. But AIDS is only one pestilence. All of you must have heard about others. Modern medicine brought the world penicillin and other wonder drugs. At first these medicines were so effective that doctors began prescribing them to cure every ache and pain and fever their patients developed. Even chicken growers regularly mixed antibiotics into the feed that their birds ate in order to keep their stock disease-free. Then, too late, we learned that disease organisms began to adapt. They became resistant to the repeated doses of penicillin and other antibacterial preparations we had been using.

"The result," he continued, "was the emergence of pestilences of epic proportions. In the mid-1990s, there were three hundred million cases of drug-resistant malaria, tens of millions of cases of drug-resistant sexually transmitted diseases like gonorrhea, herpes, syphilis, and chlamydia. Health authorities began noticing an epidemic of drug-resistant tuberculosis. Then, the ultimate horror appeared in 1976—hemorrhagic fever. Scientists named it after a river in Zaire known as the Ebola, because all the inhabitants of one entire village there died mysteriously after contracting this previously unknown and untreatable virus.

"The ebola virus caused the organs of its victims to turn to mush. They bled to death from every orifice in their bodies—a horrible death. In 1995, more than two hundred people died of ebola in the town of Kikwit in Zaire. Three months later, it broke out a thousand miles away on the Zaire-Zambian border. A strain of the virus had shown up earlier in a holding center for monkeys located in Reston, Virginia, not far from Washington, D.C. In that one place was the biological potential to wipe out the entire population of the nation's capital."

As John Edwards was talking, Maria came in with a large tray with coffee, tea, and snacks for everyone. Carl, Lori, Charley, Dave, and John all thanked her effusively, then helped themselves, but continued their conversation without interruption.

As they settled back in their chairs, Carl said, "Jack, you're really pushing my button, my friend. I've read about a lot of this, of course. Let's face it—it was hardly secret. I even wrote some of those safe-sex condom ads you saw on TV. Most of us in Hollywood pretty much took each piece of news as it came. 'AIDS is a problem, so use condoms.' 'Herpes is a problem, so use condoms.' We didn't do any campaigns about TB—we figured there was no way that people in Beverly Hills, Pacific Palisades, or Laguna Niguel were going to catch it. And as far as the ebola virus was concerned, we just figured that was somebody else's problem. After all, it was another country."

He held his coffee mug to his lips and took a slow sip. "If anybody had told us they were prophetic signs, I'm sure we would have called them nuts."

John Edwards set his own coffee mug back on the table. "You know what I like about you, Carl? Your honesty. You say exactly what you think." He chuckled. "What you say reminds me of another clear sign of the times. The tip-off this time is in the answer to a question put to Jesus by His religious enemies, the Pharisees. They asked Him what we all want to know: 'When will the kingdom of God come?' And if you'll take a look at Luke seventeen, you can see what Jesus said."

Lori found it first. "You must be talking about this part, starting at verse twenty-six." She began reading aloud. "'And as it was in the days of Noah, so it will be also in the days of the Son of Man: They ate, they drank, they married wives, they were given in marriage, until the day that Noah entered the ark, and the flood came and destroyed them all. Likewise as it was also in the days of Lot: They ate, they drank, they bought, they sold, they planted, they built; but on the day that Lot went out of Sodom it rained fire and brimstone from heaven and destroyed *them* all.'"

"That's awfully grim!" Lori said, thinking immediately of the still-unfolding tragedy on the West Coast. "But look what it says next: 'Even so will it be in the day when the Son of Man is revealed.'"

"You're right, Lori," John Edwards replied. "But for all the horror of that word-picture, you notice that Jesus equates the coming of the kingdom of God to His own return. And what is the sign of His coming?"

Lori answered, "Is it that people in the end times will behave like people behaved in Noah's time?"

"That's right, and like they behaved in the time of Lot. But go on, one more step. What does Jesus say specifically they were doing?" John asked.

"Eating, drinking, and getting married," Lori replied.

"What about in Lot's time in Sodom?"

"Let's see," she said, looking back at the page. "They were eating and drinking, buying and selling, and planting and building. But there's no mention of marriage!"

"So is there anything wrong with any of this?" John asked.

Lori thought a minute, then answered, "Not that I can think of. They were just staying alive and building for the future."

"You're absolutely right. There was nothing wrong with anything mentioned here that those people were doing," John remarked.

"Nothing wrong at all, except for one thing. I want you to look at the first book of the Bible. It's called Genesis. Find chapter six, and then verses five and those following. Start there, Lori."

Lori flipped over the pages in the Bible she was using, found Genesis, and read: "'Then the Lord saw that the wickedness of man *was* great in the earth, and *that* every intent of the thoughts of his heart *was* only evil continually.'" Lori paused, then added, "Verse six says, 'And the Lord was sorry that He had made man on the earth, and He was grieved in His heart.' That's really awful, Jack. But it's disturbing to think what God must have been feeling at the time."

"Yes, you're right. But there is something else," John said. "Jump down to verses twelve and thirteen."

Lori resumed: "Twelve says: 'So God looked upon the earth, and indeed it was corrupt; for all flesh had corrupted their way on the earth.' And then thirteen: 'And God said to Noah, "The end of all flesh has come before Me, for the earth is filled with violence through them; and behold, I will destroy them with the earth."'"

"What do you think was wrong with business as usual in Noah's time?" John asked.

After a long pause, Dave Busby said, "It's as clear as the frown on your face. Those characters were living under a sentence of death because of the way they had been living!"

"Yeah, that's right," said Carl. "But they kept on doing their own thing as if nothing was wrong." He paused, as the color drained from his face. "You know, guys, that really describes my own life in southern California—before the meteor hit."

"You and lots of other people," Dave offered. "We were all laughing and partying and doing our thing. I have to say I was there, too, Carl. I was dumping a big round ball through a hoop to entertain people, to keep their minds off the fact that the world was going to hell in a handbasket. But who's thinking about basketball now?"

"That's right," said Carl. "And Charley here was a coach. What was wrong with that? It was the way he made a living. Not everybody can be a missionary, right?"

"*Nothing* was wrong with that," John replied. "But that's not the point. All of us must realize that crime and violence were the number-one concern of the American people in the last decade of the twentieth century. Gangs of fatherless teenagers killed one another without mercy, then turned their anger on the rest of the population. There were rapes, robberies, shootings, beatings, and bombings in massive numbers. Families were broken apart. Profanity, blasphemy, and the worst kinds of vulgarity became part of the everyday language and lifestyles of the people. And promiscuous sex was epidemic.

"On top of all that, the nation gave protected legal status to people who practiced aberrant sex acts. Over a period of twenty-seven years, the American government gave protective constitutional status to the butchering of forty million innocent unborn children. It was as if the highest court in the land repeatedly jabbed its collective finger into the eye of Almighty God—as if to defy Him, to challenge Him to do something about it.

"And while this was going on, the vast majority of people were occupied with their own lives, sports, and recreations. *Lifestyles,* they called it. They gorged themselves on food and drink, spent close to four hundred billion dollars each year on pleasure, and squandered the nation's savings—then congratulated themselves on how good they were.

"When I observed this attitude of the people in America and very similar attitudes of people all around the world," John continued, "I knew that the words of Jesus were being fulfilled in my own lifetime. Sadly, I was seeing the sign of Noah and the sign of Lot."

"But, Jack," Carl interjected, "surely the United States and the countries of Europe and Asia weren't as bad as the world of Noah that we just read about."

"Maybe not," John answered, "but maybe so. People were extraordinarily violent in Noah's day, but not so violent that they couldn't hold weddings and have time for dinner. Please keep in mind that we killed more people in just twenty-seven years in this country, through abortion, than the total number of people in the whole world during Noah's day.

"Hitler, who was a demonic madman, killed about six million European Jews in the thirties and forties, during what we call the Holocaust. Supposedly sane, peace-loving Americans killed about seven times that number between 1973 and the end of the century. How violent do you suppose we have to be to parallel Noah's time?" John Edwards sighed. "And there were many more signs beside these."

"Jack," Lori said, "if it's possible, Carl and I really want to know what's coming next in our lives. Are there any signs about that?"

"I'll give you one more that is very timely, and then we're going to have to call it quits for a while," John answered. "This one will be fulfilled in the next couple of days. Let's read Luke twenty-one, verses twenty-five through twenty-eight."

Lori read the words aloud: "'And there will be signs in the sun, in the moon, and in the stars; and on the earth distress of nations, with perplexity, the sea and the waves roaring; men's hearts failing them from fear and the expectation of those things which are coming on the earth, for the powers of heaven will be shaken.'"

John said, "Do you see what Jesus said about nineteen hundred and seventy years ago, that describes today?"

Dave Busby exclaimed, "I can't believe it! Jesus said that, before He came back, the nations of the world would be in distress and perplexity because of the roaring and tossing of the sea. Good Lord!" he added in a reverent whisper. "The sea just wiped out California, and another monster wave is coming down on Asia even as we speak. Most of the ships in the Pacific are probably sunk by now. People all over the world must be going out of their minds with fear."

"We've already heard that, even before the meteor hit, people were dying of heart attacks all over L.A.," said Carl. "And that's what Jesus said would happen—men's hearts failing them from fear and the expectation of those things that are coming on the earth. We talked about all that last night. First, the meteor, then the waves, then the earthquakes, volcanoes, and radiation—then no sun for a couple of years—followed by mass starvation. It's like Jesus had a telescope—one that could see through time and space—and He trained it on the Pacific Ocean at the start of the twenty-first century."

Carl was clearly excited by what he had just said. He stood up and started pacing. "Jack, how can you be so calm about all this? Looks to me like we're living right smack in the middle of an incredible prophecy. Aren't you excited? Jesus said what was going to happen. And if we've got it right so far, looks like He could come back to earth any time!"

John smiled. "Of course, I'm excited, Carl. What I've been waiting for all my life as a Christian is about to happen. But, before it does, all of us are going to have the seven toughest years of our lives to get through. And, then Jesus will come for us.

"So, now, Carl," John Edwards said with a voice filled with love and compassion, "are you and Lori ready to meet Him when He returns?"

Carl stopped pacing and looked the other man straight in the eye. "Jack," he answered, "you know very well that we aren't ready. But we *want* to be. Will you tell us what to do?" Carl's heart was pounding. His palms were moist. He was about to cross a new spiritual frontier. He was about to find the purpose for his life. He was about to meet the same Jesus Christ who had spelled out all these truths so many years ago. The sophisticated advertising executive with all the answers was gone, and in his place was a trusting, but frightened little boy.

"Do you two both believe that Jesus is God?" John Edwards asked. Carl sat down again beside his wife. They both nodded their heads in affirmation.

"Do you believe that He died on the cross for your sins?" Again, mutual affirmation.

"Will you turn away from your sins and receive His pardon?" They looked into John's eyes and said they would.

"Will you now surrender your lives to Him as your risen Lord?" Two voices in union, "Yes, we will."

"Then," John said, "pray this prayer with me: Lord Jesus, I believe that You died for my sins. Lord Jesus, I believe that You rose from the grave and that You are alive today. Lord, I turn from my sins and I turn to You. I open the door of my heart to You, Lord. Come into my heart. Live Your life in me. Save my soul and fill me with Your Holy Spirit. Thank You, Lord, for hearing my prayer. Amen." They both prayed from their hearts. A miracle was taking place.

John Edwards rose from his chair and walked to the sofa where Carl and Lori were sitting. He placed his right hand on Carl's head and his left on Lori's. As he began to pray for them, both Carl and Lori felt something like a bolt of electricity coursing through their bodies. They raised their heads spontaneously in praise to God. Then, from deep inside, a dam of confusion, doubts, and uncertainties broke, and they poured out their hearts in praise to their newly found Lord.

For the first time in either of their lives, Carl and Lori Throneberry began to understand the purpose for their existence. Little could they imagine the adventure that now lay ahead of them.

John walked over to Charley, now standing and beaming from ear to ear. "Charley," he said, "now that Carl and Lori have committed their lives to the Lord, I would very much like for them to stay on with me for a few days, if they'll agree to it. I feel that Carl and Lori will be the first of many, and their knowledge and skills would be very helpful here. The tragedy we have seen so far is just the beginning, and I believe strongly that our government, especially with Ted Rust at the helm, can't survive the next two years. We both know what will happen next."

Putting his hand on Charley's shoulder, John Edwards said, "Old friend, I need your help too. Can you get me some surplus tents, some rations, and a lot more diesel fuel? I'm also going to need a radio expert—a broadcast specialist—who can handle all this communications gear. Do you think you might be able to help me find somebody?"

"You name it, Jack," Charley said, embracing his old friend, "and you've got it. Leave it to me."

After explaining his plans to Carl and Lori, the two new believers said they were delighted to be asked to help and that they very much wanted to stay on and continue to learn.

After a quick bite to eat, Charley and Dave took the two big trucks and set off for Albuquerque. There was so much to do . . . and precious little time.

IT WAS LATE AFTERNOON when Charley McAtee and Dave Busby stopped their trucks at the service station on the outskirts of Albuquerque. They had pulled into separate self-service islands. They were too tired to notice the price until both vehicles were full. Then they realized that the price on diesel fuel and on every grade of gasoline had been raised one dollar per gallon since they had stopped earlier that morning.

Charley shook his head. "We haven't seen the half of it yet. Prices will be going through the roof. At least there *is* fuel and I can afford it, but what about the poor people living on the edge? It's only a matter of time until we have government rationing and price controls."

Before Dave could respond, Charley said, "Anyway, I'm not going to worry about that now. We've got to move quickly. Let's drive out to the military side of the airport. I've helped coach a couple of their winning teams. During that time, I became good friends with one of the crusty old guys who is a sports fanatic. Rumor has it that he has more surplus gear than the army, navy, and air force combined. If he hasn't got tents, he'll know where he can get them."

The Albuquerque Airport had handled more civilian jets in the past twenty-four hours than it would normally receive in a year. The crisis had knit together civilian air controllers, military controllers, military ground crews, and civilian ground crews. They landed planes, fueled planes, and dispatched planes without one single incident.

The majority of the civilian aircraft had been repositioned further to the east. Now, bone-weary crews were handling a substantial part of the air traffic destined for emergency relief in California, Oregon, and Washington.

Charley and Dave drove their trucks up to the military operations center, parked, and got out. They walked into the lobby and down a poorly lighted hall to an open office. Behind the desk was a man in his mid-fifties with a mottled complexion and a mustache reminiscent of the British dragoons in the days of Gunga Din.

He leapt from behind his desk, pushed by Charley McAtee, and stuck out a powerful hand. "Dave Busby! *The* Dave Busby! One of the greatest! What brings you here?"

Dave was surprised and pleased to meet a fan under these circumstances. He shook the other man's hand firmly and said, "Hey, man, glad to meet you. But I'm the hired hand this time. Charley here is the man with the plan!"

"You old walrus!" Charley exclaimed, grabbing the hand of the other man. "I brought him here all the way from L.A. so you could get his autograph! What else?"

"Charley, don't mess with a tired old man," was the answer. "I've never processed so many airplanes in this short a time, even in combat. I know you didn't come by to shoot the breeze. So what do you want?"

"There's this place up in the hills," Charley began. "It's going to be a refuge for people trying to get out of this tragedy. I need some surplus tents, and field gear—cots, sleeping bags, field kitchens, oil stoves, rations, and mess kits. You know the drill."

"For how many people?"

"Maybe a thousand. Can you do it?"

"It'll cost you, good buddy, but I can do it."

"Great," Charley said. "Now, you get your autograph." He turned to Dave. "Dave Busby, meet Master Sergeant Tony O'Reilly, United States Air Force. Please sign a piece of paper, 'Dear Tony.'"

They all laughed when Tony O'Reilly opened a metal cabinet, pulled out a brand-new official NBA basketball, and said, "No paper, Dave. Just sign right here!"

As Dave scrawled his name across the basketball, a female corporal stuck her head into the office. "Sarge, there are five people outside who survived the meteor last night. A marine Osprey picked them off a mountain. General Gladstone sends word that they're to get VIP treatment until the secretary of defense talks to them."

Tony O'Reilly followed the corporal to the lobby and greeted Manuel Quintana and his family. They handed him a letter from General Gladstone, which he opened and read. Then they told him just a bit of their story.

"I'll be glad to help you folks any way I can," he said. "No designer jeans, I'm afraid, but I can get you some air force fatigues right now if you'll give me your sizes. Also, some toilet kits." He thought a minute. "You must want to buy your own stuff. This letter is a blanket authorization from the general. I can get the disbursement section to give you two thousand dollars before you leave. Then you can get what you want—and have some spending money left over."

Within minutes, Charley and Dave joined them in the lobby. Tragedy or no tragedy, an NBA superstar was still big news to the three boys. They crowded around Dave Busby. After a round of introductions, Charley asked Manuel the question he had been thinking about since he first heard their story: "Why were you on Mount Wilson yesterday?"

"Well," said Manuel, "I was vice president of engineering at TV station KTTV in L.A. We were having transmitter problems because of the heat, and since I'm really a hands-on guy, I went up to Mount Wilson, where we had our transmitters, to see what I could do. On the way, I heard the news about the meteor. I called my wife and told her to get in the car, pick up the boys at school, and come on up immediately."

"Manuel, you may not believe it," Charley said with a smile, "but a good friend of mine told me just this morning that he needs to hire a good television engineer. Sergeant O'Reilly has some great tents you can sleep in at the airport; or, if you're interested you can come up to my place and sleep in a real bed and take a hot shower. Which will it be?"

Manuel turned to Tony O'Reilly. "What do you say, Sergeant?"

Tony snorted. "What kind of choice is that? Charley here is loaded. You can stay in an air force tent with a pit privy located in another tent, or you can sleep in that palace he calls home. I have his number. Just sign this receipt for the money, and be sure you contact me if you decide to move somewhere else. Go on, now. You folks take it easy. You deserve some rest.

"And, Charley," he continued as they walked out together, "I'll call you in the morning about the gear you want."

Manuel and Cathy climbed into the cab of Charley's truck. The three star-struck boys climbed into the cab with Dave Busby.

To Manuel, it was as if his life was rolling down a set of tracks. What he didn't know, as the vehicles left the Albuquerque airport, was where those tracks were eventually heading.

CHAPTER FOURTEEN

ITO WATANABE FLIPPED OFF his television set. He had work to do. He was general manager of the Tokai nuclear power plants belonging to the Japan Atomic Power Company, Ltd. The reactors were co-located in Tokai Mura in the Ibaraki Prefecture, a short distance to the north of Tokyo. Both had been built in low-lying areas facing the Pacific Ocean.

Ito had begun work with Japan Atomic when the initial construction of Tokai Number One was completed in July of 1966. He was promoted to apprentice engineer in March of 1978 as soon as the American company, Ebasco, had finished installing the 1056-megawatt General Electric reactors for Tokai Number Two.

Ito soon established himself as a loyal company man. He went to work early. He came home late. Promotions came slowly but regularly. His wife and three children always took second place to Japan Atomic. As a consolation, Ito's salary was enough to provide the family with a modest, but comfortable, house and a university education for the children when they grew older.

Now, at fifty-four, Ito's hard work had finally paid off. The president of Japan Atomic Power Ltd. had personally recognized his loyalty and hard work. Ito Watanabe was now the general manager of the power plants that helped to send power to Tokyo itself.

Over the years, Ito had assured himself that without nuclear power, Japan would be at the mercy of a band of thieving desert sheiks. The Japanese industrial giant had grown because of nuclear power, not imported oil. *The work of Ito Watanabe,* he told himself, *is partially responsible for the economic victories of Japan over America. I am like a soldier in battle. Ito Watanabe is a hero of Japan.*

His portrayal of himself as a man of some achievement was no idle boast. Japan, after all, had fifty-four nuclear power plants in various stages of construction. *Of these,* Ito thought, *forty-nine are operating nuclear plants that produce 18,859 megawatts of electricity—thirty percent of our nation's electric power.* The facilities were clustered on the southern coastal areas of the island of Kyushu; on the island of Shikoku; along the Pacific Coast of Honshu, the principal Japanese island; from Shizuoka, south of Tokyo; then north of Tokyo to Ibaraki, Fukushima, and Sendai. Directly across from Tokyo on the Sea of Japan facing Korea were the Kansai Electric Power Company's installations in Fukui. In short, in Japan, nuclear power was in reach of everyone. And Ito was one of those who managed an important piece of this empire of power.

In 1995, Ito's company sent him and a group of its top engineers to Kiev in the Ukraine. Next, they went to Chernobyl. There, he learned firsthand of the cooling pipes that had ruptured, the warning devices that had failed, and the explosion of the Number Four reactor, which released into the atmosphere thirty to forty times the radioactivity of the atomic bombs dropped on Hiroshima and Nagasaki.

He traveled into Belarus and saw abandoned villages. He learned that nine years after the disaster, three million people were living in contaminated areas. But nothing had etched the tragedy more vividly in his mind than a conversation he had had with a little boy in Belarus named Sasha. Sasha's uncle had fought and survived the Afghan war. On his return home, he was ordered to go to the Chernobyl clean-up. He died a hideous death from exposure to the radiation from the reactor.

When a son was born to his surviving brother, the boy was named Sasha in his memory. Just before Ito's visit, Sasha's parents had learned after four painful bone marrow tests, that their little five-year-old had contracted leukemia from the residual radiation from Chernobyl. Dr. Valery Rizheutski, who was head of the Dispensary Research Institute for Radiation Medicine in Belarus, confided to Ito through an interpreter, "Eighty percent of the children of Belarus now have medical problems related to Chernobyl." Tears came to her eyes, and her voice faltered as she said sadly, "With eighty percent of the children affected, we have no future."

On the flight back to Tokyo, Ito was haunted by the image of Sasha. He had hated the Americans for what they had done to Hiroshima and Nagasaki. Could it be that he—the imagined hero of Japan—might one day be responsible for an even greater nuclear tragedy?

On his return to Tokai, he ordered a complete safety review of his installations. What he found alarmed him. The protective sleeves on the cooling pipes had slipped. The pipes, which had been exposed to intense radiation for years, had become brittle. *If those pipes ever burst,* he thought, *the water could drain from around the core, some of the fuel rods would be uncovered, and the heat from the radioactive decay could bring on an uncontrolled meltdown. What is it the Americans call it? The "China Syndrome"—a meltdown that runs all the way through the earth, to China.*

He looked at the massive four-foot-thick concrete walls of the containment building. Hundreds of earth shocks over the years had left hairline cracks in the massive walls. If there was a meltdown, Ito knew that the buildup of steam could explode through those walls. Then, clouds of radioactive vapor could escape into the air.

Ito was a company man. He trusted his superiors. They told him everything at Tokai was safe. But he remembered the earthquake experts who had published a widely circulated paper in Japan outlining twenty-three areas where there would be no danger of earthquake activity. One of those safe areas was the seaport of Kobe. Yet, in 1995, there had occurred in Kobe the most costly earthquake in Japan's history. Structures crumbled that expert structural engineers had certified as 100 percent earthquake resistant. *Could it be that the expert engineers have been deceived about nuclear safety as well?* Ito wondered.

He had sent a complete report to his superiors warning them of the structural dangers facing Tokai Number One and Tokai Number Two. But, as is so often the case, financial concerns and the fear of reactivating the latent antinuclear protest movement guaranteed that Ito's report would be quickly submerged.

He was torn. Where did his loyalty truly lie? Was it to the company that had nurtured him, trained him, and promoted him? Or was it to the country of his birth—the country of his beloved ancestors?

He set out to learn about earthquakes. His mentor became Katsuhiko Ishibashi, the outspoken head of the seismology division of the Japanese Construction Ministry's International Institute of Seismology and Earthquake Engineers. He learned that the dramatic increase in earthquake activity toward the close of the twentieth century was not only unusual but of very grave concern to scientists around the world. Of the thirteen largest Japanese earthquakes on record, five had taken place in the 1990s.

The first major quake of the century was in Tokyo, in 1923. Next, was an 8.9 quake in 1933. Thirteen years elapsed before the quake of 1946. Then, two years later came the next. Four years elapsed, then eight years elapsed, then fifteen years between quakes. But, something vicious began in the 1990s. On January 15, 1993, a 7.8 quake struck Kushiro, Hokkaido. On July 12, 1993, a 7.8 quake and tsunami devastated Okushiri-hima, Hokkaido. On October 1, 1994, an 8.1 quake again hit Hokkaido. On December 28 of that same year, there was a 7.5 quake in Hachinohe in northern Japan. Only nineteen days later, the costliest quake in human history struck Kobe in south central Honshu.

Ishibashi said, "Ito, we are heading for a holocaust. I fear that we Japanese must resign ourselves to our eventual destruction." When

Ito asked him to explain, the scientist told him, "Japan sits at a crucial juncture of major tectonic plates. It is located on the western end of the Pacific Plate. Touching the Pacific Plate directly at the border of Japan is the Eurasian Plate. Nearby is what is called the Philippine Sea Plate. The tendency of the Pacific Plate is to move westward and come under the Eurasian Plate. This causes violent upward thrusting and devastating damage to man-made structures near the lines where these plates intersect.

"There are several major fault lines directly under the city of Tokyo," he said. "Worse for Tokyo is the expansion of the city for three or four hundred years into landfill areas constructed toward the Pacific. During severe earthquakes, the subsoil in a city like Kobe liquefies into mud, and there is no support left for above-ground structures. An earthquake/tsunami combination would inflict incalculable damage in a city like Tokyo."

Ito listened in stunned silence as Ishibashi explained that a hundred forty thousand people were killed in the great Kanto earthquake that demolished Tokyo in 1923. Fires, he said, had reduced the city to what one account termed "a moonscape of ash and slag." Experts predicted that another devastating quake, worse than Kanto, was due to strike at any time, with property damage in excess of one trillion dollars and loss of life in the millions. However, these same experts named another target first— Ito's own area, Tokai.

Ito was shocked by this news, since he knew that his reactors could not survive the damage. He could not shut them down without permission, for they were too important to the electric power grid of central Honshu Island. If they continued to operate, his reactors could one day release enough radiation to kill most of the surrounding population. In the end, he remained the loyal company man. He kept the reactors running at peak capacity. The danger from earthquakes, he decided, must be the concern of his superiors.

Now, if the television report he had seen was to be trusted, his reactors faced two devastating blows: a giant tsunami, and earthquakes of a magnitude Japan had never before experienced.

He had been assured that the Richter scale was a reliable measure of ground motion caused by an earthquake. Each point on the scale indicated a ten-fold increase in movement. An earthquake measuring five would do considerable damage. An earthquake of magnitude six is ten times as powerful and would cause severe damage. At magnitude seven, a quake would produce widespread damage. An earthquake of magnitude eight would be a thousand times more powerful than one at five on the Richter scale. None of the earthquakes forecast for Japan in the aftermath of the meteor were less than 8.5.

As the Far East braced for the shock of a tidal wave, nature played a cruel trick. The earthquake tremors from California traveled underground around the Pacific at about two-tenths of a mile per second, or 720 miles per hour. Denying that such a phenomenon was possible, scientists had calculated seismic movement at a lightning-fast twelve thousand kilometers an hour. But, like so much in seismic theory, these earlier calculations proved wrong. Like a string of firecrackers on the Fourth of July, a massive series of earthquakes struck the Pacific Northwest, Alaska, and the Aleutians, and then headed at supersonic speed toward Japan, Taiwan, the Philippines, and Indonesia.

At noon, Ito's superiors had telephoned an order to shut down the reactors. *What possible good will that do?* he wondered. He knew there was no way to cool and protect a hot reactor core in nine hours—and that's all the time he would have before the earthquake hit. And what about the pond for storing the spent fuel rods? If the water covering them boiled off, the radiation from the damaged spent fuel pond could, according to some experts, triple the total area of radiation contamination.

If the nuclear power from his plant and others like it were to be cut off, the elevators, the electric trains, the switches, the lights, the communications, the computers in Tokyo would all stop. His superiors were wrong. It was too late to argue. He had given his best years to the company. Now, he would save what was left for himself.

He called his workers together. "My friends," he said solemnly, "a meteor has struck the Pacific Ocean near California. Earthquakes larger than anything ever experienced in history are moving toward Japan. I have heard the earthquakes may come by nine o'clock tonight—the giant tsunami by one A.M. tomorrow morning.

"Our government has not had adequate warning. They have not yet warned the people. Millions of Japanese people will die tonight. We have been ordered to shut down the reactors here at Tokai. If we do, Tokyo will lack power. The cooling pipes cannot withstand an earthquake or a tsunami, whether we shut down now or do so later. It was folly to build a nuclear power plant on this place. There will be a meltdown. There is nothing we can do about it now.

"For now, my friends," he continued, "we will install a timing device that will disengage the core beginning at seven tonight. I hope that we can avoid the tragedy of Chernobyl. Then we will gather our families and head toward the mountains. Hopefully, we will survive."

AS AFTERNOON WORE ON, it was impossible to hide from the Japanese people the tragedy that was bearing down upon them. Ito could see it unfolding before his eyes. Television commentators took the available facts and magnified them, although they did not even come close to describing the horrific events that were about to occur.

As panic set in, workers poured out of office buildings, stores, and factories. The streets were jammed with crying, pleading, cursing people. Within minutes, the roadways leading from Tokyo, which were jammed during the best of times, turned into a chaotic mass of stalled vehicles. Dozens of people were trampled to death as they attempted to board overcrowded trains out of the city. Others walked. Some rode bicycles. Anything just to get to higher ground, away from the ocean.

As panic intensified throughout Japan, more and more residents trying to leave the major cities clutched their chests and fell prostrate with heart attacks. Those who fell were trampled by the stampede of fear-crazed people.

The international airlines had seen the danger coming and had canceled all flights into Japan, Hong Kong, Taiwan, and the Philippines. Aircraft with crews near major Japanese airports were flown west to India and beyond. Airline crews in downtown Tokyo found travel to the international airport impossible. The air routes to the west were jammed with air traffic from Southeast Asia headed west.

To those like Ito who remembered the begging, pleading crowds surrounding the U.S. embassy in Saigon after the fall of South Vietnam, the scenes at Asian airports were much worse. International businessmen, diplomats, students, tourists all faced death. The night before, they had been enjoying comfortable hotel rooms, excellent food, extraordinary shopping, and famed Asian hospitality. Now, they were part of a faceless mob—unable to communicate with the rest of the world, fighting to escape sure death.

As was the case in Los Angeles, some went stark-raving mad. Others prayed. Some decided to spend their last evening eating, drinking, and enjoying the pleasures of the night.

AT 9:00 P.M., AS IF SOME huge beast had emerged from under the sea, the giant Pacific Plate plunged beneath the Eurasian Plate, thrusting it upward one hundred fifty feet in the air. The first breaks were in the north throughout Hokkaido. Tokai was next. Buildings and roadways collapsed in seconds. Thousands of flimsy houses began to blaze from thousands of fires ignited by overturned kerosene stoves. The water pipes at Tokai Number One and Tokai Number Two broke apart like clay pots. The containment walls shattered in scores of places. The overheated cores began meltdown. It was only a question of time before a cloud of poisonous radiation would engulf every man, woman, and child within ten miles.

But the big one was Tokyo. When the plates beneath it jumped, it seemed that hell was unleashed on earth. Downtown buildings swayed and then collapsed. The fill dirt from centuries of dumping into Tokyo Bay suddenly liquefied. The high-rise apartments, the airport, everything man-made no longer had support. It all collapsed and crumbled.

All electricity was out in the city and its suburbs. The only light was from the wind-whipped flames bursting up from hundreds of thousands of shops and dwellings.

Yet, the roaring beast was still not satisfied. Wave after wave of violent shocks ravaged the entire island nation. Virtually every nuclear facility in Japan was in a crisis meltdown condition. Roads were destroyed. Power lines and telephone lines were down. Every railroad train had been derailed. Bridges and overpasses were twisted rubble.

Millions of people crawled out of the rubble of the cities and villages. They groped about in the dark, grateful to be alive. To them, an even greater horror was yet to come.

Early Saturday morning, while it was still dark and their nation was in ruins, they heard a roaring noise in the distance. Then the great wave broke over them. They were picked up five hundred feet in the air, then smashed back to earth again. They were turned over and over again by the violence of the waves until their bodies were like jelly. Their lungs gasped for air while their ear drums exploded with the pressure.

They couldn't see. They couldn't hear. Nothing had prepared them for the horror of being seized by this malevolent force.

The angry wave poured inland as far as the mountains. Nothing living in its path survived. Then it retreated to its boundaries, pulling with it the bodies of people and animals, the rich topsoil, and all those things that people, when they were alive, had counted precious.

As the giant wave receded, a man-made peril began. A cloud of radioactive steam rose from the remains of Japan's infrastructure. It traveled across the Sea of Japan and the Korea Strait to Korea. Korea's water became radioactive. Its lakes, its streams, its reservoirs were now poisoned.

The cloud spread beyond Korea to the Yellow Sea and the East China Sea to the heavily populated coastal cities of China. From Shanghai to Beijing, the reservoirs received radioactive aerosols. The streams and rivers were polluted with radioactive particles. The grass was radioactive, and the milk was radioactive.

In one brief moment, 250 million people in Korea, China, and Japan had received sufficient radiation to cause death, or lingering illness from cancer and leukemia. In one night of horror, Japan had ceased to be a nation. Almost 97 million people had died from the earthquakes, the fires, the tidal wave, or nuclear radiation. Its infrastructure was demolished. Its housing was demolished. Its financial wealth was gone. Part of its precious topsoil was washed away. Much of the rest was damaged by seawater.

Yet, Ito Watanabe and his wife and children survived. Kubi Nomura and his wife had survived. The Japanese government had survived. They had overseas assets. They would rebuild.

CHAPTER FIFTEEN

MANUEL AND CATHY QUINTANA fell exhausted into the king-sized bed in Charley McAtee's regal guest suite. They slept the sleep of the dead. There was not even a flicker of remembrance of the horror they had survived—just twelve hours of blissful, undisturbed sleep.

They woke refreshed, then sat bolt upright in bed, shocked at their unfamiliar surroundings. Suddenly they remembered—they were in Albuquerque at the home of a friendly man whose name they had forgotten. After they washed the sleep from their faces, they slipped on the thick, oversized terry cloth robes and slippers their host had left for them, and went down the hall into the spacious living room.

"Well, good morning," Charley McAtee boomed out. "I'm so glad you could rest. In case you forgot, I'm Charley McAtee, and you are my most welcome guests. Would you like some coffee and breakfast?"

"We can't begin to thank you enough for your help, Mr. McAtee," Cathy said. "But, in answer to your question, we are starved, and breakfast sounds great! Are our boys still asleep?"

"Are you kidding? There's no way those fellows are going to sleep long when there's an NBA star around the house. The last I heard, they were outside shooting hoops with Dave. They've already had their breakfast. Come on, let's go to the kitchen." As they walked down the hallway, Charley turned to Cathy and said, "By the way, please call me Charley. I've never been too much on formalities."

A half-hour later, when the last of the eggs, sausage, wheat toast, and fresh fruit had disappeared from their plates, Manuel and Cathy recounted for Charley the highlights of their ordeal atop Mount Wilson.

The usually loquacious coach sat in stunned amazement, then shook his head and said, "You folks have seen the pit of hell and lived to tell about it. How did you survive?"

"We are alive today because of the hand of God," Cathy answered softly.

Manuel nodded assent. "It's true. We have no other explanation."

"That's wonderful," said Charley. "Are you both believers?"

"Yes, we are," Cathy said. "A couple of days ago, I'd say we were just casual church-goers. But, after what the Lord has taken us through, my husband and I are all His. And the boys too. Every part of us belongs to the Lord. I suppose you might say we were 'born again' on that mountain."

"I watched a lot of television news while you folks were asleep," Charley responded. "A huge tidal wave and massive earthquakes have been hitting all over the Pacific. Nobody has any clear idea yet how bad things really are, but the preliminary guess is that maybe five hundred million people have died since this thing started."

Cathy and Manuel reacted instantly to the huge numbers. "No, Charley," Manuel said. "That can't be possible!"

"I'm afraid so, Manuel. And property damage is—well, it's so enormous they stopped counting at ten trillion dollars. It looks like huge portions of California, Oregon, Washington, Hawaii, and Alaska are gone. The U.S. death toll, according to what I've been hearing, is something over thirty million—and that's just a preliminary guess."

He looked at his two guests. "Manuel, you and Cathy don't have any idea how special and how blessed you really are."

Manolo's eyes clouded over as he tried to take in the magnitude of the situation and the realization that, for some unknown reason, he and his family had been spared. "Charley," he said after an emotional pause, "it's almost too much for us—all this—all we saw—all that's going on in the world right now. We're here today in your beautiful house, eating breakfast and drinking coffee as if nothing happened. But all our friends and neighbors, all our relatives, all the people we loved back in California are . . . now dead." He brushed tears from his eyes. "There has to be some purpose in this. There just *has* to be—and some way we can pay back what has been done for us."

"Manuel, there *is* a purpose. And, what's more, I'm absolutely certain that you and Cathy will find it before long. That's the way God works.

"But for now," Charley continued, "I wonder if I couldn't get you two to help me with something. I have an old friend up in the hills who has this tremendous communications setup. He's got satellite dishes, radio and TV transmitters, and all kinds of high-tech stuff that he uses in his ministry. He told me yesterday that he's been looking for a qualified technician who can help him run the show up there. Would that have any appeal for you, Manuel?"

"Are you kidding?" Manolo smiled. "That sounds like just what I need right now, to help me adjust to what's been happening. I don't know about tomorrow or the next day," he added with a laugh, "but it sure sounds good *today!*"

"That's great," said Charley. "My friend's name is John Edwards. We call him Pastor Jack, and I know he's going to be thrilled to meet you. Along the way, maybe he can help you two sort things out."

"Charley, you're terrific," Manuel replied. "Cathy and I both need some time to sort out our lives. But, aside from that, I'll need some basic tools if I'm going to be helping anybody. All my gear—well, you know. If I can help this guy for a few weeks, it would be my pleasure. I'll write out a list of what I need."

"We would be honored, Charley," said Cathy.

Charley finished his coffee and headed for the door with the list Manuel had given him in his hand. "For now, why don't you two take it easy while Dave and I go and pick up some supplies and the gear you need?"

CHARLEY AND DAVE WERE SHOCKED at the prices on goods in the stores and shops in Albuquerque. Gasoline was now nearly $4.00 a gallon, lettuce was $6.00 a head, tomatoes were $2.50 a pound, and medium-sized apples were $1.50 each. But when they commented about the high cost of things as they made their rounds, the explanation was always the same. One grocer said, "Stuff is harder to get now, you know. All produce from California has stopped. The fruit we've been getting from Washington and Oregon is gone. Supplies are tight and getting tighter. In a week there may be nothing left. You'd better get used to it!"

At the gas pump, the story was a shortage of tankers to carry oil and gas. But everywhere they went, there was one clear message: human greed had triumphed. There was actually remarkably little grief about the tragedy. In most cases it just seemed that this was an opportunity for the merchants to make a quick profit.

Charley had already taken delivery on the soybeans he had purchased, and he kept them under lock and key in a rented warehouse nearby. After completing their shopping, he and Dave loaded a hundred sacks of beans onto the truck and headed for the airport.

When they arrived, Charley made his way to the office of Master Sergeant O'Reilly. "Tony, did you get the gear I wanted?" he asked.

"Charley, where's your faith, old boy? You know I did. But I gotta tell you, the price has been bumped a little on us."

"What do you mean 'bumped a little'?"

"Oh, like about double." Tony smiled.

"Double?" Charley shouted. "Double! Are you crazy?"

"Hey, come on, Charley," Tony O'Reilly said. "I don't set the prices. I take my ten percent and, other than that, charge you just what it costs me. You know that. Prices on everything have gone through the roof. With the West Coast and Asia both gone, where are they going to get these things anymore? These tents were made in China, and chances are we won't be getting any more of them, either."

"Okay, okay," Charley conceded, waving his hands in the air. "How much?"

"Well, Charley, it's five hundred bucks a tent. The mess gear adds about five hundred more. Times a thousand setups makes an even million dollars."

"Whew!" Dave Busby whistled. "A million dollars for some lousy government surplus?"

"One million in cash," said Tony. "No checks. The banks aren't clearing checks right now."

"Tony," said Charley, "you know I don't keep that kind of money around. Everything I have is in banks or brokerage accounts."

"Charley, old friend, everything you *used to* have was in banks and brokerage accounts. If that's all you've got, you're in trouble, pal. Have you got any gold?"

Suddenly the crisis assumed new meaning for Charley. Up until then, he had been the strong one, the caring friend, the dispassionate observer. He had a house, a car, some trucks, and two hundred thousand bushels of soybeans in a warehouse. But seeing millions of dollars of his liquid assets—stocks, bonds, insurance policies, contracts, even bank accounts—disappear overnight changed things dramatically. If his assets were frozen, or perhaps lost forever, he would still survive. But his attitude of cool detachment would have to change.

Charley sat down on the corner of Tony's desk and folded his arms across his chest. "How much is gold worth today?" he asked.

"My people are selling at three thousand an ounce, right now, and buying at twenty-eight hundred. Tell you what. I'll round it out for

213

you. We can do the deal for three hundred fifty-seven ounces, if you've got it."

Charley breathed a sigh of relief. "I've got it," he said. For years, he had been accumulating gold as an inflation hedge. He had stored at least a thousand ounces of the yellow metal at his house. In a world suddenly thrown back to primitive barter, at least he had that means of survival. "Dave and I will be back to pick the stuff up at one o'clock this afternoon. But one more thing—Tony, can you loan us a couple of your biggest trucks and a couple of drivers for about six hours? We're going to need a little help hauling all that stuff up to the site."

"No problem, Charley. See you at one. Pleasure doing business with you."

With that, two stunned former athletes retraced their route back home.

AT TWO O'CLOCK ON SATURDAY afternoon, the convoy set out for El Refugio, along with Charley, Dave, the Quintana family in Charley's two trucks, and four heavy-duty former military vehicles. The narrow road was all uphill, with a lot of slow-moving traffic. It took them four hours to reach El Refugio.

The land where John Edwards had built his home and conference ground was vast and beautiful. There were seemingly endless vistas of purple mountains and rolling valleys punctuated by scattered forests, cultivated fields, manicured lawns, and a large sparkling pond at the bottom of the hill. At the far side of the property was a small river that wound, snakelike, from one end of the valley to the other. "If there is a heaven on earth," Manuel whispered to Cathy, as Charley's truck pulled to a stop in the driveway, *"this* has got to be it!"

John Edwards, who had heard the rumbling of the trucks, came to the door and looked out. Charley jumped down from his truck and called out to their host. "Jack! Come on out here and see what we've brought you."

John Edwards hurried across the lawn, rubbing his hands together in delight as he looked at the military vehicles. The drivers had already jumped down from their trucks and were starting to unload.

"Charley, you're the best!" John exclaimed. "I can't believe my eyes!"

"All compliments are gratefully accepted," Charley said, grinning. "Now, tell us where you want this stuff."

John Edwards directed the unloading of supplies. Boxes of perishable items were stacked in a barnlike structure near the house. Tents and other supplies were quickly stacked up next to the building and covered with tarps. When the supplies were unloaded, John Edwards asked the drivers to stay for dinner. They were all anxious to get back on the road before dark, so they declined. But John insisted on sending them on their way with bags of chips and cans of soft drinks.

As the army trucks started down the driveway, Charley said, "I've got something else you've been wanting."

"Is that right, Charley?" John Edwards asked. "What could that be?"

Charley turned toward the Quintanas, who were standing uncertainly by his trucks. "I brought you somebody you've been wanting to meet. Come with me."

The two men strode across the lawn to the waiting family. "Pastor Jack, this is Mr. Manuel Quintana and his family from L.A. This is Cathy, Miguel, Ricardo, and Juan. These folks are getting to be kinda famous, you know. They're the ones the army found sitting on a mountaintop after the meteor hit. They spent last night at my place, and I've been twisting Manuel's arm to come up here and give you a hand. He's a certified broadcast engineer. Until two days ago, he was in charge of engineering at a TV station in L.A. You may have to persuade him, Jack, but I think he may be the one you've been looking for."

John Edwards extended his hand and smiled broadly. "You folks are an answer to prayer. The Lord must have a very special plan for you all, to bring you out of that inferno alive and looking so fit."

He reached over and grabbed Miguel, the oldest son, by the shoulder, then drew all three boys together in his arms. "You fellows are very, very special. Do you know that?" They nodded, looking up into John Edwards's shining eyes. "You are all very welcome here, my friends. Welcome to my ranch, and welcome to what I believe God has called us to do in the wake of this week's disaster."

"Thank you, sir," said Manuel. "We were so lucky to meet Mr. McAtee and Mr. Busby last night. The boys couldn't believe it. They got to shoot baskets with one of their all-time favorite Lakers stars this morning. But really, our heads are swimming from all that's been going on the last couple of days."

Just then, Carl and Lori Throneberry came out of the house and walked across the driveway toward the group. They were wearing well-worn jeans, cowboy boots, and work shirts that John Edwards had come up with, and they looked more like a couple of ranch hands than displaced Angelinos.

Lori threw her arms around Charley's waist, and Carl walked over and gave Dave Busby a bear hug. "What's going on, Charley?" Carl asked. "Looks like you've brought some more homeless wanderers our way!" He and Lori introduced themselves to the Quintanas and made a mental note of the names and ages of each of the boys.

"Cathy," Lori said, "I'm so glad you've come. Hanging out with these guys is okay, I guess, but I've really missed not having another woman to talk to!" The men all laughed, then quickly admitted that it would be nice to expand their small group with another couple. "We sure sympathize with everything you must have gone through," Lori continued. "Carl and I were on one of the last flights out of L.A. Thursday morning. We knew we were lucky to get out of there when we did, but now we understand that it was more than just luck. Pastor Jack and Charley and Dave here have been so good to us. We've learned so much about ourselves and about what the Bible says about all this. We know now that God was responsible for our getting out of L.A."

"I feel the same way," Cathy said.

"We'd like to know more about you folks," said Carl. "How did you get here?"

They stood in amazement as Manuel and Cathy recounted their incredible deliverance. As they talked, John Edwards led the whole group back up the driveway and into the house. Never missing a beat, Manuel described their flight out to the desert camp, then down to Albuquerque, and everything they had done up to that moment. By the time he and Cathy had related all the essential parts of their story, they were all standing around in John Edwards's large, comfortable living room.

"Ever since we got out of Los Angeles," Carl said, "I've been haunted by one thought: *Why Lori? Why me?* You know, I've wanted to know why we were allowed to live when so many millions had to die. What purpose was there to our lives? I bet you all must be wondering the same thing."

"Oh, yes," Cathy agreed with great emotion. "That's exactly what I've been feeling for two days. I'm very grateful, but I can't figure it out."

"Carl," said Manuel, "when that great big fireball roared down on us, man, I thought we were dead for sure. You better believe we want to know why we were able to live through it. I, too, keep thinking, *Why us?* Why wasn't it somebody more worthy than us?"

"Well," John Edwards said, "none of you should ever doubt that God has placed His mark on your lives. You wouldn't be here under these circumstances if there wasn't something very special going on."

"I believe that," said Manuel. "But what about you, Lori? Have you found the answer yet for you and Carl?"

"Yes and no," Lori replied. "We don't know everything yet. But we have come to faith in Jesus Christ since we've been here, and we believe that is part of it. I also feel that Carl's skills are going to be useful to Pastor Jack in his work here at the ranch—especially in light of what's coming next."

"What do you mean?" Cathy asked. "What's coming next? What more could happen?"

Dave Busby laughed. "Hold on to your hats, folks. For the past two days Lori and Carl have been getting a college education in history, prophecy, theology, and everything else you can think of. If you get them started, you may not be able to make them stop!"

"Dave Busby!" Lori laughed. "You're just an old troublemaker!"

"We really are brand-new at all this," Carl said, smiling at Dave and Lori, "but from what we've been hearing, the events of the past forty-eight hours are dramatic revelations of God's plan and of His wrath on the earth. If John and Dave and Charley are on track in what they've been telling us—and we believe they are—then what's coming is that Satan is going to run wild on the earth before long. That's what Lori was talking about."

"Okay, but what do you mean, Satan is *going* to run wild?" asked Manuel. "Something has been running wild already, hasn't it?"

"Good point." Dave Busby laughed.

"Hey, come on," said Carl, "let's sit down. If you and Cathy are really interested, Manuel, I suggest we let our expert here tell us what he feels is coming next. Pastor Jack has been working on this for, well, a long time, and I think you'll be interested in his take on it."

As they were settling into their chairs, Maria appeared at the door. She looked at Cathy and asked if she spoke Spanish. When Cathy said she did, they immediately broke into an animated conversation. It was obvious that Maria was welcoming the new visitors. Cathy translated for those who didn't understand Spanish. She told the group that Maria had even offered to help take care of the boys and provide some amusement for them while they were there. Cathy thanked her profusely before Maria retired to the kitchen to prepare snacks and beverages for everyone.

John Edwards had been listening intently and decided it was time for a short briefing on what was taking place at El Refugio. "Folks, the world is being torn apart by a series of natural disasters. Clearly, they are the worst in human history. Don't want to give you all the bad news at once, but I'm expecting a series of volcanic eruptions to come next.

"As you all know only too well, the people of this country are in shock. There's no money anymore—at least, not as we know it. There will be shortages of everything. In a few months, all of the world's grain reserves will be depleted. From this, I expect a scarcity of food more severe than this world has ever experienced. People will be rioting and looting. They will give up everything they have to secure peace, employment, and food. Then, the Bible tells us, a world leader will appear who will offer the people those things.

"This new world leader will claim to be a messiah, a savior, but actually he will be a puppet of the devil. There's also going to be a second figure who has the ability to perform magical feats before the whole world. This second man will eventually control all the money in the world."

"Wait a minute, Jack," Manuel said. "Play this a little slower, will you? I've never heard of any of this. Is all this stuff in the Bible?"

"That's right, Manuel. Every bit of it is in the Bible. As a matter of fact, whole books have been written about a diabolical world dictator called the Antichrist. He got that name because he will try to perform for Satan what Christ performed for God."

"Wow, I hope he fails," Cathy said.

"Of course he will fail, Cathy," said John Edwards. "But not before he has done terrible things to a lot of people on earth."

"And you feel," Manuel asked, "that this character may be showing up pretty soon?"

"Yes, I do," John Edwards replied. "Very soon. That's why I don't have as much time to talk about it as I'd like."

"Come on now, Pastor Jack," said Dave Busby. "You're not trying to give them the stripped-down version, are you?"

John Edwards laughed. "No, Dave, I'm not. What we're getting set up for right now are the practical applications. That's what El Refugio is all about. But Manuel asked if the Bible talks about the false messiah, and the answer is yes, definitely. The apostle Paul called him the 'man of sin' who exalts himself against everything that is of God. But the most vivid description was written by the apostle John in the Book of Revelation. As you probably know, this book contains a lot of images that are a bit hard to decipher, but it's not too hard to understand if you have the key. Want to take a look?"

"Sure," said Manuel. "Why not? We've got some time on our hands!"

John Edwards handed Manuel, Cathy, and Miguel copies of the Bible and suggested the three boys might like to look on together.

"Okay," he continued, "turn to Revelation, chapter thirteen. Manuel, here's where we see a description of an animal called 'the beast.' This is the Antichrist. Now, look at verse two and read what it says."

Manuel began tentatively, "It says, 'The dragon gave the beast his power and his throne and great authority.'"

"Good," said John. "This is the man I was talking about. But if the beast is the Antichrist, as I've already said, who do you suppose the dragon might be?"

"Must be the devil," Manuel answered.

"Yes, that's exactly right. And who is the devil?"

"Well, he's an evil spirit," Manuel said, "a real powerful evil spirit."

"That's true, in part, but did you know that Jesus called him the Prince of the Earth? When the devil came to Jesus to tempt Him, the evil one offered Jesus all the kingdoms of the earth because he said they belonged to him. He was lying, in part, but Jesus turned him down as if the offer was true. This beast figure will accept from the devil what Jesus rejected.

"Now, please read the second part of verse three."

"'The whole world was astonished and followed the beast,'" Manuel read. Then he added, "Whatever the devil gave him, the world sure bought it. He becomes the leader of everyone."

"That's the way I see it too," replied John Edwards. "Now, look at verses seven and eight."

"'He was given power,'" Manuel read, "'to make war against the saints and to conquer them. And he was given authority over every tribe, people, language, and nation. All inhabitants of the earth will worship the beast—all whose names have not been written in the book of life belonging to the Lamb that was slain from the creation of the world.'"

John continued, "This beast is to be given power over all the inhabitants of the earth. Everybody is going to venerate him."

"But, Jack," Carl said, "we're making this sound so modern, but it was written—well, the Roman Empire was still at its height when John wrote this book—so don't you think the apostle John might have been talking about some Roman emperor? Didn't the emperors claim to be God?"

"Carl," John answered, "you make a good point. The apostle John may very well have used a Roman emperor as a model. After all, one of them exiled John himself to that tiny island. However, the power of Rome only went so far. It didn't control India or China or Africa. And remember, the beast controls everybody. So, in my opinion, this beast hasn't received power yet. But he will soon."

Cathy and Lori were thinking the same thing, but Lori spoke first. "If he has the devil's power for a time to hurt the saints, does that include us?" she asked. "Because we're certainly not saints!"

"It includes all those who belong to Jesus, Lori, and who refuse to worship the beast. But there will be many who will resist him. I hope that includes all of us. That is the reason for El Refugio. I've built this place as a center to encourage resistance to the evil that is coming. This is something I've been planning for the last five years."

"And you want me to help out?" Manuel exclaimed. "It sounds like you all are planning to get yourselves killed."

"Maybe. Maybe not. But, one thing is certain if you play ball with the Antichrist."

"What's that?"

"The Bible says that everybody who goes along with the Antichrist will share his fate," John replied.

"What fate is that?" Manuel asked.

"God said the fate of the Antichrist is a lake of fire forever."

"Doesn't sound like too great a choice, does it?" Manuel shook his head. "Either take a chance on getting killed by the beast if you resist him, or burn forever in a lake of fire if you decide to go along. That one's gonna take a little thought!"

"Charley," Dave Busby interrupted, "what about this character with all the money? Tell us about him."

John Edwards laughed. "Okay, Dave! Take a look at Revelation thirteen. Here is a picture of another beast. In some ways he appears to be like Jesus, but he talks like the devil. Read verse twelve."

Dave read: "'He exercised all the authority of the first beast on his behalf, and made the earth and its inhabitants worship the first beast.'"

"What do you think that means, Dave?"

"Well, it sounds to me like there's going to be a second beast who comes on like a religious dude. In reality, he's also a big honcho—a political leader or maybe a prime minister. He acts in the name of the big guy, but like his helper . . . a surrogate."

"That's right," John Edwards said. "But, if you read further, you will find that this religious dude, as you say, can do spectacular magic tricks that make people on earth think he represents God. Then, he plays the ultimate trick and tells them to worship a statue of the Antichrist, which he has made to talk."

"Wow!" Miguel Quintana said, quickly covering his mouth with his hands. "Sorry!"

Everyone exploded with laughter. "That's okay, Miguel." John Edwards chuckled. "That's exactly the reaction people will have when it happens. Talking about some powerful beast who does magic tricks sounds like Saturday morning cartoons, doesn't it?" The boys laughed as John Edwards made a sinister face and mimicked the movements of a robot. "But it will be worse than anything on TV. His magic will be very real, very powerful, and very deadly."

"I'm wondering who's going to buy this magic, Charley," Carl said. "If he sets up an idol, it seems to me that people like Orthodox Jews, dedicated Christians, and devout Muslims aren't going to buy it. Most of these people don't go in for idol worship."

"Again, you're exactly right, Carl, but they'll have to pay a terrible price for remaining true to their convictions. If they're caught, they will be executed. But this prime minister for the Antichrist has one more trick up his sleeve, and it will be worse than all the others. Look at verses sixteen and seventeen."

Carl read, "'He also forced everyone, small and great, rich and poor, free and slave, to receive a mark on his right hand or on his forehead, so that no one could buy or sell unless he had the mark, which is the name of the beast or the number of his name.'"

"You know, folks," Charley chimed in, "Dave and I tried to use a check to buy the tents and mess gear for this place. Guess what? My checks were no good. All the bank accounts and brokerage accounts I own are frozen. It's so easy to take away most of a person's money in a crisis like this."

"I know how this system can work," Carl interjected. "My agency did the original campaign to sell the idea of smart-cards. These cards, which look like any other credit card, contain a tiny chip that tracks your bank balance and is debited or credited with purchases and deposits. No checks, no cash, no hassle. But we found out that people were worried about having these pieces of plastic lost or stolen. Guess what the solution was? A tiny surgical implant—a paper-thin computer chip no more than a quarter-inch square. The thing can be inserted very easily under the flesh of your hand by any physician, and it can be read by a simple recognition device—a sort of hand ID-reader. Now, I'm told, they can do the same thing with a laser tattoo. So simple and convenient, we thought it was fabulous."

"Everybody will think it's fabulous, Carl," John replied. "When everybody is out of money, the world government of the Antichrist will start the financial ball rolling by issuing each person credit on a chip. There will be no sale transactions for anything unless the purchaser has the laser chip tattooed on his hand. From then on, a giant network of super computers can monitor every movement, every purchase.

"Just think about it," he added. "Every time you buy groceries, gasoline, a movie ticket, or a book, the system will keep a record. The government will know everywhere you go, everything you earn, and everything you spend. From there, it would be easy to have monitoring stations where you would have to check in regularly like a parolee or a felon on house arrest.

"For someone out of favor with the government," he continued, "the credit balance could be reduced to zero by the powers that be. Then the individual couldn't buy, couldn't sell, couldn't eat, couldn't travel. He would be at the mercy of the dictator. And just as you say, Carl, until the scientific breakthroughs of the nineties none of this would have been possible. Now, the Antichrist and his religious, financial cohort can control the population of the entire planet."

"Except us," Charley whispered.

"Hopefully," said John Edwards, "and not just us. Many people like us all over the world will resist the Antichrist. Charley, why don't you read Revelation seventeen for us, the fourteenth verse?"

"'They will make war against the Lamb,'" Charley read, "'but the Lamb will overcome them because He is Lord of lords and King of kings—and with Him will be His called, chosen, and faithful followers.'"

"Folks," John said somberly, "during the next few years, the Satanic forces are going to do everything in their power to destroy God's people. It will seem for a time that they're winning, just like it seemed for a time that Adolf Hitler was winning—or, more recently, that the Communists were winning. But, the forces of the Antichrist will lose because Jesus Christ is more powerful than Satan."

Lori overheard little Juan Quintana whispering something to his brother, Ricardo, and asked him to say it out loud. "Go ahead, Juan," she said. "Tell everyone what you said. That was good."

Juan's lips were moving, but he had his head down, and no one could hear him, so Lori asked him to repeat it again, louder.

"Good is stronger than evil!" he boomed out, and everybody smiled or laughed at the sudden exclamation.

"Whoa, Juanito!" Dave Busby laughed. "Right on, pal. Good job. How do you know that?"

"'Cause the Bible says that God is good," he said, "and God is stronger than the bad guys."

As the adults remarked about this delightful insight from the group's youngest member, Lori placed her hand on the boy's shoulder. "That's right, Juan. That's the best part of all, isn't it?" All three boys looked at Lori and smiled.

"Thank you, Juan," said John Edwards. "I'm so glad you know that, and I think it's important for all of us to remember that God is the one who will win in the end. One time Jesus said, 'Don't be afraid of those who can kill only your bodies—but can't touch your souls! Fear only God who can destroy both soul and body in hell.' That comes from the Gospel of Matthew, and it's very important. Right, Juan?" The boy nodded.

"You know," John Edwards began again, "I believe that the motto we all need to live by is spelled out clearly in the lessons we've seen in the Scriptures. We are called, we have been chosen, and we are to be faithful. That's why each one of us is here. We have been called and chosen. Now, it's up to us to be faithful."

"Called, chosen, faithful," said Dave Busby. "I like it—the new team motto!"

John Edwards closed his Bible and stood. "Dinner will be ready soon." He turned to the Quintanas. "Let me show you to your rooms."

As if on cue, everyone stood up, stretching and yawning. Manuel said, "I'd just like to ask one last question. I understand what you're saying about the Lord's power. But these two agents of Satan you've been telling us about—do you really think they can pull off some kind of worldwide dictatorship?"

"Manuel, I believe they can, but only for a relatively short time."

"Next question," Carl joined in. "Can you pull off what you are trying to do here?"

"With the Lord's help, we will—or we'll die trying, Carl."

"Jack, if Cathy agrees," said Manuel, "you can count me in. I'd be happy—and lucky, too, I might add—to help you out with your communications and equipment."

"It's more than luck, Manuel," said John Edwards. "It's a calling, and there's work for all of us here. We'll have to get moving quickly. I fear that we're going to be looking into the face of the Antichrist very soon."

CHAPTER SIXTEEN

SUNDAY MORNING WAS two hours away when the exhausted United States cabinet reconvened in the White House Cabinet Room. President Ted Rust was presiding. By his side was his new vice president, Mark Beaulieu. Late the night before, after a lengthy session of the crisis management team, Secretary of Defense Al Augustus had approached Beaulieu with congratulations. He found the man charming, sporting a warm smile and ready wit.

In the midst of the casual banter, Augustus had made an off-hand remark. It was innocuous, inconsequential. But as he looked into Beaulieu's eyes, expecting a twinkle or a grin, he saw something else. The eyes of the new vice president stared back, cold as ice, without feeling. Al felt as if he were looking at someone else. Then, as if a slide had been changed in a projector, the cold expression vanished, and Mark Beaulieu's face was once again filled with the charm and warmth for which he was noted.

As they parted, Al Augustus thought, *Maybe I've been up too long, or maybe I'm hallucinating. But, no, I felt it. It was cold and icy. It was evil. There is something very disturbing, something sinister about that guy.*

Before Ted Rust opened the meeting, Al Augustus again looked at Mark Beaulieu. All he got back was the warm smile of a friend. Perhaps he had been mistaken. Perhaps not.

"We will open this meeting," President Rust began, "with a presentation by our science adviser, Dr. Eisenblatt, of satellite photographs taken during the past twenty-four hours."

Dr. Eisenblatt stood up. His thin shoulders were stooped, his face lined with fatigue. "Ladies and gentlemen, I must tell you that the earth has been convulsed during the past forty-eight hours by the most devastating disaster in human history.

"Much of the devastation occurred at night," he said. "And, even with our infrared photography capabilities, the satellite pictures are of poor quality. Most of the electric power throughout the Pacific area is no longer functioning. However, there are battery-powered satellite transmission facilities in the area that have sent back fragmentary information."

Ted Rust stopped him, "Doctor, I suggest we begin with the United States."

"As you wish, Mr. President," he said. Pointing to a staffer across the room, he directed, "Please dim the lights."

In the presentation that followed, the cabinet endured scene after scene of dead bodies, wrecked ships, collapsed buildings, and forest fires out of control. They were led through countless pictures of panic-stricken people, crazed with fear, trying to escape from hell on earth.

An aide entered the room quietly and handed a note to Dr. Eisenblatt. He read it quickly. "Ladies and gentlemen," he said softly, "I have just learned that only moments ago three dormant volcanoes in the Cascade Range—Mount Shasta, Mount Hood, and Mount Rainier—have all erupted. This means that people in Seattle, Tacoma, Portland, and northern California who escaped the floodwaters by moving to high ground may be killed by the hot gas and debris from these explosions.

"With this information, Mr. President, I would calculate that the death toll in America may reach thirty million people."

What happened next was like a reprise of their first cabinet meeting. "Oh, my God," Ted Rust moaned. He tried to stifle his emotions but could not help sobbing aloud. Benjamin Benares gently led him from the room.

As before, Al Augustus resumed his place as head of crisis management and did not miss a beat. "Please continue, Dr. Eisenblatt."

"We have now learned that, in addition to the three volcanoes in the continental United States, twenty-three more have erupted from Chile to Indonesia. The eruption of Mount St. Helens in 1980 sent ash into eleven states—enough to cover a football field to a depth of a hundred and fifty miles. During nine hours of eruption, Mount St. Helens sent out five hundred and forty million tons of ash. If this figure is multiplied by twenty-six, we can estimate that fourteen billion tons of ash will enter the atmosphere, along with five hundred and twenty million tons of sulfur dioxide and aerosols.

"This is just a rough estimate of how many billions of tons of ash will be thrown into the atmosphere from these explosions," the scientist said, "not to mention the airborne debris caused by the meteor. We know that the stratosphere will be darkened for as long as two years and that the entire earth will be covered with gritty volcanic ash. The streams, reservoirs, agricultural fields, and city streets—everything will be affected."

"Doctor," Al Augustus interjected, "is this absolutely certain? The atmosphere all over the world will be filled with grit?"

"That's right, Mr. Secretary."

"Well, what about jet airplanes? Will they be able to fly?"

"The volcanic ash would soon destroy every turbine engine exposed to it," said Dr. Eisenblatt. "For a period of time, it seems, flight will be restricted—if not eliminated altogether."

"Then, what about land-based vehicles like automobiles?" Al Augustus persisted.

"In my opinion," Dr. Eisenblatt continued, "the volcanic ash would work its way into every engine or piece of machinery exposed to it. Obviously, a closed system water-cooled engine would be less susceptible than an air-driven turbine."

"How long are we talking about?"

"The ash will fall for several weeks. Perhaps a month. Then, it must be cleaned up. We will be faced with removing as much as two feet of ash and sludge from much of the United States. Some of it will never be removed. Eventually, it will be washed away and will settle at the bottoms of the rivers, the lakes, and the oceans."

"You mean that we can't fly for the next month or two?" Al Augustus snorted.

"Not in jets. For that matter, I wouldn't consider flying in a piston airplane for at least a week, except in a grave emergency."

The stir in the room was growing louder. "But what about national defense?" the secretary of defense asked.

"Not to be flip, Mr. Secretary, but that may be about the only good news I can offer. I don't believe we'll need to worry about war for some time," he said with a wry smile. "Most of our weapons of war are already out of commission, and those that remain simply will not function in this type of environment."

"You mean that the ships are sunk, the planes can't fly, the tanks will break down, and the barrels of the artillery pieces will be corroded?" Augustus asked.

"I'm afraid so."

The secretary of state spoke up. "My European counterparts are calling for an immediate summit to deal with this crisis. Are you saying there cannot be a meeting?"

"Mr. Secretary," Dr. Eisenblatt replied, "within a few hours, all global travel by jet airplanes must, of necessity, be terminated. I cannot promise how reliable satellite communications will be through clouds of volcanic ash. I'm afraid that soon satellite photographs will no longer be possible."

"But we must meet to make plans!" The secretary of state was clearly getting upset.

"Mr. Secretary," the vice president interjected, "may I suggest that a summit meeting of heads of state may be premature. We haven't been fully apprised of the damage in Japan, China, and the rest of the Far East. Our own West Coast, Hawaii, and Alaska have been decimated. We can expect flooding in our East Coast and Gulf cities. The banking centers are unable to function. I believe that we lack adequate knowledge of the extent of the problem. It may take days before governments gain control over their own resources. Then we can take a more reasoned look at a plan to put the world back together."

Despite his earlier misgivings, Al Augustus found himself agreeing with the logic of the new vice president. "I must concur with the vice president's analysis. I suggest we focus in on the domestic crisis for now. Any objections?" There were none.

"Assuming that Dr. Eisenblatt is correct," he continued, "we need to take emergency action to protect the nation's machinery from the corrosive effects of volcanic ash. I recommend that all civilian and military aircraft be grounded pending analysis of the effect of falling debris. We should warn factory owners to take steps to shield equipment from outside air. All military gear should be placed under protective covering. Buildings should be shut and sealed. Intake valves and ducts need to have extra protective filters—and those need to be cleaned or replaced almost every hour.

"And, of course, we must broadcast on every available outlet a warning to the population about the airborne dangers facing us in the next few days. We will adjourn for now and reconvene tomorrow. We've all got work to do!"

AL AUGUSTUS AND JAMES WONG walked out of the meeting together. Al motioned to an empty office, and they went in and sat down.

"Jimmy, what's your take on Beaulieu?"

"The guy's obviously brilliant," Wong responded. "Did you hear his put-down of State?"

"That's true, but do you sense anything—well, a little creepy about him?"

James Wong thought for a moment. "Actually, now that you mention it, there was this one incident."

"What happened?"

"I was talking to him about China, and at some point I simply mentioned that Buddhism had come to China from India, and suddenly his eyes changed. So help me, Al, somebody else was staring out at me. Then, as quickly as it happened, there was Mark Beaulieu, gracious and urbane as ever. It was spooky."

Al Augustus became very animated. "Jimmy, that same thing happened to me last night! We were having a friendly chat, and I made some off-hand remark. I don't even remember what it was. Then, there were those eyes—icy cold. I felt a chill go through me like you wouldn't believe."

"Do you suppose, Al, that his appointment is not just happenstance? I remember the things that were said about him several years ago. He was just a crazy leftist kid, then he went to India. Got his wild oats out of his system, I suppose, and came back the very soul of moderation. If there was ever anybody on a greased track for the vice presidency, it was Mark Beaulieu. Valery puts Benares in as chief of staff—then Beaulieu." James Wong scratched his head and added, almost as an afterthought, "It's also apparent that our leader is about ten steps from the funny farm. Al, I don't like any of it."

Al Augustus's expression became very serious. "Jimmy, do you believe in God?"

James Wong was surprised by the suddenness of the question. "What do you mean? Why that? I've believed in money most of my life—not much time for religion."

"Sure, Jimmy," Al went on. "I know that's your front. But I sense something else. Something that goes beyond the polish, the Chinese character, and the smell of money."

"Not much use in putting up a front anymore, is there? When you die, a front dies with you. When I was a boy in China, a Christian missionary who spoke Chinese introduced me to God. At that time I asked Jesus to come into my life. From the way I've lived since then, though, no one would ever have guessed it. But if you're serious, Al, yes, I believe."

A tear ran down Al Augustus's cheek. He was mentally and physically exhausted. Millions were dead, but to him had been entrusted the care of the survivors. Only by his foresight and leadership had the lives of tens of thousands of men, women, and children been spared. He could not carry the burden by himself anymore.

"I've never told anybody about this, not even my wife. But our stories are much the same. When I was ten years old, in a summer church program, I invited Jesus into my heart. Since I became an adult, my 'religion' has been running companies and being a player in public affairs. But with the turn things have taken in the past two days, Jimmy, all that stuff has come back to me, and I have a gut feeling I had better renew my vows while there's still time. I can't speak for you, but I have a feeling we're going to need all the help we can get from here on out."

Chapter Seventeen

U NTIL THAT WEEKEND, NO ONE during the nineteen hundred and seventy years since the time of Jesus had ever witnessed a sea gone mad; no one had ever seen the destruction that would take place on earth when just a small piece of the heavens was shaken loose.

Even great students of the teachings of Jesus never fully realized the significance of the words of their Lord. Now, everyone knew—but for hundreds of millions of people, the knowledge had come too late. This was the end of the age, and many would not survive it.

In his study, laid out rather like the bridge of a sailing ship at the top of the winding stairway in his expansive mountain home, John Edwards struggled to assimilate all that had been happening over the past weekend. Radios, televisions, computers, and a half-dozen satellite dishes on the property of El Refugio fed information into that room, spilling out billions of bytes of data per second.

John listened, deciphered, and made notes—often more like a machine than a man—on a simple yellow legal pad. He was attempting to put the pieces of a great puzzle together—no easy feat. Every free moment he had, he spent in his mountaintop study, writing. On Friday night he wrote:

> When the meteor plunged into the Pacific Ocean last night, it set off a giant wave a mile high that traveled away from the center of impact in a 360-degree circle. The giant wave moved out from the Impact Zone at a speed of five hundred miles per hour, then slowed to three hundred miles per hour at a point two thousand miles away from the impact. As it traveled, the wave height diminished somewhat so that, by the time it reached Japan, its vertical height was five hundred feet.
>
> The earthquakes resulting from the violent impact caused further dislocations in the ocean. Nothing could impede the movement of the first great wave. From then on, the tsunami wave action caused by earthquakes surrounding the Ring of Fire resembled a billiard ball careening off the sides of a pool table.
>
> The Pacific Ocean became a seething caldron as the tsunami waves collided and reinforced one another, in turn sending repeated shock waves north, south, east, and west. Low-lying land areas ringing the Pacific were not lashed by one giant wave, but by repeated waves roaring upon them from unexpected directions and striking at unexpected locations.

He sat and reflected on what he had just written. It was as if the sea had gone mad. Its movements could not be predicted, could not be anticipated. Nothing could be done to quiet it as it raged on uncontrollably, angrily punishing over and over the land mass that contained it.

John Edwards reached over and opened his well-worn Bible and scanned the pages he had read so many times regarding the end of the age. His eyes drank in the words that Jesus Christ had spoken to His disciples in A.D. 30, that before His return, the "sea and the waves will be roaring."

At that time, He had said, "Men's hearts will fail them for looking at what is taking place on the earth, because the power of the heavens will be shaken." Now, here was the fulfillment and the final revelation of those very words.

DURING THE COURSE of the weekend, John Edwards filled page after page with his hasty scrawl and shorthand notes, and little by little he developed a striking portrait of what had taken place in Asia. He recorded the devastation in Japan. Sixty minutes later, the giant wave struck the island nation of Taiwan with its full fury. The capital of Taipei in the north and the great seaport of Kaohsiung in the south were completely inundated. Although some of the Taiwanese people succeeded in escaping to protected mountainous regions in the center of the island, loss of life was beyond measure.

John Edwards wept as he watched satellite feeds from the East showing the destruction. It was the same story again and again. The series of islands making up the Philippines were blasted, and tens of thousands died in only a matter of minutes. In some villages, no warning was possible. In the major cities, warning was unnecessary. Where, he wondered, could people on flat land go to escape a five-hundred-foot wall of water bearing down upon them at three hundred miles per hour?

China, with a population at the last census of 1.2 billion people, is the most heavily populated nation on earth. The largest percentage of Chinese live in the two-hundred-mile region abutting the Yellow Sea and the East China Sea. Roads in China are primitive. The preferred mode of transportation for the average Chinese is the bicycle, Edwards knew, so the possibility of flight from the coming devastation was out of the question.

The government in Beijing had had almost twenty-four hours to alert its population that a meteor would strike the Pacific. But, like their Japanese counterparts, they seemed unable to believe that something occurring near California could have an impact on the people of China.

Even if the Chinese government had given people a warning, what would have happened to two hundred million refugees traveling inland on bicycles with no shelter, no food, and no health facilities? The movement of one million refugees out of the war-torn nation of Rwanda in 1994 had created one of the worst human catastrophes of the twentieth century. John Edwards shook his head. It was impossible to fathom a refugee situation multiplied one hundred, two hundred, or even three hundred times. The logistics would have been an impossible nightmare.

So, John Edwards saw that, not really knowing what action to take, the Chinese government chose to take no action at all. Only those few people with satellite dishes had any warning. Those who depended solely on the government-controlled media had no warning whatsoever.

For most of the weekend, he did not sleep. He sat in front of his television, watching with increasing sadness the news reports of the devastation taking place. The big wave slowed somewhat as it laid waste the Ryukyu Islands, then it surged across the East China Sea, and slammed into the China coast. The people had no notice. The wave hit about two o'clock in the morning when virtually everyone was asleep. Its height was roughly two hundred feet at landfall. The devastation was unspeakable.

He watched infrared satellite pictures of the walls and roofs of dwellings collapsing. He could imagine people lying in beds or on mats, crushed to death. He could almost hear the screams and cries that would have been quickly silenced by the raging seawaters.

He thought of the biblical story of a night in Egypt when a death angel walked the land and selectively killed every firstborn male child of the Egyptian people. In this night of horror along the seacoast of Asia, there was no selectivity. Everyone died . . . the old, the young, the healthy, the infirm, the rich, the poor, the good, the bad.

The main wave traveled about a hundred miles inland before its fury was spent. A secondary wave, spawned by the first, yet of terrible ferocity, flooded the Yellow Sea in a north/south direction, bringing further devastation to the west coast of Japan, then swamping Pusan and Masan on the Korean coast, pouring into Inchon Harbor and from there into Seoul. It devastated the Tiangsu and Shandong provinces of China and the coastal area of Bo Hai.

Little was left of Shanghai, the great port city of China. The thriving port, which had realized thirty-five billion dollars in annual trade just the year before, was laid waste. The proud shops jammed with Western merchandise and the latest fashions were gone. Row after row of elegant buildings that spoke of the days of European colonialism were demolished. It appeared that the entire population of Shanghai had perished under the wall of water.

As the weekend progressed, it was evident from the reports that John Edwards was receiving that the raging angry waves of the Pacific would show no favorites. Hong Kong and Macau were devastated. There was huge loss of life and property across the low-lying coastal areas of Vietnam. The coasts of Australia, New Zealand, and Indonesia were overwhelmed by giant waves.

Water was compressed by the Malacca Straits and gained even greater power.

The island nation of Singapore had achieved its physical growth through vast landfill projects. When the column of water coming through the straits hit, Singapore, for all purposes, ceased to exist. Abnormal tidal action swamped the low-lying areas of Thailand, Myanmar, Bangladesh, India, and Sri Lanka.

Since all of the world's oceans were connected, John Edwards knew that in the past, even a relatively mild tsunami in Asia had caused high water several days later in the Thames River in England. He thought of the times he had tossed a stone in the pond to teach his own children about wave movement and the way concentric motion developed. First, there was an upward splash, then concentric waves of water undulating outward from the splash site, then higher water lapping upward over the bank of the pond around its edges. It was an invariable pattern in nature.

The displacement of water caused by the impact of a three-hundred-billion-pound meteor had an effect on the seawater levels all over the world beyond anything that had ever been experienced in history. To be sure, the land mass of South America, North America, and Asia touching the Pacific had felt the full fury of the impact of the meteor. The action in the Pacific caused not only the Indian Ocean to rise, but also the Atlantic Ocean, the Mediterranean Sea, the Baltic Sea, the Caribbean Sea. In fact, all bodies of water connected to the Pacific rose dramatically in the hours after impact.

The damage in the Pacific to life and property was horrible beyond calculation. The flood damage in the rest of the world, John Edwards estimated, would amount to hundreds of billions of dollars. He paused for a moment from his writing. For he realized another horror had been unfolding over the weekend as well—a horror that would affect the earth for months to come—the eruptions of volcanoes all over the world.

"IN ANCIENT DAYS," John Edwards wrote, "primitive tribes felt that volcanoes were caused by angry spirits. In order to appease these spirits, they devised elaborate rituals and offered sacrifices. Sometimes they even hurled young women into the molten lava in a volcano's crater to win favor with the savage monster that they imagined lurked within."

As recently as 1979, President Suharto of Indonesia had taken part in the ritual sacrifice of eighty animals as an offering to the volcano, Mount Agung, by the people of Bali. Modern, urbane Westerners preferred to think that human and animal sacrifices were relics of the past. But John Edwards knew it was not so. "To this day," he wrote, "the uneducated peoples in rural areas hold an annual festival to offer rice and tonics to propitiate what they perceive as the spirits that lurk behind the fiery caldrons deep in the bellies of volcanoes."

John Edwards watched an interview of a well-known scientist who offered expert opinion that in the first year after the meteor struck, the world would endure from six to eight hundred volcanic eruptions, from the approximately fifteen hundred potentially active volcanoes worldwide. The scientist stated that almost three-quarters of the active cones were located along the juncture of the Pacific Plate and the tectonic plates that bordered it. The presence of these volcanoes in Chile, Peru, Ecuador, Columbia, Guatemala, Nicaragua, Mexico, the West Coast of America, Alaska, Japan, the Philippines, and Indonesia had reinforced the popular term, "The Ring of Fire."

The scientist briefly described the relationship between earthquakes and volcanoes. Earthquakes, he said, were caused by the shifting of the earth's giant continental and ocean crusts, which floated on a fiery hot core of molten rock and metal called magma. The cohesive force of gravity and the centrifugal force of the earth's spinning motion through space served to hold the molten portions of the earth's core in place. Nevertheless, the sheer weight of the earth's crust with its continents and oceans created enormous pressure on the core. That intense pressure, coupled with intense heat, created the potential for extraordinary explosions all over the globe wherever cracks developed in the earth's mantle.

John Edwards copied a portion of the man's words on his yellow pad: "Over time, molten magma seeps through the cracks in the tectonic plates to form large domes. These domes are like balloons being filled with volatile liquid. The pressure builds and builds until they finally erupt." In the margin, he wrote, "The force of a volcanic eruption is beyond anything that has ever been created by any device known to man."

But, John Edwards knew that volcanoes did not erupt only on land. Far more eruptions occur unnoticed under the floor of the Pacific

Ocean. A *National Geographic* special he had once seen described the vast eruptions of lava from under the ocean floor that brought into being the islands and island chains dotting the Pacific Ocean. According to the documentary, islands could appear out of the depths of the water, then blow apart and sink once again beneath the sea from whence they came. But the earth remained volatile and alive beneath them.

Rolling his chair back to the computer in the corner, John Edwards slipped an encyclopedia on CD-ROM into the drive and searched for information on the dates and places that he remembered in part. The most famous volcanic eruption, he noted, took place in 1883 when Mount Krakatoa—which lay eighty-seven miles west of Jakarta, Indonesia, in the Sundra Strait between Java and Sumatra—erupted. The explosion could be heard twenty-five hundred miles away. Reports indicated that atmospheric shock waves from Krakatoa traveled around the planet three times. Skies all over the world were darkened for months because of the cloud of thick ash thrown up by the explosion.

In 1815, when Mount Tambora on the island of Java in Indonesia erupted, it threw fifteen square miles of ash and debris into the atmosphere. Vast portions of the Pacific islands were coated with two feet of thick volcanic ash. The atmosphere was said to be so clouded from volcanic debris that sunlight did not break through. The weather patterns were so disrupted in the American northeast that ten inches of snow fell in June and ice was said to be one inch thick in August.

When Mount Pinatubo erupted in June of 1991, gas and aerosols spewed up eighteen miles into the air. Ash from the explosion fell in Vietnam and Cambodia and even as far away as Singapore and Malaysia. The explosion caused the ground to tremble in Manila. People in the vicinity of the Subic Naval Base and Clark Air Force Base were terrified as red-hot molten lava poured down the mountainside and streams turned into raging muddy torrents.

In the Pacific Northwest of the United States, a thousand-mile chain of volcanoes called the Cascade Range extends from northern California to British Columbia. The last eruption occurred at Mount St. Helens in the state of Washington in 1980.

"Volcanoes," he scrawled in the margin, "kill by what is called *nuee ardente*—the glowing cloud of blistering hot ash, gas, and solid debris; by hot and cold blasts; by hot lava flow; and by mud flows known as lahars. They spread sulfur dioxide in the atmosphere, which creates natural aerosols that wreak havoc on the ozone layer. They send ash and gas into the stratosphere, where they can block out the sunlight for months—even years."

In the year 2000, fully five hundred million people lived in areas directly at risk from volcanic explosions. The thought was staggering.

"IT STARTED SATURDAY EVENING and continued into Sunday morning," John Edwards wrote in longhand, "on what Christians call the Lord's Day. It seems that hell itself has visited earth." He noted that the hideous booms began in Guatemala as a roar from the bowels of the earth, then blew the top off a long-dormant volcano, and launched a plume of fire, steam, and ash twenty miles into the sky. "Then," he wrote, "as if some giant conductor were leading a symphony of evil, a second volcano, more powerful than the first, answered from Mexico.

"In quick succession," he scribbled as fast as his hand would move, "Mount Shasta, Mount Hood, and Mount Rainier rose up and expelled their fury. Then, on and on around the Ring of Fire, one after another, the world's most powerful mountains erupted in a concerto from hell, flinging death and destruction high into the air."

The first, he saw, was Mount Katmai in Alaska; then, Mount Pribilof in the Aleutians; as well as Mount Kiska and Mount Okmok. Soon, they were followed by Mount On-Take in Japan; Mount Canlaon in the Philippines; Mount Semeru, Mount Slamet, and

Mount Raung on the island of Java in Indonesia; then, back again to Mount Lascar in Chile, Mount Cotopaxi in Ecuador, Mount Ruiz in Colombia, and Mount Arenal in Costa Rica. And, once again, around the Ring of Fire toward the west, a new series of violent explosions began to rend the planet.

"Earth trembled. It seemed to wobble in its orbit as though it had gone out of control. The ground throughout the earth shook. The noise seemed unbearable to those alive to hear it. Shock wave after shock wave circled the globe. Sheer terror gripped those in Europe and America. After what had already happened, one reporter asked, was it possible that the earth would actually break apart and everything living would die?

"The sun, the moon, and the stars have been extinguished," he poured out on the paper before him, "by a thick mantle of volcanic ash. The temperatures will quickly begin to drop slowly all over the world. Though we may not feel the worst of it for some time yet, the global winter has begun. In time, it will change the balance of nature on earth."

The writers of the Holy Bible referred to the grace of God as extending to *thousands of generations*. Those same writers again and again told of a time coming in history that would be filled with gloom, suffering, and darkness. It was to be such a short time that they referred to it as the *day* of God's wrath.

John Edwards realized that up to the time of the meteor, no one had fully comprehended how horrible the day of God's judgment could be. Even writers inspired by God Himself could only intimate what would happen. He had not understood until now. But now every living person would know. For nineteen hundred and seventy years, God had demonstrated His grace. During five years of intense effort, His people had gone to every nation, urging people to receive His offer of salvation.

He had set a "day of wrath" and that day was ended, John Edwards now realized. It began on Thursday night. It ended three days later on

Sunday morning. Almost two thousand years earlier, God's Son, Jesus Christ, was arrested on a Thursday night, crucified on a Friday, and lay dead through Saturday to early Sunday morning. Could it be that the weekend of the wrath of God toward earth had followed the pattern of the weekend that brought redemption?

John Edwards brushed tears from his eyes. He turned the page of his yellow pad, then wrote, "We know that as dawn was breaking on the Sunday we call Easter, Jesus Christ rose from the dead. Could that not also be part of the pattern? Could there not also be a resurrection for Planet Earth? Jesus Christ promised His disciples, 'When you see these things come to pass, lift up your heads . . . for your redemption draws near.' Surely there will have to be redemption for us now, after all that has happened."

He leaned back in the big leather chair and breathed in the crisp morning air as the first rays of the sun began to filter in through the windows of his study. "Redemption will come, indeed," he said aloud, "and soon. But not until this planet, which has at long last tasted the very wrath of God, first tastes the wrath of Satan."

PART TWO

CHAPTER EIGHTEEN

B ENJAMIN BENARES PULLED into his driveway about nine
o'clock Sunday morning. He unlocked the front door to his
row house on Nineteenth Street near Connecticut Avenue and
let himself in. He jumped with fright as he caught sight of a man in a
dark suit sitting in the corner of his living room.

As his eyes adjusted to the dim light, he saw that it was his old
friend, Tauriq Haddad. Haddad wasted no words. "Benjamin, my
son. I heard of the breakdown of the president again last night. I fear
he is so unstable that he is no longer of any use to us. Since tomorrow is his birthday, I have brought a special present that I would like
you to give him. It is tightly wrapped now. Under no circumstance—
and this is very important—under no circumstance whatsoever are
you to untie it."

"I understand," said Benares.

"Just before you present the package to him," Tauriq continued,
"pour the substance in this small bottle onto the ribbon on top of the
box. Will you do that?"

"Yes, Tauriq." He asked nothing further. He knew questions would
have been out of place.

"And, Benjamin, tell the president it is a very special gift that must
be opened by him personally when he is alone. If you will, please,

leave the gift on his desk, then ask for a White House driver to bring you here to your home to pick up some work papers. Then you can send the car back to the White House. After he has gone, go out the back of your house. One of my drivers will be in the alley, waiting for you. You will then disappear from the United States."

"So soon?" Benjamin asked.

"Yes," said Tauriq. "It is for the best. But remember, do not untie the ribbon that holds the top on the box."

At that, Tauriq Haddad stood, walked toward the kitchen, and out the back door.

AT 8:00 O'CLOCK MONDAY morning, key members of the White House staff gathered in the Oval Office to wish President Ted Rust happy birthday. They toasted him with glasses of nonalcoholic wine, munched cookies, and sang "Happy Birthday." Benjamin Benares placed his gift for the president in the middle of the president's desk. Just before entering the office he had emptied the tiny vial of liquid onto the ribbon, as he had been instructed to do. Now, he whispered to the president, "Sir, I have brought you a special gift from my home in India. It would embarrass me to have you open it in front of the others. Would you please—*please*, sir, wait until you are alone to open it?"

"Of course, Benares. How thoughtful of you! All the way from your home in India. Will Valery like it?"

"Of course, she will, sir. I feel she will be overjoyed. But now please excuse me, sir. I have urgent matters to attend to."

Benjamin Benares opened the door of the Oval Office and walked quickly downstairs to the side entrance of the White House. "I have left some very important papers at my home," he told the duty officer. "Would you please get me a car and driver?"

"You are in luck, Mr. Benares," the security officer said. "There's one outside now. The driver knows where you live. By the way, I just heard that there is flooding along the Tidal Basin. Tell the driver to keep to the high ground or you won't make it."

Benjamin Benares sat in silence during the ten-minute ride home. He told the driver to return to the White House, then lingered at his front door until he saw the vehicle turn the corner. He carefully turned the key in the lock, opened the door, and walked through the house toward the kitchen.

As he passed through the door to the kitchen, two powerful arms pinned his arms to his sides. Something cold touched his temple, and then a .22-caliber bullet ripped through his skull. One of Benares's assailants unscrewed the silencer from the barrel of the weapon and placed the gun in the dead man's hand. On the kitchen table, under a sugar bowl, the other man placed a computer-generated suicide note that replicated Benares's handwriting. Then they carefully opened the door and went out. Shiva had claimed his first victim.

A second and third were not far behind.

WITH ALL OF THE TRAGEDY crowding his world, Ted Rust appreciated every little bit of kindness shown him on his birthday. He was anxious to see the present his new chief of staff had brought him. He had heard of some of the beautiful crafts created by the people of India. Perhaps this would be something rare and expensive. Perhaps that was why Benares was embarrassed for the others to see it.

So, before his first appointment, he sat down at the desk and pulled the package toward him. And, as he did, the ribbon, already weakened by drops of acid, fell away from the box. As he leaned forward to see what had happened, the top of the box flew back, and a cobra's head reared up in his face. Frozen in horror, Rust remained immobile, and the creature struck like lightning, burying its fangs deep in his neck.

President Ted Rust pushed himself away from the desk and slammed his fist down on the buzzer to summon his secretary, but when she entered the room the president was already sprawled out in his chair in a near-paralyzed state. When she saw the five-foot cobra coiled on top of the desk, she screamed and ran out of the room.

Seconds later, a team of Secret Service agents took control of the situation and called for emergency medical help for the president, who already appeared cold and lifeless. One agent then pulled his .38 service revolver and fired three shots directly into the serpent's body.

But the severe wound it had sustained only served to enrage the creature, and it slithered off the desk and charged the agent. Another agent appeared with a riot gun. One of the officers screamed out, "Blow that sucker's head off!" The blast of the shotgun shattered the glass doors. The headless cobra lay writhing at the agent's feet.

By now it was too late for President Ted Rust. The venom injected in his neck had entered his brain within seconds. There followed an almost instantaneous paralysis of his autonomic nervous system. He stopped breathing. Within minutes, Ted Rust was dead—the first American president ever to die by snake bite.

Thus, Shiva had claimed his second victim. There was one more yet to come.

THE CHAIRMAN OF THE Federal Reserve System, which has responsibility for the money supply of the nation, has been thought by many to have power second only to the president.

The board of governors of the Federal Reserve System had been in marathon session all weekend, trying to coordinate a monetary policy to mitigate the crisis. They had worked night and day to devise a plan that they could coordinate with their counterparts in other developed nations. They had conferred with officials of the World Bank, the Bank for International Settlements, the International Monetary Fund, and the heads of major banking institutions.

As the crisis deepened, a workable solution eluded them. The magnitude of the financial crisis simply could not be grasped while the tragedy unfolded. All they could do was monitor the situation, keep a steady hand, and keep looking for a solution.

The meeting adjourned, and the chairman stepped outside and entered his waiting limousine. He sat down first, then put his feet down. He felt something spongy under his feet and was about to complain to the driver when he felt the fangs enter his calf.

"There's a snake in the car!" he gasped. "Help me!" he called out.

"Mister, this is Washington, D.C. There ain't no snake in *my* limousine!"

The chairman opened the limousine door and fell out on the sidewalk. Several men ran over to help, then jumped back in shock when they saw, sitting on the backseat, a coiled and fully flared cobra.

"Great Gawd Almighty!" screamed the driver. "Call a doctor! There's a snake in my limousine! Hurry! This guy's dying!"

Keeping a wary eye on the strange passenger in the backseat, he opened the front door, turned on the key, and lifted his cellular phone outside. He dialed 911, but they did not believe him. Finally, after more than ten minutes, he was able to summon an emergency ambulance. The chairman of the Federal Reserve died on the way to the hospital. Shiva had claimed his third victim.

CHAPTER NINETEEN

A T ANY OTHER TIME, the entire nation would be in deep mourning over the loss of two presidents in less than a week. But people's personal worries far outweighed the deaths in Washington, D.C. They were reeling from the loss of millions of lives on the West Coast, a shattering economic crisis, broken communications, and ongoing flooding.

Although the worst of the disaster caused by the meteor was over, the displacement of the oceans was still making its presence felt around the world. By Monday parts of London were underwater. The famed dikes in Holland had burst, and seawater was pouring into the low countries. There was serious flooding occurring in the French seaport cities along the English Channel and in the Mediterranean. The major ports of Italy, Malta, and Sardinia, along with Tunis, Algiers, and all the ports of North Africa experienced abnormal tides, as did Athens, Istanbul, Tel Aviv, and Haifa.

The effect on the East Coast of the United States, while less severe, still caused considerable problems. Boston's Logan Airport was closed due to flooding, as were New York's Kennedy and LaGuardia airports. The public, however, would soon have to deal with closures of all U.S. airports as a result of volcanic ash. Floodwaters swept lower Manhattan, closing Wall Street and shorting out underground telephone and electric lines. Low-lying parts of Philadelphia, Wilmington, and Baltimore were covered with water.

Further south, the business district of Norfolk, Virginia, was under several feet of water. Ships in port at the Norfolk Naval Base were rising to a dangerous point above the man-made structures. Charleston, Myrtle Beach, Jacksonville, Daytona, Palm Beach, Fort Lauderdale, and Miami all had four to five feet of seawater flowing in the streets. Life was difficult and becoming extremely dangerous as structures began to collapse. Hot electric wires were falling into the rising waters, and power plants were being shut down for fear of major accidents.

Cities along Florida's west coast were inundated by the rising tides, as well. The line of devastation continued around the Gulf of Mexico, reaching Mobile, New Orleans, Galveston, Houston, Brownsville, and the resort towns along the coast of Mexico.

On top of all this, crime was skyrocketing in the cities, and armed militias were being called into service to halt the bands of outlaws and thugs who were preying on the thousands of displaced persons. These were not normal times, and the death of two presidents within days of each other seemed merely one more piece of a terrifying mosaic of human suffering.

What the people wanted was strong leadership, and many felt that in Mark Beaulieu they had finally found their man. As for the new president, he understood that he had finally achieved the destiny that had been prophesied long ago in Andra Pradesh Province, and he played his role with consummate skill.

First, he visited the grieving widow of President Ted Rust, before the eyes of the world. The meeting had all the pathos and theatrics of a soap opera. With tears streaming down her cheeks, Valery Rust clutched the hands of the new leader and thanked him that he had been there for the nation in this time of need. Privately, he had already offered her the post of secretary of health and human services. She jumped at the chance and immediately began making plans to install her radical sisters in key government posts.

After the courtesy call, Beaulieu arranged for the body of Ted Rust to lie in state in the Capitol Rotunda, along with that of his predecessor. Next, he arranged a solemn funeral procession down Pennsylvania Avenue, and then an elaborate memorial at Arlington National Cemetery, where the bodies of both ex-presidents would be interred with full military honors.

The following morning, the president called the attorney general and demanded a full investigation into the appalling lack of security that had allowed a cold-blooded assassin like Benjamin Benares to be placed in such a sensitive position in the executive branch of the United States government. Two FBI agents were immediately dispatched to the office of Percy DuVal, the head of White House personnel, to make preliminary inquiries into clearance procedures used in the hiring of Benares.

DuVal gave them the thin folder on Benares. Copies were made of all documents in the file and given to the agents. As they signed the hand receipt, they promised DuVal a return visit, and walked out. Fifteen minutes later, Percy DuVal left the office. He drove the two blocks up Pennsylvania Avenue to his favorite restaurant and left his car running at the curb.

The owner was all smiles. "Good day, Mr. DuVal. Have you come for an early lunch?"

"No, Georgio," he said. "I just remembered a call I have to make, and my cellular phone isn't working. I need to use your phone."

"No problem, Mr. DuVal. Please help yourself."

On the third ring, a familiar voice answered. With a hand cupped over the receiver, DuVal said, "Two FBI agents just left my office. They took the file on Benares. Said they'd be back with more questions. What have you got me into?"

"My very dear friend," answered Tauriq Haddad, "you must not worry. Everything will be taken care of. It's a very simple matter, I assure you. Meet me in one hour in the parking lot of the Key Bridge Marriott."

"Okay," said DuVal, as he scribbled the words, "Parking lot—Key Bridge Marriott."

Later that afternoon, a Fairfax County deputy sheriff found DuVal's car parked along a rural road near McLean, Virginia. Inside was the body of the White House personnel director, a shotgun between his legs and his face partially blown off. The medical examiner ruled the death a suicide; there would be no further investigation into the death. However, there was no mention in the examiner's report of the red welt that encircled DuVal's neck. But to those who knew India, this was the mark of the Thuggees, followers of Kali, the consort of Shiva. Shiva had claimed another victim.

With the supposed suicide of Percy DuVal, the investigation into the appointment of Benjamin Benares had only one lead—the Secret Service supervisor who was directly responsible for the security check of Benares. He insisted he was following orders relayed to him through Percy DuVal directly from the president of the United States. He passed a polygraph exam and convinced his superiors he was telling the truth; but his transfer to a low-security farm-belt office job effectively ended his career.

The FBI investigation was quick, but it seemed to satisfy the nation's curiosity, and the national media quickly turned to issues far more pressing.

AT 8:00 O'CLOCK THURSDAY evening, President Mark Beaulieu was to make his first television address from the podium of the House of Representatives to a joint session of the Congress. His address was to be televised to the nation. Immediately after being sworn in, he had fired the White House director of communications. Then he fired the speechwriters, the entire public affairs office, and the entire press office. His congressional staff had not yet gotten settled into the White House, so Mark Beaulieu did something unusual. He wrote his own speech and handled his own arrangements for radio and television coverage. At the same time he made sure that what he had to say would be taped and retransmitted to the rest of the world. It was clear that he planned not merely a message to the American people but a global address that would provide a rallying point for the wounded, the down-trodden, and the dispossessed of the world, along with a new vision for global unity.

As he began his address, an almost supernatural intensity came over his features. His charisma was thrilling. His logic was flawless. His words were electric.

"I speak to you tonight, my very dear friends, not as citizens of the United States or Great Britain or Germany or China or any single nation, but as citizens of the world. For we have suffered together, we have toiled together, we have wept and worked together for one great and noble end—the healing of a broken world. Tonight I speak to you all as one people, one race, one generation dedicated to trans-forming that which is dead and dying, and destined by our fate and our common fortunes to make a world where men and women can live together in harmony."

Mark Beaulieu was the very essence of calm self-assurance. The words flowed like honey, and even hardened media commentators were visibly charmed by his remarkable charisma and brilliance. He never missed a line, never dropped a phrase. He was perfect.

"You and I have survived a time of tragedy by the very will of God who has given us a new mandate to unite as one, as brothers and sisters around the world. We are one, we are the world—we are the family of all mankind."

"Tonight I stand before you in the name of a new order of unity and cooperation in the world and a new alliance of peace that will affirm what you and I believe. No more divisions that separate us. No more wars that destroy us. No more starvation or famine or pain.

"No longer can we stand by silently while honest men and women are being denied the dignity of work. No longer can the fruit of our toil be taken from us by men driven by greed and corruption. No longer can we condone the exploitation of our suffering so that only the corrupt and greedy can live.

"What I bring you tonight, my dear friends," he continued, "is a message of hope for a world dedicated to peace; and thus, I am announcing the formation of a new coalition—a world Union for Peace. Instead of the United Nations, which has failed time and time again to deliver the unity it has so often promised, I lift up to you the Union for Peace. The UP, so named because it will lift us UP—UP from poverty. UP from slavery. UP from repression. UP from tyranny and war.

"In coming days we will work together to abolish the engines of war, to eliminate the armies, navies, and air forces that prey on weakness and exploit our pain. Security is not a remote or regional concern, but a common bond, and instead of giving allegiance to single nations with private armies, our worldwide Union for Peace will guarantee that peace is universal. A world at peace . . . a world united . . . a world that is one.

"We have survived the greatest tragedy in the history of man. But this is not the end. It is the beginning of a new age, which will rise UP from the floods, UP from the earthquakes, UP from the volcanoes. Tonight, I release you from outmoded nationalism. I release you from outmoded traditions. I release you from outmoded and unrealistic secularism. I release you into a life of total freedom within the Union for Peace." Then he lifted his open right hand in the universal sign for peace. On his palm was a bright red dot. Those who watched saw the dot glow intensely bright. They were transfixed by its hypnotic power. Somehow, it was more than a sign. It seemed to be some kind of psychic signal.

Then there was a stir behind the president as the popular Speaker of the House of Representatives stepped down from his seat and hurried to the speaker's platform. The president turned, then stepped aside as the Speaker approached the microphone.

"Mr. President," he said, "ladies and gentlemen, please forgive me. But, like you all, I have been challenged tonight in a way I have never been challenged in all my life. What I have heard here tonight has given me new hope and a feeling of pride I thought I would never feel again. I am, quite frankly, stunned by the vision that President Mark Beaulieu has just described and I, for one, say 'Amen, Mr. President!'

"I say, 'Count me in!,' and I say *yes* to the people all over this nation and the world who applaud you. I say *yes* to the Union for Peace, and *yes* to our common hope. In times like these we need a savior. Tonight I am convinced that our time has come—and a savior has indeed come for us all."

At that, the crowd that had been assembled at the Capitol for the address broke into spontaneous cheers and loud applause as the Speaker grabbed the right arm of the president and lifted it high to the crowds and the television audiences around the world. Then, waving and holding up both arms in a victory salute, Mark Beaulieu said good night. The speech was ended. But its impact had only just begun.

The radio, television, and print media went wild. The effect of the president's speech was overwhelming, and around the world, phone circuits were jammed with calls, faxes, and data communications. Commentators described the new American president as charismatic, compelling, magnetic, and electric. World leaders started falling in line immediately, one after another, competing to see who would be first to embrace the Union for Peace.

Mark Beaulieu was being billed as the one natural leader for the world.

Those in Washington—seasoned political operatives, cynical reporters, members of Congress from both the Left and the Right—had never seen anything like it.

By the next morning, all over the world, as if by some stroke of magic, there was a veritable forest of posters, billboards, bumper stickers, and yard signs, all printed in red letters that proclaimed "Yes to UP!" and "I Support the Union for Peace."

UPON HIS RETURN TO THE WHITE HOUSE, Mark Beaulieu accepted the hearty congratulations of the White House staff and a group of Capitol Hill dignitaries who had gathered to offer their praise. He then entered the Cabinet Room, where he received a standing ovation from the men and women around the big table.

"Thank you, ladies and gentlemen," he said as he took his seat. "I know that the events of the past few days have left us all a bit rattled, so I will make this meeting very brief. I want to thank each of you for your dedicated service to my predecessors. You've been stalwart in this time of great crisis, but I feel that the United States needs a new sense of direction. As of this moment I am asking for the resignation of each of you, along with all other government personnel who served at the pleasure of the previous heads of state. Your resignations will all become effective as of nine o'clock tomorrow morning."

"But, Mr. President," the secretary of energy, Marsha McGovern, spoke up, obviously alarmed by this turn, "so many resignations can only lead to chaos in the government. The people will be horrified, and there will be many more problems than you can imagine. There must at least be a reasonable period of transition. You simply cannot do this."

"Thank you, Madame Secretary," the president said, "but I believe I have all the bases covered for a very smooth transition. There is one last thing, however," he continued. "I would like Secretary Augustus and Secretary Wong to continue in their present posts, if they will agree to do so. Gentlemen," he said to Wong and Augustus, "we can talk now. Thank you, ladies and gentlemen. This meeting is adjourned."

Al Augustus moved quickly to the front of the room. "Mr. President, this is sudden. But if you're making such a big change, why have you decided to keep Jimmy Wong and me on the cabinet?"

"Because, Mr. Secretary, you have the loyalty of the armed forces, and Secretary Wong is important to me for our continued good relations with Asia." Beaulieu looked from one man to the other. "Will you stay?"

"Of course, Mr. President," James Wong said.

"I will as well, Mr. President, if you wish," Al Augustus said. "Do I have authority to continue to deploy resources for the ongoing crisis management operations?"

Mark Beaulieu was already thinking of his next appointment and hardly listened to the secretary's question. "Certainly," he replied hastily, "continue as you see fit. But stick to your game plan." Even the wiliest of men make mistakes. For Mark Beaulieu, president and future leader of the world, this would prove to be one of the biggest.

As soon as they left the cabinet briefing room, Al Augustus pulled James Wong aside in a small alcove.

"What do you make of *that?*" Wong asked.

"First of all," Al answered, "he's cleaning house, putting his own guys in everywhere. It's a coup d'état as big as Hitler and the Reichstag."

"I can see that, but why keep us around?"

"Simple. He knows that the military is loyal to me. Said so himself. When he starts blending our forces into this Union for Peace he's talking about, he's going to want to use me as his Judas goat—to lead the lambs to slaughter."

"Maybe," James Wong replied, "but don't you think he's going to figure out at some point that you're on to him?"

"Maybe. Maybe not. He may very well have a blind spot. He's got some sort of incredible power, that's clear; but he probably figures that because of this power, he can persuade anybody to do anything he wants. If I play along, he may not realize that I understand where he's coming from."

"What about me?" James asked. "What do you think he wants me for?"

"The Asian connection. All of Asia is flat on its back right now. He's probably planning some global money scheme, and he needs you to sell it to the Pacific Rim."

"Yes, but I'm not inclined to do that, Al," James Wong said. "Just how long do you think I can cooperate?"

"As long as possible, I hope. After that, when it gets to the point that you can no longer sell the lie, we had better get you undercover. Whoever is pulling the strings on this operation is a cold-blooded killer. We've had proof of that in no uncertain terms. They'll take you out in a heartbeat if you get in their way."

James Wong winced at the thought.

"I'm going over to the Pentagon to meet with the Joint Chiefs," said Al Augustus. "Want to come sit in?"

"Are you kidding?" James Wong said. "You *know* I do."

AL AUGUSTUS AND JAMES WONG entered the conference room reserved for the heads of the United States armed forces. Military officers with stars and gold braid and row upon row of military decorations worn proudly on their chests stood at attention as the cabinet officers entered.

"Gentlemen," said Al Augustus, moving rapidly to his chair. "I've just come from a meeting with the president. I have full authorization to continue with crisis management operations. That, of course, includes the protection of our troops and our military equipment from the volcanic ash and flooding we've been experiencing."

"Tommy," he continued quickly, "is there any place in the United States where the ash hasn't been falling?"

"Yes, sir, there is," the chief of staff of the air force replied. "The jet stream has moved south so that it's now flowing across the California Coast, up over Nevada and northern Colorado, then almost due east.

That means maximum fall of ash is taking place in the far West, the Midwest, and the East Coast. Other fallout is blowing from Texas all across the Southeast. For some reason, though, there is a reasonably clear pocket down in New Mexico and parts of southern Colorado."

"Very good," Al Augustus replied. "I want to move as many of our assets into that clear pocket as we possibly can. Tommy, I want you and General Clark to work together on this. Deploy whatever army and air force units you can muster, and let's get a base set up outside of Albuquerque. Now, whatever you do, don't get tangled up with the emergency relief operations down there. This is to be strictly military. But I want the Eighty-second Airborne out of Fort Bragg, plus all the C-130s based at Pope Air Force Base. I want a squadron of F-117s out of Langley moved down there as well. Send the Second Armored and the First Cav out of Fort Hood, and the Mechanized Division from Fort Riley. If either of you has further recommendations, I'll be glad to consider them."

"What about tactical nukes, sir?" asked the air force chief. "Don't you think we ought to send them along as well?"

"Good point, Tommy," Al Augustus said, "You'll also need all the communications gear, food, hospital equipment, spare parts, and ord-nance you can get your hands on to sustain a protracted stay. We want to haul as much of that stuff as we can by rail. I'll issue an emergency order so that you can commandeer the rolling stock you need."

He turned to the chief of Naval Operations. "Admiral, can you put the three new Sea Wolf submarines into the water for an extended cruise?"

"In three days, Mr. Secretary. With a full complement of weapons."

"Perfect. I want each of us to have in our possession the necessary authorization codes to contact the three skippers. Admiral, I want these three boats to be under my direct command.

"For the rest, use all maximum efforts to mothball your assets so that this corrosive ash can't destroy them. Keep your personnel on full alert to wash the ash down as soon as it falls. Got it?

"Finally, my liaison for this operation will be a general officer who has been on the ground in Albuquerque. He is General Archie Gladstone. I know this is a bit unusual, but I'm recommending Gladstone to the president for the temporary rank of Lieutenant General. If the president agrees, Gladstone will assume that rank within days. I'd like you all to please give him your full cooperation. Thank you, gentlemen."

As they walked out, James Wong winked. "Al, you're always three steps ahead of the rest of us. I hope you can stay ahead of our very dear friend, Beaulieu."

"Hang on a second, Jimmy. I have an urgent call to make."

He plugged into a secure line and asked the operator for General Archie Gladstone at Fort Bragg. "Archie, this is Al Augustus."

"Yes, Mr. Secretary. How can I help you?"

"Archie, there is an urgent matter of national security. Can you get up here to Washington right away?"

"None of our jets are flying, Mr. Secretary. I have a little single-engine plane that can make it, but it may take me four or five hours to get there."

"Fine. I know it's late, but come directly to my house. You can spend the night—what's left of it—when you get here."

"Yes, sir. On the way. See you tonight."

As Al Augustus left the Pentagon, he wondered, *Who, beside Jimmy and Archie, can I trust? Is there anyone I can confide in who won't betray me?*

As they stepped outside, Al grasped Jimmy Wong's hand. "I'm counting on you."

"And I'm counting on *you*, Al. See you tomorrow."

THE INSISTENT CHIMING of the doorbell woke Barbara and Al Augustus in the middle of the night. Barbara sat up in bed and nudged her husband's shoulder. "Someone's at the door," she whispered.

"I know," he mumbled into his pillow.

"You know?" she said in surprise.

"Forgot to tell you," he said groggily as he swung his legs out of bed. He stood up and reached for his robe, which was on a nearby chair.

"Well, who is it?" she asked.

"Gladstone," he said, heading toward the door. "General Archie Gladstone."

"Gladstone? The head of the relief effort in New Mexico?" she asked.

"That very one," he said. At the door, he turned and added, "I needed to meet with him, and it couldn't wait. I'll put him in one of the guest rooms." He walked back over to the bed, bent down, and gave her a kiss on the cheek; then he left the room and headed downstairs.

Barbara sighed deeply as she lay back in bed. She and Al had been married over twenty years, and she loved him deeply. She didn't know what the meeting with Gladstone was about, but she knew that, whatever it was, it was for the good of the country.

As Al walked down the stairs, their German housekeeper, Evi, was coming down the long front hallway, tying her robe. "Who is that, ringing and ringing?" she asked grumpily. She had been with the family so long that she felt perfectly free to express her feelings.

"It's business, Evi," Al said. "I'll get it."

As she turned and walked back down the hall toward her room, she was muttering to herself in German.

"I'm sorry," Al called after her.

Then he turned and opened the door. "Come in, General. I'm very glad to see you. Flight up go all right?"

"Thank you, sir. Yeah, no problem. But, at the risk of seeming impertinent, what in blue blazes is going on up here?"

"Long story, Archie. But come on, let's sit down where we can talk." Al led the way to the living room and turned on two lamps. "Make yourself comfortable. Do you want something to drink?"

"A little soda with lime would be great—thanks."

Al returned a few minutes later with lime and soda for both of them. He handed Archie his drink, sat down across from him, and said, "Archie, what I'm going to tell you is absolutely top secret. Can I trust your silence?"

"You know that, sir, or you wouldn't have asked me to come up here at this unholy hour."

"That's right, Archie. Well, here's the story," Al Augustus began. "As you know, we had one president commit suicide. The next was killed by a snake bite, and then the man who left the cobra on the president's desk was murdered. They say he committed suicide, but don't you believe it. Now, we've got this ex-campus radical in the White House, and if you heard the speech tonight, you know he's got some mighty big plans.

"Tonight, when we met after the telecast, Beaulieu fired the whole cabinet, except Treasury Secretary James Wong and me. In his speech, he indicated he planned to turn our entire military over to some utopian outfit called the Union for Peace. Archie, I don't know about you, but it sure looks and sounds to me a lot like Hitler, all over again."

"Exactly," said Gladstone. "Except this time it's happening in America and not Germany." Archie Gladstone rolled the cut-glass goblet between his hands. "I don't disagree with anything you're saying, Mr. Secretary. I did see the speech, but I wasn't exactly sure what was going on. There was something weird—almost hypnotic—about that man. But from what I hear, not a lot of people would agree with me on that."

"Well, I certainly agree, Archie," said Al Augustus. "But so far, things are going just fine for our side. Beaulieu has given me carte blanche for crisis management. That includes getting our troops and equipment out of the corrosive ash from those volcanoes. The air force meteorology guys say there's an ash-free pocket near you in New Mexico and another in southern Colorado. I'm moving in what amounts to a combat-ready strike force. Totally undercover, you understand. Maybe we'll never need it—I *hope* we'll never need it. But, along with three big nuclear subs and a good stock of tactical nukes they're laying on right now, we'll have some powerful bargaining chips in our hands if things should—well, get out of hand."

"That may prove to be very important, I'm afraid," Gladstone agreed.

"But, Archie, you're going to need two more stars so I can put you in charge of the outfit. Would you go for that?"

"Naturally, but I'm not up for two, Mr. Secretary."

"You leave that to me. Any hesitation about jumping into this thing?"

"No, sir," he said. "I'll gladly command the units, but when it comes to turning guns on our own boys, or even some world force, that's going to take a lot of getting used to. We'll have to see what happens as this thing plays itself out. But, Mr. Secretary, I can promise you that I will keep my mouth shut about this conversation. I'll keep the units in my command in top-notch shape, and I believe you know you can count on me to do the right thing when the time comes."

"I do know that, Archie," said Al Augustus, "and that's why you're here. But that will have to do for now. One day, we're going to have to fight for our freedom against enormous odds. For now, get used to the thought.

"Now, come on," he said, grabbing Archie's hat and flight bag, "and I'll show you where you can sleep tonight."

CHAPTER TWENTY

J OHN EDWARDS FLIPPED on his high-powered satellite receiver. He and his guests gathered around the large-screen television set to watch the nationwide address by the new president, Mark Beaulieu. But as they listened, John Edwards began shaking his head, registering surprise and alarm at what he was hearing.

"What's the matter, Jack?" asked Carl.

"This is terrifying, Carl," he said, "and no one in the audience appears to see what's happening. Parts of this speech are virtually word-for-word from one of Adolf Hitler's speeches at Nuremberg! I don't suppose there's anyone alive who remembers or who would care, but this sinister, seductive rhetoric he's using—it sends chills down my spine!"

They all listened intently to the rest of the speech. When they saw the upraised hand and the glowing red dot in the president's palm, Cathy grabbed Manuel's hand. "What does it mean, Manolo?" she whispered. "It's so weird."

John Edwards turned. "I'll explain it in a minute," he said, then turned back to the television screen.

When the Speaker of the House began to praise the president and his plans for global unity, John Edwards stared intently at the TV screen. His gaze was so fixed that several in the group wondered what he was seeing that was so compelling.

After the conclusion of the remarks, and as the crowd in the Capitol was cheering, John Edwards turned to his little band and said, "This is a momentous time, my friends, and it confirms so much that we have been talking about. That symbol in his hand is not just a badge or a tattoo. It's the third eye, which means that Mark Beaulieu has invoked the powers of Satan himself."

"What do you mean, 'third eye,' Pastor Jack?" asked Cathy Quintana. "I haven't heard that term before."

"Cathy, you've probably seen Indian women who wear the mark of Vishnu on their foreheads, the dot that is sometimes white or yellow, or more often red." Cathy nodded. "Well, among other things, that dot is a symbol of a third eye—a spiritual eye. Some say it is the eye of cosmic consciousness that comes from their pagan gods. I'm certain the dot on Mark Beaulieu's hand represents the same sort of thing.

"What we heard was not the man on the screen. They were the words of a powerful demon speaking through the man he now controls. By his actions and his words, he gave permission for the host of demon power to be released on earth for five months. Did you notice he used the phrase, 'I release you,' four times? This means he released demon power to the four corners of the earth. Everyone will suffer. There will be no place to hide."

"When the five months of intense suffering and agony are over, the very man that you just saw on television, now possessed by a powerful demon prince, will be possessed by Satan himself. I have no doubt that President Mark Beaulieu will become the political leader of the entire planet. I am sorry to say it, but the man you saw, the president of the United States, will one day very soon assume the power of the Antichrist."

"Jack," Carl asked, "how do you know these things from just that one speech?"

"Carl, I watched his eyes. His eyes told it all. I don't know if you noticed, but they actually changed. One minute they were the eyes of President Mark Beaulieu. But the next, they were the eyes of a demon. Beaulieu can seem very kindly, but I believe that if anyone crosses him, he will be capable of exploding in an uncontrollable demonic rage."

"But, Jack," Carl said, "surely you must be basing your opinion on something more than that. I watched his eyes and sure, I saw some very animated and even contradictory expressions, but—the eyes of a demon?"

"Perhaps you're right, Carl," John Edwards said, sitting on the edge of the sofa. "I saw his eyes and the red dot on his palm. But, also, I feel clearly that the Lord told me in my spirit that this is the man."

"This guy is the president of the United States of America," Manuel spoke up after listening quietly to the ongoing debate. "How can the U.S. president be some character in a book by the apostle John?"

"Manuel," John replied, "I have absolutely no biblical authority to back me up on this part. Much that John wrote in Revelation about the Antichrist makes it look like he would be a Roman emperor more than anyone else. But there's one thing to keep in mind. All the modern European nations are continuations of the Roman Empire. The United States is the offspring of Great Britain, France, and Spain, not to mention Germany, Italy, and other European countries whose people settled here. The U.S. is the end and the greatest expression of Western civilization that sprang from the Roman Empire. The world has looked to the United States for leadership for almost a hundred years; so why *wouldn't* our president be the most likely candidate for world leader—or world emperor?"

"Pastor Jack, I have a question too," Cathy said looking across at John Edwards. "What do you mean that demon power is going to be released on earth?"

"Revelation predicts five months of demonic torture for everyone on earth who doesn't belong to the Lord," he answered. "That means we in this room are all safe, but it will be hell on earth for everyone who is not a believer in Christ for the next five months. Chances are, the entire world is going to seem like a giant lunatic asylum. We saw the signal just now on television. I believe that was the very moment in which the demon hordes were released to torment people all over the earth."

THE MORNING AFTER HIS SPEECH, President Beaulieu sent the nominations for his new cabinet to the Senate. Without question, it was the strangest assortment of nominees ever presented for confirmation in U.S. history.

For secretary of education, the president had selected a Buddhist monk who shaved his head and dressed in a saffron robe and sandals. For secretary of agriculture, he asked for a shepherd from Nevada who lived alone in the hills and spoke broken English. The man's only known "credential" was that he had once played jai alai in Las Vegas. For secretary of energy, he named a Lebanese Shiite Muslim who was a member of the terrorist group, Hezbollah, and ran a filling station in Dearborn, Michigan.

For drug czar, he picked a man who had spent his life crusading for the legalization of all narcotics. For secretary of state, a professor of Eastern religions from Harvard University who had close ties to Shoko Asahara, the leader of the Japanese cult of Shiva worshipers known as Aum Shinri Kyo, or Supreme Truth. They had been linked with a poisonous gas attack in a Tokyo subway in 1995. And he chose for attorney general a militant black feminist attorney who advocated abolishing the death penalty and closing all prisons.

It was as if the new president was deliberately attempting to ridicule the agencies of the United States government in order to create sentiment for their destruction.

In contrast with the changes in the administration implied by the president's strange nominations, his request that Al Augustus be reconfirmed as secretary of defense and that James Wong remain as secretary of the treasury seemed odd only because they were so logical and appropriate. But perhaps most surprising was that his new appointments were totally out of character with his previous persona. All except the man he selected to control the nation's money supply. For the post of chairman of the Federal Reserve board, he nominated the brilliant international banker, financier, and philanthropist, Tauriq Haddad.

By the time the nominations hit the floor of the United States Senate, that famed deliberative body more closely resembled a ward for the criminally insane. The presiding officer on that day was a junior senator from Massachusetts, who sat on the dais talking to himself and slapping an invisible being that was leaving wet teeth marks on his hands.

The majority leader was banging his hand on his desk, yelling, "Stop it! Stop it!" while the minority leader was pacing up and down the aisle, jerking his head violently from side to side, his hands shaking as if from palsy. Other members were slapping and rubbing parts of their bodies as if they were being bitten by invisible beings. While all this was going on, other members either calmly sat at their desks in the Senate chamber watching in bewilderment or fled to the safety of their offices.

But scenes just like this were being repeated not just in the U.S. capital but in cities and villages all over the world. Some people were walking about calmly, while others were cursing, biting themselves, striking themselves, and rolling on the ground, begging invisible tormentors to leave them alone. The vehicles that were making their way through clouds of volcanic ash were swerving violently on roadways as their drivers wrestled with invisible assailants.

Pharmacies sold down to bare shelves their supplies of painkillers. Prozac, Valium, Librium and other tranquilizers were soon exhausted. But all to no avail. Nothing would stop the torment that was driving men and women insane. Those who were not being attacked tried to offer assistance. Not only were their overtures not appreciated, but they also found themselves being physically and verbally assaulted by the sufferers. There were cries and curses everywhere. The entire world had seemingly gone mad. There was no relief in sight.

In this milieu, naturally all meaningful work stopped. Farmers could not plant or harvest. Factories could not produce. Salesmen could not sell. Some people were tormented all night long, and in the morning they would appear with bite marks all over their bodies. Others developed welts from poisonous stings by invisible insects. The minute sleep would come, another torment and another horror would wake them. Millions of men, women, and children went about during daylight hours like zombies.

Others could sleep, but they could not work. Every time they began a task, they suffered sharp, excruciating pains that no pain-killer, no antibiotic, no salve would heal. Before long, the mental torment far exceeded the physical. People lived through hell every day in their own minds. All they knew were pain, torment, and curses.

As a result of these disturbances, an extraordinary phenomenon developed. The only group of people who could produce or get restful sleep were those sealed by God. All others were under unrelenting assault. Those who had always considered spiritual matters beneath their dignity or something to be postponed until later often seemed the most undignified and disturbed of all. Those who were fully committed to God's side were able to continue their work.

The mental and physical torment by unseen demons was more than some people could bear. They alternately cursed God, then begged to die. After a few days of torment, many were driven completely insane. The torture continued, but their minds seemed disconnected from what was taking place. Suicide attempts were increasingly common. People shot themselves, hanged themselves, took poison, and jumped from bridges. Yet, whatever they tried was unsuccessful. Nothing could save them from the torment. Even death would not come.

To add to the misery, volcanic ash was everywhere. Streets were filled with muddy goo. The air was polluted. Not only were streets filthy, offices were filthy, homes were filthy, furniture was filthy, people were filthy. And little by little, they were also beginning to feel the effects of the temperature inversion brought on by the clouds of smoke and ash in the air. No sooner had the agonizing heat broken than temperatures began to fall all over the country. They had gone from the blistering heat to an unrelenting chill in such a short period of time that even this change had become a sort of hell for many.

At one point John Edwards compared what was happening to the play about hell written by the French existentialist, Jean-Paul Sartre. The play was called *No Exit*, and no description could have been more apt for the world engulfed by demon hordes. There was no escape, no release, no death—no exit.

Those who knew their Bible realized that the torment was only going to last five months. But those who suffered believed it would never end. On television, on radio, in every type of printed literature, appeals were made to those who suffered. The message was simple: If you are tormented, surrender in faith to Jesus Christ, and the devil's torment cannot touch you any longer.

The message was so straightforward. Yet, people writhing in agony chose to curse God and His messengers rather than accept the only way out of their misery. Incredible as it might seem, they deliberately chose to suffer demonic torment rather than humble themselves, turn from evil, and receive God's pardon.

AS SECRETARY OF THE TREASURY under President Mark Beaulieu, James Wong redoubled his efforts to free up the stalled credit mechanisms of the United States. He knew that the overlapping functions of the Treasury Department and the Federal Reserve created a murky situation, at best. But to avoid catastrophe, James

Wong determined to encourage as close a relationship as possible between the two institutions.

When Tauriq Haddad took office, James Wong accomplished coordination of his efforts with the new chairman. He found this shadowy figure as enigmatic as his boss. Tauriq Haddad was at once urbane, charming, fascinating, and coldly calculating. He could be gracious and self-effacing, or aloof and totally lacking in basic human emotions. *He is exactly like Mark Beaulieu*, James Wong thought. *There is something wrong with this fellow's eyes. Somebody else is living there inside him.*

However, James could not let his suspicions stand in the way of doing his job. So, working together, he and the brilliant Middle Eastern financier quickly developed an interim financial plan for the United States. They worked in apparent harmony, but James could see looming ahead a deadly confrontation over Haddad's long-range plan to introduce a global financial system based solely on numbered computer accounts. He knew that one day his opposition to Haddad's plan would cost him his job—and possibly much more. But being a man of conviction with an inherent sense of honor, the secretary simply steeled himself for the anticipated encounter.

What they set in place for the short term was relatively simple. The banking system of the United States was temporarily disengaged from international clearing houses. The West Coast banks, plus those in Hawaii and Alaska, were written off. Force majeure was declared to block any claims under the Federal Deposit Insurance Corporation. All West Coast corporations were declared bankrupt and de-listed from various stock exchanges. Claims against surviving banks, brokerages, and other corporations by the estates of those who had died were held in suspended accounts pending the presentation of documented proof.

All contract claims and debt claims relating to the stricken region were placed in suspense for one year. Wong and Haddad followed the same method in regard to the investments of U.S. citizens and companies in Asia, the claims of Asians against U.S. assets, and the de-listing from U.S. exchanges of the stock of Asian firms that had traded as American Depository Receipts, or ADRs. The accounting task was monumental. But working under simplified regulations, teams of accountants and auditors—thousands of them all across the nation— brought the chaotic mess to some order. Banks and exchanges opened under new guidelines within thirty days, and little by little the economy began to stabilize.

Massive losses had taken place that were irreversible. The volatility of commodity prices, currency prices—in fact, all prices—meant that trillions of dollars worth of options and other derivatives must either be canceled or the entire financial system would be destroyed. Wong and Haddad took the only way out. They declared all derivative contracts to be invalid. Traders must start again. To some, the physical losses meant bankruptcy. To others, the cancellation of crushing financial obligations was like manna from heaven.

Both men realized that the immediate inflation of prices following the disaster was temporary. But what they feared was a long-term depression with factories closed and millions out of work. So, they agreed that interest rates would have to be lowered and generous credit would be made available to member banks by the Federal Reserve board. The Fed would then purchase one hundred billion dollars of treasury notes, which, in turn, provided funds to the federal government to pay for disaster relief, the ongoing clean-up, and other vital services.

James Wong could not fault Tauriq Haddad's performance. Their joint operation was masterful and enormously successful. But it was clear that Haddad had a much more sinister agenda. For now, he needed a prosperous America to pay for his global schemes. It would be only a matter of time before he enslaved the American economy and used it to enslave the world.

JAMES WONG ACCOMPLISHED in thirty days what some men could not have done in thirty lifetimes. He wanted to leave Washington for a rest, but he was unable to do so because of what had happened to his wife.

Joyce Wong, the former Joyce Cumberland, came from old money. She had grown up as the daughter of privilege. Her passion was for the outdoors. At ten, she was winning blue ribbons in equestrian events. At twelve, she won a junior sporting clays skeet tournament. She was also an excellent swimmer, played tennis, and was a low-handicap golfer.

Blonde, tanned, with beautiful but prominent features, Joyce looked every bit the patrician. Her clothes were always the most expensive, yet her look was understated elegance. Before the chaos began, her name often appeared in programs as a patron of major southern California charities—art museums, symphonies, charity auctions, and hospital events.

For Joyce Cumberland Wong, this was all there was in life. She was never ostentatious, but she took for granted a mansion filled with costly antiques, Impressionist paintings, and imported Oriental carpets. She believed that memberships in exclusive clubs, high-powered imported cars, a staff of servants, and a circle of equally privileged rich friends were normal. She had never known anything else.

No one would say that Joyce was immoral, or even amoral. She cherished the standards and values of her class. She was, pure and simply, secular. She lived life on only one level—the level of the materialist. She was extraordinarily self-assured. She knew who she was, and she liked that person very much.

When the torment came, Joyce Cumberland Wong believed that she could handle it. A few insect bites could not faze her. But as the onslaught grew more intense, she began to break. She could not sleep. She could not eat. Her mind and body were tormented. Her face became gaunt. Black circles appeared under her eyes. Her appearance was, for the first time in her life, unkempt. She would walk the floor at night and scream for relief.

Her husband was among the unaffected, and he tried to persuade her that her torment would cease if only she would surrender her life to Jesus Christ. But she rebuffed his entreaties. She was Joyce Cumberland, not some weakling who had to prostrate herself before some bleeding Messiah. The Cumberlands could endure pain. But *never* would a Cumberland become one of those weird holy rollers!

So, as the difference between her own condition and that of her husband grew more and more pronounced, she began to hate her husband. While she suffered, he was totally without pain. He was always well-rested and content while she was on the brink of insanity. He kept talking to her about Jesus until she couldn't stand it anymore. One night she exploded in rage, "You smug little Chinaman! My family told me not to marry you! I hate the very sight of you! I want you out of my sight!"

Later, she apologized. She tried to explain that she was blinded with pain. James forgave her for her words, but the wound remained. Whatever love they had once shared was gone. The real Joyce Cumberland had burst through, and James Wong knew that when the time came to make a stand, his wife would choose possessions, power, and lifestyle—she would not choose him.

CHAPTER TWENTY-ONE

A FTER ABOUT THREE WEEKS, the volcanic ash had either settled to the ground or entered the upper atmosphere. This meant that jet travel between twenty thousand and twenty-nine thousand feet, though still dangerous and ill-advised, was marginally possible. Given the opportunity to begin taking their program to the world, Mark Beaulieu and Tauriq Haddad boarded the expensively equipped presidential 747 with its specially constructed engine filters and began a string of whirlwind meetings with leaders around the world.

For the people at El Refugio, it seemed ironic that the man who was to become the Antichrist had to choose a Christian flight crew, Christian security detail, and a Christian advance team. Because of the demonic assault, no other trained specialists were available to fill these key posts.

At every stop on their itinerary, the crew found that airports were open for very limited periods of time due to the limited number of torment-free specialists available to work air traffic control.

Beaulieu and Haddad found each of the world leaders they met desperate for solutions. Everywhere, the message was much the same. The president of Germany echoed the sentiments of all the world leaders when he said, "Mr. President, you are the most gifted leader in the world today. We are desperate people. Our economy is in shambles. The mood of the country is ominous. The torment, the cold, the darkness, the lack of basic necessities will bring on revolution and bloodshed. We want you to formulate a plan to restore peace and economic stability to the world."

The leaders of every nation told Mark Beaulieu what he most wanted to hear: "If you do as we ask and restore the peace, we will gladly join the Union for Peace. To secure peace, we will agree to place our armed forces under a unified command. What other arms are left, we will destroy. We will demobilize all other military forces. And, especially, we want you to be our leader. You must become the president of the Union for Peace. You must be the leader of the new world order."

For his part, Tauriq Haddad was singularly successful. The leaders of central banks all over the world agreed that credit must be restored to the world economy. They agreed on emergency measures. But Tauriq's principal goal was not to restart credit; instead, it was to implement a totally new financial system. To his delight, he found no objection to the proposal that they work together to formulate a new system of finance that would do away with cash and checks. It was to be a system that would eliminate national currencies in favor of one unified, global currency, under the finance directorate of the Union for Peace.

THE PRESIDENTIAL VISITS extended as far east as was feasible; then, because of the devastation in the Pacific region, the entourage retraced their steps back through the Middle East. En route, they stopped in Baghdad and were warmly greeted by the new president, Ibrahim bin Ishmael. Bin Ishmael claimed to be a descendant of the first Ishmael, the son of Abraham by the servant girl, Hagar. The first Ishmael was thought to be the progenitor of all the Arab people.

This unusual leader was an Arab mystic who was persuaded that the heritage he had received from his family—the family of Ishmael—was superior to that of the camel driver, Mohammed. Thus, he spent many hours in solitary prayer vigils, seeking supernatural revelations that would equip him to offer new religious truths to his people.

When Ibrahim bin Ishmael looked into the eyes of President Beaulieu, he did not see a man at all. Instead, he saw a white city in the desert. He saw marching armies. He saw people falling down in worship. At that precise moment, he received the revelation that he had been seeking. Something strong and powerful and seemingly all-wise had entered his being. Consequently, he was not merely willing to follow the political leadership of this president from America, he was also willing to worship him.

After they had spent time discussing the concept of a global union to secure peace for all people, Ibrahim bin Ishmael said knowingly, "I want to take you, my friend, to the place at the mouth of the Euphrates River where all civilization began. I will show you Ur of the Chaldees where Abraham, our father, was born. And then I will show you ancient Babylon, the great capital city of Nebuchadnezzar."

The official party flew in a squadron of helicopters to the ancient site. As they walked the ruins, Mark was lost in thought: *I have been here before! I feel a sense of history . . . of destiny!* He knew without question that he was part of the great unfolding of the struggle of human civilization that had begun in Akkad and Ur, along the banks of the Tigris and Euphrates rivers.

But it was not until they reached the site of Babylon itself that Mark Beaulieu truly realized his destiny. As Beaulieu, Haddad, and Bin Ishmael walked through the desert ruin and the partially finished reproduction palace begun many years ago by Saddam Hussein, he saw it clearly. At Babel, all of the people on earth had been divided from one another by the barrier of language. Now he was here. President Mark Beaulieu would accomplish what no other human had ever achieved. He would unite all of the people on earth into one great union . . . a Union for Peace.

Mark Beaulieu felt a power far greater than anything he had ever known fill his being. He had attained his destiny. He would lead the world. In his mind's eye he saw gatherings of troops and armies as vast as the sea. He saw bombs falling and weapons firing. Millions of men of war would go forth under his leadership to destroy those who would oppose the Union of Peace. Now he knew how it was supposed to be. Now he understood his destiny.

President Mark Beaulieu was interrupted from his reverie by the voice of an excited Ibrahim bin Ishmael. "My friend, I see it now!" the Iraqi leader proclaimed. "Rising from this very place will be a great palace and a magnificent capital. Babylon will be restored, and the destiny of all mankind will rise from its slumber. Here, in this very place, will be the capital of the world—*your* capital! The world headquarters of the Union for Peace."

As bin Ishmael spoke Mark Beaulieu could see it too. There were lavish, tree-lined boulevards. Stupendous buildings with giant marble columns that towered a hundred feet above the heads of the people who thronged there for his leadership and his judgments. The Congress Hall for the Nations. His personal headquarters. And at the very center, elevated above all the other structures, would be the temple of the Church of World Peace. Yes, it would be large, stately, imperial, and capped by a dome covered with glistening twenty-four-karat gold. It would be *his* temple! His *destiny!*

And inside the temple, built to resemble the Jefferson Memorial in Washington, only much larger, would be the statue. He saw the scene in his mind's eye: Worshipers were prostrating themselves before it. As Mark gazed into the mists of that enchanted vision, the picture in his mind snapped into focus. The statue was speaking. It was his face, his body, his voice. The statue in the temple to be built in Babylon was—it was *him!*

"My friend," he said to the Iraqi leader, "I share your enthusiasm. But if we were to build the center for our Union for Peace here, how long do you estimate it would take?"

"If cost were no object, Mr. President," he said, "we could easily conscript a hundred thousand or more of the most skilled construction workers from around the world. We could import equipment, materials, and mobilize vast resources from everywhere to complete the project in record time. Giant cranes and earth-moving equipment would be needed. We could hire artisans, engineers, craftsmen—the very finest in the world. I believe that in three years we could erect— here on the place where we now standing—the physical structure for the government of the world."

Beaulieu turned slowly. Where there was only barren earth and sand, he saw great towers and soaring columns. Where there were coarse, scruffy weeds, a vast city would arise. "In three years, Haddad and I can build the political and economic structure for the greatest government of mankind in all recorded history." As the two leaders clasped hands, they said in unison, "We will build it together."

On the flight back to Washington, Haddad and Beaulieu were intoxicated by the prospect of what lay ahead. As they were enjoying a delicious dinner and a bottle of vintage wine, Tauriq Haddad remarked, "It will be a palace fit for the Messiah himself."

"That's an interesting expression," the president replied. "Why do you choose it? And what do you know of the Messiah?"

"Why do you ask?" said Tauriq.

"My mother Rebekah died when I was a small boy. But I remember that she often spoke to me of the Messiah—the one who would come as savior of the nation of Israel and the world. His name, she said, was to be Immanuel—'God with us.' She told me that observant Jews were constantly speaking as if the Messiah could return any day— to restore the glory of their nation. Yet, no one ever came."

Tauriq Haddad looked deep into the eyes of Mark Beaulieu and said softly, "I am glad that you possess this knowledge, my very dear friend. But I suspect you know much more than you are saying. For when you meditated at the feet of Shiva, you received a vision, and you knew, even then, that there was a destiny ahead of you.

"For you, my very dear friend," Tauriq Haddad said, as he turned his head and bowed slowly before his leader, "are the messiah. *You* are god come in the form of a man."

CHAPTER TWENTY-TWO

SECRETARY OF DEFENSE Al Augustus lost no time while President Beaulieu was out of the country on his extended mission. Before he left the country, the president had signed off on giving Archie Gladstone his second and third stars, promoting him to the rank of lieutenant general. Congressional approval was perfunctory. The president also signed an executive order authorizing the secretary to take all necessary action during the crisis to protect United States military installations.

With the gradual thinning out of the volcanic ash, it was now possible to begin deployment of aviation units as well as ground units into the Ash-Free Zone. Augustus had located a virtually abandoned military storage depot in southern Colorado near Pueblo. The commander's operations task force was able to report that the Pueblo depot took in 22,500 acres, with some 922 igloos, or weapons storage bunkers, of which 102 were storing 2,475 tons of deadly mustard gas. The facility also housed two completely equipped 400-bed portable military hospitals. In addition to the ammunition storage igloos at the depot, there were also a thousand unused buildings.

The Pueblo Depot had been the site, years earlier, for the destruction of the Pershing intermediate-range nuclear missiles.

Secretary Augustus determined to position his forces on the east and west foothills of the Sangre de Cristo Mountains—Spanish for the "blood of Christ"—which divided Albuquerque in the west from Pueblo in the northeast.

As the buildup began, traffic toward the staging areas accelerated dramatically. Trains were now moving. Truck convoys with armaments, equipment, housing and shelter materials, as well as food and expendable items, filled the roads. Huge quantities of fuel, ammunition, and rations were in transit day and night. Now that limited low-level flying was permitted, the flood of supplies in and out of Albuquerque increased at an even faster pace.

General Archie Gladstone had never before visited the Pueblo facility. He hardly knew of its existence, but he was delighted by the spacious accommodations, which he deemed easily large enough for two or more reinforced combat divisions. But what else he learned after his own detailed inspection amazed him.

He called Al Augustus on a secure line. "Mr. Secretary, I thought all Pershing missiles were supposed to have been destroyed here by the end of 1991 under the terms of the treaty President Reagan signed with the Soviets."

"Of course they were," said Augustus. "There *are* no more Pershing missiles."

"Well, there are now," said Gladstone.

"What are you talking about? There can't be any Pershing missiles at Pueblo."

"Mr. Secretary, I just counted ten fully intact Pershings here at Pueblo. What are your instructions?"

Al Augustus paused briefly, then answered, "Don't tell anybody about them. After the base is completely secure, I want you to make them operational. Are the warheads there too?"

"Negative. But I know where they're located. When I obtain the warheads, where do you want the missiles targeted? I suppose you know they're quite capable of reaching Washington from here?"

"Yes, Archie," he said, "I know their capability. For the time being, don't target any place. I pray that no one will ever have to set off one of those horrible things. However, it'll make a good bluff when we have to deal with our weird friend at the White House.

"By the way, General," Augustus continued, "I've located seven of the Little Giant antimissile systems. I'm told they're twice as effective as the Patriot. They can knock out incoming missiles a hundred and fifty miles out. Right now, they're on their way to you. One day you may need them. But remember, your orders are that your units are to be engaged in an extended maneuver to avoid contamination of our assets by falling ash—nothing more. Is that understood?"

"Understood, sir. And thank you."

Archie Gladstone had his work cut out for him, and he needed to recruit a large staff—and quickly. After two months of the torment, and with continuous demonic attacks, it had become clear that certain people were affected by the torment and certain ones were not. Only the unaffected were capable of performing any meaningful work. It was also clear that the presence or absence of torment depended on an individual's religious beliefs. However, employers who wanted to hire only torment-free workers ran into legal problems when it appeared that they were hiring solely on the basis of religion. Fortunately, the bureaucracy had coined the terms "affected" and "unaffected," and under emergency legislation passed to deal with the crisis, unaffected workers were given preference in sensitive positions. Thus, with unaffected officers assigned on temporary duty to assist him, General Gladstone accomplished in record time the orders that had been given to him by the secretary of defense.

PRESIDENT MARK BEAULIEU arrived back in Washington just in time to face a major political campaign. Not only was his seat up for grabs, but so were the seats of all of the members of the House of Representatives and a third of the Senate.

Many powerful groups bitterly opposed taking the United States into a new world government. There was even more vocal opposition to massive disarmament followed by merging the remaining forces of the United States into a multinational peacekeeping force. To complicate the matter even further, the president was having to deal with vocal and sometimes dangerous domestic discontent. Incumbent administrations get blamed when things go wrong, and things were certainly wrong all over the world. The so-called "misery index" dipped so low that it could scarcely be measured. The president's approval rating fell to a non-electable 40 percent.

Mark Beaulieu scheduled a major television address exactly four months and twenty-nine days after the beginning of the torment that had been driving the earth mad. After his usual promise of peace, economic security, full equality, and world brotherhood, he made a stunning announcement. "I know of your suffering and your pain. I have prayed for you—for each citizen of America, and each citizen of the world. My god has assured me that, as a token of his favor, he will cause the curse to be lifted off the world at my command.

"Therefore, I command that at one minute past midnight this very night, all spiritual forces that have been tormenting the earth shall return from whence they came. I command them to set you free." He opened his right hand toward the camera, and the red dot glowed brightly, as before. He then closed his right hand into a fist, and the light was apparently extinguished.

At precisely one minute past midnight on the thirtieth day of the fifth month, all demonic torment ceased. God, not Satan, had been blamed for the torment. And for this great deliverance, Mark Beaulieu received all the praise. He was hailed as a righteous man, a holy man, a powerful and compassionate leader. Overnight, the polls showed that his approval rating had soared to 90 percent. His election was assured.

But, Tauriq Haddad still wanted more. He wanted control of the United States Congress. He wanted to replace many of the incumbents with his own hand-picked people. Tauriq organized what he called "Truth Squads" to travel to each congressional district and to demonstrate face-to-face to incumbent congressmen how undesirable it would be for them to continue in high public office. The majority saw the "truth" right away and announced their plans for retirement.

In addition, the news was widely circulated of sitting members of the House and Senate who were severely wounded while being robbed at gunpoint by juvenile criminals. In some cases, their automobiles malfunctioned at high speeds. Some were arrested for dealing in narcotics. Photographs were widely circulated of other members accepting bribes from known criminals.

By October, less than a month from the fall elections, roughly half of the incumbent members of both houses of Congress had declared their intention to resign.

It was eminently clear that the new chairman of the Federal Reserve board was not making the slightest attempt to maintain even a thin veneer of political neutrality. He emerged as campaign manager, traveling companion, and chief confidante of President Mark Beaulieu. The new president declined to fill the now-vacant vice president's office, and he did not replace the late Benjamin Benares as chief of staff. Tauriq Haddad became, in effect, the surrogate president, chief of staff, and vice president.

Two weeks before the election, Mark Beaulieu was scheduled to deliver a rousing speech at a giant patriotic rally at Soldier Field in Chicago. Tauriq Haddad arranged the entire event, complete with flags, banners, marching bands, and an enormous pyrotechnic display of an American flag to be set off at the end of the president's speech.

The event was carried on national television with arrangements for retransmission worldwide. Everything, down to the wild applause of the crowd, was carefully orchestrated. Nothing was left to chance—nothing, that is, except the unexpected.

At the closing of the president's speech, he stood before the blazing American flag. But, just as the crowd rose in a thunderous ovation, a swarthy man in the front row pulled a .44 Magnum from under his coat and screamed, "Death to the New World Order!" He fired a volley of five shots at the stunned leader. With the sixth shot, the gunman turned the weapon on himself and ended his own life.

Four of the five bullets scored direct hits on the president. He was wearing a bullet-proof Kevlar shirt, but his head and neck were unprotected. The first shot missed, the second and third struck him in the chest and did no damage; but the fourth struck him in the neck, and the fifth ripped into his face and tore away part of the scalp. The scene was even more horrifying than the assassination of President John F. Kennedy in 1963 because high-definition color cameras with telephoto lenses were trained directly on the president's face at the time. The audience saw every horrifying detail as the popular young president instantly fell dead to the platform.

When the screams and pandemonium of the event finally ceased, a strange hush settled over the stadium. The pyrotechnic flag burned itself out, the sporadic hissing and popping of the fireworks casings adding to the surrealism of the moment. Immediately the stage lights came up full. Secret Service agents hurried about trying to cordon off the area, but it was now too late for protection. The president of the United States lay dead, murdered before the stunned eyes of the world. No one spoke. No one in the crowd even moved.

After several solemn minutes, a lone figure strode across the platform with a wireless microphone in his hand. In the quiet, his hard leather heels echoed loudly on the wooden platform. It was Tauriq Haddad.

"Our leader is dead," he said solemnly. "But god loves us too much to leave him this way. I tell you, god will bring him back to life again—here, before the eyes of you all! I, god's prophet, declare it so. When I speak the word, President Mark Beaulieu will live again!" The chairman turned on his heel and strode to the lifeless, blood-soaked body lying on the platform and shouted, "Mark Beaulieu! I say to you, live!"

At his command, a single bolt of lightning crackled from the sky and struck the body of the fallen president. People screamed and gasped at the suddenness of the blast. Slowly, Mark Beaulieu rose to his feet. He no longer seemed human. His face—in fact, his whole body— seemed to emanate a luminescent aura that made him appear to the dazzled crowd as supernatural . . . angelic.

Instantly Tauriq Haddad fell to his knees, looked up reverently into the face of the president, and said into his wireless microphone, "You were dead, but now you live. You are the one sent by God. You *are* god!"

Without saying a word, Mark Beaulieu raised both his hands as a sign of blessing on the crowd. Suddenly there was loud weeping as most people fell to their knees in spontaneous worship of the resurrected leader. Throughout the crowd, some people began to howl and moan. Others clasped their hands and moved their lips in silent prayer. No one spoke against him. All who were assembled there that night were convinced that they were looking at the very face of god's anointed. All, that is, except a few dedicated followers of Jesus Christ and a small handful of Orthodox Jews.

Television news, the newspapers and news magazines, and the online services all focused on the extraordinary events at Soldier Field. Universally, issues of spirituality were on everyone's lips. Theological professors from the University of Chicago, Yale, Harvard, and Princeton were interviewed on all the television networks.

To a person, each declared why, in his or her considered opinion, the events at Soldier Field fulfilled perfectly Christian prophecies of the Messiah. The leading professor of Christian apologetics at the University of Chicago summed up the feeling of his colleagues, saying, "I can say without hesitation that Mark Beaulieu embodies all that we have hoped for in the Messiah. Last night, the entire world witnessed god become man, and man become god."

In a world that had been racked by every conceivable disaster, the appearance of the god-man was nothing short of a miracle from heaven. Here at last was the savior they had waited for and dreamed of through the long and difficult months. Here was the one man who could bring solutions to their problems. Here was the god who could rule over them, bringing peace and prosperity, and make the world new. Life itself would be reborn. How could anyone stand in his way?

In the presidential election, no one *did* stand in his way. Mark Beaulieu won every state and took every vote in the electoral college. Candidates he had endorsed won a solid majority in both the House and the Senate. His hand-picked people would soon be selected Speaker of the House, majority leader, and whip of both houses of Congress. For that matter, his chosen representatives were also selected as the minority leader of the Senate and minority leader of the House. For all practical purposes, Mark Beaulieu had taken absolute control of the government of the United States of America.

Beaulieu controlled the money, the budget, the FBI, and the prosecution of criminals. An independent judiciary might be able to block elements of his program, but it soon became clear that with absolute control of Congress, he could pack the Supreme Court and then take from the courts as much appellate jurisdiction as he pleased. After all, if the courts were denied jurisdiction over certain classes of cases, then they could hardly rule against the president in sensitive matters.

Although the United States Constitution made it clear that the president was commander-in-chief of the armed forces, Mark Beaulieu scrupulously avoided confronting the military at this time. He had plans for the military, but not for now. He had given the popular secretary of defense a relatively free hand to muster forces and maintain U.S. military readiness. And so it would remain—until the time came to rein him in.

IN DECEMBER, A GREAT GATHERING of the nations was held in Rome. The principal issue to be discussed was a proposal for international adoption of the charter of the Union for Peace. Agreement was unanimous. The ruling heads of every nation on earth marched to the platform and signed the document. Then, a voice-vote was taken to proclaim the American president, Mark Beaulieu, president of the Union for Peace and Tauriq Haddad the general secretary. Again, the vote was unanimous with no abstentions and not so much as a quibble to the contrary.

Immediately following the vote, the delegates approved the assessment of $25 billion in suitable proportions from the nations of the world for the purpose of constructing the headquarters of their new organization at the site of ancient Babylon. They had already approved the offer by their new president of temporary quarters in one of the buildings of the U.S. government in Washington, D.C., but they seemed elated at the prospect of a world headquarters in the Tigris-Euphrates Valley, where civilization itself had begun.

IN JANUARY, MARK BEAULIEU and Tauriq Haddad turned their attention to domestic issues. Since his radical days, Mark Beaulieu's life goal had been to destroy Western civilization. He believed it was his destiny to crush the powers of greed and corruption that dominated in the West. Now, he believed, the path to the fulfillment of that destiny—the destiny assigned to him by Shiva—lay straight ahead of him.

In a few short months, he had successfully undermined the entire process of democratic government in the United States, and he was well on his way to replacing the Christian religion. To Tauriq Haddad was given the task of seizing absolute control of the money supply of the world. Now, Mark Beaulieu realized that his next target must be the destruction of the American family.

Thanks to the destruction in the West, mayhem in all the cities, and the ash from the volcanoes, which had spread everywhere, America was in desperate need of physical cleansing. Mark Beaulieu, a one-time Peace Corps volunteer himself, ordered the conscription of all young people between the ages of eight and seventeen to serve as members of the Peace and Beauty Battalions.

Although most parents did not relish the thought of their boys and girls being taken from home to live in hastily built government compounds, they were delighted as street after street became sparkling clean under the diligent labor of tens of thousands of eager young cleaners. It was soon evident that the public loved the Peace and Beauty Battalions, who marched dutifully through their cities, carrying their brooms, mops, and buckets.

What they did not know was that every child received three hours per day of instruction in what was called "Shiva Consciousness." The children were taught to pray in Sanskrit. They started with meditation, then learned mind control, levitation, and astral projection. They were taught that Lucifer was the god of light and that the God of the Bible was the cruel and evil god of darkness. They were taught over and over that their loyalty was to be to the Union for Peace, and not to their families or friends. They were taught that their parents were reactionary, repressive, and old-fashioned, and because they were old, they were unable to understand the spiritual revelations of the New Age.

They learned to express ridicule, disgust, and hatred for Christians and Jews. They returned home thoroughly versed in the occult. Some had become demon-possessed. In their closing ceremonies, several of the most advanced walked into a blazing fire to meet Satan, then walked out unharmed.

Like every tyrant before him, Mark Beaulieu realized that to control the future, it was first necessary to control and corrupt the youth. For the young people from eighteen years of age and up, he devised another plan. There would be enormous festivals held indoors and outdoors. To help the young people achieve Shiva consciousness, the drinking water available was laced with hallucinogens. There were prayers and chants to Shiva followed by wild dancing.

The participants were told to be free, to cast aside all inhibitions from the past. "A New Age is dawning of peace, love, and freedom," they were told. "Your bodies are gifts of God for free expression. There is no right. There is no wrong. Just let yourselves become lost in the peace of lord Shiva."

The results of government-sponsored hedonism were not unexpected. Drug addiction and group orgies became accepted. Out-of-wedlock pregnancy soared, as did sexual disease and even deaths. Public displays of sexuality and nudity became pandemic. The young stopped studying. They stopped working. Across America, by the millions, the nation's youth—the hope of its future—entered a euphoric nether world that was part psychic, part psychedelic, and patently self-destructive.

Whatever they did to themselves was not the issue. They were no longer a potential threat to Mark Beaulieu and the Union for Peace. That was why he jammed through Congress legislation that completely legalized the distribution and use of previously banned chemical hallucinogens. At the same time, Congress voted to grant privileged status to those who engaged in even the most bizarre sex acts—pedophilia, incest, and bestiality. All forms of pornography were legalized—including the sexual exploitation of children. "In the new America," the posters read, "anything goes!"

AS PEOPLE BEGAN TO RECOVER their senses from the suffering that had been inflicted on them by the hordes of demons, something else happened as well. Those who had suffered began to turn on those who had not suffered. First, there was envy, then bitterness, then physical violence. Over and over again, the same words were heard, "While we suffered, the unaffected made money. We couldn't work, so the unaffected took our jobs. The unaffected caused our suffering to happen, so that they could grow rich. They're responsible for five months of hell. Now, they've got to pay!"

Since so many of the affected by demon powers were called "good Christians," the angry mobs were hard-pressed to blame Christians in general for their sufferings. So they narrowed the charge. Those responsible were the "goody-goody fundamentalists." It was the fundamentalists who were unaffected, not the good Christians.

Soon they devised a term "fundamentalist unaffected" to identify the real enemies, and the acronym F/UN began to be spray-painted on cars, fences, mailboxes, houses, and places of business. People with the F/UN label found their houses fire-bombed, their businesses ransacked, their families terrorized.

When they appealed to the police, they found no support. Over and over again, they were given the same stock answer: "Folks are all stirred up because they were affected and you weren't. Now, you're going to have to pay for what you've done!"

There no longer seemed any doubt that the F/UN people were different from everybody else. They dressed differently, they talked differently, they acted differently. Clearly, the country would be better off without them. "Who knows what these smiling, profiteering people might try next," some reasoned.

All over the nation, it became clear to the Christians that the land that once was theirs had been taken away. They were treated as outcasts and renegades—enemies of society. Some had begun the trek to the place in the mountains they had learned about on satellite TV. Others believed the trouble would soon blow over, so they elected to stay behind. But they were wrong.

To be sure, things were going to get infinitely better—but before they did, there was a much worse fate in store.

CHAPTER TWENTY-THREE

A S THE MONTHS DRAGGED BY under the dreary gray skies, the seasons blended one into another. The ice and cold of winter were more intense than ever before in living memory, and spring and summer never came. Without the sunlight, there were crop failures throughout the world. Some varieties of food plants could grow under these conditions, but serious shortages of cereal grains developed.

Those nations that, in the best of times, lived day-to-day, experienced famine more horrible than any they had ever known. Children deprived of vitamin D from the sun developed rickets. In the absence of sunlight, bacterial organisms began to thrive, which produced, in turn, worldwide epidemics of influenza and tuberculosis.

Nuclear radiation released from the meltdown of the Japanese reactors had caused a much more serious pollution of the water supplies of Asian nations than had been originally anticipated. Multitudes of people began experiencing the growth of skin tumors, cancer of vital organs, leukemia, and other life-threatening illnesses.

Adequate food, medicine, and financial resources no longer existed anywhere on earth. It was impossible to take care of the nutritional and health needs of the vast population of the world. Without specifically saying so, President Mark Beaulieu and Chairman Tauriq Haddad were quite satisfied to see the drastic reduction in the number of people populating the planet. While their public pronouncements always professed sympathy and compassion for the suffering, privately they blocked the expenditure of any funds for medical or nutritional relief. They showed no grief when they learned that the death toll from famine and disease had exceeded one billion people.

For the anniversary celebration of his inauguration, almost two years after the volcanoes erupted, President Mark Beaulieu announced a major address to the world. He stood in the assembly hall of the Union for Peace Building in Washington, D.C., looked straight into the television cameras, and said, "The world has suffered long enough in cold and darkness. I have come to the earth that you may walk in the light, not in darkness. At my command, the clouds that have covered the earth the past two years shall be rolled away, and there shall be light."

He did not, of course, announce the results of confidential meteorological reports indicating that the clouds of aerosols that circled the earth, made up of sulfuric acid and other photochemical compounds, had been almost totally absorbed into the upper atmosphere. The reports indicated that in a matter of hours the sun would have begun to break through—without help from anyone. But President Mark Beaulieu had no intention of announcing that piece of news, and no one in science would have thought to preempt him.

Instead, he held out his right hand to the camera. The red dot on his palm began to glow. "Let there be light!" he intoned majestically, then walked off the platform to wild applause. By morning, the rays of the sun were breaking through in Washington. Within twenty-four hours, people around the world were beginning to feel the sun's welcome warmth.

Once more the god-man, the world leader, had brought deliverance to the earth. He had proven he was worthy of worship. He could control demons. He had come back from the dead. Now he had shown that he could control the atmosphere surrounding the planet.

Tauriq Haddad lost no time in capitalizing on what had taken place. At exactly 8:00 o'clock the following evening, he arranged a global telecast to announce that President Mark Beaulieu, the god-man, had appointed Federal Reserve chairman, Tauriq Haddad, as the presiding bishop of the Church of Eternal Peace. Churches and temples were to be built all over the world so that worshipers could come to pay honor to the god-man.

In his new role, then, Bishop Haddad arranged for the construction of hundreds of lifelike statues of President Mark Beaulieu. Inside each one was installed an elaborate artificial intelligence apparatus designed to duplicate, and in some instances to exceed, the functions of the human brain. Not only could these statues hear and understand human speech, but they could also give logical answers to questions posed to them.

The statues were placed on high platforms in Temples of Eternal Peace that were hastily constructed all over America and then in strategic locations around the world.

Worshipers flocked to the temples. They would praise and adore the statues, then bow down before them. They would ask the statues questions. The answers that came back were so reasonable and so logical that multitudes believed they had heard from the oracle of god himself.

It was partly the product of the latest technology. It was partly demonic. It was partly a snake-oil and medicine show. But the people loved it. They had found their god, and nothing could shake their confidence in him. Secretary of Defense Al Augustus recalled to James Wong the words of the apostle Paul that so vividly described them as people, "who exchanged the truth of God for a lie, and worshiped and served the creature rather than the Creator."

Beaulieu and Haddad had won. It seemed that nothing could stand in the way of these two men who were empowered by Satan to subjugate the world. Thus, the time had come for their next move.

The people loved President Mark Beaulieu. In their eyes he could do no wrong. When contingents of troops from India, Pakistan, Saudi Arabia, and Turkey began appearing on the streets of American cities, no one was alarmed. In fact, they warmly greeted the men and women wearing the teal blue jumpsuits, combat boots, and white helmets. On the breast pockets and the backs of each uniform were the bright red letters UP on an orange field surrounded by a circle of white stars.

But after the arrival of the troops, mysterious things began to happen. Prominent citizens started disappearing—public officials, lawyers, educators, businessmen. On a given day, these people would be very much in evidence, but the next day, they would disappear without a trace.

As alarm increased across the nation, the president announced a plan to combat the disappearances. To provide safety for the citizens from abduction by unidentified assailants, each person was to be given an identification card. The concept was simple. Convenient boxes were established all over a town or city. After 6:00 P.M., monitors would indicate whether or not each person was safe at home. If someone broke the electronic zone around his home after 6:00 P.M., he would have to log in at the safety box nearest his home. If he had not logged back in at some zone box within five hours of departure, safety squads would begin a search to see if foul play had occurred.

It all seemed so kind and thoughtful, until people began to realize that they had been surrounded by an electronic cage of fiber optic cables, electronic sensors, and reporting stations all connected to a powerful network of super-computers. At first, the periodic safety checks seemed inconvenient but benign. It remained so until people around the country who failed to check in on time returned home with swollen, puffy faces and bruises as a result of beatings administered by troops of the Union for Peace.

One of the early victims of a brutal beating was Vince D'Agostino, the former chief of staff to ex-president Rust. After quitting his job,

Vince had decided to go back to practicing law again, with a small firm in Washington, D.C. Both he and his wife, Angie, had been among the unaffected, something for which Vince thanked God every day. Of the eight lawyers in the firm, he was the only one who was un-affected. As a result, he had single-handedly held the office together.

Eventually, though, the other lawyers, all of whom resented but needed Vince, turned on him. It became so unpleasant that, as much as possible, Vince started working at night, when he knew he would have the office to himself. One night, he forgot to log in at the zone box. At midnight, three men appeared at his office.

Having been a street-tough kid, Vince could still hold his own in a fight. But not when it was three against one. By the time the fight was over, Vince had two black eyes, several fractured ribs, and bruises all over his body.

He arrived home at two in the morning. Angie, a late-night person, was sitting in the living room reading a book as Vince turned his key in the lock.

"Hi, honey," she called out.

The response was a muffled groan.

Concerned, she hurried across the living room to the hallway, where her husband was standing, holding on to the doorknob. She took in the black eyes and the torn clothing and instinctively reached out for him. "Oh, dear God," she said, "what happened?"

Vince shrank back from her touch. "Don't hug me—please," he gasped. "My ribs. I think they're broken." He tried to take a deep breath and winced. "It was the UP police—they made it clear they didn't like my not checking in."

"Come sit down," she said and gently led him by his arm to the couch. As he very slowly sat down, she said, "I'll get an ice pack for your eyes, and we should get you to a hospital about your ribs."

Vince reached up and took her hand. "No hospital. These are probably hairline fractures. They'll heal on their own." He looked up at her. "But I could sure use that ice."

"I'll get it," she said.

As she turned to leave the room, Vince called, "Angie?"

She stopped and looked at him. "Yes?"

"I know we've talked about staying in D.C. and toughing it out," he said. "But I don't believe it's possible anymore. We've got to get out. Now."

"I know," she said. "And I completely agree—especially after what they did to you tonight," she added angrily. "But where will we go?"

Vince could feel his left eye closing up. "Get the ice pack, and then we'll talk. I have an idea. . . ."

WITHIN A YEAR, THE POLICE from the Union for Peace had established population monitoring zones throughout North America, then around the world. There was no longer any pretense that the action was for the good of the people. The world had become one vast police state.

The military were, of course, exempt, as were members of the president's official family. Their license tags carried the UP designation, as did their identification cards. Equal privileges were extended to members of diplomatic missions to the Union for Peace. Groups who lived in very remote areas were ignored. It was simply too much of a logistical headache for the Union for Peace militias to track down every remote trapper and logger. The government felt that it held the ultimate weapon, which would bring in the strays when the time came.

WHILE THE FORCES OF EVIL were at work, there were others growing in number who were working equally hard, and in secret, to counteract everything the Union for Peace was doing.

Lieutenant General Archie Gladstone had established what he called the Western Defense Zone. His stated mission was to protect military assets from volcanic ash. But, in fact, he had created a military state within a state. He had called on the genius of the grizzled Master Sergeant Tony O'Reilly to assemble absolutely monumental depots of food, fuel, and ammunition, all well-hidden in mountainous regions of the country. General Gladstone positioned two armored divisions in Pueblo, along with a paratroop division and a mechanized division west of the Sangre de Cristo mountains.

His airplanes were dispersed into camouflaged bunkers in Albuquerque. Then, with utmost secrecy in a maneuver known only to a select few, General Benjamin ordered the ten Pershing missiles to be transported from the Pueblo depot and deployed with nuclear warheads in deep ravines over a wide area to the west of the Sangre de Cristo mountains.

Meanwhile, Albuquerque had almost tripled in size since the beginning of the chaos. It was not just the presence of over a hundred thousand military personnel that had caused this expansion. Civilians from all over the country were being drawn there by the thousands.

Manuel Quintana had succeeded in arranging two more satellite up-links at El Refugio. With these, he could access satellite transponders at times of the day when they were not in use by others. Pirate transmissions known as "The Voice of the Mountains" were broadcast around the world. They were filled with news reports not available from other sources. They warned of the insidious dangers represented by the Union for Peace. They particularly warned Christian believers to stay true to their convictions, whatever the price. They repeated, time and again, the biblical messages that described with great precision the nature and plan of the Antichrist.

The director and producer of these television and radio programs was Carl Throneberry. At the same time, he used all of his considerable skills to create pamphlets, leaflets, and newspapers. He, Lori, and a small staff created these pieces on two sophisticated desktop publishing computers. Printed material was sent in digital form by satellite telephone all around the world to thousands of cell groups of what came to be known as the Christian Resistance.

The leaders of the Union for Peace soon realized that a powerful underground had grown up that could not be manipulated by the controlled media. Despite all their efforts to infiltrate and block efforts of the Christian Resistance, they were powerless to crush it.

Thwarting their attempts was the fact that, by this time in history, more than sixty million households in the United States alone had personal computers, most equipped with modems and color fax capabilities. These computers, in turn, were connected via the Internet to tens of thousands of World Wide Web sites, site-based servers, networks, and home/office machines. For a police state to silence such an enormous network of interconnected data links, computers, copiers, facsimile machines, and printers, it would first have to totally disrupt its own means of communications. And that was not an option.

To be sure, some people in the resistance could be arrested and tortured. Some were. Some data links could be monitored and shut down. Some were. But all the ingenuity of Satan himself could not block the flow of truth to those who wanted to hear it. However, the flow of truth from the Voice of the Mountains and the Christian Resistance had no effect on those who determined in their hearts to cherish the lie instead of the truth.

As repression grew more intense across the continent of North America, but before the massive road checkpoints appeared, families used what liberty they still had left to rent trucks and trailers and head to enclaves throughout the country where Christians had gathered. Lori's parents and sister, as well as Carl's mother, were safely ensconced in just such an enclave.

As the months passed, John Edwards's tiny household swelled to more than ten thousand people. John was alternately delighted at the prospect of helping so many people, yet horrified at the thought of providing them with safe drinking water, food, and shelter over a very long period of time.

Fortunately, many of the arrivals came with motor homes, RVs, tents, and trailers. He now had thousands of willing workers, but where could he find the large equipment to build adequate long-term accommodations for so many?

Then, one of those unexplained "accidents" happened, which had now become a routine part of life at El Refugio. Manuel and Cathy had driven into Albuquerque to pick up some electronic components. As they parked the pickup and started into the store, Manuel turned around abruptly and almost knocked down a soldier wearing fatigues and walking hurriedly down the sidewalk. As Manuel steadied himself and tried to catch the other man before he fell, he saw the three stars on his lapels. He recognized him as the officer who had helped him so long ago—Archie Gladstone.

"General Gladstone," he said, "please forgive me. I hope I didn't hurt you."

The general shrugged, "That's okay. Not your fault."

"General," Manuel said, "do you remember us? I'm Manuel Quintana, and this is my wife, Cathy. You saved our lives."

Archie Gladstone had so much on his mind that the memory came slowly. Then, suddenly he remembered. "Quintana. Oh, yes, of course! You're the couple we picked off the mountain in the Osprey. How are you doing?"

"We're doing fine, General. How about you?"

He shook his head and laughed. "Busy. I'm commander of the Western Defense Zone. As you probably know, the secretary of defense ordered a major deployment of combined forces to Albuquerque to escape the volcanic ash. By the way, the secretary never got to meet you, but we've talked about you more than once. He'll be out this way before long. I'd love to set up a meeting."

"That would be great," Manuel said. He reached into his shirt pocket and pulled out a pen and a pad of paper to write down a phone number, paused, then asked "Tell me, General, were you among the affected or the unaffected?"

Archie Gladstone laughed. "The unaffected, but that hasn't made me too popular with some of my colleagues. How about you?"

Manuel breathed a sigh of relief. "Unaffected—all of us. General, we're living up in the hills in a place called El Refugio. When we started, there was just a handful of people. Now it's more like ten thousand, from all over North America. All of them are unaffected. They had to get away from the terrible things that were—that are—" he corrected himself, "happening."

"I understand perfectly," Archie Gladstone replied. "I'll bet you folks could use some help, if there are that many of you. Tell me— what can I do for you?"

"General, we need power tools, earth-moving equipment, trenchers, well diggers—that sort of thing."

"I'll have that and a whole lot more sent to help you in less than a week. I'll also see about sending you the equipment you'll need to set up a sewage-processing plant. But first, how do my people get up to your place?"

Manuel drew a map on the small pad of paper. "It's about three hours north and west of Albuquerque," he said, as he sketched roads and turn-off points. "You go north, then west, and follow the lights."

"The lights?" he said. Archie Gladstone looked at the map, then at Manuel, then back at the map again. "Oh, the lights!" he roared. "Well, *that* explains it! My pilots and AWACS guys have been reporting strange weather phenomena down this way—some sort of unexplained luminous columns in the sky over this precise area. We thought they were reflections off the clouds, or some sort of aurora caused by the volcanoes. But now I know better.

"I'd say that your ten thousand unaffected guests have something a lot more powerful than my four divisions defending them." He laughed. "When the showdown comes, Manuel, I'll probably be asking *you* folks for help!"

CHAPTER TWENTY-FOUR

BUILDING THE WORLD headquarters of the Union for Peace was the most costly construction project of all time, far exceeding its preliminary budget. It included a huge airport, a complete network of roads, a state-of-the-art hydroelectric plant and compatible power systems, sewers, water collection and storage facilities, a high-tech telephone exchange with satellite up-link capacity, and all the basic infrastructure needed to support a city of a million people. Full-grown trees were imported at great expense to line the broad boulevards. There were graceful fountains, statuary, beautiful hanging gardens, and immense public parks.

Most of the public buildings were constructed of gleaming white marble. The palace and grounds designed for the leader of the world were the rival of the royal palace of France at Versailles. Nothing in history—whether the hanging gardens of Nebuchadnezzar, the court of Kublai Khan, the pyramids of the pharaohs, or the lavish splendor of the Roman Empire—compared to Babylon. Overnight, it seemed, the desert bloomed, and Babylon became an oasis to the entire world.

At the center of it all was the temple—the Mother Church, as it were—of the Church of Eternal Peace. In the temple was a gigantic figure of a man draped in a toga. His left hand was resting possessively on a giant globe, his right hand was raised with the palm upright. The red dot in the center of the palm radiated light and heat like a glowing ember of coal.

This statue was bigger, grander, and more sophisticated than the other statues of Mark Beaulieu that had been placed in temples around the world. The creators of this remarkable system had spared no expense. They had incorporated technologies beyond anything previously known to science. The statue represented the stunning culmination of a three-year crash program by a dozen of the world's leading experts in cybernetic andromorphology. Of course, the world was told nothing of the technology. The statue, after all, was held forth as the embodiment of the spirit of Mark Beaulieau.

Their great creation was equipped with sensors that made the apparatus seem so lifelike that it even appeared to be breathing. Its eyes moved, the lids opened and closed naturally, and the pupils of the eyes dilated in response to changing light, precisely as human eyes would do. Its head could turn and nod, its mouth could move, and its arm and head motions were fully computerized to simulate human actions. Every motion was fluid and lifelike. Nothing about this amazing creation seemed artificial.

What observers found to be most remarkable about the statue was that it could think and reason, carry on natural conversations, and coordinate all of its bodily motions in perfect harmony with the thoughts being expressed. Bishop Haddad would stand before the lifeless statue. Then he would make an incantation and call for his satanic lord to enter the statue and give it life. When Haddad activated the remote control device in his pocket, every single man and woman standing before it was convinced that the spirit of the god-man, Mark Beaulieu, had entered the statue. Every word spoken was believed to be divine.

The great dedication festival was drawing near. But before the celebration of their great achievement could take place, Mark Beaulieu had an obligation to fulfill.

"Tauriq," he said, "I want you to bring the prime minister of Israel to Washington for a meeting." The invitation of the president of the Union for Peace could not be ignored. Within forty-eight hours, the prime minister of Israel was ushered into the presence of Mark Beaulieu. And then, after the customary exchange of pleasantries, the president said, "Mr. Prime Minister, your nation, for reasons of its own, has elected to decline membership in the Union for Peace. Israel is the only nation on earth to scorn our offer, and I want to know why."

The Israeli leader was clearly uncomfortable in these surroundings. He coughed, shuffled his feet, then offered several totally specious reasons why Israel had declined affiliation with the UP. Both men knew the real reason. The Orthodox in Israel were adamantly opposed to surrendering Israeli sovereignty to a world body controlled by what they called "goyim." Even with more than thirty political factions represented in the Israeli government, they all knew that if the Orthodox delegates to the Knesset withdrew from the shaky coalition currently in power, the entire government would fall.

To avoid further embarrassment for his guest, Mark Beaulieu changed his direction. "The real reason I wanted this meeting," he said, "was to arrange a treaty of peace and friendship between the Union for Peace and the nation of Israel. I understand perfectly well why it isn't politically expedient for your government to join our Union. However, we want to offer to the entire world the same type of Free Trade Zone that now exists between Israel and the United States. With this treaty, Israeli products can be bought and sold in any market in the world—completely free of customs and duties. This freedom of trade will be impossible so long as your country maintains a separate currency. Therefore, we propose that you abandon the shekel and accept the global standard—the world currency—as your standard."

The Israeli leader was terrified at the prospect of political and economic isolation. However, the prospect of a peace treaty delighted him, and he accepted with alacrity, subject only to Knesset approval.

The proposal to begin using the currency of the world seemed a small price to pay for the promise of peace. Little did he know what was coming next.

For three years, Tauriq Haddad had worked with his counterparts in the major industrialized nations to create a system to control global credit. Much of the groundwork had been laid for him by the scientific advances of the 1990s. Computing power had accelerated to such a degree that by the end of the decade, a small desktop computer could store more data and perform more simultaneous calculations than could previously be accomplished by a multimillion-dollar mainframe system that would fill an entire room.

Oddly enough, it was a celebrated television commercial from the late 1990s that was often credited with fueling the microminiaturization craze that led to these new developments. That commercial for a new generation of high-tech software had been written and produced at JPT Worldwide by Carl Throneberry based on a concept that, at that time, was entirely theoretical. The commercial only hinted at what was to come: the new devices actually achieved what the ads had unwittingly promised.

But for the first time in history, mankind had in its possession equipment powerful enough and fast enough to monitor the earnings, spending, and the entire wealth of six billion people. It was in 1995 that a consortium of banks introduced to their customers a smart-cash card. The concept was simple. A balance was coded into a computer strip on the card by the issuing bank. Each time there was a purchase, the checkout machine would reduce the balance by the appropriate amount. When the balance reached zero, the card could be renewed at the bank or by an automatic teller machine.

With this arrangement, a customer could leave larger balances in his principal bank account and use the cash card instead of hard currency. The system pleased customers, but it meant that the anonymity of purchasing by cash was eliminated. The advantage of the cash card was obvious. There were no verification mechanisms, no cumbersome receipts to sign. And, there was no cash for businesses to count or have stolen. With each transaction, the amount was automatically debited from the individual's account by the bank's computer and credited to the account of the business establishment recording the sale.

This technology from the last century seemed like a boon to a man with the vision and the aspirations of Tauriq Haddad. But his own plan moved well beyond this point. He planned for there to be one standard for pricing, but no currency. The wealth of each individual would still be recorded in his or her name, but approval of the monetary authorities would be required for every transfer of funds from individual accounts.

Each day-to-day purchase would be transacted by the smart-cash card, which carried a limited renewable balance. Once the balance was drawn down, there could be no further purchases with the card unless government computers cleared the account for replenishment. Haddad persuaded the Parliament of the Union for Peace to make the use of gold, silver, or paper currency illegal. To trade in any way or by any means except that prescribed by law was punishable—by death.

As the technology improved, the danger of losing one's cash card was obviated. A small microchip tattoo on the back of the hand carried all the same information found on the card and was essentially theft-proof.

In his elaborate plans for the opening ceremonies of the world capital at Babylon, the bishop planned to dedicate the great Temple of Eternal Peace and the statue it contained. The statue would then call for the creation of a new world monetary system. The people would be told that it was for the purpose of eliminating greed, ensuring a fair division of labor, reasonable profits, and doing away with crime, especially in the narcotics trade.

And, he thought, *there will be one more thing: Only those who are willing to swear allegiance to the president of the Union for Peace will be eligible to receive the computer tattoo.* Without registration, their bank accounts, brokerage accounts, pension funds, insurance policies, and Social Security would be frozen. Without registration, wages could not be credited from an employer to the account of an employee. People could work, but they could not be paid for their work.

With no credit, it would be impossible to pay real estate or personal property taxes. Therefore, the property of those not officially registered would, within a short time, be forfeited to the government. In short, absolute compliance with government directives and procedures was obligatory. No one could refuse to cooperate.

With this move, suddenly the wealth of the world was under his control. Tauriq Haddad knew that the instinctive need for survival and the love of money would quickly overcome any doubts about the allegiance of the people to the god-man, Mark Beaulieu.

BEFORE LEAVING WASHINGTON to take up residence in his new capital, President Mark Beaulieu called his cabinet and top aides together.

"My very dear friends," he began, "I'm leaving Washington for the great capital of the Union for Peace in Babylon. But before I go, I want you to know that you and your spouses, or you and a special friend of your choosing, will be my personal guests for the opening ceremonies. I am planning a fortnight of festivities that none of you will ever forget. The White House travel office will put together all the details for our entourage. Then you will be flown on one of my private aircraft from Andrews Air Force Base. You will stay at my personal palace."

The men and women gathered in the room were elated about the prospect of seeing the new capital and going there as guests of their leader. After the meeting, President Beaulieu pulled Al Augustus aside. "This is the moment I've been waiting for, Mr. Secretary. I know that, as secretary of defense, you want world peace as much as I do. So you will be pleased to know that immediately after the dedication of my new capital, a portion of the armed forces of all the member nations will be placed under the command of leaders chosen by the Parliament of the Union for Peace. Through limitation of the very possibility of armed aggression, we will be able to proceed with our plan to destroy weapons of war all over the world. The remaining military forces of all nations throughout the world may then be demobilized. We will enter a new millennium of peaceful coexistence.

"Mr. Secretary . . . Al, my friend," he said, warmly, "your excellent work in crisis management and your sage counsel concerning military affairs and the deployment of our forces during these difficult days have been invaluable to me. I'm now giving you the task of fulfilling our mission for peace. I have every confidence that you'll accomplish this task as you did the other."

Al Augustus knew now that he was dealing with a demonic megalomaniac. Al realized that somehow this man had been blinded to his defense secretary's true loyalties. The appearance of cooperation was essential now, so he clasped the president's hand warmly and bowed from the waist.

"Mr. President," he said with feigned deference, "I will carry out your wishes in a fashion that even you will not believe possible. Now, sir, what is your pleasure? Shall I stay here and begin my mission now, or would you prefer that I join your party in Babylon?"

The president paused for a moment. "The work here is very important, that's true, but you'd be missed at the ceremony. And you'd be sorry not to have seen the spectacle that Bishop Haddad and I have prepared for this occasion. Perhaps you should go ahead and begin your work now, but then rather than coming in the larger plane with the official party, you can fly to Babylon on my smaller personal

Global Express airplane. After a brief stay at the capital, you'll return refreshed and better able to finish your mission here. Does that sound agreeable?"

"Mr. President," Al said, "it will be done precisely as you have described." Gratified by the exchange, Mark Beaulieu turned imperiously on his heel, and the two men parted company.

AS SOON AS HE RETURNED to the Pentagon, Al Augustus called for an emergency meeting of the Joint Chiefs plus all of the service secretaries.

"Ladies and gentlemen," he began, "I've just come from a meeting with the president of the United States. He has told me that immediately following the dedication of the capital of the Union for Peace in Babylon, he desires to merge the armed forces of the world into a unified command based on the orders of the Parliament of the Union. All other forces will be mustered out and their weapons scrapped." Al Augustus looked quickly around the room and added, "I'd like your comments."

"Mr. Secretary," the chief of Naval Operations began, "this plan is outrageous! There's no question in my mind that this is simply a shortcut to tyranny! Once this is done, the sovereignty of the United States is ended. How can we allow this to happen?"

"I disagree, Mr. Secretary," the chief of staff of the army answered. "We must never forget that the military are to be under civilian rule. Beyond that, I believe that our president is not a man, but a god. I, for one, have every intention of following his direction to help bring peace to the world."

Each of the service chiefs responded in turn, and after a heated debate, Al Augustus asked those who agreed with the presidential directive to stand and those who disagreed to remain seated. To his amazement, all stood except the chief of Naval Operations and the commandant of the Marine Corps.

"For those of you who are standing, I want an immediate plan of implementation on my desk by 0900 tomorrow morning. It'll be your call, so don't worry that I or anyone else will be second-guessing you. What units should we place in a multinational command? Where should these units be deployed? What units should be demobilized, and which weapons destroyed? You need to understand that it is crucial that you focus on command integration within the Union for Peace. Is that understood?" Each officer indicated that he or she understood the task at hand.

"As you know," Al Augustus said, "I've personally assigned four divisions and several air wings to a military depot in the West. These units will be demobilized at my express order, along with the three Sea Wolf submarines now at sea.

"As we begin this operation, I'm going to need weekly reports on your progress. This may be the biggest challenge of all, and we have extensive work to do." Then he added, "The gentlemen who are sitting will please report to my office at the conclusion of this meeting."

Later, in his office, Secretary Augustus told his private secretary that he was not to be disturbed under any circumstances. He walked over to the television in the corner, switched on CNN, and turned up the volume. He motioned the admiral and the general to seats close to him.

"Gentlemen," he said, "are you affected or unaffected?"

"Unaffected, sir," came the answer from both.

"Are you willing to die for freedom?" Again, the answer was affirmative.

Then he whispered, "We must stop this madness. Come to my home at this address at eight tonight. Please wear civilian attire and be very discreet. If it appears you're being followed, lose your tail before coming in. But, please, do come."

At that point he turned the volume down slightly on the television and raised his voice. "The news today seems much better, don't you agree? We're living in momentous times, and you're very fortunate to be where you are today. Gentlemen, it's vital that the president have your loyalty. He's given us the key role of bringing about world peace. I respectfully request that each of you rethink your attitudes on this matter." He stood and shook the hand of each man and said, "Thank you. You are free to go."

AT EIGHT ON THE DOT, both officers arrived in separate staff cars displaying the UP license plates. Al ushered them into the study.

"Gentlemen," he began, "our nation is in grave crisis. Over the past few years, the government has been seized by a subtle coup d'état. Now, if we go ahead with the plans being proposed by the president, we will also be surrendering the military might of this nation to the devious plans of a world dictator. The real tragedy is that all this is happening without a shot being fired!"

"What can we do, Mr. Secretary?" the admiral asked.

"It's simple. Tell your colleagues that I persuaded you to follow civilian leadership despite your misgivings. Then, do everything in your power to slow this thing down."

Over the next hour Al Augustus shared with them a plan to frustrate the use of American arms by the multinational force. It was simple, but the logic was impeccable, and so natural that not even the devious mind of Tauriq Haddad could have perceived the methodology. As the two officers rose to depart, Al Augustus said soberly, "Do you remember what happened to the military officers who tried to destroy Adolf Hitler?"

The men nodded. "Yes, indeed," said the marine officer. "Dispatched before they knew what hit them."

"Precisely," said Al Augustus. "The president has informants in every part of the administration. But, even so, he hasn't yet put his full spy network into place. When it's fully activated, your lives will be in grave danger. So, please hear me: From this moment on, you are on your own . . . but you are not alone."

TREASURY SECRETARY JAMES WONG and his wife, Joyce Cumberland Wong, were welcomed on board Air Force One as part of the American delegation flying from Andrews Air Force Base to Babylon International Airport. The secretary of state and the secretary of defense were to arrive later on the president's personal Global Express courier. Because of the ranking of protocol, the Wongs were seated in the forward compartment used by the president himself.

During the seven-hour flight they were served a delicious seven-course dinner accompanied by an assortment of vintage wines. As she sniffed the aroma of twenty-five-year-old cognac, Joyce snuggled back next to her husband. "Now," she said, "*this* is the life. I can't understand why you can't warm up to President Beaulieu. He's a great man. He can give us the moon if you'll just give him a chance! Why do you resist?"

"I know how you feel, Joyce," James said. "But everything is not as it seems. We've endured terrible tragedies over these last few years and months, and on the surface it seems we're coming out of it. I'm worried. Things are moving too fast, too soon."

Indeed, James Wong's words were prophetic. After their arrival, they were whisked in a black stretch limousine to the palace, where they were taken to the most elegant suite of rooms they had ever seen. The walls were of pink and white marble. Exquisite antique Persian rugs covered the floors. The fragrance of jasmine filled the rooms. The fixtures throughout were of eighteen-karat gold.

Joyce walked slowly through the rooms, stunned at the opulence of what she saw. "Jimmy, can you believe this?" she exclaimed.

"It *is* amazing," her husband agreed.

As she entered the bedroom, with its huge, ornate, canopied bed, she noticed a jeweler's box on the hand-carved dressing table. "What's this?" she asked, going over and picking up the box.

On the top was a perfumed note that said, "To Joyce Wong, from Mark Beaulieu."

Joyce opened the box, then gasped in amazement. Inside was the most extraordinary necklace she had ever seen. Dozens of flawless white diamonds and at least a hundred karats of beautifully cut sapphires were set in an eighteen-karat gold collar. It was something Cleopatra might have worn.

"Jimmy, look!" she exclaimed. "It's from the president!"

"Wow!" the treasury secretary said, stunned by the magnificence of the piece. "That necklace must be worth a million dollars in old currency. Probably more. But we can't keep it."

As he spoke there was a knock at the door. James Wong walked through the suite, followed by Joyce, and opened the door. There stood Mark Beaulieu.

"Jimmy and Joyce," he said, coming into the large sitting room, "I'm so glad you made it. How nice to see you. And, Joyce, I hope my small gift pleases you."

"Oh, Mr. President, it doesn't just *please* me. It *overwhelms* me. It's beautiful!"

"But, Mr. President," Jimmy Wong spoke out, "we can't accept anything so extravagant. It's . . . well, it's too much!"

"Nonsense, Mr. Secretary." The president smiled condescendingly. "This is just the beginning. You are in a very key position. You are the man destined to lead my efforts in the Far East. This bauble—this trinket—is just the first installment of what you have coming. It's only a token of what I intend to do for you and your beautiful wife, Joyce. But now, please rest. I know that you've had a long journey, and there's so much to do."

When Mark Beaulieu left, he closed the door gently behind him, and Joyce turned around playfully. "Jimmy, what did I tell you?" she purred. "This man is going to give us the moon!"

She walked into the bedroom, to try on the necklace in front of a mirror. James Wong immediately began searching the living room for a listening device. He found one in the return duct of the air conditioner. The microphone was, in turn, attached to a tape recorder that activated whenever a light was turned on in the room. Every word they spoke would be recorded and analyzed by experts.

James then walked into the bedroom, where his wife was preening before a large mirror. "There's no question, my love, that the president is a wonderful friend," James lied. Then, pulling his wife by the hand, he said, "I need a shower. We can talk later."

Inside the bathroom, he turned on all the water faucets. "Joyce, this place is bugged. I found one, and there may be others. Believe me, every word we say here is being monitored."

"I don't care about bugs, Jimmy. I have nothing to hide, and there's nothing to be afraid of. Why don't you simply face the fact that you're suspicious by nature, get over it, and accept the president's offer? I want my life back," she said as she sat down on a chaise longue in the sumptuous bathroom. "I want to go back to where we were before everything . . . went wrong. I want it all, Jimmy, and Mark Beaulieu can give it to us!"

James Wong shook his head in frustration. "Joyce, what this man wants is total allegiance, total worship, total adulation. No compromises. He's not interested in you or me at all. We're totally expendable. Why can't you see that? What he wants in return for these trinkets and these little trappings of power is just too high a price to pay."

Joyce looked at her husband as if she had never seen him before. "You *do* have a price, don't you?" she asked seriously.

James sat down across from her on the edge of the marble tub. "Perhaps," he said after a brief deliberation. "Everyone works for a price, I suppose. The workman is worthy of his hire. But, Joyce, my price is too high for this kind of thing, and I won't sell my soul for a sapphire necklace and a marble palace."

"You could have everything," she said. "It's not just the necklace. He wants us to be in charge of the Far East. It could be the opportunity of a lifetime."

"Not at these prices, my love. I want none of it."

She jumped to her feet and bolted out of the bathroom, shouting, "James Wong, you are a fool!"

As careful as James Wong thought he had been, he had not been careful enough: Every word between James and Joyce had been monitored by listening devices that filtered out the sounds of running water. Mark Beaulieu immediately began planning a big surprise for his reluctant secretary of the treasury.

Parties, banquets, and entertainment were lavish and endless, all calculated to satisfy every sensate desire of the guests assembled from all over the world. Each day there were festivities, games, sports, and recreation. Night after night was filled with dining, drinking, dancing, and dalliances, along with wild and decadent entertainments. Every palate was delighted. Every taste was satisfied.

Then, midway through their two-week celebration, came the highlight of the event. After enormous fanfare and buildup, the guests were assembled in the marble temple before the statue. Bishop Tauriq Haddad pressed the remote control, and the massive statue of the world leader came to life. To the applause and delight of the crowd, the statue spoke of peace that would last a thousand years. He spoke of a new age more glorious than anything previously imagined by mankind. With a masterful gesture, he outlined the plans for the immediate implementation of a global peace-keeping force and a crime-free, drug-free currency system.

The already intoxicated crowd cheered and applauded again and again.

Then came the big surprise of the evening. Bishop Haddad strode slowly up the steps to the platform beside the great statue. In his hand he held a small laser device. "My very dear friends," he said, "we celebrate here tonight the beginning of the new age of power, of praise, and of prosperity. We have seen marvels this week no one could imagine a very short time ago. But unseen in all of this has been the emergence of a new economic age as well. Among our guests is the distinguished secretary of the treasury of the most powerful economy on earth. He and I have worked together to bring the world economy to this point, and to establish the new economic order.

"And so, now, Secretary Wong," he said, motioning for James Wong to join him on the platform, "it falls to you to receive the honor of being the first person on earth to declare here before this assembly that the Lord Mark Beaulieu is your god, and then to receive on your hand the mark that will, from this day forward, allow you to buy and sell and trade as a citizen of the world. Mr. Secretary, please come forward."

The crowd cheered and applauded. Joyce Cumberland Wong whispered, "Jimmy, this is wonderful! You are to be the first in the world. Go, Jimmy! Go up and get the honor you've been working for all these years!"

James Wong walked forward through the crowd with his head down. As he stepped onto the platform, he lifted his eyes and looked around at the sea of faces.

"Ladies and gentlemen," he said. "Mark Beaulieu is a man. Nothing more. He is not God. He is not divine. He has no power over your souls, and I do not believe that his spirit is inside this statue. I can't tell you how it works, but I know it's activated by a computer, and that's how it's able to mimic human behavior."

Surprisingly, Tauriq Haddad did not attempt to stop or interrupt James Wong. His eyes burned like fire, but he simply smiled as the treasury secretary made his statement.

"I am a Christian believer," James continued. "Jesus Christ is my Lord, and I will not acknowledge any other, even if it should cost me my life."

There was hushed silence in the hall. Then the features of the statue changed to something hideously evil—it seemed more the head of a serpent than that of a man. Flames shot from its mouth, and both of its massive hands rose into the air: "Kill! Kill!" it roared. "He has condemned himself by his own words. Let him die in torment. Now!"

The men and women in the crowd were terrified but uncertain. What was happening? What had provoked this outrage?

Al Augustus was standing toward the back of the crowd, but he could do nothing now to help his friend. But never, for the rest of his life, would he forget what happened next. The floor beneath James Wong dropped open, and he slid down into a room below the temple floor. Before the floor sprang back into place, the agonizing screams of James Wong rang out across the vast marble hall.

For several chilling minutes, he screamed in pain from whatever tortures he was enduring in the chamber below. Guests stood mute, listening in agony and terror as his cries echoed against the walls of the temple. Then the sounds suddenly ceased with a sickening finality. An ominous silence filled the huge hall.

No one who had been there would ever be free from that moment—from those screams. From that moment on, similar screams would echo time and again from the lips of others who, like James Wong, refused to admit that a demon-possessed man was now their lord. Now they knew, but now it was too late. Up to that hour, Mark Beaulieu had contained Satan. But from that moment on, Satan contained Mark Beaulieu. The Antichrist had been loosed in fury upon the earth. Fortunately, his time was limited.

A SHOCKED AND GRIEVING Al Augustus received immediate clearance to return to the United States to pursue the "peace effort." But in the darkness of the cabin on his flight back across the Atlantic, he repeated in his mind over and over his promise to avenge his friend, James Wong. *Jimmy, I'll make him pay. Jimmy, I'll do it for you. With all my strength, somehow I'll take that monster down.* What Al Augustus, in his grief, did not realize was that in his own strength he could never destroy a spiritual being as powerful as Satan.

When he landed at Andrews Air Force Base, he immediately called his wife. His conversation was terse and to the point. "Thank God, you decided not to go to the inauguration, Barbara," he said. "It was beyond description."

"What do you mean?" she asked. Al could hear the alarm in her voice.

"I'll tell you later," he said, "when I see you in Albuquerque. We're going on an extended vacation."

"Al—"

"No questions. I'll explain it all later. I'm making arrangements now, and I want you on a flight out of Andrews tonight. Someone from Andrews will call you with the exact flight time."

"But—but—" Barbara sputtered.

"Hey," Al said cheerfully, "I told you when you married me, you'd never be bored!"

Barbara couldn't help laughing. "You got *that* right," she said.

"See you in Albuquerque," Al said, and hung up.

After making arrangements for Barbara's flight, Al drove to Patuxent River Naval Air Station where a navy two-seater fighter was waiting to take him to Albuquerque. As soon as he was strapped in the forward seat, the pilot took off without pausing for clearances. They made the flight in record time. But as they approached Albuquerque, Al Augustus noticed unusual luminous columns in the sky to the west of the city. He had read about clouds of angels. Could that be what he was seeing? Could these be angels?

Jimmy, he thought, *I'll do what I can. But, maybe God has something for us that's a lot more powerful than anything I can do.*

CHAPTER TWENTY-FIVE

LIEUTENANT GENERAL ARCHIE Gladstone was on hand in Albuquerque to greet the secretary of defense on his arrival. "Mr. Secretary, how was the ceremony in Babylon?" he asked.

"It was pure hell, Archie," Al Augustus blurted out as they hurried across the tarmac to the waiting staff car. "There was a big statue of Beaulieu in a monstrous temple. Tauriq Haddad introduced a world credit system that would only be available to people who agree to worship Beaulieu as god!"

"You must be joking," said Gladstone, as they jumped into the back of the staff car. "Beaulieu is an American president. What does he think he's doing? He used to be a congressman, and now he wants people to believe he's god? Do you mean we can't have any money unless we call him a god? He must be crazy!"

"Worse than crazy, Archie. When Haddad tried to get James Wong to be first to sign up, James had the courage to refuse. He said Jesus Christ is God, not Mark Beaulieu. Then, in front of our eyes, the head of that giant statue suddenly changed into something more like the head of a cobra, with scales and a hideous expression, and it began shouting, 'Kill! Kill!' Then, James was dropped through some kind of trap door into a torture chamber under the auditorium, and they killed him. There's no telling what they must have done to him down there. He was yelling and screaming, and we could hear the whole thing. But then all of a sudden the noise stopped. Archie, it was horrible!"

"Sir," Archie said, "you've had a long, hard trip. Are you sure you saw a talking statue turn into a snake's head? Could it have been some kind of mass hypnosis?"

"General," Al said sternly, as the car sped out onto the highway, "my eyes are great and, trust me—I know what I saw. We're dealing with the devil incarnate here. There may have been some doubt about who this guy was when we first started dealing with him, but there's no doubt anymore. Are all our troops deployed?"

"Yes, sir, they sure are. From Pueblo to Albuquerque, on both sides of the Sangre de Cristo."

"How about the Pershings?"

"All deployed in relatively safe locations."

"Now, for the big question, Archie," Al Augustus said. "Are the troops loyal?"

"I would say so, sir," Archie Gladstone replied. "At least seventy-five percent of them are unaffected."

"That's not enough," said the secretary. "I still have presidential authority to begin troop demobilization. Archie, I want you to tell the twenty-five percent that they're being mustered out as part of a worldwide force reduction. That's from the top. Give all of them pay vouchers and military transportation back to Dallas. After that, they're on their own. I suppose they'll be able to get on in the new regime, but that'll take time. In the meantime, we've got to get our people all together."

"Yes, sir."

"And, Archie," the secretary continued, "I will personally take charge of this Western Defense Zone. Soon, I will no longer be secretary of defense. Do you have a problem with that?"

"No problem at all, sir." The general was silent for a moment. "Sir, we're isolated. We lack many things. It may be like the Alamo all over again. But if we don't resist here and now, there will be nobody left to do it. So I am with you. Let's do it!"

They clasped hands in friendship. "With God's help we will win," Al whispered.

AFTER THE INCIDENT WITH James Wong, Mark Beaulieu was never the same again. The execution had the desired effect. Instantly all men and women, not only in that crowd in Babylon but also in every nation and every town, bowed to the powerful god-man who now seemed to hold the destiny of the world in the palm of his hand. He was celebrated and praised by both high and low, but the veneration he received gave him no peace. The human part of him had entered its own private hell. Night after night, Satan would rage within him. He would walk the rooms of his palace screaming and crying out in agony. He could never rest.

In public, especially on his worldwide television broadcasts, the world saw only the handsome face of their leader. But when he was alone, his expression would change. His face was drawn and contorted, and the rage that welled up inside him was that of Satan himself. His countenance was hideous beyond comprehension.

Alone, raging through the halls of his great capital, he would smash priceless pieces of furniture and hurl objects at subordinates who displeased him. And they all displeased him. Relief came momentarily whenever he could witness the agonizing torture and death of some helpless individual who refused to worship him or to acknowledge his power. His beautiful palace became a charnel house of horror. First, there were tens, then hundreds, then thousands whose screams and cries bore witness to the satanic cruelty that now ruled the world.

During most of his life, Mark Beaulieu had been celibate. He was not homosexual. He was not heterosexual. He simply was nonsexual. His lifestyle was neither ascetic nor particularly carnal. Rather, he was entirely dedicated to another calling.

This was, perhaps, his charm. To most women who knew him, he appeared to be pure and unapproachable. He seemed like some exalted figure from ancient mythology. He was, at one moment, the innocent boy whom women wanted to mother. Alternately, he was the ideal lover secretly desired. He was a man who seemed to combine unblemished purity with wanton sensuality.

Immediately after the death of James Wong, Beaulieu took Joyce Cumberland Wong as his consort. He did not woo her. He did not marry her. He took her. He took others as well.

Under the driving influence of Satan, the leader of the world began to engage in every imaginable form of depravity. The imperial palace became the home of mass orgies. Orgies with men and women, orgies enhanced by drugs, orgies involving sadism, even orgies with animals.

As a diversion, Mark Beaulieu copied a page from the lecherous life of the Roman emperor, Nero. He sent his agents all over the world for the purpose of abducting beautiful teenage girls who would be brought to the palace, subjected to one night of unspeakable acts, then turned over to the pleasure of his equally depraved bodyguards and staff. When the head is corrupt, the body also will be corrupt. The poison from Babylon began seeping into every level of society and virtually every corner of the world.

The agents of Mark Beaulieu—many of them possessed by demons—unleashed a reign of terror on the world that eclipsed the Holocaust of Adolf Hitler and the Stalinist purges in Russia combined. The earth was filled with the cries of the victims of the Antichrist. Forcible abduction, rapes, robberies, savage beatings, torture, and mass executions became the norm, not the exception. In a short while, many could no longer remember a time when it was not horrible to be alive.

In the days of Adolf Hitler, Central Europe was under the heel of a madman, but the rest of the world was free. Outside the hell of Nazism, there were strong champions who would one day bring liberty. There had always been a neutral place, a country such as

Switzerland or Sweden, to which the oppressed could flee for help. There was, somewhere, a ray of hope. There were always civilized norms—a Geneva Convention—which offered at least a basis for an appeal.

But, under the Antichrist, there was no place of refuge. No neutral country. No recognized champion to fight for the rights of the oppressed. All the world was in the thrall of the one being in the universe who knew no mercy and whose only desire was the torture and annihilation of the entire human race.

The irony of it all had become clear. The people of the world had consciously and deliberately chosen to be ruled by the prince of evil rather than the Father of good. Now, they had no second chance.

THE ANTICHRIST SET HIMSELF in Babylon as the ruler of the world, but it was still not enough for him. One prize still eluded him. How could he be the god of all, so long as Christians and Jews continued to worship Jehovah? And how long could his reign endure if there was a time-honored outpost anywhere in the world belonging to his enemy?

Israel had accepted his peace treaty. Nevertheless, it maintained an internal system of finance that was beyond the reach of Tauriq Haddad. All of that must be changed, the leader announced. The Antichrist's emissaries traveled to Jerusalem to arrange an official visit for the president. He was to be accompanied by a large entourage. Some drove into Israel in advance of his arrival. Others went by private jet or by helicopter. He flew into Lod Airport in his personal jet, then took a jet helicopter directly to the Temple Mount.

Accompanied by the prime minister of Israel and his own officials, Mark Beaulieu walked to the place directly above the Holy of Holies at the Temple of Solomon. A large stage with a podium had been set up there, from which he was to deliver an address to the world. Banners snapped in the wind, military jets flew a respectful salute overhead. Television cameras from news organizations on every continent were covering the event.

After the perfunctory greetings by several local dignitaries, the leader began his address. "I greet you, citizens of Israel, in the name of the Union for Peace. I have struggled to bring peace to this world, and I've accomplished this task. My associate has brought a crime-free, drug-free financial system to the world. Because of his work, illegal sale of narcotics has been put to an end.

"Today, however, I stand before you in celebration of the crowning achievement of my life. For I have come in peace, to declare before you all that I am your messiah. I am the anointed one of Israel. I am, as it has already been declared by the prophets before me, god come in the flesh. As you honor me with your worship, I vow to shower on your nation the promised blessing that has so long eluded you. Centuries of insult, humiliation, death, and dishonor have plagued your people. Today, that bondage of despair is broken as I declare to you the heritage you have so earnestly desired. Although I cannot live here with you in Jerusalem, I have brought my statue to be set up at this holy place. When you come here, you will be able to see it and worship it in my place. It is the very likeness of your god and leader. It will impart my wisdom to you."

Little by little, waves of conversation, protest, and angry reactions were beginning to swell among the crowd. Those who had accompanied the Antichrist tried to cheer and applaud their leader, but they were too few and the crowd was too large. Their cheers were silenced and eventually stopped. Mark Beaulieu raised his hands like Caesar calling for the applause of the crowds, but there was no applause. Finally, a black-robed Orthodox rabbi leapt up in the midst of the crowd and yelled out, "This is blasphemy! What you are saying is wrong. We will never worship an idol; we will never bow to your statue. You are not our Messiah. You are an impostor! You are the tool of Satan!"

Immediately other Orthodox Jews in the crowd began to rise to their feet, yelling and shouting, and throwing stones at the men on the podium. Armed guards raced to the defense of the leader and fired their weapons in the air to quell the disturbance, but to no avail. The last thing Mark Beaulieu wanted to do was set off a riot. Spewing profanities, the Antichrist hurried to the safety of his helicopter and ordered his pilot to make it a quick flight back to Lod Airport.

On board his jet transport, the leader was out of control. His features changed to those of Satan. "I hate them all!" he roared. "I detest them! I will destroy them! They are human scum. They are not fit to live. I will kill them! I will kill them all!"

From that moment on, his overriding passion became the destruction of Jerusalem and the subjugation of the Jewish people.

AS THE UNIVERSAL CREDIT PLAN of Tauriq Haddad went into effect, the unaffected citizens of the world were faced with an impossible choice: Either they would be forced to deny their deeply held beliefs or become starving vagabonds.

To the vast mass of people, those who had been among the affected, there was no moral dilemma. They had, for some time, acknowledged that the American president was god incarnate. They had seen his miracles, they had attended his church, they had been uplifted and inspired by his wisdom. In truth, they were already a part of the Antichrist system. If an oath of allegiance and a tattoo were all that was needed to receive access to money, nothing could hold them back.

It was a very simple process for each of them. A person would give the oath, receive the laser tattoo, then trot happily off to the supermarket. Each one wanted peace, job security, and a stable world. For the first time in years, these things were attainable. Why listen to the crazed fundamentalists with their silly talk about Satan, demons, God's judgment, and the "mark of the beast"?

But for the unaffected, reciting an oath of allegiance to a satanic representative was very serious. For a time, many of them refused the oath and the mark. As the months wore on, the cries of their starving children, the lack of work, the impending loss of home and possessions, took their toll. One by one, many slipped quietly into the local offices of the ministry of finance of the Union for Peace, swore the oath, and received the laser tattoo.

No bells sounded. No lightning bolts struck. There was no angel standing with drawn sword. It was all so natural. It just took a minute or two to get back to real life . . . a warm dinner, a secure future, happy children.

But something precious had left their lives. They had turned their backs on God and become slaves of Satan. It was like Adam when he ate the forbidden fruit. One bite seemed so harmless, so ridiculously simple. Yet, Adam had listened to his wife and his belly, and he lost Paradise.

ALL OVER THE WORLD, there were those among the unaffected who chose to lose everything material rather than deny their faith. First, their food supplies ran out. Without money they were forced to compete with rodents and wild dogs and cats for scraps of rotting garbage.

When their utilities were disconnected, they were forced to endure burning heat or freezing cold. In time, real estate and personal property taxes came due, and the rule was that failure to make payment meant immediate forfeiture of all personal assets. There was no grace period. There was no second chance. Without money to make the payments, they lost everything and were evicted.

They wandered the city streets and the countryside. Their clothes were ragged, their appearance unkempt. Occasionally, there would be an outdoor fountain or, perhaps, a stream where they could wash themselves.

Their eyes grew hollow and sunken. Their shoes were soon worn out. Their clothes became soiled and ragged. But somehow they survived. Through it all, they were determined to fight and to win. In their hearts they knew that someday, somehow, the worldwide kingdom of the Antichrist would have to fall.

AL AUGUSTUS HAD WAITED to call Mark Beaulieu until he and Barbara were settled safely in New Mexico. Then, when he called, he had learned that Mark Beaulieu was in Israel. Finally one afternoon, when seated at Archie Gladstone's desk at their secure headquarters in New Mexico, Al Augustus grabbed the telephone and once again dialed the private line of the president of the world. The Antichrist himself answered the phone.

"Mr. President," Al said, "this is Al Augustus. I'm in the United States at my compound in Albuquerque."

"Al, my friend, it's good to hear from you," Mark Beaulieu answered. "I haven't talked to you since the dedication. I want you to know how much I appreciate your being there with me."

"You don't seem to understand, Mr. President," Al said. "I saw what you did to James Wong, and I want you to know that I am out. I want nothing more to do with you or your sadistic plans. I intend to resist you and, one way or the other, to see that you fail in your mission."

Suddenly the voice on the phone was no longer that of President Mark Beaulieu. It was, instead, a roar from hell. "You miserable little traitor! You know no one can resist me! I will crush you like a grape and feed your body to the birds. I will have vengeance!"

The sound was terrifying, but something rose up within Al's spirit. Something supernatural. "Listen to me, you snake-headed freak," he shouted in return. "You've been a loser from the very beginning. Jesus Christ is the winner, and I'm on His team. And, just for the record, I have eighteen Poseidon missiles aimed at the heart of Babylon at this minute. If you try to come after me, I'll blow you back to hell where you belong!"

When Al Augustus slammed down the phone and turned around, General Gladstone grabbed him by the arms and shouted, "Yes! Mr. Secretary, that was fantastic! You couldn't have said it better."

"Thanks, Archie," he said, and grinned. "For the first time since this chaos started, I know that God is on our side and the victory is in our hands."

"You're right, Mr. Secretary. Even though you and I may know that ultimate victory is assured, I'm sure that in the upcoming months we'll have our share of heartaches, sacrifices, and loss of life. But, sir, the battle is joined!"

As they turned to go, Al Augustus put his arm around Archie Gladstone's shoulder. "Archie," he said, his eyes twinkling, "just one more thing. Please don't call me 'Mr. Secretary' anymore, will you? In case you didn't notice, I just officially resigned!"

AFTER THEIR FORCES WERE DEPLOYED, Al Augustus wasted no time in arranging a visit to the sanctuary in the mountains he had been hearing so much about. He wanted to see El Refugio for himself and meet the prophet known as Pastor Jack. But even more, he wanted to know the source of the luminous columns of light that stood high above them.

A few years before, Al Augustus had been known as a hard-nosed businessman. He was a shrewd negotiator and a tough competitor. His friends said he was a man who went for what he wanted and took no prisoners. Those same traits had served him well in the Defense Department, but after what he had seen in Babylon, he was a changed man. He would use every conventional weapon available to him, but that did not mean he was unwilling to consider help from unconventional sources as well.

The command helicopter made the journey from Albuquerque to El Refugio in forty-five minutes. He was met by a young woman who showed him around for a few minutes until Manuel Quintana could catch up with them. Manuel was finishing the morning satellite up-link operations, but the brief delay allowed Al Augustus to get the lay of the land, and what he saw amazed him.

Tents had been erected in neat rows along well-drained and carefully graded streets. Other streets were lined with white-washed stores and shops. He was surprised to see both a high school and an elementary school. In many ways the place had the feeling of a frontier town, with a thriving and bustling community doing business and carrying on their lives. There was an obvious spirit of harmony and cheerfulness among the people. Everywhere he walked, people greeted him. But this was also the most high-tech frontier town anyone could imagine. Everywhere he looked, Al saw computers and other advanced electronic equipment.

Underground cables carried power from a central generator to provide electric power to key locations in the complex. There were larger structures built of adobe and wood at various locations. These were combination kitchens, dining halls, and places of community worship. The presence of ultramodern communications equipment stood in marked contrast to the rustic simplicity of the rest of the complex.

The order, cleanliness, and the utility of the place all bore silent witness to the strength and organizational abilities of El Refugio's founder, John Edwards.

To Al Augustus, one detail seemed particularly surprising. At El Refugio there were no weapons: no pistols, no rifles, no automatic weapons, and no artillery. *Are these people pacifists?* Al wondered. *Do they have hidden caches of weapons that aren't visible to the casual observer?*

"Mr. Secretary," someone called to him. Al Augustus looked around and saw a handsome man in his late thirties jogging across the road from the communications complex. As the man drew closer, Augustus recognized Manuel Quintana from photographs he had seen. Archie Gladstone had briefed him—must have been years ago!—about Manuel's incredible story of courage and survival.

"Sorry to get delayed, Mr. Secretary," Manuel said, shaking hands with Al Augustus. "We lead a simple life here," he added, slightly winded, "but not everything we do is very simple."

"I can see that." Al Augustus beamed. "This whole place is remarkable," he said, "but I'm especially pleased to meet you, Mr. Quintana. I've never met anyone with such an incredible story of survival. You are a true American hero."

Manuel shrugged off the compliment. "My wife and boys are the heroes," he said. "I'm just a fellow who was protected by the hand of God. But, come on. Let's walk up the road and meet the founder of El Refugio, the man we call Pastor Jack. I think he's up there just beyond that clump of trees taking care of some new arrivals."

When they reached the place, there was a small group of people—obviously a family of new arrivals—unpacking boxes and bags from the back of their car. Several meters away, just at the tree line, Al could see a man with his shirt off pounding tent pegs into the ground with an eight-pound hammer. *That must be Pastor Jack,* Al thought. When the last pegs were placed, Jack tossed the hammer aside and slipped on the denim shirt that had been lying on the ground beside him. But as John slid his arms into the sleeves, Al couldn't help staring. Here was a man in his seventies with the lean, muscled torso of a prize fighter. Between his chest and his right shoulder was a ten-inch scar. *War wound,* Al thought, *or maybe a street fight.*

"Mr. Secretary." John Edwards smiled as he approached, buttoning his shirt. "Forgive my appearance, but these folks here just arrived from Illinois, and we needed to get them set up with a place to stay."

"That's quite a war wound on your chest there, Mr. Edwards," Al Augustus said.

"Oh, it's not exactly a war wound," said Pastor Jack. "Years ago I fought light heavyweight in amateur tournaments. In my last fight, my opponent went after this right shoulder with everything he had. It took three operations to repair the damage, but now it works fine, in spite of the scar. But enough of that," he said. "I see you've got some great company here. Manuel is one of our leaders, and a real hero. So, what do you say, would you like to take a look around?"

"While you're taking the tour," Manuel said, smiling at Al Augustus, "I have to get back to work." With a wave of his hand, he was off. "Hope to see you later," he called over his shoulder.

"Count on it," Al called back.

There was another surprise in store for Al Augustus.

"I want to show you around," John Edwards said, "but first I need to have a few words with my chief of staff." He nodded toward a short, bearded man who was approaching them.

"You have a chief of staff?" Al asked in surprise. "This really *is* an organized set-up."

John Edwards smiled. "It's just a nickname, really. But in another place, at another time, he actually had that title." There was a twinkle in his eye as he added, "I have a feeling you might have known each other then."

Al squinted at the bearded man as he approached. Then his mouth dropped open in surprise. "Vince?"

"Al!" Vince D'Agostino exclaimed. "What are *you* doing here?"

"I could ask you the same question."

"Well," Vince said, grinning, "between being Catholic and having a reputation for slapping presidents, I couldn't get a job in D.C." Then his expression grew serious. "One night I was beaten up. I knew then that Angie and I had to get out—and fast. I had heard about Pastor Jack's group out here, so I volunteered my services."

"And in the nick of time too," John Edwards said. "This place was growing so fast, I needed someone with Vince's organizational abilities. And," he continued, winking at Vince, "we got an additional bonus—his wife, Angie, is now teaching in our elementary school."

Al shook his head. "I can't get over this."

"Yeah, it's pretty amazing, isn't it?" Vince said. "Anyway, if I'm not interrupting, I need to talk to my boss over here"—he nodded in John Edwards's direction—"for just a minute."

"Take your time," Al said.

After a quick conference, John Edwards rejoined Al, and Vince went off to work.

"Now, for that tour," John Edwards said.

Al Augustus and John Edwards were immediately drawn to each other through mutual respect. In a sense, they were both men of war, although their means and methods were very different. As they walked, Al commented on the apparent absence of guns and weapons at El Refugio.

"We decided at the beginning," John Edwards responded, "that it would be an exercise in futility to try to resist the forces of evil with the little peashooters we could bring together. So we just asked the Lord for His protection, and He has answered our prayers."

"Are you referring by any chance to those luminous columns we see?" Al asked.

"That's right," he said. "What you see above this place—and I know this may be hard to believe, but it's true—are angels. According to the Bible, they are messengers of God sent to watch over His people. I must tell you, Mr. Secretary, I am very grateful for the deployment of your military forces out here, but our primary trust is in the Lord's army."

"I'm glad to know you've got your priorities right, Mr. Edwards." He smiled. "I believe every word of what you're saying, and I know that God has a hand in what's taking place here. There's no other explanation for what I see.

"But please call me Al," he added after a brief pause. "The fact is, I parted ways with the administration once and for all when I came back from Babylon. I don't need their title anymore!"

"All right," John Edwards said. "And you can call me Jack, if you like."

"I'd like that, Jack," he said.

As they made the rounds of the compound, John Edwards pointed out the basic structure of the settlement and showed Al how the infrastructure was being maintained. Water and sewage facilities were all state of the art. They had storage facilities for everything from automobiles to diesel fuel, and six barns of various sizes where grains, cereals, and the dairy products produced by the residents of El Refugio were processed and stored. In the upper meadows there were close to seven hundred head of cattle, along with a smaller number of sheep and goats. In addition, John Edwards kept two saddle horses in the stables behind the house. Riding not only kept him fit but it gave him the ability to keep in touch with the crew that looked after the place and supervised farming operations in the lower valley.

Even though they had provided for themselves very well for the past few years, the number of refugees was still growing, and it was becoming increasingly difficult to get by on what they had. The two men eventually ended up at John Edwards's house, and Maria brought them both glasses of iced tea on the terrace.

As they talked, Al's face grew somber. "What you're doing here and what General Gladstone and I are doing in the Western Defense Zone are all well and good," he said. "Together we're a military and a spiritual rallying point. The very fact of our existence can offer hope to people all over the world.

"I have tremendous stores of materiel and a great fighting force," he continued. "I even have nuclear weapons at my disposal. But we both must understand that my forces are puny compared to the combined armed forces of the Union for Peace. We can win one, maybe two, battles. But if Beaulieu ever gets his mind off Babylon and comes after us, without outside help we're dead. Frankly, I believe what Beaulieu would do to us would be worse than death."

"Al," John Edwards replied, "I moved here to provide a refuge for God's people who would be fleeing the oppression that has just recently settled on the earth. I've been hearing of groups of believers all over America who are receiving supernatural guidance from God. God warns them just before the UP patrols arrive to arrest them. Time and again, their lives are spared. Some of them go into hiding.

PAT ROBERTSON

Sometimes the police are actually diverted moments before making an arrest. The lives of these people are in jeopardy every single minute—yet they're growing stronger, not weaker."

"I believe what you're telling me," Al Augustus answered. "My troops need to hear this. Would you consider coming down to Albuquerque to speak to them? We'd also like you to come up to Pueblo where so many of our fighting men are quartered. These are brave men and women, but they're also smart enough to know that one day their supplies will run out and, without some kind of intervention, they'll be helpless. Without God and these angels," he said, looking up, "their end is certain. Will you help us?"

"You and General Gladstone have helped us," John Edwards answered, "and we'll help you. We know that it's your presence that has kept the UP troops away from here and allowed us to do our job. Now we will pray that God will permit His angels to fight along with your forces."

Al stood to go and the two men shook hands. As they walked down the broad natural-stone steps that led from the house to the driveway, John Edwards put his hand on Al's shoulder and said, "By the way, Al, this may encourage you. About twenty-seven hundred years ago, a great prophet named Isaiah foretold the destruction of ancient Babylon. He said that Babylon would never be built again. Despite the marvelous spectacles you've seen over there in the desert, the work still isn't finished. I believe the Word of God. It will never be finished. Whether or not either of us lives to see it, one day it will be utterly destroyed—and Mark Beaulieu and his henchman along with it!"

As they walked the half-mile to the helicopter pad, the two men agreed to work and to fight together. They paused just beyond the tarmac, and John Edwards reached out and took both of Al Augustus's hands in his own, then he bowed his head. "Father God," he said, "I am here by Your command. You have given me ten thousand to care for and feed. I pray for each of them, and I pray for these brave men and women in the resistance all over the world.

"And, Father, please accept my special thanks for my new friend, Al Augustus. Give him supernatural wisdom to withstand his enemies. Strengthen him and his forces. Send the angels, dear Father, to fight for him. Give us victory over the evil one. In the name of Jesus. Amen."

As they looked up into each other's eyes, both men knew that God had heard and answered their prayer. They embraced as if they had been friends for years, and Al turned and walked the short distance to his waiting helicopter with new optimism and enthusiasm.

"We'll work out a schedule," he called back over the sound of the revving engine, "so you can come and speak to the troops. I'll send the chopper to pick you up. God bless you!" He jumped into his seat, buckled himself in, and was soon back in the air headed for Albuquerque.

CHAPTER TWENTY-SIX

Supplies were getting tighter at El Refugio, and many of the most commonly used items were becoming harder and harder to obtain. Thanks to the foresight of John Edwards, the people had a fairly good supply of the basic necessities. In addition to the fresh foods, grains, and vegetables that they were able to produce, they also had quantities of dried foods that had been shipped in from Albuquerque. There was ample fresh water, and they had sewage disposal facilities, modest housing, and a diesel-fired electric generator that served the whole community. But electronic components, along with printing and paper supplies, were harder to find.

By now, Carl Throneberry had established a dynamic network involving millions of people all over the world who were active in the Christian Resistance. Despite shortages, they were existing as a far-flung community under a primitive system of barter. Fear of death or imprisonment did not prevent an underground economy based on the exchange of goods for services or exchanges based on gold and silver. Regardless of government rules, there were people living under the Antichrist system, as there have been in every system, who were willing to enter an underground economy, buying and selling for profit.

Carl and Lori, working with their three assistants, produced the television and radio programs sent out around the globe in a dozen languages under the title, "The Voice of the Mountains." The digital technology available to them gave them the ability to transmit in one minute a burst of digital "bits" that contained as much information as the entire daily edition of the *Wall Street Journal*. This, in turn, meant that one of Manuel's transmitters could fire a burst of television, audio, or print to an unused satellite transponder, which would bounce the signal down to thousands of tiny and easily disguised satellite receivers in America and other parts of the world. These messages could then be relayed by personal computer, printed booklets, videos, and audio cassettes. Consequently, all of the outposts of the Christian Resistance not only had a unifying voice, but also had a clearing house for vital information.

Carl and Lori seldom got more than four hours of sleep per night, but somehow it was enough. Together with their staff, they wrote and assembled not only the printed materials, such as newspaper articles and pamphlets, but also the audio and videotapes that poured out to the world from El Refugio. Never had the two of them felt more personally fulfilled. Yet they were often overawed by the enormity as well as the danger of the task that confronted them.

Working with John Edwards, Carl and Lori developed a system they called "Mass Survival." Before them were giant maps on which were pinpointed areas in the United States and in other parts of the world where there existed a clear majority of unaffected people. They sent out coded messages describing the safest routes for people to take to these locations. Miguel, Ricardo, and Juan Quintana were key players as well. Every evening they would gather up the data that came in over the computers, phones, and fax machines and transfer the information to maps and charts on the walls. Their colored pins, flags, and arrows gave the planning bunker more the look of a life-size game board than a war room.

As more and more refugees streamed into the designated safe zones, the unaffected majority grew substantially stronger. This meant two things. First, the unaffected majority overshadowed the military forces of the Union for Peace to such an extent that day-to-day repression was severely restricted. Second, and more important, the unaffected community could now build houses, plant crops, make tools, sew and repair clothing, make furniture, and somehow come up with all the necessities of life, completely outside the monetary system imposed by the Antichrist. They were able to set up schools and hospitals in many places, and even crude utilities to meet the needs of all the people without ever resorting to central credit.

In time, various communities began specializing in certain types of products that were exchanged with other communities in a thriving underground system. Some of these communities were discovered, and some of the leaders were arrested, tortured, and executed. The world system moved against the communities when they were able. The UP soldiers demolished their buildings and butchered their inhabitants. But the unaffected were tenacious; the resistance continued.

Month after month, Carl, Lori, and the communications team at El Refugio continued sending out warnings, intelligence bulletins, messages of encouragement, and the information needed for the suffering to survive.

But one day, when they saw that their operational supplies would soon be depleted, Carl spoke to John Edwards about the situation. John suggested that perhaps a trip into Albuquerque would help solve the problem. However, Carl said that it wouldn't be enough.

"I've tried every place I know in Albuquerque," Carl told him, "and nothing is available. My old advertising agency would have exactly what we need, and lots of it. The home office in L.A. is gone, of course. But they still have the office in Dallas. Last I heard, my old friend Larry Rossiter was operations chief. We were quite a team in the old days. I'm pretty sure he's one of the affected. But Larry's okay. There's a bond between us. He'd help me out. So, what do you say? Maybe I should go."

"Carl, you'd have to be out of your mind to try something like that!" John Edwards replied. "You know as well as I do that Dallas has become a center for the Union for Peace. If you go to Dallas, you'll almost certainly be arrested. You don't have proper identification. You're an outsider." He put his hand on Carl's shoulder. "And if they arrest you, my friend, they will surely kill you. You're a wanted man."

"John, you may be right, and believe me, I'm not discounting the dangers. But you know that millions of people are depending on us for their very survival. If we don't get supplies now, everything here stops. Our entire printing operation will be out of business. Our mission will be over."

"How does Lori feel about this crazy idea?" Pastor Jack asked.

Carl looked a little sheepish. "Well, I haven't exactly told her yet. If she thinks I'm going to Albuquerque, she won't be as worried. Hopefully, I'll be back before she realizes that I went a little further than that."

"You've got to tell her," John said. "She has to be part of the decision-making process."

"You're right," Carl said. "I will."

"One more thing, Carl," John persisted. "What assurance can you possibly have that the supplies you want are available in Dallas? That you can arrange some kind of shipment back across the border? Or that your old friend is even alive?"

"I made a contact in the resistance with someone who worked at the agency until about the time the new economic policy went into effect. They laid him off then, but he arranged to . . . well, borrow some stuff we needed a time or two. I'll contact him and see if he can set something up with Larry."

"Next question," said John Edwards. "How will you get there?"

"Well—" Carl paused. "I've called Tony O'Reilly, and he said he'd get me a motorcycle with the UP logo. I'd have more flexibility than if I was driving a car." He shrugged. "I don't have it all figured out yet, but with O'Reilly's help, and the help of the resistance along the way, I think I can make it over there and back."

"Carl, I don't know if you are brave or just foolhardy, but if you feel that this is what you must do, then go ahead. Please be careful, but rest assured that we all will be praying that the Lord will keep you safe in this dangerous mission."

They shook hands, then embraced, and Carl was gone.

AS CARL EXPECTED, LORI WASN'T HAPPY about his making the trip. "Not only is it dangerous because of the UP patrols," she exclaimed, "but you haven't been on a bike in twenty years! As far as I'm concerned, that's the biggest danger of all."

In the end she agreed, and during the next twenty-four hours, Carl, Lori, and a small group of insiders laid out a strategy for the dash across the frontier to Dallas and back. They made calls to underground operatives in Texas and set up a contact point where Carl could meet Larry. They would exchange gold for the supplies, and provide a map for the drivers to deliver the goods to El Refugio. They worked throughout the day, went over maps and laundry lists of the supplies they wanted, and Carl recited everything he needed to do to get safely through the lines.

After supper, the group prayed for Carl. John Edwards handed Carl a leather money belt containing gold coins, then sent him on his way. He took one of the four-wheel-drive vehicles and drove past Albuquerque to the airport staging area. He parked, then walked into the building housing the office of Master Sergeant O'Reilly.

When O'Reilly looked up and saw Carl in the doorway of his office, he got up and walked immediately over to the locked cabinet, shifted the bolt, and pulled a large box off the bottom shelf. "It's all here," he said, handing the package to Carl, "identification papers, a UP uniform, and a weapon. There's no way you could get gas over there—another reason why a car is out of the question. So I've had the fellows rig you up the UP bike with a full tank of gas and two auxiliary tanks. You can barely make it on that, so no side trips."

"Thanks, Tony. How much am I going to owe you for all this?"

"You can't afford it," O'Reilly said, smiling. "You people are doing such good work up there, this one's on the general. But, Carl, take care of yourself."

After suiting up in the enemy uniform, Carl donned an old jumpsuit for the short ride to the border. He didn't want to be stopped by the guards on his own side. He paused just long enough to familiarize himself with the brakes and gears, then mounted the bike and cautiously maneuvered his way back past the airport, around the edge of town, and on toward the eastern boundary of the Defense Zone. Just a mile or so from the crossing point, he ducked behind a dilapidated old shed and put the jumpsuit in his saddlebag. He checked his uniform, put on the UP helmet and goggles, then headed out again.

I must be crazy, Carl thought. *Here I am a copywriter for disposable diapers, acting like a member of the OSS. What on earth have I gotten myself into?*

His stomach was churning as he presented his fake ID card to the sentry at the outer sector. Carl waited nervously while the guard checked him over, but then the man gave the clearance, saluted, and waved him through the checkpoint. Carl jammed his machine into gear and set out into no man's land. He didn't know if he had gotten through because his disguise was perfect or because a lone cyclist was not a very grave threat. Or because of John Edwards's prayers. In any event, he knew he had to move fast if he was going to get the job done.

Carl traveled steadily, straight through the night. It was a grueling twelve-hour trip, and he was exhausted by the time he reached Dallas. More than anything, he wanted to stop and rest, but he could not afford the luxury. His money was no good anymore, so he couldn't even stop for breakfast.

What he saw in Dallas amazed him. Everywhere he looked there were life-sized pictures of Mark Beaulieu. Across the streets were banners proclaiming the slogan of the Union for Peace, "Strength Through Unity." Personnel carriers with armed troops were positioned at strategic street corners. Pairs of uniformed troops patrolled each city block.

Worse than that, however, was the general dinginess and drabness of the city. It was as if Dallas had been turned into a black-and-white movie. People walked along with their heads and shoulders drooping, their faces toward the ground. The icy breath of a satanic dictator had chilled the heart of this once-great city.

Carl checked his watch and saw that it was exactly the time he had agreed to meet his contact. He drove along side streets until he reached the prearranged point on Mockingbird, just a block off the Central Expressway where his contact would be waiting. Carl pulled up at a combination gas station and convenience store. Someone wearing a helmet with a visor and a bulky motorcycle jacket stepped from behind a trash dumpster. Carl presumed it was his friend, Larry. He walked toward a gasoline pump and motioned for Carl to come over. Signaling for Carl to be silent, his contact proceeded to pump enough fuel to fill all three tanks of Carl's bike, then hopped on the back and yelled, "Step on it, man. Let's get out of here!"

At that moment Carl realized the voice was not that of his friend, Larry. But there was no time to think or speak. *I'm just going to have to trust this guy,* he thought. What surprised him was that his contact apparently had no intention of paying for the gas. The clerk inside the store hit a red button, which notified a nearby UP motorcycle patrolman, who immediately took off in hot pursuit.

Carl's contact yelled directions from the back of the bike and, to Carl's surprise, motioned for him to slow down. As the UP patrolman got closer, Carl's passenger shouted, "Turn right!" Carl swung the bike sharply to the right and down a narrow alley. Then his passenger shoved Carl's head forward and shouted, "Duck down!" as they sped down the alley.

The patrolman saw the glint of piano wire that had been stretched across the path just as it caught him in the neck and threw him hard to the ground. He broke his neck and died instantly. His motorcycle slammed to the ground and skidded another fifty feet before coming to a stop against a wall. As instructed, Carl had stopped at the end of the alley. His contact jumped off the bike and ran over to the dead man.

"Quick! Give me a hand!" Carl, who had been looking on in amazement, got off his bike. His contact pushed open the door of an abandoned shed, and the two of them rolled both cycles inside. Next, they brought in the body of the fallen trooper and closed the door behind them. The contact quickly stripped off the dead man's helmet, boots, and uniform, and then rolled the body under a tarpaulin beside one wall.

As Carl watched, the cyclist stood, pulled off his own helmet, and a cascade of long brown hair tumbled out. Carl saw that it was not a young man at all. In fact, *he* was a woman!

"Where's Larry?" Carl asked, winded and shaken by what had just taken place.

"They were on to him," the woman answered. "It was too dangerous, so he sent me to fill in." She held out her hand. "My name is Nicole, and I used to work with Larry. Now I'm a sort of freelance, you might say."

"Nicole." Carl smiled. "I must say, I've never seen anyone handle themselves the way you just did. You're pretty tough. Where did you learn ... well ... *this* ... ?" he asked, pointing to the body of the slain UP officer and the motorcycle in the corner.

"That's a long story," she said. "I was in the army for a while, and that's where I learned to 'trap a monkey,' as we used to say. The gas, the wire, the whole thing was a set-up—the best way I could come up with to lure the patrolman off his beat so I could get his uniform and his motorcycle."

As they talked, Carl learned that Nicole had done a lot of things in her thirty-three years. A rebellious teenager, she had run away from home. Eventually, she had ended up in Dallas, where she tried working her way through college. When it became apparent that she could no longer afford it, she had enlisted in the army in order to get the rest of her education paid for. What she hadn't counted on was how good she would be at it, or how much she would love it. She had learned guerrilla fighting in Central America. She was an airborne-qualified paratrooper, and could handle a gun as well as a man. She was a natural combat leader.

When the Union for Peace came along she was one of the first to join up. But later, when it became clear that there was something sinister about it and that President Mark Beaulieu had something much bigger in mind than she had at first expected, she made an emotional decision to work for the downfall of the Union from the inside. She became a trained operative. Nicole had worked to undermine Central Command as well as UP missions in the West, and she had an impressive list of hits to her credit.

"I was on the right side," she said, "but not for the right reason."

"What do you mean?" Carl asked.

"Well, to put it simply, I hadn't accepted Christ into my life." She pushed her hair back from her eyes. "I came from a really religious background, and I rebelled against it all. My parents were always talking about the Bible, and they sent me to Bible study, but I just didn't want to listen. And nothing my parents did could make me listen. Boy, was I headstrong!"

Carl nodded. "I can identify with that," he said. "What caused you to change?"

"Funny you should ask," Nicole said. "It was one of the 'Voice of the Mountains' pamphlets you guys put out." She described what was in the pamphlet, then added, "Deep in my heart, I always knew that everything it said was true, which I suppose is why I got out of the Union for Peace when I did and started to work for its downfall. I didn't have any moral reason at first, but when I read this pamphlet, I changed, and I accepted Christ for the very first time."

"Nicole," Carl said with tears welling up in his eyes, "I thank God for you! You saved my life today. On top of that, you've helped me set things up to get all the supplies we need delivered to El Refugio. But you've given me something else that means the world to me. You have shown me that my life has a greater purpose."

She gave him a puzzled look.

"You see," he said, "I was the one who wrote that pamphlet that helped turn your life around. Sure, I've been writing ad copy all my life. I'm an old copywriter, and I can sling it with the best of them. But Jesus grabbed hold of my wife, Lori, and me one day and set us both off on a new path. He pulled us out of the way of the meteor that hit Los Angeles, and He's put us in the path of many blessings since then. You're the hard evidence I've needed that . . . well, that it was the right thing to do."

Nicole gave Carl a warm embrace, then said, "I'm so glad it means that much to you. You found that God has given you a calling, and through it, you've been able to touch millions of hearts all over the world. You've helped people keep up their spirits who are living under the terrors of the UP. But the real gratitude should be all mine, Mr. Throneberry. You expressed from your heart the only words that could have changed my mind and given me back my life. If I've helped you get a sense of perspective, I'm glad, but you've given me the joy of knowing Christ for myself. In that sense, you're really the one who saved *my* life."

As they talked, Carl tried to persuade Nicole to come back with him to El Refugio. "We can use a strong leader like you, Nicole," he said. "And chances are pretty good that you're going to be a wanted woman around here for a while, so you'd be much safer on our side of the fence."

Nicole agreed. She needed to get away, and she was willing to help out any way she could. So they worked out a timetable and decided to make their way back to El Refugio shortly after nightfall. In the meantime, Carl would spend most of the day napping and resting while Nicole slipped out, transmitted the gold Carl had brought in his money belt, and completed the business transactions for the supplies.

Finally, after sunset, the two-person UP patrol mounted the motorcycles and made their way carefully out of Dallas traveling westward toward Albuquerque. They arrived at the Western Defense Zone just as the sun was coming up over the mountains the following morning. They passed through the sentries on both sides with no delays and walked into Sergeant O'Reilly's office dead tired and covered with dust, but delighted to have survived the journey.

"Sergeant," Carl said. "I made it safely, thank the Lord. And I brought you back your motorcycle with a hundred percent interest!"

When Carl and Nicole arrived at El Refugio, Lori was at the head of the pack, as more than a dozen of their friends gathered around praising the Lord and clinging to the two weary travelers. Questions were flying faster than Carl could think or speak, but when he paused to introduce his new friend and fellow adventurer, he got the greatest surprise of all.

John Edwards, who had seen the commotion from the upstairs window, came down and joined the group on the lawn. He approached them with his hands together at his waist, almost as if he had been praying. But from that moment on, no further introductions were needed. The crowd seemed to separate on cue, and the whole scene moved as if in slow motion. As John approached Carl's friend, Nicole, she saw his face, saw his outstretched arms, and ran to meet him.

"Daddy," she cried as she embraced him.

"Nicole," John Edwards sobbed into her long brown hair. "You're here. Thank God, you're safe! I was afraid I'd never see you again!"

Over the next two hours, the crowd in John Edwards's spacious den continued to grow until the room was packed. Sitting side by side on the long sofa, the beloved pastor and his long-lost daughter told of the differences that had separated them years before, and how Nicole had simply disappeared and stopped writing or calling home. What made the moment so touching was that they had not spoken to each other from that time to this, and they were learning about each other while surrounded by, and being supported by, people who had given their lives to the Lord. John Edwards and his daughter were rebuilding a relationship that only God could have put back together again.

At one point, Carl interrupted, "Nicole, back there in Dallas . . . I had no idea!"

"Me either," said the young woman. "I didn't know my father had moved out here after Mother died. I didn't know anything about El Refugio. And all I knew about the Voice of the Mountains was those few pamphlets I read—I guess I was too busy with other things! So this was all a surprise for me too. But, Mr. Throneberry, I thanked you before for writing those words that brought me back to Jesus. How can I ever thank you now for bringing me back to my daddy?"

No words were needed. That moment said it all.

FORTUNATELY FOR THE COMMUNITIES helped by Carl and Lori in the weeks that followed, the Antichrist was focusing his attention more and more on his own debauched lifestyle while ignoring minor seditions in the hinterlands. A systematic approach to worldwide terror became less and less a viable option for the leader of the corrupt Babylon.

But, debauched or not, and systematic or not, the Antichrist had a score to settle. There was rebellion in this Western Defense Zone. His former secretary of defense had not only betrayed his trust, but had also insulted and blasphemed him. He raged in the palace whenever he recalled the insulting telephone call when Al Augustus had announced his odious intentions.

Beaulieu knew that the renegade Al Augustus commanded forces that had three types of nuclear missiles: intercontinental, intermediate, and theater. He feared a nuclear confrontation. His newly created Babylon must not be destroyed. His grand capital must endure for a thousand years as the center of his worldwide dominion. Babylon was the symbol of his power. If somehow Babylon was destroyed, then he feared his kingdom would be at an end.

But for now, he was emperor of the world. His one goal must be to annihilate that outpost of rebellion lest it spread like a cancer. He was willing to gamble that Al Augustus would be unable to make good his threat of a nuclear strike. Therefore, he sent orders to his American commanders to begin action against the Western Defense Zone immediately.

WHEN THE FIRST INTELLIGENCE report came in, General Gladstone rushed excitedly into the office of Al Augustus. "Al, our aerial reconnaissance shows the movement of a military force of over five hundred thousand men moving toward us from Texas!"

"Are they equipped with U.S. or foreign weapons?" Al asked.

"Well, they seem to be U.S.," Archie replied, "but what difference does that make?"

"Maybe a lot of difference," Al Augustus said cryptically. "Are you well dug in?"

"Yes, sir," he said proudly. "You bet we are!"

"I imagine," Al Augustus mused, "they will get their artillery within range, position their infantry, and then hit us head on. But we hold the high ground, and they don't have much room to maneuver."

"You're right," Archie replied, "but we can look for cluster bombs, concussion bombs, napalm, even laser-guided missiles coming in here. High ground or not, our guys will go through hell before it's over!"

"I know that, Archie, but if we don't hold here, there is no place else. This is it. Get your fighters upstairs now! Take out their AWACS, then the bombers. With five-to-one odds against us on the ground, maybe we'll at least have a fair fight in the air."

Within minutes, the F-117 Stealth fighters screamed into the heavens from Albuquerque. The Union for Peace had two lumbering AWACS radar planes and one smaller Hawkeye. For some reason, they had given the aerial eyes no fighter escort. It took just three air-to-air missiles from the F-117s, and the UP forces were electronically blinded.

Then the skies over Texas came alive as aerial dogfights unfolded that were reminiscent of the battle for Britain in World War II. Archie Gladstone's pilots fought as men fight who must win or die. The UP pilots fought like uninspired robots. Trails of smoke etched the sky as dozens of UP planes exploded and fell to earth.

Nothing the UP sent up ever got through. When the score was tallied, it was UP losses–49, Western Defense Zone–5.

The UP forces now had no radar surveillance, no air cover, and no possible air bombardment of the skillfully entrenched positions of Archie Gladstone's ground forces.

When the Antichrist heard of the loss of most of his air wing, he raged in fury. Then, like Hitler before him, he refused the advice of his ground commanders to postpone the attack until a new air wing could be brought up. "They are weak, sniveling cowards!" he roared. "Any general who fails to attack will be executed!"

Acting on the orders of their demonized commander in chief, the UP generals had massed their armor in a broad attack line. Behind it, they positioned the rocket launchers and the heavy artillery pieces. Both sides had battlefield-nuclear capacity, but both rejected their use for fear of retaliation and the subsequent dangers of fallout.

Archie controlled the air and could have begun bombing and strafing runs over the enemy forces. He could not understand why Al Augustus had ordered him to refrain from doing so.

Archie and Al flew by helicopter to a high lookout post. Just before the order was given for the UP gunners to commence firing, the artillery pieces and rocket launchers went into action across the front, and suddenly there was a series of dramatic explosions! The breech of each gun had exploded when it fired its first shell. As the rockets and missiles started to leave their tubes and launch pads, but before they were airborne, they exploded.

From the initial salvo, not one field piece or launcher remained intact. All were destroyed.

Archie Gladstone was awestruck! *That sly fox,* he thought. *Al Augustus is always three steps ahead.*

"Al," he said, "I don't get it. What happened out there?"

"It seems, General," he said with a smile, "that my friends in the Pentagon were successful. It was really very simple. Before I left for Babylon, I requested that a paper-thin coating of high-explosive Plastique be painted on the breech or in the barrel of every rocket launcher, missile launcher, and artillery piece that we turned over to the combined world forces. From the looks of things, I would say that they did their job quite well!"

"Sir, it is a pleasure to serve with a man like you. The UP ground troops are helpless before us. What do you suggest we do next?"

"General," he said, "if you'll look up at the sky, I believe you'll have your answer."

As they looked up, they saw that the luminescent columns stationed over El Refugio had begun to move across the Sangre de Cristo Mountains. Suddenly, majestically, they poured down toward the east and the south.

It was indescribable! The columns seemed like beams of pure white light, yet they also appeared to be cascades of colored light. They were brighter than the most intense laser beams ever created, yet they were full of the colors of a thousand sunsets over the mountains.

They reached the assembled army of the Antichrist. Where there once had been tanks and trucks, suddenly there were piles of ash. Where soldiers once stood, there remained only charred spots on the desert floor.

In less than sixty seconds, it was all over. The luminescent columns seemed to stream backward, as if pulled upward by a great vacuum. Once again, they stood high above the mountain home of El Refugio.

Archie Gladstone was speechless. He fell on his knees, raised his hands, and cried aloud, "I praise Thee, O God of my fathers!" Then he stood.

"They're all gone!" he said. "There is nothing left of that huge army but black spots and ashes. I saw it with my eyes, but I don't know what happened!"

"Archie," Al said reverently, "I've lived a long time, and I've seen many things, but never have I seen anything like that. I used tricks and gimmicks to blow up some field pieces, but my tricks aren't enough to beat Satan. What we just saw *can* do it."

He slapped the general on the back. "Archie, old boy, what we saw was the power of the angels of God! They were only waiting for someone to stand up to Satan's boy in Babylon, and, when they saw that we would stand, they took over and did the rest!

"Just think about it: we knocked down a few planes, but we didn't have to kill a single soldier. The angels did it all! They're moving with us. From now on, we'll begin to break out of here and attack the system."

THE ANTICHRIST MADE HIS ATTACK against the rebel outpost at the Western Defense Zone a widely publicized event. But by the same token, the humiliating defeat at the Sangre de Cristo Mountains was also widely publicized. The controlled media suppressed the story, but they could not suppress the rumors that spread among the people like wildfire.

Now, there was doubt. A tiny band of rebels had annihilated five hundred thousand UP troops. It was said that angels were involved.

Could it be that angels existed that were more powerful than their god-man? Could it be that they who had sided with the Antichrist had made the wrong decision?

The battle at Sangre de Cristo became a turning point. The unaffected throughout the world were given hope, but something strange began to happen to everyone else. Every man, woman, and child who had received the laser tattoo began to break out in boils. Not just a few boils. There were boils and skin eruptions on their faces, their chests, their backs, their legs, even their feet. Walking became unbearable . . . sleeping was impossible.

Then came the mouth sores. Around the walls of the mouths of each person whose hand was tattooed, there developed strange, pus-filled canker sores. Their tongues were raw and inflamed and began to swell. They found it excruciatingly painful to eat and to swallow.

Through their pain, they swore allegiance to their god-king, Mark Beaulieu. Through their pain, they cursed and reviled God for bringing such suffering upon them.

In Babylon, it was no different. The body of Mark Beaulieu was covered with sores, as was the body of his consort, Joyce Cumberland Wong. The body of Tauriq Haddad burned with pain.

The form of the Antichrist appeared. He shook his fist at heaven, and roared, "I will defeat You! I will pull down Your throne! We've won! We've won! You are the loser, not me!"

"Tauriq," the Antichrist said with Mark Beaulieu's voice, "the final showdown is at hand. We will assemble a mighty army from all over the world. Then we'll summon all the forces of our lord, Lucifer, and his principalities and powers.

"We will march to Jerusalem. We will subjugate that city and take it from Jehovah. We will defeat the rebels on earth, and we will defeat the angels in the air. The prize, Tauriq, is not just earth—it is the very universe itself!"

BUT AFTER THE BATTLE of Sangre de Cristo, a temperature inversion took place over the Tigris-Euphrates Valley. The air did not move, and the sun beat down unmercifully. The first week, the temperature was 90 degrees Fahrenheit. The second week, it reached 100 degrees. And, the third week it was over 110 degrees. By the end of the month, the heat varied between 120 and 130 degrees. It was becoming unbearable.

The land baked in the hot sun. The marshes of the Shatt-al-Arab between Iraq and Iran dried up completely, as did the mouth of the Tigris-Euphrates rivers. The branch of the Euphrates River that flows through Iraq slowed to a trickle, then dried up completely.

The Antichrist raged within his palace. He had all the money in the world. He had at his disposal the finest medical minds of the world. Yet, no amount of money or science could cure the sores on his body and in his mouth.

And nothing he could do would stop the blazing heat that was obliterating the grass and the trees, and causing the life-giving water within Babylon to evaporate. He and his people were being scorched to death. He hated God for what was happening. He cursed God. He raged against God. But the heat wave continued, and the sores grew worse.

The final battle was coming. He would march on Jerusalem at the head of his armies. "Then," he said to Joyce Cumberland Wong, "I will win! At last I will have my revenge!"

CHAPTER TWENTY-SEVEN

THE INITIAL CONTINGENT of troops from India boarded the UP warships at Calcutta, bound for the seaport city of Karachi in Pakistan. Several hours later, similar units boarded from Madras. Within a day and a half, a naval convoy loaded with trucks, tanks, artillery, ammunition, and thousands more troops set sail from Bombay.

They disembarked in sequence at the port of Karachi in Pakistan, then marched overland through the mountains to the north and west. They took the route that led through the Kajack Pass, which was used centuries before by Alexander the Great when, following his great victory over King Porus at the Indus River, his rebellious troops forced him to give up on further conquests and return home.

The enormous motorized column reached the Afghan plains near Kandahar, then rolled like a deadly serpent across Iran. All along the route, they were joined by Iranian contingents. Soon, their numbers exceeded two million men and five thousand battle tanks. To observers of the scene, the number of troops was so vast that it might just as well have been two hundred million.

They crossed into Iraq, up through the arid marshes of the Shatt-al-Arab, then into the plains west of the dry riverbed of the Euphrates. By first light they were joined by another massive contingent that had come through Iran from the Central Asian nations that had once been part of the former Soviet Union. There they rested, refurbished their equipment, and awaited further orders from the leader of the world.

As their first order of business, joint air, naval, and marine forces from Europe were ordered to eliminate all resistance from the Port of Haifa on the Mediterranean. When the Israeli defenders refused to give ground, the Antichrist ordered the forces of the Union for Peace to break off the fighting and withdraw. Then he ordered one neutron bomb to be dropped over Haifa.

Seconds after the blast, all human life was gone. The port facilities of Haifa were taken over, intact, by the Union for Peace without a struggle.

That one neutron bomb was the first and last of the campaign. The Antichrist wanted Jerusalem intact. He also wanted the Jews of Jerusalem to be alive when he entered the holy city. He had no desire to kill them. He wanted them to bow down before him, to beg him for mercy, to acknowledge that he—not Jehovah—was the one true god. Over and over he savored the sweet victory that lay ahead of his forces.

When Haifa had been cleared of radiation, convoys of vessels from Marseilles, Naples, Trieste, Constanza, Odessa, and Istanbul began crowding the limited port facilities of Haifa to unload their cargo of tens of thousands of troops, armor, and supplies belonging to the Union for Peace.

The high command in Babylon had coordinated the troop movements so that the huge force from the east would enter Israel from Syria through the Golan Heights. The troops from Turkey and Europe would enter at Haifa, then move southeast through the mountain pass inland from the coast.

The forces would join at the broad and fertile plain of Jezreel.

On the west of the Jezreel plain was the silent sentry that for centuries had guarded the Via Maris north from Egypt and south into Israel and Egypt from ancient Assyria. At this place, the Via Maris was intersected by the road south from the harbor at Haifa.

This military outpost had been built and demolished no less than twenty times, and was now nothing but a ruin, a "tell" or mound, bearing witness to its four-thousand-year history. Its name was Megiddo. By virtue of being rebuilt so many times, they called it a hill or "mountain." Hence, the name Mount Megiddo. The name in Hebrew is *Har Megiddo*, and in Greek, *Armageddon*.

As the invading ground forces were gathering, the sky over northern Israel was filled with airplanes. The kill ratio was decidedly in Israel's favor, but that was not enough. There was no way that a tiny nation could send into battle enough fresh missiles, replacement aircraft, and replacement pilots to match the combined air power of the military forces of the world. The Israeli pilots fought like supermen, but that was not enough. Soon, the Antichrist controlled the skies. From a military perspective, the battle was now his.

On the ground it seemed that the skies and, consequently, the battle belonged to the might of the Antichrist. But, in the skies above the skies, another battle was being waged with much greater intensity.

Although Satan had remained in Babylon, he had ordered his lieutenants to maintain control of the heavens at all costs. But this was fast becoming an impossibility for them. The Archangel Michael had been sent by Almighty God with the largest contingent of angelic powers ever known in the history of the world. As Israeli planes were seemingly losing control of the lower atmosphere, their allies above were winning the fight.

In this battle for ultimate control, the armies of the Lord of the Universe did not lack fresh warriors. One by one, the principalities and powers of Satan's host were bound and removed from earth. Soon, Michael had cleared every satanic alien from the skies. However, no one realized what was happening in the heavens. Things had become so grim that it appeared as if Satan had defeated God. But there were some serious surprises ahead.

Israeli ground troops gave up territory grudgingly, but little by little they were forced to pull back to form a defensive perimeter around

Jerusalem. The threat came not just from an advancing army of vastly superior forces from the north; the Antichrist had also summoned troops from Libya, Ethiopia, and the Sudan to move across the Sinai to invade Israel from the south. A giant military movement was underway that would soon envelop the entire nation of Israel and then surround the city of Jerusalem.

Israel lay prostrate at the feet of the tyrant, Mark Beaulieu. As Israeli troops pulled back, they took as many of their civilians with them as possible. But only limited evacuation could be accomplished under battlefield conditions.

The combined forces of the Antichrist had gained the access points to Jerusalem from all sides. Behind them lay a population that had been raped and plundered. To all appearances, the nation of Israel was as good as dead. Within twenty-four hours, Jerusalem would be overrun. For weeks, the Israelis had fasted and cried out to God, but no answer had come. They were helpless, isolated, seemingly alone. The might of the entire world was against them. The end had come.

Then, something began to happen. The ground began to shake. No bomb had been detonated, but the effects of a neutron bomb were clearly visible in the forces of the Antichrist. Pieces of flesh began to fall from the soldiers' bones. Their eyeballs began to rot in their sockets. Their internal organs slowly began to turn to mush, and they fell, gushing blood, one after another.

Bodies of the dead and dying were piled all over the hills and valleys surrounding Jerusalem. Dark clouds gathered over the city, and rain began to fall that soon turned to hail. First there were pellets, then baseball-sized stones of ice, then round chunks of ice that weighed as much as fifty pounds. There was no place for the remaining forces of the Antichrist to hide. They were literally stoned to death.

THE FINAL ACT BEGAN with a mighty angel, who descended into Earth's atmosphere and blew a trumpet blast heard around the globe.

Then, he shouted with a voice that reverberated through the heavens, "NOW!"

At his command, fire from heaven poured down upon the city of Babylon, the capital of the Antichrist. All was obliterated. Powerful angels swooped down from the sky and seized Satan, Mark Beaulieu, and Tauriq Haddad. They also seized Beaulieu's consort, Joyce Cumberland Wong. As they rushed them toward the eternal lake of fire that had been prepared to hold Satan and his legions, they passed a figure going the other way.

He was powerful . . . youthful . . . remarkably handsome. His entire being glowed with supernatural light. As they passed, Joyce Cumberland Wong looked at his face. "Jimmy! Jimmy, it's you! Jimmy, please help me. Please don't let them take me to hell! Jimmy, I love you . . . you know I've always loved you!"

She was pathetic. To James Wong, she looked like a frightened old hag covered with sores, but her anguish was heart-rending.

"Joyce," James Wong said, "you never loved me. You never loved anybody but yourself. I offered you a better way, but you cursed me. You've made your choice, and I have no power to change it. Good-bye forever, Joyce."

Then in a flash, he was gone. Instantly, she was in a lake of fire with the devil and the Antichrist . . . forever!

All over the world, those who had pledged allegiance to the Antichrist were instantly changed. Underneath the human facade was a spiritual being, a being that once had been made in God's image. What now emerged was not the image of God, but the image of Satan. They were grotesque caricatures of God's creatures. The boastful and proud were now visible as satanically inspired liars. Cowards. Irreversibly damaged. They were, as Dante had so vividly portrayed them in *The Inferno*, the damned. Lost forever.

They bore the mark of Satan; now they were destined to be with him forever. They screamed, fought, and struggled. But, like a person who carries the putrefying carcass of a dead rat to a garbage can, the angels carried these wretched creatures away from earth to the garbage dump of eternity. Time and again each of them had been offered a better way, but each in his or her own way had rejected it. Each had been given a free will. Each had exercised that free will to make a choice. Now, there was no second chance. Now, there would be no exit.

THE RESIDENTS OF EL REFUGIO watched the news coverage of the unfolding events with fascination and amazement. But several had questions. Some of the things they had seen that day seemed to contradict Scripture. Finally, when his curiosity got the best of him, Dave Busby asked John Edwards to explain a few things.

"Pastor Jack," he said, "I don't get it. Nothing happened at Megiddo. I thought the war to end all wars—or the mother of battles, or whatever—was supposed to happen at Armageddon. But they shot right by there like nobody's business!"

"That's right, Dave," John Edwards said. "Despite the popular notion of the last several years, the Bible never speaks of a 'Battle of Armageddon.' It says that the forces coming against Jerusalem will *gather* at a place called Armageddon. That's what we've been seeing the past couple of days. True to Scripture, this is exactly where the Antichrist joined his forces. But the actual battle to be fought was never to be the 'Battle of Armageddon.' It's the 'Battle of Jerusalem.'"

"Wow!" Dave said. "That's where they are now. Oh, brother!"

As the men and women at El Refugio and at other outposts around the world witnessed the unfolding events of the end of the age, they could not be certain exactly what had happened, or when. It all took place as fast as the blink of an eye. Somehow, at least in the closing moments, the time sequence of heaven blurred the elapsed time on earth. Events took a much longer time to describe than they took to happen, and they were not sequential. But they happened just as John the Apostle had described them two thousand years before.

John Edwards offered an interesting metaphor. "You know, Albert Einstein said in his theory of relativity that time slows down the faster an object moves through space. An astronaut hurtling through space at speeds approaching the speed of light might perceive from his on-board clocks that he had traveled in space for six months. But on returning to earth, he might discover that two hundred years has passed in his absence. So, time is not constant," he said. "It's relative. I suspect that's why Saint Peter could say that one day at God's level is like a thousand years to those who live on the earth."

At one point, the Antichrist had wanted maximum worldwide television coverage of his triumph in Jerusalem. So, by satellite telecast and by every sophisticated means available, the world was allowed to witness the columns of UP troops rolling toward Jerusalem. The world was told that the Union for Peace had been victorious over the Israeli Air Force. When it looked as if the battle was going against them, both Carl and Lori Throneberry grew visibly agitated.

Sitting on the edge of her seat, Lori said, "People, I know what the Bible says about Israel winning, but without some kind of miracle, it seems to me they're goners. Unless they want to do themselves in, like the defenders at Masada, or blow themselves up with an atomic bomb, I don't see how they can get out of this alive."

Just as she spoke the words, the satellite picture went dead.

"Lori, that miracle may be happening," Carl said. "It wasn't a bomb, though. I'll bet anything our little friend in Babylon just cut the feed. There's something happening that he doesn't want the rest of the world to see."

Charley McAtee, who had joined them earlier, said, "We all got a taste of what the Lord did east of here, didn't we? That air force general can't stop talking about it. I think you're right, Carl. Something big is brewing in Jerusalem right now—just wait and see!"

As people went back to their regular duties, Manuel Quintana tried his best to pull down another satellite broadcast or to learn something more about the war in the Middle East. He was completely unsuccessful. Then, after several hours without any news, the residents of El Refugio heard a trumpet blast that seemed to reverberate through every fiber of their beings. They ran to the windows of their homes and to the doors of their tents to see what was happening. There was a tremendous shout that echoed from one end of the mountains to the other.

"Carl," Lori whispered excitedly, as she and Carl stood looking out of the open french windows in John Edwards's living room, "what was that word? Did you hear it? It sounded like 'Now!'"

"Yes, it sounded like that to me, too, honey," Carl whispered back. "I think we're in for something really big!"

As they thought about what they had heard, the television flashed back on, and the transmissions resumed again. Racing back to the giant television in the living room, Lori and Carl could see that the cameraman was trying to focus his lens on a bright object glowing like the sun above the Mount of Olives to the east of the Temple Mount in Jerusalem.

Then, as if on cue, the sky above El Refugio began to glow with an intense light.

Carl looked at Lori. Something was happening to her before his eyes. Her hair was full and golden. Her face was the face of the beautiful girl he had fallen in love with years ago. Then she began to glow in a translucent radiance he had never seen before in his life. She looked angelic.

"Lori," Carl said, reaching out to her, "you are the most beautiful creature I have ever set eyes on!"

"Carl," she said with a radiant smile, "you should see yourself!"

Without realizing what had happened, both of them had been transformed in the twinkling of an eye. Carl stood tall and handsome. His body was lean and muscular. His hair was shimmering. He, too, had a translucent glow, and they were both clothed in pure white linen.

"Lori," he said, "what the Bible promised is happening. I feel such incredible peace. I love you, Lori, and I know we'll be together for all eternity."

She took his hand. "For all eternity, Carl."

Every single person at El Refugio had been transformed in a moment of time in the same manner as Carl and Lori. There were now no handicaps, no deformities, no sorrows, no arthritis, no deafness, no disease. Only youth and vigor, laughter and joy. It was like an unveiling. The veil of mortality had been lifted. Transformed spiritual beauty was there for everyone to see.

But the unveiling of God's children was not confined to El Refugio. All over the world the homeless and the oppressed who had refused to deny their Lord were being rewarded. Their glory reflected the glory of God. In turn, the earth itself was radiating the glory of God's people. The flowers burst into bloom, the birds sang, the animals were at peace. Even the poisonous snakes were no longer a threat.

The promise of God had been fulfilled. The era of peace had begun. Peace between God and man. Peace between man and his fellowman. Peace between mankind and nature. No living being would hurt or destroy God's earth anymore. No longer would the youth of the world be trained to fight and kill in war. For the first time since creation, there truly was peace on earth and good will among men.

Then the people of El Refugio saw what seemed like a gigantic shimmering space-craft coming down to orbit the earth. It was a giant, jeweled cube about fourteen hundred miles on each side, suspended between heaven and earth. It was the New Jerusalem. It was to be the home of God and His Son, Jesus Christ. And it was to be forever the home of all those who had come to faith in Christ.

Manuel Quintana, Cathy Quintana, and their sons, all holding hands were slowly lifted up to New Jerusalem. They sang as they went. Dave Busby and Charley McAtee were right alongside. Carl and Lori, holding each other's hands, rose majestically into the sky.

John Edwards, his work at last completed, was lifted from the earth and welcomed into the joy of his Lord along with his daughter, Nicole, now transformed in radiance—the daughter he had once feared that he would never see again.

Vince and Angie D'Agostino were lifted into the air.

Al and Barbara Augustus were there as well, arm and arm, and Archie Gladstone ascended to the New Jerusalem at the head of four divisions from the Western Defense Zone. Not one of God's people was left behind. They rose from every part of the planet. Like glorified rivers of light, they streamed into the New Jerusalem and entered into God's rest.

The old age had ended, and the reign of Jesus Christ and His saints had at long last begun.

ABOUT THE AUTHOR

PAT ROBERTSON is the founder and chairman of the Christian Broadcasting Network, Inc., founder of Regent University, The Center for Law and Justice, and International Family Entertainment, Inc. Robertson is the author of twelve books including *The Turning Tide* and *The New Millennium*. His *New York Times* bestseller, *The New World Order,* was the number one religious book in America in the year of its publication, as were *The Secret Kingdom* and *Answers to 200 of Life's Most Probing Quesitons.* Robertson was named among America's 100 Cultural Elite by *Time* magazine. He and wife, Dede, have four children and thirteen grandchildren. They reside in Virginia Beach, Virginia.

ALSO BY PAT ROBERTSON

The Turning Tide

Shout It from the Housetops

The Secret Kingdom

Answers to 200 of Life's Most Probing Questions

America's Date with Destiny

Beyond Reason: How Miracles Can Change Your Life

The Plan

The New Millennium

The New World Order

THIS IS JANUARY...
BRING IT ON!

AS FEATURED ON THE 700 CLUB

BRING IT ON

BOLD ANSWERS TO TODAY'S TOUGH QUESTIONS

PAT ROBERTSON

ISBN: 0-8499-1712-3

Is Christianity relevant to today's issues? Pat Robertson tells inquiring minds to bring on the real questions and he'll answer with the hard-hitting truth. Based on the most popular segment of the 700 Club, this new book answers hundreds of questions from life issues to end times. Bring it on.

Pat Robertson

Community Baptist
Church